'Is your pulse always this rapid?'

'You make me nervous,' Summer admitted, wishing he would let her go.

'I wonder why?'

James's tawny glance slid from her face to the rounded contours of her breasts under the cream crêpe de Chine, and his strong hand slipped from her wrist to imprison her fingers.

'Relax,' he said softly.

Summer had never been more aware of a man's body. Her own was supple and firm now, but close to him she felt fragile, and as she was thinking how easily he could overpower her, he lifted his free hand and very gently brushed her cheek with the backs of his fingers.

Although she was now more experienced than she had been the last time this happened, other men's kisses were no preparation for the arms and lips of the man she had loved in secret for almost two years.

But she knew it was not a kiss to be taken seriously. There was nothing she could do but pretend it had meant as little to her as it had to him . . .

SUMMER'S AWAKENING

BY

ANNE WEALE

WORLDWIDE ROMANCE

London • Sydney • Toronto

The lines on page 127 reprinted by kind permission of the Society of Authors as the literary representative of the estate of A. E. Housman and Jonathan Cape Ltd. publishers of THE COLLECTED POEMS OF A. E. HOUSMAN

First published in Great Britain in 1984
by Worldwide Romance,
15–16 Brook's Mews, London W1A 1DR

Australian copyright 1984
Philippine copyright 1984

© Anne Weale 1984

ISBN 0 263 74754 9

Set in 10 on 10 pt Linotron Palatino

Photoset by Rowland Phototypesetting Ltd
Bury St Edmunds, Suffolk
Printed and bound in Great Britain by
Cox & Wyman Ltd, Reading

Most fat people need to be hurt badly before they do something about themselves.
    Jean Nidetch, *The Story of Weight Watchers*

PROLOGUE

SHE woke in a panic, her aunt's loud commanding voice still ringing in her ears as she sat up, fumbling for the light switch.

It was only after the light had revealed the flower-printed Pratesi sheets and her bare arm, golden-brown from weeks in the sun, that she was able to shake off the vivid reality of her nightmare.

With a shuddering sigh of relief she sank back on the down-filled pillows in their expensive cotton cases. Her aunt was dead. She was free. The years of servitude were over.

Until her arrival in Florida, she had never heard of Pratesi, the luxurious Italian bed-linen bought by kings and sheikhs, movie stars and millionaires. Now, after almost three months in the beautiful Spanish-style house on Bay Shore Road, she was accustomed to such things.

A few hours earlier her dinner had been served on gold-rimmed plates made by Lenox, the only major producer of fine china in the United States and suppliers to four of the nation's Presidents. She could remember the controversy when a 4,372-piece set, commissioned by Mrs Ronald Reagan, had been delivered to the White House at a cost of more than two hundred and nine thousand dollars.

Now Lenox china and Baccarat crystal were part of her own changed life-style; and it was amazing how quickly one became accustomed to the best.

For a while she lay looking at her bedroom, contrasting the spacious elegance with the small, cold, north-

facing room she had slept in throughout her teens.
Since her return to America, her father's country and
the setting of her happy childhood, she had tried to
forget the intervening years of exile. But now and then
a bad dream, such as the one she had just had, would
revive some of the painful memories stored in her
subconscious mind.

But the most wounding memory had nothing to do
with her aunt, nor was it one she could push to the
back of her mind. There was never a day when she
didn't remember that crushing humiliation and the
man who had inflicted it on her.

The bedside clock showed half past one. Before
turning out her light, a couple of hours ago, she had
been reading an article by a beauty editor about the
mental and physical benefits of an experience called
sensory isolation which involved floating in ten inches
of heavily salted and therefore very buoyant water in a
dark and sound-proof flotation tank. According to the
editor, who had tried it, the experience was marvel-
lously relaxing.

Feeling wide awake and restless, she wondered if
floating in a heated swimming pool under a starlit
night sky might be equally soothing.

A few moments later she was in her white-carpeted
bathroom, pulling off her nightdress. She had been in
and out of the pool all day and her bathing-suit was
hanging from the shower tap. Before reaching for it,
she paused for a moment to look at herself in the
full-length mirror.

A tall girl with sun-streaked blonde hair, long
brown legs and a curvy figure which she would have
liked to be slimmer, but which she wasn't displeased
with.

She thought: Why do I need a bathing-suit? Nobody's going to see me. I can swim as I am.

It was March, and at night the house was centrally
heated. By contrast, the air in the garden made her
shiver and hurry to the pool. A little vapour rose from
its glass-calm surface, a sign that the water would be

warmer than the air.

She dropped her towel on a chaise-longue, stepped out of her thongs and loosened her terry-cloth robe. The garden was completely private, flanked by the spacious grounds of two other mansions.

Naked, she stepped into the pool, descending the submerged steps until, with a sigh of pleasure, she sank into the water like a woman relaxing into the arms of her lover.

As a little girl, she had been brought up on fairy-tales and poetry. As she swam up and down the long pool, snatches of moon-poems came to her.

> A ship, an isle, a sickle moon—
> With few but with how splendid stars
> The mirrors of the sea are strewn
> Between their silver bars.

Presently she rolled on to her back, feeling her hair drifting like seaweed in the water. The air was cool on her wet breasts. She felt like a mermaid, star-gazing.

'Do you make a habit of skinny-dipping in the small hours?'

The mocking male voice rang out from somewhere behind her, making her slack body jerk in a convulsive and panic-stricken movement to bring herself upright and turn to see who had spoken.

He was by the side of the pool, wearing a long white robe with a hood hanging from the shoulders. Just for an instant, with his arms crossed inside the wide sleeves, he looked like a tall monk standing there.

Then she recognised him.

The man who had once made her normally calm, quiet nature seethe with violent, angry emotions. The only person for whom she had ever felt hatred.

The last man in the world she wanted to find her naked, alone, at night, in his swimming pool:

PART ONE

CRANMERE

BETWEEN its impressive main gateway and the great English country house known as Cranmere Park, a three-mile-long drive, lined by beech trees, wound its way through acres of pasture grazed by a herd of white Charolais.

Designed in 1710 by Sir John Vanbrugh, the architect of Blenheim Palace, Seaton Delaval and a number of other historic mansions, the house had been sited on a rise to command fine surrounding views. The last mile of drive was uphill so that when, on a blustery morning in November, Summer Roberts pedalled her bicycle into the stable-yard behind the house, she was pink-cheeked and out of breath.

Leaving the bicycle in a coach-house still filled with the horse-drawn vehicles used by earlier generations of the Lancaster family, she followed a gravelled path which led round the east front of Cranmere to what was known as the Garden Door.

This opened into a wide corridor where, on a row of strong pegs, hung a motley collection of ancient Burberrys, oilskin waders, game-bags, tweed Norfolk jackets and heavy wool jerseys; together with all kinds of headgear and, ranged in a row on the mud-resistant flagged floor, many different sorts of foot-wear from wellington boots to rubber galoshes.

On the opposite wall, grouped round the doors to the lavatory and the room where flowers were arranged, was a fine set of early sporting prints which, in a less splendid household, would have hung

15

somewhere more important than the downstairs cloakroom.

Probably none of the Lancasters had realised that the prints were rarities. Although in recent years two of Cranmere's most important oil paintings had been auctioned at Sotheby's, the great house was still full of treasures, many of them unrecognised except by Summer and Lady Emily who were interested in such things.

At the inner end of the cloakroom was a door leading to the Great Hall. Before passing through it, Summer paused to remove her outdoor clothes and to change her warm, fleece-lined boots for a pair of brown leather Oxfords which she kept at Cranmere as house shoes.

She was twenty-two—an age at which most young women spent time and money making the best of themselves. But she had been actively discouraged from giving any thought to her appearance.

Among her assets were long-lashed, intelligent grey eyes, a flawless complexion and a beautiful low-pitched speaking voice. But as she never used make-up and still wore her long thick fair hair in the pigtail dictated by her aunt—although now it was wound like a Catherine-wheel and pinned to the back of her head—her best features were usually less noticeable than her worst ones.

From lack of money and other difficulties, she dressed very badly in drab, shapeless, serviceable clothes. Today she was wearing a loose navy needle-cord pinafore over a grey roll-necked jersey and thick ribbed wine-coloured hose. Her house shoes and boots were brown. Her shoulder-bag was black—the leather-look plastic beginning to wear thin in places.

Although she had passed through the Great Hall every day for the past eighteen months—except for the week when her aunt had had her second stroke—she never failed to be impressed by its lofty magnificence. A modification of Vanbrugh's dramatic design

for the entrance to Castle Howard, the Yorkshire seat
of the Earl of Carlisle, the hall at Cranmere was lit by
windows in a cupola eight feet above the black and
white marble floor.

On her way to mount the Grand Staircase, she
checked when a voice said, 'Good morning, Miss
Roberts.'

'Oh . . . good morning.'

Somewhat surprised to see the late Marquess of
Cranmere's butler in this part of the house at this hour,
she would have continued on her way had he not said, 'If
I might have a word with you . . .'

'Certainly.' Something in his manner made her add,
'Is anything wrong, Mr Conway?'

Although the Marquess and his family had always
referred to and addressed the head of the household
staff by his surname alone, Summer felt it would have
been inappropriate for her to follow their example. She
was not a servant as such, but she was an employee,
and the butler was a man in his late sixties, old enough
to be her grandfather.

'No, no, nothing's wrong,' he assured her. 'It's merely
that his Lordship arrived late last night. He wishes to see
you, Miss Roberts. You'll find him in the library.'

'His Lordship?' For a moment, she was nonplussed.

During her time at Cranmere, 'his Lordship' had
meant either the Marquess of Cranmere or his son, Lord
Edgedale.

But the heir and his wife had been killed in their BMW
on the Autoroute du Sud the previous sum-
mer; and, at the end of October, the old Marquess
had died in his private apartments in the south
wing.

Summer's social life was so restricted as to be non-
existent. She didn't know any of the county people who
came to the house as guests; nor did she mix with the
village people. Nevertheless, she knew there were two
schools of thought about the Marquess's death. One
was that, after thirty years of heavy drinking, he had
finally succumbed to cirrhosis; the other that, with

no grandsons to succeed him, he had died of despair at the extinction of his line.

Recognising her puzzlement, the butler said, 'His late Lordship's other son, Miss Roberts. Lord James as he was when he lived here.'

She had known, but momentarily forgotten, that another son did exist. Emily had told her about him. He had left Cranmere under a cloud, sent packing by his father, the nature of his offence unknown. Neither she nor Emily had expected him to reappear so soon after the Marquess's death, if ever. He had been what was known as 'a bad lot'.

'You say he arrived very late. Has Lady Emily seen him?' she asked.

'I shouldn't think so, Miss Roberts. It had gone ten o'clock when his Lordship telephoned from the airport, and it was midnight by the time he arrived here. He was up in good time this morning, looking round the house and making himself known to those of the staff who don't remember him. But as far as I know he hasn't yet seen Lady Emily.'

'You say he rang up from the airport. That suggests he's come back from abroad. Do you know from where?' she enquired.

The butler shook his head. 'His Lordship hasn't mentioned his whereabouts during his absence.'

Was that a very gentle snub? Did Conway consider it improper for her to express curiosity about her new employer's activities during the years since his father had summarily disowned him? Or did the butler's impassive expression mask an equally sharp curiosity, and perhaps a degree of apprehension?

In recent years the Lancasters had suffered various reverses, culminating in the untimely death of Lord and Lady Edgedale on their way from Paris to the French Riviera.

Who could say what misfortunes might not occur now that the title and estate were in the hands of a black sheep whose only motive for returning might be self-interest?

'As he doesn't know I've arrived, I'll just go up and say good morning to Lady Emily before I present myself to him,' said Summer.

Today, as she climbed the wide, shallow steps of a staircase conceived as something more than merely a means of access between one floor and another, she had no eyes for the lace-like intricacies of the wrought-iron balustrade, or the vivid green of an immense malachite urn displayed on a pedestal where the first flight joined the second.

Her mind was concentrated on Conway's startling announcement and its possible repercussions. It could be—she certainly hoped so—that the new Lord Cranmere's arrival would be a good thing for the house and everyone in it.

A misspent youth didn't necessarily mean he must be a dissolute adult. He might have reformed and become quite respectable and staid.

Yet if that were the case, why had he never come home? Never made any effort to repair the breach with his family?

However angry his father had been with him all those years ago, the fact that his elder son had failed to safeguard the succession must have mellowed his attitude to his younger son, so had Lord James ever attempted to make peace with him?

She was forced to conclude that no olive-branch had ever been proffered. Which in turn suggested that James Lancaster was not a man who attached much importance to blood ties or, probably, to his own responsibility as the last of his line.

The important question was: What would be his attitude to Emily? Would he be kind and protective? She would be appallingly vulnerable if it turned out that the newly-arrived Marquess was still the 'bad lot' he had been in his salad days.

Summer, who had personal experience of what it was like to be defenceless, felt her hackles rise at the thought of Emily being in the same situation.

She herself had had no one to turn to. At least Emily

had her to stand by her. But for how long?

Originally, she had come to work at Cranmere on a part-time basis. For the past twelve months her hours had been ten until five, often seven days a week. Her hours and the salary she received were a matter of mutual agreement, mutual good-will. She had never had a contract. The new Lord Cranmere could dismiss her tomorrow, if he wished.

Or even today, she thought wryly.

While spending the Christmas of 1718 at Castle Howard, Sir John Vanbrugh, its designer, had written to the Duke of Newcastle: *There has fallen a Snow up to one's Neck . . . In short 'tis so bloody cold, I have almost a mind to Marry to keep myself warm.*

In most of the architect's houses, including Cranmere, the state rooms faced south, the private apartments to the north. However, since central heating had been installed, those private rooms at Cranmere were no longer as arctic as they must have been throughout the first two hundred and fifty years of the house's history.

Although it was now quarter past ten in the morning, when Summer entered her bedroom she found Lady Emily Lancaster still cosily ensconced in her four-poster bed.

This was not unusual. An inveterate bookworm, she often read far into the night and, in consequence, was prone to oversleeping. Her breakfast was brought to her on a tray at half past eight, and usually she stayed in bed, reading, until Summer's arrival.

Emily suffered from asthma. If she had an attack when Summer was not there to help her, she could press a bell which would summon Mrs Wright, the housekeeper.

After the death of Miss Margaret Ewing, Summer's aunt, whom she had cared for and nursed from shortly after her first stroke until the end of her life, Lady Edgedale had invited Summer to move from her aunt's cottage to a room at Cranmere.

For reasons of her own Summer had declined this suggestion; although she sometimes felt guilty at leaving Emily by herself, particularly since the tragedy on the Autoroute.

Had Emily been at all nervous of sleeping far away from the servants' quarters, Summer would have stayed with her. But in spite of her physical frailty, the child was anything but timorous. As long as she had Cyprian with her, and could read until she felt sleepy, being alone in her part of the house didn't bother her in the least.

Cyprian was a large woollen caterpillar, knitted with green and black wool and stuffed with kapok by Emily's former Nanny. Now that she was nearly fourteen, she was inclined to be sheepish about her love for her toy. But Summer understood her feelings—she had once loved a threadbare white rabbit with a red felt coat, a carrot attached to one paw. She could still remember her sense of outraged betrayal when, returning to the cottage after a term at university, she discovered Miss Ewing had burnt him as a piece of unwanted clutter.

'Summer! You'll never guess. Something terrific has happened,' Emily exclaimed delightedly, as soon as she saw her.

Although small for her age, much too thin and with no present claim to prettiness, in moments of animation she had an evanescent charm which made Summer think that one day she might be a beauty. She had red hair and hazel eyes and, in summer, a tendency to freckle. In winter she always looked pale and what Mrs Wright called 'peaky', meaning not well.

'Oh, really? What?' Summer asked.

At first she didn't connect her charge's excitement with the news imparted by Conway.

'My wicked Uncle James has turned up—and he doesn't seem wicked at all. He seems very nice. I like him,' Emily announced.

'When did you meet him?'

'Last night. He saw my light from the Blue Room and he came and introduced himself.'

'Wasn't that rather alarming?'

'I did wonder who it could be when I heard his footsteps in the passage, but it obviously wasn't a burglar—they creep about with a torch, and he knew where the light switches were. I could hear him coming from miles away. He walks like General Cadbury.'

Summer had met the General, an old man of upright bearing and piercing glance. She had seen him marching about the village, glaring with disapprobation at youths in black leathers slouched astride powerful motorbikes, eating fish and chips from polystyrene dishes.

She would not have expected the wastrel James Lancaster to bear even a slight resemblance to the stiff-necked, reactionary General. But Emily was an observant child and if she said he did, he must do so.

'What makes you like him?' she asked.

'Lots of things. He has a nice smile . . . and nice teeth.' Emily always noticed people's teeth. 'He reminded me of Lion Gardiner. I mean I should think Lion probably looked a lot like James. He says I needn't call him Uncle.'

From this it was clear to Summer that her charge's first description of him as 'very nice' had been an understatement. To be likened to Lion Gardiner, who had recently replaced the Chevalier Bayard as Emily's current beau ideal, he must be a man of quite exceptional charm.

But was that charm natural or calculated, Summer wondered uneasily.

While Emily's father was alive, he had run the estate and the home-farm, in consultation with his father. After the Edgedale's bodies had been brought back to England and interred in the family vault in the parish churchyard, the old man had interviewed several prospective farm managers. None had proved suitable and, up to the time of his death, a nucleus of loyal and conscientious staff, who had never worked anywhere else, had kept the place going as before.

Whether, because of his long estrangement from his younger son, Emily was now her grandfather's heir, Summer had no idea. It was only just over a fortnight since the second funeral. Since then the future of the Castle and its occupants had been a matter for conjecture.

One thing was certain—in no circumstances would a child of thirteen have any immediate control over such an inheritance. It would be in the hands of trustees until she was eighteen or more.

But it could be that her trustees would, from now on, include James Lancaster; or that, by virtue of his ability to save the family from extinction, he could overset a will made in Emily's favour.

Much as she hoped that it might be a worthier motive which made him seek out his niece so soon after his arrival, and exert himself to make a good impression on her, Summer had an uncomfortable intuition that his midnight visit to Emily's bedroom had been a deliberate strategy of some benefit to himself.

He won't win *me* over so easily, she thought to herself, before asking, 'How long did he stay? What did you talk about?'

'Oh, ages . . . an hour at least. We talked about all sorts of things. Just imagine . . . it's eighteen years since he was last here. He was seventeen when he left, so that makes him thirty-five—eight years younger than Daddy.'

'Did he tell you where he's been in the meantime?'

Emily shook her head. 'He didn't say, but he has an American accent so perhaps he went there to seek his fortune.'

'Or to Canada,' Summer suggested, her more prosaic turn of mind making her wonder how a youth of that age, brought up in privileged circumstances, would have managed to scrape a living in his first few years on the other side of the Atlantic.

Deep down, at the core of her being, she was as romantic as Emily. It was she who had introduced her pupil to Bayard, the brave but gentle French knight, and more recently to Lion Gardiner, the English colonist who had played a stalwart part in America's early history and given his name to an island off the tip of Long Island.

But the soft heart of Summer's nature was something she kept to herself, hidden by layers of reserve and a down-to-earth, practical manner. Even with Emily, she tried not to show how easily certain lines of poetry, or Kirsten Flagstad singing Wagner's *Liebestod*, could move her to tears. Even *Tie a Yellow Ribbon* could make her cry if she let it.

'Yes, his accent could be Canadian,' Emily agreed. 'I can't tell the difference. Can you?'

'I expect I could when I lived in America. Not now. It's years since I've spoken to any Canadians or Americans.'

'That's rather odd—don't you think?—the fact that you're an American with an English accent, and James is an Englishman with an American or Canadian accent.'

Summer's response was a preoccupied 'Mm'. After a thoughtful pause, she said, 'He didn't mention being married, or having children of his own, did he?'

'No, he hardly said anything about himself. He wanted to know all about me, and what had been happening here since he went away. He knew about Daddy and Mummy.'

Five months after the accident, Emily could speak of her parents without distress. Indeed, the nature of her relationship with them had meant that, for her, being orphaned had never been the shattering trauma which Summer had experienced at the age of ten.

Looked after from infancy until she was eight by a nanny, and thereafter by a series of governesses, she had had much less contact with her parents than children in ordinary households. They had been like an uncle and aunt to her; not the constant, loving companions whom Summer had lost and still missed, many years later.

'How did he know? Did he tell you?' she asked.

'No, but he read about Granpa in the *New York Herald Tribune*. Did you know Granpa had had two wives?'

'I had no idea.'

'The first one was an American, and they were divorced. James knows her—she lives in Palm Beach. Did you ever go there?'

'No, not that I remember. Palm Beach is in Florida. We went almost everywhere else, but never to Florida.'

Summer's father had been an artist who specialised in painting murals on the walls of rich people's houses. He had worked all over the United States and in Europe as well, and Summer had hazy memories of Paris and the Riviera.

Looking back, it surprised her that he had never had a commission in Palm Beach, one of the wealthiest resorts in the United States. Perhaps he had painted some murals there, either before she was born or when she was too young to remember that phase of the happy, footloose life which she and her mother had lived with him.

One of her ambitions—really more of a pipe-dream because she had little hope of ever being able to achieve it—was to retrace her father's footsteps, taking photographs of his work to illustrate a memoir of him.

'James says it was because of Granpa's first wife being a well-known American that they gave him an obituary notice in the *Herald Tribune*,' Emily went on. 'Otherwise American readers wouldn't have been interested in him, and he—James, I mean—mightn't have heard he was dead for ages. You see, he doesn't use his title in America. The old lady—Granpa's first wife—is the only person who knows he has anything to do with us.'

'I see. Why is she well-known?'

'I asked him that, and he grinned and said because

she'd had almost as many husbands as Elizabeth Taylor. Granpa was the first one, but they didn't have any babies and they didn't get on, so after four years she ran away with a Frenchman. I wonder if Mummy and Daddy knew about her. I never heard them talking about her.'

'They must have known, I should imagine. I'd better go down to the library—Conway told me when I arrived that your uncle wanted to see me there. I don't suppose I'll be long.'

'Oh, is James up already? I thought he'd still be in bed, or I should have got up and had breakfast with him. He told me that flying through several time zones would upset his body clock; and that when he did go to bed he'd probably sleep through till lunchtime. He wasn't at all tired last night.'

'Conway said he was up early, and it's certainly high time that *you* were up and about, my little slug-a-bed,' Summer told her, with a smile. 'Come on: out you hop, or you won't be washed and dressed in time to see the programme about Vienna.'

Since becoming Emily's tutor, she had often made use of the BBC's television programmes for schools and also the more advanced programmes for Open University students.

Lord and Lady Edgedale had seemed untroubled by the fact that her tuition of their daughter inevitably was biased in favour of Summer's own preferred subjects, and lacked the balance and scope of a normal education.

Emily had never gone to school because her asthma was caused by a condition called airways irritability, and was thought to be exacerbated by frequent exposure to colds and similar infections. Summer had sometimes wondered if that diagnosis could be wrong and the asthma was actually psychosomatic; triggered by activities and people Emily disliked, such as riding and two of her governesses.

'Miss Banks was a fresh air fanatic. She was always dragging me out for long boring country walks,' she had once confided, telling Summer about her predecessor.

Summer had been sympathetic—her parents had liked sunny climates. Before coming to England to live with her mother's unmarried elder sister, her only experience of cold weather had been spending Christmas in Switzerland, in a warm and snug wooden chalet.

The memory of her first winter in Miss Ewing's cold and draughty cottage could still make her shudder. No matter how low the temperature, her aunt had insisted she must always have her bedroom window open. The only heating in the bathroom had been from an inadequate oil stove. And every Saturday and Sunday afternoon, when she would have liked to curl up by the fire with a book, she had been forced to go out for a chilly trudge round the countryside. She had no intention of imposing a similar regime on Emily.

They never walked in bad weather, and rarely and not far on fine days. They both preferred mental exercise to any form of physical exertion.

'Perhaps we should skip lessons today and spend it with James,' said Emily, as she wriggled her way from the centre to the side of the double bed.

Summer said, 'He may want you to spend the day with him. Perhaps that's why he wants to see me—to ask if you can have a holiday.'

Emily flung back the bedclothes. The winter before her mother had bought her two frilly Victorian-style nightgowns, but she hadn't liked them, complaining that they rode up round her chest during the night. She preferred pyjamas.

Her chest was still flat, her hips and thighs bony and boyish. Physically she was still pre-adolescent, but not emotionally. Already she was longing to meet a real-life person who embodied the qualities of her historical heroes.

Remembering herself at the same age, Summer thought it might be a condition common to all lonely girls. Perhaps lack of affection in childhood or, in her own case, having it and then losing it, always made girls start to dream about love prematurely.

It seemed an aeon since she had first yearned to know what one of her favourite poets, Robert Browning called 'the wild joys of loving'. But so far her experiences with men had been limited to a couple of disastrous blind dates during her time at university.

The tall double doors of solid Spanish mahogany were closed when she went to the library to present herself to Emily's uncle.

Knowing that a light tap might not be audible if he were at the far end of the room, she clenched her fist and rapped on the panel hard enough to hurt her knuckles.

As she was straining her ears to hear herself bidden to enter, both doors were suddenly swept open and she was confronted by a very tall man who, after looking her up and down, said, 'Good morning. Who are you?'

Disconcerted by the question, as well as on several other counts, she instinctively stepped back a pace.

She was tall herself, but he was taller by at least eight inches. A giant of a man, with broad shoulders, but not thick-necked with heavy jowls like his father and brother. His looks were so different from theirs that, if the butler's recognition hadn't proved him to be who he said he was, she would have thought him an impostor.

'I—I'm Summer Roberts . . . Emily's tutor,' she stammered.

He seemed to find this as unexpected as she had found him. His left eyebrow lifted, and his eyes repeated their comprehensive appraisal.

All over the house there were portraits which showed that, for many generations, the Lancasters had been men with a predisposition to early baldness, rather protuberant pale blue eyes, and fair complexions becoming florid in middle-age.

Their wives' looks had varied enormously; but the male line had run true to form—until it produced this startling mutation; a deeply tanned, black-haired man with strange tawny-coloured eyes under heavy lids. Or perhaps it was only because his height obliged him to look down at people that his eyes seemed narrowed and preternaturally watchful.

'You know who I am, Miss Roberts. How do you do?' he said briskly, offering his hand.

Long ago, when she was a little girl, Thomas Roberts had taught her to shake hands firmly. He detested limp-fingered hand-clasps.

The ninth Lord Cranmere had a grip like her father's; warm and strong and rather more prolonged than most people's handshakes. But her father had always smiled when he grasped the hand of a stranger —from what she remembered of him, a smile had been his most characteristic expression.

Emily had given her the impression that her uncle was also a man whose approach to life was good-humoured; a man who smiled easily and often.

Yet he wasn't smiling at this moment. His expression was rather *un*friendly.

He let go of her hand, stepped aside and, when she had crossed the threshold, pulled the two doors together behind him.

'Come and sit down,' he invited. 'Conway has just brought me a pot of coffee. Shall I ask him to bring another cup?'

'Yes, please . . . if you would,' she assented.

She never felt hungry in the morning—a cup or two of black coffee was all she ever had for breakfast. It was not until nearly mid-morning that she began to feel peckish.

He moved swiftly ahead of her, making for the desk with the house-telephone. Of all the rooms in the Castle, the library was Summer's favourite. A long and lofty apartment, lit by the tall rounded windows which had been one of Vanbrugh's hallmarks, it contained half a dozen desks, several tables and two

folding racks made to hold portfolios of drawings. In
between there were chairs and sofas, and a number of
revolving bookstands.

However, the bulk of the books were housed on the
shelves which lined three sides of the room, with more
shelves up on a gallery reached by two identical circu-
lar staircases. At the far end of the room were double
doors to match those he had opened for her. There
was also a secret jib-door fooling the eye with rows of
books which looked real but were actually painted on
the wood.

Artists called the technique *trompe-l'oeil*, and while
this particular example had been painted in the early
nineteenth century, it was a device she knew her
father had used.

Once, in a house they had rented—she couldn't be
sure but she thought it had been in Virginia—he had
painted a small *trompe-l'oeil* especially for her.

She had been in bed, having measles or maybe
chickenpox, and he had lain flat on the floor, painting
something on the baseboard. Not until he had finished
was she able to see what it was—a hole in the skirting
with a little brown mouse peering through it.

With its beady black eyes and fine whiskers, the
mouse had looked so convincing that when, later,
Summer had gasped and exclaimed, 'Mommy!
There's a mouse in the corner!', her mother had
thought it a real one.

Now, whenever she passed the jib-door, the happy
memory would bring a smile to her lips. But not this
morning. This morning all her attention was focussed
on the tall, authoritative man who had suddenly entered their lives, but with what effect—good or bad—
remained to be seen.

Having made a brief call to Conway in the butler's
pantry, he invited her to sit down on one side of a
large partners' desk while he took the chair on the
other. Between them, the worn leather surface was
littered with interesting relics of earlier generations of
Lancasters.

A malachite inkstand presented by Tsar Nicholas of Russia, with the urn on the Grand Staircase and other tokens of esteem, to the fifth Lord Cranmere. A silver wax jack once used in sealing letters. A black papier mâché folder for blotting paper with a matching pen tray holding pens of turned ivory which might have lain there, their nibs rusting, for a hundred and fifty years. A brass carriage clock . . . a bronze model of a mare and her foal . . . a round ebony ruler . . . the minutiae of a splendid heritage.

The first thing he said was: 'I gather you don't agree with Johnson that "nobody who does not rise early will ever do any good", Miss Roberts. My niece tells me she doesn't usually start her school work until around ten or ten-thirty. Why not at nine?'

There was nothing overtly censorious in his tone of voice, but nevertheless there was criticism of her methods underlying his opening remarks. She felt it was an ominous beginning to her relationship with him.

Outwardly composed, inwardly nervous, she answered, 'Because I believe in the theory that people fall into two categories—night-owls and larks. Emily's an owl. She loves to read in bed. If she went to school she would have to conform to conventional school hours. But she doesn't go to school, and I see no advantage in forcing her to get up early—any more than I'd make her write with her right hand if she happened to be left-handed.'

He picked up the ebony ruler and began to revolve it between his long, sun-burnt fingers. She wondered where he had acquired his deep tan.

Certainly not in Canada or the northerly parts of America where, according to the news on the radio, the winter weather was being more severe than usual. Perhaps he had been in Palm Beach with the old lady Emily had mentioned.

Summer had noticed his use of the phrase 'around ten or ten-thirty' where an Englishman would have said 'about ten'. But his transatlantic accent was not a

strong one; and not, she was fairly sure, Canadian.
After twelve years away from her homeland—and
having left it as a child—her ear was no longer tuned to
the many different kinds of American accents. The
way he spoke reminded her of the voice of Alistair
Cooke, the British-born, Yale and Harvard-educated
broadcaster who helped her to keep in touch with
events in her own country. But the actual timbre of
James Lancaster's voice was more like that of Sir
Douglas Fairbanks, one of the few Americans to have
been knighted by the Queen of England.

'And are you also a night-owl, Miss Roberts?' he
asked her.

'Yes, I am, as it happens.'

'I see,' he said, on a dry note.

The implication was obvious. He thought it was for
her own convenience that she let Emily lie late in bed.

Striving to keep her tone equable, she said, 'But if
you remember, the great Dr Johnson prefaced his
advice by saying, "I have, all my life long, been lying
till noon"—and surely no one would describe him as a
failure?'

A fugitive gleam of amusement appeared in
the lazy-lidded eyes meeting hers across the wide
desk.

There was even a hint of a smile at the corner of his
well-cut mouth as he said lightly, 'Touché,' and then,
'I can see I shall have to pick my quotations with
greater care for the context.'

'Are you always an early riser yourself, Lord
Cranmere? Emily said you were expecting to sleep
until lunchtime.'

'Oh, you've been up to see her, have you? I thought
you'd just arrived. Yes, I'm normally up around six. I
don't need very much sleep—I never have. When I
was Emily's age, I was friendly with old Barty Hicks.
He's probably dead now. He was a poacher by trade
and, as you know, they work at night. I used to spend
many nights with him, not only on this estate but
sometimes on neighbours' land.'

'You helped poach your father's game?' she exclaimed in astonishment.

Moments ago, there had been a smile in his eyes, now she saw something else—a swift, cold glare of displeasure. Only for a fraction of a second but, while it lasted, oddly frightening.

At that point the butler appeared with a cup and saucer for her, and a plate of the chocolate biscuits which she and Emily had with their mid-morning break.

Watching Conway pour out the coffee, she could only conclude that the younger man had been annoyed by what he considered an impertinence. But why mention his youthful misdeeds if he wanted to keep her firmly in her place? He hadn't seemed to mind her Johnsonian riposte. Why had her spontaneous comment on his poaching made him angry?

As the butler withdrew, she helped herself to the cream and sugar he had placed on her side of the desk.

'Not for me, thanks,' said the Marquess, when she would have passed them across to him.

When he also refused a chocolate biscuit, she thought he might produce a cigarette to smoke with his cup of black coffee. Then she noticed there was no trace of nicotine stains on his fingers as there had been on his brother's.

Not only were they unalike in looks, but their general appearance was different. Lord Edgedale had been a countryman who hadn't shared his wife's liking for London. Although well turned out when hunting, or in evening dress, at most other times he had been an untidy-looking man who frequently cut himself shaving and who suffered from scurf in what was left of his hair.

Whether his younger brother was always as well-dressed and spruce as he was this morning, she had no means of telling. Even though he had the physique to make a cheap suit look good, she felt sure that the one he was wearing was the American equivalent of a bespoke suit from Savile Row. She could see that the

buttons on his sleeves were the kind which un-
fastened and she knew this to be a sign of superior
tailoring. His shirt cuffs were fastened by discreet flat
gold links. Unlike his father and brother, he didn't
wear a signet-ring on his left little finger. Perhaps if he
hadn't left home in disgrace the year before, he would
have received one at his coming of age.

'Tell me about Emily. As you know, I talked to her
last night and formed an initial impression. But I'd like
to hear your opinion of her.'

She realised she should have foreseen he would ask
her this and prepared a considered judgment, neatly
expressed.

To give herself time to think, she said, 'Do you mean
academically or generally?'

'Both.'

'Well . . . I'm not in a position to compare her with
her contemporaries, but by the standards of my day
I'd say she's extremely bright. She enjoys learning. I
don't have to push her. Sometimes I have to restrain
her from overdoing it. As a person, I think she's a
darling . . . sensitive, generous, full of fun—'

Before she could list any more of Emily's good
qualities, he interrupted her.

'You make her sound a paragon. Has she no faults in
your estimation?'

Again his tone was so dry as to make it obvious he
suspected Summer of sycophancy.

She lifted her chin. 'Everyone has faults, Lord
Cranmere. I feel it's a negative attitude to dwell on
children's defects rather than their virtues. If you'd let
me finish, I should have added that Emily is inclined to
be untidy and she has a quick temper. But considering
that thirteen is a notoriously awkward age, she's very
easy to handle and I think she has great potential—
even though, at the moment, she has no clear-cut
vocation.'

'She tells me that asthma has prevented her from
going to school. How often does she have these
attacks?'

'Very seldom. But if she were in a different environment she would probably have them more often.'

'But that theory hasn't been tested?'

'No.'

'What are your qualifications as a tutor, Miss Roberts? Are you a graduate?'

'No. I was at Somerville for a short time, but I had to come down for family reasons.'

'You must have been an exceptional scholar to be given a place at one of the Oxford women's colleges. Why did you have to relinquish it?'

She hesitated, unwilling to discuss a subject which she felt couldn't be of any real interest to him.

'The aunt I lived with was taken ill. There was no one else to look after her.'

'Are you still looking after her?'

'No, she's dead now.'

'Isn't it possible for you to go back to Oxford?'

'I don't know—I haven't enquired. I don't particularly want to go back. It was going to lead to a teaching career, and that's what I'm doing.'

'But your present pupil won't keep you occupied indefinitely, and then what?'

Was this the first hint that dismissal was hanging over her?

She said quietly, 'I'm sure I shall be able to find another post when my time here comes to an end. I imagine you don't mean to make any drastic changes until you've been here long enough to make wise decisions, Lord Cranmere. I'm sure you're aware that Emily has already had two bad shocks this year, and that it would be better for her to get over losing her grandfather before there are any more disturbances in her life.'

'Were she and her grandfather fond of each other? He must have mellowed since my time if they were'— was his sardonic comment.

'No, perhaps not precisely fond,' she admitted. 'But he was her only close relation after she lost her parents. I've no doubt you and she will have a much warmer relationship . . . given time. Have you any daughters?'

He rose abruptly from his chair. There was restlessness in the way he thrust his hands into the pockets of his trousers and took two or three strides away from the desk before suddenly swinging to face her.

'No daughters. No sons. No wife. My motto is: He travels fastest who travels alone.'

It didn't surprise her to learn that he was a bachelor. He didn't look like a family man. In spite of his elegant clothes, there was something . . . untamed about him.

'But now that the future of your family hinges on you—' she began.

'My family, if and when I have one, won't be living here,' he informed her. 'I prefer the New World, Miss Roberts. I've made a life for myself there and I've no intention of sacrificing my achievements on the altar of tradition. I came to England for two reasons; first, to disclaim the title and, secondly, to meet my niece and take responsibility for her until she can look after herself.'

Summer blinked at him incredulously. This was a turn of events she hadn't envisaged. She couldn't believe he was serious.

'How can you disclaim the title?'

'Easily. Lord Home disclaimed his in order to become Prime Minister. So did Lord Hailsham when he wanted to sit in the House of Commons. All that has to be done is to send an instrument of disclaimer to the Lord Chancellor. I shall do that later today.'

'But why? What's wrong with a title? What's wrong with tradition?' she protested, still too shocked to think before she spoke. 'If you don't want to use it, you needn't. But to throw it away . . . to reject it—'

'I don't think what I choose to do is your concern,' he said coldly. 'And I don't expect you to discuss it with anyone else. I particularly want to avoid the kind of sensational publicity drummed up by the tabloids. No public announcement will be made until after I've left the country. Meantime, in private, I prefer to be called by the name I'm known by in America. James Gardiner. Spelt G-a-r-d-i-n-e-r.'

When she didn't speak, he went on, 'It's been my name for ten years. I adopted it as my legal surname before I became an American citizen.'

Summer found her voice. 'What made you choose the name Gardiner?'

The broad shoulders shrugged. 'It was the name of a man I admired when I was a boy. An English military engineer who went to America as a colonist in the seventeenth century.'

She said huskily, 'Lion Gardiner of Gardiner's Island.'

'Yes—how do you know about him?'

'There's a book up on the gallery—*Lion Gardiner And His Descendants*. Emily has read it. He's rather a hero of hers.' She refrained from adding—and of mine.

'Is that so?' His expression was warmer than it had been some moments earlier. 'I should think she and I are probably the only people who have opened it since it found its way here. I must—' He was interrupted by the telephone. 'Excuse me.'

She was already on her feet when, putting his hand over the mouthpiece, he said to her, 'This is a long distance call which may take quite a while. We'll continue our conversation later.'

On her way back to Emily's room, Summer still found it hard to credit his intention to repudiate his heritage.

Clearly he had done well for himself in America. Equally clearly he still felt resentment and bitterness towards his father. Perhaps he had been harshly treated. But it was a long time ago—too long to bear a grudge. There had been times, in her teens, when she had hated her aunt. Now that she was older, she pitied her.

Madame de Staël, the brilliant society hostess whom Napoleon had banished from Paris, had been correct when she wrote, *Tout comprendre c'est tout pardonner*. To understand all is to forgive all.

It had been old Dr Dyer, the local GP, who had been her aunt's medical adviser, who had made Summer understand her aunt's sour, relentless nature and, understanding it, forgive its effect on her own life.

As it happened, later that day Dr Dyer came to Cranmere, first to attend to a housemaid who had scalded her arm, and then to give Emily a polio booster.

He was semi-retired; the practice being run by his son except for a few special patients and calls to Cranmere.

When Emily told him about her uncle's arrival, which perhaps he had already heard about while he was downstairs, he said, 'I wouldn't mind having a pound for every time I patched up Lord James, as he was then. He was always risking his neck in some foolhardy escapade.'

Emily's hazel eyes widened. 'What sort of escapades?'

The old man chuckled. 'You'll have to ask him. I can't tell you. A doctor must respect his patients' confidences.'

As he spoke there was a knock at the door and the subject of their conversation joined them.

He had lunched with his niece and her tutor, but had spent the afternoon in conclave with the senior partner of his family's lawyers, whom he had summoned from London early that morning.

'Dr Dyer! I heard you were here. How are you? It's good to see you.'

Watched by Emily and Summer, the two men exchanged cordial greetings. For the second time that day she saw the American, as he was now, employing the same potent charm she had seen him exert on his niece at the lunch table.

Towards her his manner had been courteous, but she had felt that he would have preferred to lunch with Emily à deux. Indeed, Summer had suggested going back to the cottage for her lunch, leaving them to spend the rest of the day alone together. Then he had explained that the lawyer was arriving at two, and Emily had insisted she must eat with them.

Trying hard to be fair to the man, in spite of her intuitive conviction that he hadn't taken to her, she acknowledged that perhaps he hadn't actually 'exerted' his charm upon Emily, in the sense that a confidence trickster exuded false charm to gull his victims.

Perhaps with people *he* liked, James Gardiner always was a charming, warm personality. Unfortunately, before they had finished shaking hands, she had sensed that he was writing her off as a dowdy, uninteresting female. And she had to admit that even before she had met him, she had to some extent prejudged him—and not favourably.

Presently, after ten minutes' conversation, Dr Dyer said he had another call to make.

'I'll see you to your car,' said James Gardiner.

A few minutes after the two men had left the room, Summer noticed that the doctor had forgotten his gloves. But for Emily's disability, she would have asked her to run after him. However, running, or even hurrying, could make the child start to wheeze, so it was Summer who hastened to catch him up.

By the time she reached the end of the West Corridor where it joined the Gallery overlooking and surrounding the Great Hall, the men were on the other side, almost at the top of the Grand Staircase.

The acoustics of the Gallery were such that people on opposite sides could speak to each other across the abyss without raising their voices. She had already overheard the doctor talking about Barty, whom she took to be the local poacher referred to by James that morning.

She was about to call out 'Wait a minute' when she heard the younger man say, 'Have you had much to do with this hulking great girl who teaches Emily?'

'Summer? Yes . . . know her well. Her aunt was a patient of mine. A difficult, embittered woman, and not always kind to her niece. Summer has had a tough

time of it since she lost her parents and came to
England. She was born and brought up in America.
She's a very nice girl, you'll find. A bit overweight, but
that's—'

'Overweight! She's as fat as a pig,' was James
Gardiner's caustic interjection. 'She never stops eating. Chocolate biscuits with her coffee this morning.
Two servings of dessert at lunch. She must weigh as
much as I do, and most of her weight is blubber.'

They were descending the stairs now, their backs to
the spot where Summer had instinctively paused
when she heard his question to the doctor.

She had not intended to eavesdrop but, while Dr
Dyer was replying, she had been unsure what to do.
Already James Gardiner had referred to her in terms
which must cause him embarrassment if he realised
she had overheard.

Now, after his brutal description of her being 'as fat
as a pig', she was literally frozen with shock.

Dr Dyer said, 'I seem to remember you used to be
able to pack away an amazing quantity of food, James.
You always made very short work of any cakes and
buns my wife offered you, after I'd stitched you up—
or extracted pellets from your backside,' he added,
with a reminiscent guffaw.

James did not join in his laughter. His tone incisive,
he said, 'I'm not sure that a girl who's an uncontrollable glutton is a suitable mentor for Emily. How serious is her asthma? I was under the impression that,
with the development of inhalants, it was now as man-
ageable as diabetes. Isn't Ian Botham an asthmatic?'

'Yes, he's had it since he was a youth, and it hasn't
stopped him becoming one of England's greatest
cricketers,' agreed the doctor. 'Personally, I think
Emily's asthma is something she will grow out of.
Meanwhile, in my opinion, Summer is an ideal person
to have charge of her. They've established a bond of
affection which you'd be most unwise to break. I'd go
as far as to say that Emily is fonder of Summer than
she ever was of her mother. You didn't know Lady

Edgedale. She never struck me as having a maternal nature. She was very good-looking, and my wife thought her vain; more interested in her clothes and in going to parties in London than in spending time with her daughter.'

'Not accusations which anyone could level at Miss Roberts. She doesn't appear to give a damn what she looks like. However, if you feel she's good for Emily, at least for the present—'

Summer heard no more. The sound of their voices was fading, and she had recovered the power to move and was going back the way she had come.

Still clutching the leather gloves, but with her errand driven out of her mind by the scalding humiliation of being called that *great hulking girl . . . fat as a pig . . . an uncontrollable glutton . . .* she walked blindly along the corridor; her footsteps making no sound on the long row of Persian rugs laid end to end, a lane of time-mellowed colour on the wax-polished floorboards ranged with seventeenth-century chairs, antique chests and fine lacquer cabinets.

Halfway along, she realised she couldn't go back to the schoolroom. She had to have time to recover before Emily saw her. At the moment it was all she could do not to break down in tears.

Fat as a pig . . . fat as a pig . . . the cruel words rang in her ears, making her cringe with chagrin. How could she ever face him?—knowing that he held her in contempt; that he didn't see her as a woman, only as a shapeless hulk, a great greedy lump of blubber who couldn't stop stuffing herself.

Her throat tight, her vision blurred, she stopped by the huge gilded mirror which reflected the break in the corridor where a short landing led to stairs going up to the schoolroom floor and down to a lobby between the gun room and the billiard room.

For a long time she had avoided catching sight of herself in full-length mirrors or shop windows. The only mirror she looked in was the one above her bathroom basin; a small rectangle of glass which reflected her head and neck when she brushed her teeth and washed her face, night and morning.

Now, as she forced herself to look at what other people saw—her outward and visible persona; not the real Summer Roberts, her inner self—a low groan of shame and despair burst from her quivering lips.

Because all he had said was true. She looked a fat slob . . . a mess.

How many times had she told herself: Tomorrow I'll start a serious diet. Tomorrow I'll cut down on sugar . . . stop eating chocolate . . . peanuts. Next week I really will start to get into shape. Starting next month, without fail, I'll begin a whole new regime; no snacks, no second helpings, no eating biscuits in bed.

Promises . . . secret pledges . . . New Year resolutions . . . good intentions. None of them ever fulfilled because, every time, she had lacked the willpower to starve herself. If it had been for just a week or two, she might have managed it. But not for the months and months it would take to dissolve the fat which had been slowly accumulating all through her teens.

And now, all at once, it was too late.

Today, when she wanted so badly to be slender and graceful, and turned out with casual elegance, she looked even worse than usual.

As her chest heaved with suppressed sobs and she felt her control giving way, her ears caught the sound of hurried footsteps crossing the marble floor of the Great Hall.

He was coming back! Perhaps on reaching the car Dr Dyer had noticed his gloves were missing. Guessing that, with his long legs and muscular physique, James Gardiner would mount the staircase much faster than he walked down it, for an instant she was overcome with panic. She wanted to run, to hide, to find a dark, secret place to curl up and cry as she had, long ago, under the bedclothes, when she first came to England and knew that never again was she going to be kissed goodnight.

But she had been only ten then. Now she was twenty-two. Too old to cry. Too old to show her feelings.

By the time James Gardiner came round the corner from the Gallery, she was moving slowly to meet him, her emotions under control.

'Dr Dyer has lost his gloves—ah, you've got them. Good.'

As he took them from her, he scarcely glanced at her face.

She watched him striding away, his broad upper back tapering to a lean waist and hips, his well-brushed glossy dark hair just touching the back of his shirt collar.

In that moment her usually pliant and amiable nature was swept by violent emotions quite foreign to her normal temperament. She felt anger, and fierce hostility and, above all, a burning desire to retaliate.

How, she had no idea. The desire, though strong, was vague, expressing itself in the thought: I'll show you. You wait, Mr Gardiner. I'll show you . . . damn you!

It was dark when she cycled back to the cottage near the village school of which, at one time, Miss Ewing had been in charge.

Summer put her bike in the shed at the end of the garden. The back yard she had called it at first, before Aunt Margaret had corrected her.

The door at the rear of the cottage led directly into the kitchen-cum-breakfast-room. There was no dining room and only a very small sitting room. ('Not living room, Summer. In England we say sitting room or, in a larger house, drawing room.') But as they never entertained, the lack of space hadn't mattered.

In all the years she had lived there, until Miss Ewing's first stroke, they had never had anyone to supper, or even to coffee and biscuits. To a child whose parents had delighted in impromptu parties for the friends made everywhere they went, Miss Ewing's belief in keeping herself to herself had been incomprehensible.

Since her aunt's death, Summer had made some improvements to the warmth and comfort of the cottage. The practical side of her nature, repressed by her aunt's insistence that she concentrate on her studies, had finally found expression in hanging more suitable wallpaper—small spriggy designs by Laura Ashley—over the ugly patterns chosen by Miss Ewing.

She hadn't enough money to make all the changes she would have liked, but gradually it was becoming a more welcoming place to come back to and spend her solitary evenings.

The absence of a television was no hardship to her, but lately she had been thinking it would be nice to have a cat. Until Emily's grandfather had died, she had seen herself staying at the cottage for at least the next three or four years. Marriage, or living with someone, had not been in her mind for a long time—not since that last blind date organised by well-meaning girl-friends.

Sometimes at night, before sleeping, she would let her imagination conjure romantic fantasies in which, slim and beautiful, she played the part of the mysterious Barbara dei Trechi whose love affair with the Chevalier Bayard resulted in the birth of his only known child, a daughter; or of Mary Wilemson, the Dutch girl whom Lion Gardiner had married while he was serving in the army of the Prince of Orange and whom, a year later, he took to Massachusetts with him.

Some of her father's forbears had come from Holland, and perhaps that was why, of the two passionate day-dreams she had so often replayed in her mind at night, she had always identified best with Mary, the pioneer bride unafraid of the dangers and hardships as long as she had Lion to protect her.

Now James Gardiner's coming had made it impossible for her ever again to think of Lion Gardiner without seeing, in her mind's eye, the compelling dark

face of the man who had adopted his surname in preference to his own patronymic. And with the thought
of him would come the wounding echo of his indictment of her as a gross, ungainly frump; someone who
would never see a man's eyes light with desire when
he looked at her, or surrender to real-life embraces as
ardent as those she had invoked in her day-dreams.

That night, as she lay in bed after putting her light
out, watching the full moon appear and disappear as a
rising wind drove ragged clouds across the winter sky,
her mind was full of a vengeful determination to make
James Gardiner eat his words.

She had had nothing to eat since coming home, and
only two cups of black coffee instead of her usual glass
of milk with supper, and a mug of hot chocolate at
bedtime. Knowing that she didn't need any more food
that day after eating a substantial lunch at the Castle,
she had been determined to begin her new regime
immediately.

But as sleep eluded her, as she tossed and turned in
the narrow single bed with the cheap mattress which
her aunt had bought twelve years ago and which now
needed replacing, she began to feel hungry.

Tantalising thoughts of the pork pie and cheese in
the refrigerator, the cakes and biscuits stored in tins in
the pantry, tempted her to go downstairs and assuage
her appetite with a late-night binge, as she had so
often in the past.

Secret orgies of compulsive eating had been a feature of her life ever since the abrupt termination of her
time at university. With her aunt partially paralysed
and no longer in charge of the domestic arrangements,
she had been able to build up a store of chocolate bars,
bags of what as a child she had called potato chips but
now knew by the English term crisps, jars of peanut
butter and jelly (called jam in England), tins of salted
cocktail nuts and many other goodies.

While her parents were alive, she could remember
being given fruit and celery to munch rather than
crackers. The English called them biscuits, and

produced probably the finest variety of them of any country in the world; ranging from Bath Olivers, invented by a Dr Oliver who had lived in the city of Bath in the eighteenth century, to currant-filled garibaldis, buttery Scottish shortbread and chocolate-coated digestives.

Once she had opened a packet of biscuits, she could never restrict herself to eating only one or two. Often she would demolish the entire packet.

It was the same with a slab of chocolate. The taste of the first two squares would excite a hunger for more—and more—until the whole slab had gone.

As well as the pork pie, with its thick pastry crust, the refrigerator contained a tub of liver pâté which she liked to spread on hard water biscuits. Thinking about it made her salivate. Yet at the same time she was remembering James Gardiner's scathing remark about her gluttony.

Her body craving the pleasure of crunching the brittle biscuits and feeling the soft, creamy texture of the pâté on her tongue, she fought to control the mounting urge to have one last, final, never-to-be-repeated debauch.

The cottage did not have a telephone. At half past eight the next morning, Summer walked to the public telephone a short distance away and dialled the Castle on the line which would be answered by Conway.

'This is Miss Roberts. Would you ask Lord Cranmere if he wants Lady Emily to have a free day today, please,' she asked.

'His Lordship has already left for London, Miss Roberts. He isn't expecting to return till tomorrow evening.'

'Oh, I see. In that case I'll come as usual.'

As she returned to the cottage she felt pleased with herself for having resisted temptation the night before. But she knew she might not have the will-power to resist again tonight. Somehow, she had to get rid of all the fattening snacks.

It seemed a sin to dump them in the bin to await the weekly rubbish collection. Nor was it practicable to stand at her front gate, handing them out to the children on their way to school. They would think she had gone mad. She could imagine the grins they would exchange with each other, the muffled sniggers.

Suddenly she thought of the old people's houses at the far end of the village; a complex of low-rent bungalows built round a communal social centre and the house of the Warden and his wife whom the residents could contact if they were taken ill or needed any kind of help.

Half an hour later, with everything eatable, except eggs and vegetables, packed in a large cardboard box balanced on and tied to her bicycle basket, she set out for the old people's community centre.

The comfortable room where whist drives and other activities were held was never locked during the day although there was seldom anyone there before mid-morning. Summer knew that a number of local farmers' wives left surplus produce there and other people took old magazines, unwanted paperbacks and anything else which might be useful. If any of the old folk happened to see her arriving with a large box and leaving without it, they wouldn't pay much attention and the contents would be distributed by the Warden to the most suitable recipients.

'James has gone to London,' said Emily, when Summer arrived at the Castle. 'I wish we could have gone with him,' she added wistfully.

She had often begged her mother to take her, but had always been refused on the grounds that the traffic fumes would activate her asthma and that, in any case, Lady Edgedale would be too busy to take her sightseeing. To the suggestion that Summer could do that, her mother had again demurred.

The family's town house had been demolished by a bomb during the air raids of the Second World War. After the war a block of flats had been built on the site,

one of which they used as a *pied-à-terre*. But it wasn't
large enough to accommodate Lady Edgedale, her
Spanish maid, her daughter and her daughter's tutor.
Or so she said. Summer suspected that she hadn't
wished to be encumbered with them. Dr Dyer had
been right in describing her interest in her child as
perfunctory. She had gone through the motions of
being a fond mother while at Cranmere, but in London
she wanted to concentrate on shopping and social
engagements.

'Did your uncle spend the evening with you?'
Summer asked.

'Part of it. Mr Darblay, the lawyer, stayed the night.
I had dinner with them, but afterwards they had more
business things to discuss. Instead of Mr Darblay
going back on the train this morning, he's gone with
James in the car he hired at the airport. James has to
see Granpa's stockbroker and his bankers. He's afraid
there are going to be tax problems which he'll try
to explain when he gets back. It's something to do
with Granpa not expecting Daddy to die before he
did.'

From time to time Summer had read newspaper
articles about the crippling death duties and the tax on
repairs which put the future of many of Britain's
historic houses in jeopardy. She wished now she had
studied the articles with closer attention.

In their unfinished conversation yesterday morning
James Gardiner had not made it clear if, as well as
disclaiming the title, he meant to cede his claim on the
estate. He had said his disclaimer wouldn't be publicised till he had left the country, which suggested that
he didn't mean to stay in England long.

On the other hand, he had told her his second
reason for coming to England was to take responsibility for his niece till she could fend for herself. The
two statements seemed contradictory. How could he
protect Emily's interests from the other side of the
Atlantic?

'I wonder if, unbeknown to your grandfather, your

father and your uncle kept in touch with each oṭ...
she speculated aloud.

'I shouldn't think so,' said Emily. 'In fact, no . . . I'ṃ.
sure they didn't. The first time I heard him mentioned
was after Mummy had been to London and met a man
who had been at Eton with James and who asked her
about him. That was why she asked Daddy if he
thought James was still alive and would ever come
back. I remember he said, "God knows", and then,
"Certainly not while Father's alive". I think it was
horrid of Granpa to thrash James for every least thing.
I don't wonder he ran away.'

'He does seem to have been rather unruly as a boy,'
Summer pointed out. 'He admits he went poaching
with an old man called Barty Hicks, and that often they
took game on this land.'

Having said this, she wished she hadn't. She might
detest the man herself, and still harbour doubts about
the integrity of his motives towards his niece; but he
was Emily's only relation and therefore it was better
for her to think highly of him, at least till he had
disproved his right to her confidence.

For the child's sake, Summer was sincere in hoping
that he would never hurt her as savagely as he had
lacerated her own *amour propre* the day before.

'Oh, I don't count poaching as wicked,' was Emily's
dismissive answer. 'I suppose it's stealing in a way—
but it's not like taking things from people's houses, or
from shops.'

By one o'clock, having had her mid-morning coffee
without milk, sugar or biscuits, Summer was
famished.

For lunch that day they had chicken consommé
followed by Dover sole with carrots, braised celery
and sauté potatoes, and for pudding baked apples
with cream.

It took all her resolution not to take a bread roll when
John, the young footman, offered them to her. She
also refused the potatoes and ate her apple without
cream. The cook, Mrs Briars, had baked four apples for

them, but Summer didn't have a second one, nor did she have cheese and biscuits.

To her relief neither Emily nor John seemed to notice any change in her habits. She rose from the table still feeling hungry but virtuous.

At four o'clock her will-power was severely tested when there were hot buttered crumpets, dripping with butter, for tea. Every afternoon, in winter, there would be either buttered toast or freshly baked scones, brought up to the schoolroom in a covered silver dish with a hot water compartment.

But crumpets with home-made raspberry jam were one of her particular weaknesses. She almost groaned aloud when Emily lifted the lid from the covered dish and the fragrance of toasted crumpet and melted butter wafted to her nostrils.

For some time before tea arrived she had been debating whether to admit to Emily that she was dieting, or to give some other reason for her apparent lack of appetite.

During her last year at school and in her brief time at Oxford, when girls who were sylphs compared with her were always worrying about their figures, she had tried several different reducing diets. Each time something had happened to make it impossible to stick to them. During the time she had known Emily she had made no further attempts to lose weight and had probably put on some pounds.

She said, 'I'm not going to have a crumpet today. It will spoil my appetite for supper. I'm having a piece of fillet steak tonight.'

It turned out to be a well-chosen white lie.

Emily said, 'Oh, are you? We had it last night. I shouldn't have known what it was but Mr Darblay asked James if American beef was as good as it was reputed to be, and he said, "On the whole—yes. But no better than this excellent fillet." And he asked Conway to give Mrs Briars his compliments.'

While Summer averted her eyes, Emily bit off a mouthful of crumpet and munched enjoyably for some moments before going on, 'Then they had a long talk about meat. James explained to Mr Darblay that porterhouse steaks took their name from the places where travellers used to stop for meals on long coach journeys, and that Texas Longhorns were originally bred from cattle from Andalusia which were used to the heat and lack of water in southern Spain. That was why they were able to stand being herded as far as a thousand miles to the railroad centres. I asked James if he had worked as a cowboy when he first went to America. He laughed and said no, that was one of the few things he hadn't done. But I can imagine him riding the range in jeans and a Stetson, can't you?'

Summer murmured agreement and drank some tea which, without sugar, tasted horrible.

In spite of James Gardiner's urbane appearance the day before, it wasn't impossible to visualise him in the hard-wearing clothes of a cowboy, his long legs comfortably extended in American working stirrups rather than short English hunting stirrups.

But the image which came to her mind, remembering the tanned, raw-boned face, was not of him as a cowboy but as the other major protagonist of the American legend; the wild, war-painted Indian warrior defending a way of life which was doomed to extinction.

Obviously there could be no American Indian blood in James Gardiner's veins; and yet, with his high, slanting cheekbones and aquiline nose, the cast of his features bore more than a passing resemblance to the proud, hawklike faces of some of the so-called redskins.

In her mind's eye it was easy to see his black hair flowing to his shoulders, held in place by a band above his eyebrows and whipped back by the wind when he rode, like the mane of his pinto. She could see his tall frame clad in buckskins, or naked except for a breechclout, his shoulders like polished bronze, powerful biceps swelling his arms as he drew his bow to kill an animal or an adversary.

Even in the clothes he wore now, there was something about him which suggested a hard, tough man with a streak of ruthlessness in him. That he had no understanding of or compassion for other people's weaknesses had been clearly demonstrated yesterday.

'Summer! What *is* the matter?' Emily exclaimed.

Her train of thought broken, Summer said hastily, 'Nothing. Why?'

'You had such a strange, angry look on your face. Not a bit like you. Whatever were you thinking?'

'I—I was thinking about the Red Indians. The cruel things they used to do to their enemies and prisoners . . . and the equally terrible things which were done to many of them.'

'James says America is an incredible country to live in, but I shouldn't have liked it in those days . . . never knowing when an arrow might come whizzing through the window. He says that a lot of things Americans eat, such as corned beef and pot roasts, derive from the days of the settlers. Even hamburgers are a modern form of the minced beef the early colonials used to eat with their fingers.

'Did he mention whereabouts in America he was living while he was talking to Mr Darblay?'

'No, he spoke of all sorts of places; Vermont, Montana, North Carolina—but not as if he lived in any of them. He says I'm too skinny. If you're not going to eat them, may I have one of your crumpets?'

'By all means. Have them both, if you can manage them.'

Summer poured herself some more tea and wondered how long it took to learn to like it without sugar.

Prior to her illness Miss Ewing had done all the catering. After it, Summer had taught herself to cook for them both. However, that night she didn't have the fillet steak which had been her excuse for abstaining from crumpets and fruit cake. Her supper consisted of a boiled egg, two crispbreads from a packet bought on her way home, a raw tomato and an orange.

For the second night in succession she went to bed

feeling hungry, and wishing she had some bathroom scales to show whether her self-denial was beginning to show some results. Although she had got rid of all the high-calorie snacks which had been in the house the night before, the rest of the crispbreads were a lure, and she longed for a glass of milk to quieten her rumbling insides. Two pints were delivered every morning, and she decided to cut down to four pints a week, or just over half a pint a day.

Usually she slept very soundly, rousing only when her alarm clock began to buzz. That night she woke several times and next morning felt tired and listless.

On her way to Cranmere, the exertion of cycling against a head wind made her feel oddly shaky. By the time she arrived she was longing for a cup of sweet milky coffee and something to eat, but she knew she would have to wait until eleven.

Emily greeted her with the news that shortly before her bedtime James had telephoned from London to ask how she was and say goodnight.

'Wasn't that nice of him?'

'Very,' Summer agreed.

'He's expecting to be back about four.'

Clearly Emily was looking forward to his return as much as Summer was dreading it. She would have preferred never to have set eyes on him again. Her pride was still raw. She felt that, as long as she lived, she would never forget the sound of his voice calling her an uncontrollable glutton who didn't give a damn what she looked like.

By mid-morning the trembly feeling had worn off and she managed to restrict herself to black coffee, without biscuits. But it seemed forever to lunchtime.

John was off duty that day, and so Conway waited on them.

'Ooh, potted shrimps . . . lovely,' said Emily, when the butler placed a small bowl of pink morsels drowned in butter in front of her tutor.

Summer ate her first food of the day with mingled

relish and guilt; the latter because of the butter and
because she had taken a bread roll to counteract the
richness of the first course.

The second was roast grouse—'Probably the last
this year, Miss Roberts', said Conway—garnished
with watercress and accompanied by gravy and game
chips, with a green salad.

She was not keen on game, possibly because the late
Lord Cranmere had liked all his birds to be hung until
they were extremely high. But at present she felt so
ravenous that even the ripe, slightly undercooked
flesh of the grouse tasted good to her.

Usually, when her plate was removed there was
nothing edible left on it. When she had first come to
England and found some of Aunt Margaret's dishes
strange and unappetising, she had been told not to be
faddy and was made to eat every last crumb of whatever had been put in front of her, so that leaving a
clean plate had become an ingrained habit.

Today she left all but two or three of the game chips,
causing the butler to enquire if they were not to her
liking.

'There's nothing wrong with them. I'm just not very
hungry today.'

She could imagine the sardonic expression with
which James Gardiner would have reacted to this
statement, had he been at the table. Conway kept
his thoughts to himself. Perhaps, returning to the
kitchen, he would say something such as, 'Wonders
never cease, Mrs Briars. Miss Roberts isn't hungry.'
But, if so, she wouldn't hear him.

The pudding was a chilled orange compote, giving
her her first taste of sweetness since the day before
yesterday. Having eaten the thinly sliced fruit, she
was about to drink the syrup left in her bowl when the
echo of a scornful voice saying *fat as a pig* made her
hesitate and put down her spoon.

During the afternoon it began to rain and Summer
foresaw a wet ride home. Fortunately, she had a black
plastic cape and a sou'wester in her saddle-bag, and

there were wellington boots she could borrow in the downstairs cloakroom.

Conway was clearing away their tea things when the schoolroom door opened and James Gardiner walked in.

To Summer's astonishment Emily leapt to her feet and ran across the room more eagerly than she had ever greeted her father. They had not been a demonstrative family and, although this man was her uncle, he was still virtually a stranger.

Even more surprisingly, he scooped her up in his arms, whirled her round in a circle and set her back on her feet.

'Hi there. How've you been?' he asked, smiling, before turning to say good evening to Summer and the butler.

In fact it was still afternoon, but the unrelenting heavy downpour had made them draw the curtains earlier than usual. Lit by one lamp and the leaping flames in the hearth the schoolroom looked very cosy.

'Would you care for some tea, m'Lord?'

'No, thanks, Conway. I need something more potent than tea after driving from London in this deluge.'

'A Scotch on the rocks perhaps, m'Lord?' A faint smirk showed that the butler was being facetious.

'A double Scotch without the rocks would be even better. Ice is fine when it's hot, but not in this climate.'

James Gardiner raked back a lock of wet hair which had fallen forward across his forehead. Then he produced a linen handkerchief and dried his hands on it.

'I got drenched in a five-yard dash from the car to the house.'

'You're going to get soaked going home. Why don't you stay the night, Summer?' Emily suggested.

'No, I must get back. I have things to do. My cape is completely waterproof.'

'You can't cycle in this, Miss Roberts. You'll be half blinded by the rain. I'll drive you home,' James Gardiner offered, taking up the traditional English male stance on the hearthrug, with his back to the fire.

However, as the room also had radiators, he only
blocked the firelight, not the heat.

'Thank you, but it isn't necessary. I often cycle home
in the rain. The trees along the drive will shelter me
from the worst of it.'

'You live near the schoolhouse, don't you? That's
half a mile from the gates, on a major road. Visibility is
very poor tonight, and you could be knocked down.
I'll drive you—when I've had my reviver. Wait a
moment, Conway'—this as the butler was about to
leave the room. 'Bring me a cold beef sandwich with
my Scotch, would you, please? If there's no beef,
chicken or Cheddar will do.'

'Certainly, m'Lord.'

With Emily holding the door for him, the old man
carried the laden tray from the room.

Summer had glimpsed a flash of irritation on the
younger man's face which she attributed to his dislike
of the butler's repeated use of his unwanted title. Perhaps he held strong views which allied him more with
the Left Wing element of the country's political system.

'So what have you two been doing with yourselves
today?' he asked, as his niece returned to the fireside.

She curled up in a corner of the large shabby slip-
covered sofa which faced the hearth, as it had in his
time and before.

Having described their activities, she said, 'What
have you been doing, James? Did you stay at the flat?
I've never been there.'

'The flat is in Belgravia, near Eaton Square. I stayed
at the Savoy which is nearer the City where the people
I had to see have their offices.'

'Did you go to the theatre last night?'

'No, I dined with a friend at his club.'

'Daddy belonged to the Turf Club and Boodle's, but
he mostly used Boodle's. So did Granpa.'

'A bastion of undeserved privilege and reactionary
minds,' was her uncle's dry comment. 'My friend is a
scientist. He belongs to the Athenaeum.'

The reference to undeserved privilege seemed to

support Summer's thought that he might be a staunch Left Winger. If he were, it would increase her dislike of him.

She had an instinctive fear of people with extremist views which they almost invariably sought to impose on everyone around them. Kindness and tolerance were the qualities she admired above all others.

The Lancaster family's motto was *Nemo me impune lacessit*. No one attacks me with impunity. James Gardiner had told her that his personal motto was: He travels fastest who travels alone. Looking back to her formative years, Summer knew that if her parents had a credo, it had been: *Live and let live*. Their friends had been drawn from all walks of life, many different religious sects and more than one racial background. Her father would have thought it as foolish to condemn a man for being privileged as for being poor.

She was seated in a high-backed basket chair with cushions of the same faded, rose-patterned chintz as the cover on the sofa. On the opposite side of the hearth was a deep wide-armed club chair, also slip-covered. Presently James Gardiner lowered his tall frame into it, stretching out long legs which made her uneasily conscious of the width of her thighs, made more noticeable by being in a sitting position.

She could never sit with her knees crossed. Except when she was alone with Emily, she tried to remember to sit like the Queen when she was being photographed; with her lower legs slanted to one side and crossed at the ankle. Nothing could make her legs look slim, but in that position they looked less like the legs of a billiard table, as they did when planted squarely in front of her with a space between her fat knees.

As she listened in silence to Emily chattering to her uncle, her mind was at work on the problem of how to avoid being driven home by him.

When Conway returned with a silver tray in place of the wooden one he usually brought to the schoolroom, she rose, saying, 'If you'll excuse me for a few minutes, I'll take some books back to the library. Mr

Renfrew doesn't like us to accumulate too many up
here.'

'Who is Mr Renfrew?'

'He's a retired archivist who came to live near here
some years ago, and discovered that the library had
never been properly catalogued. He's been working
on it ever since.'

'For a salary or for love?'

'I've no idea.'

Conway cleared his throat. 'If I may venture to
answer your question, m'Lord, I believe Mr Renfrew
receives an honorarium for his services. His health is
not good and he doesn't come on a regular basis. This
week he's confined to bed with a chill.'

As she made her escape from the room with an
armful of leather-bound volumes, Summer hoped
James Gardiner hadn't spotted Emily's look of puzzlement at the mention of Mr Renfrew. In fact the archivist had never expressed an objection to books being
removed from the library—it wasn't his place to do so.
Besides, as he was aware, both Summer and Emily
were people with an inborn respect for all books, old
or new.

Young as she was, the child could be trusted to
handle a rare and perhaps fragile volume with the care
it deserved. Although sometimes careless with her
clothes and other possessions, she never had to be reminded to wash her hands before touching the books
in the library, or indeed those in her own bookcase,
given to her as Christmas and birthday presents.

On reaching the library, Summer didn't spend time
replacing the books in their correct places on the
shelves. She left them in a pile on a table before
hurrying to the downstairs cloakroom.

The early morning weather forecast had made it
seem advisable to unbuckle her saddle-bag and bring
it indoors with her. Quickly she changed her shoes for
a pair of wellington boots which she knew would
accommodate fat calves.

She was unfolding her cape when the cloakroom

door opened so suddenly that she jumped and gave a little gasp.

'Where do you think you're going?' James Gardiner demanded.

It took several moments for her to recover from being startled. To her annoyance, he had managed to make her feel as guilty as if she had been doing something wrong—instead of relieving him of the trouble of turning out again when he would much rather be lounging by the schoolroom fire.

'I'm going home, Lord Cranmere . . . I beg your pardon, Mr Gardiner,' she corrected herself. 'I happen to want to get back early tonight, and I saw no reason to spoil your enjoyment of your drink.'

'Do you usually leave the house without saying goodnight to Emily?'

'No, I don't,' she admitted, her colour rising. 'But in the circumstances, I—'

He interrupted her. 'I don't know how long it takes you to ride home in normal conditions, but it would take longer tonight—considerably longer than waiting for me to drink my Scotch and run you home in the car.'

'Possibly.' His autocratic manner was beginning to make her angry.

After what she had heard him say about her, she would always feel latent hostility towards him in any circumstances. It only needed a little extra aggravation to bring that hostility bubbling to the surface, like a saucepan of milk boiling over.

She said, 'Frankly, I'm not very keen on being driven by people who drink and drive.'

'It takes more than one double Scotch to impair my judgment, Miss Roberts, and it's my first drink today. I don't start before lunch like your previous employer.'

Later, when she was reviewing the altercation, she thought it a curious way to refer to his father's heavy drinking. She concluded he had meant to emphasise that it was he who now held hire-and-fire power over her. As if she needed reminding!

'However, it's still in the glass, and I'm still as sober as you are,' he went on, reaching for the dark green waterproof coat which his brother had worn for fly-fishing, and taking a flat brown tweed cap from the peg above it.

It was the kind of cap worn for country pursuits by landowners all over England. It fitted his head well enough, but somehow it didn't suit his face. It went with a ruddy complexion, not a sub-tropical tan; with eyes of blue, grey or brown, but not with tawny gold irises; with an Anglo-Saxon physiognomy, not the sharply carved features of his face.

He was the last of a line which could be traced back to the early fifteenth century. Yet when he had shrugged on the coat and put on the peaked tweed cap, he looked extraordinarily un-English. He looked what he had become; a tall, tough, decisive American who liked to give orders and have them obeyed, not defied.

'And you needn't feel you're being a nuisance,' he went on. 'As anyone who knows me will tell you, being the son of a peeress doesn't make me one of Nature's gentlemen. I do things for *my* convenience; rarely for anyone else's. It would upset my plans for you to be knocked down tonight, and also I want to discuss them with you.'

She hadn't seen the car he had hired, but she thought it unlikely it would be a large estate car with room for her bicycle in the back.

She said, 'What about my bike? I shall need it tomorrow.'

'If it's fine, you can walk for a change. If not, we'll send someone to fetch you. Don't stand there arguing, Miss Roberts. Get that cape on and let's get started.'

Fuming, she did as he told her. A few minutes later she was in the leather-scented interior of a Jaguar, and he was dashing round to the driver's side of the limousine.

Summer couldn't afford to buy a car, even a second-hand model, but since her aunt's death she had learned to drive. There was a driving instructor living in the village—he worked in the nearest town, but he lived not far from her cottage. He had a daughter who had sat for her 'O' level examinations the previous summer, and some weeks before the exams, he had asked Summer if she would give the girl some private coaching in the evenings. She had agreed, if he would teach her to drive. Somewhat to her surprise, she had passed the test the first time and could now hire a car if ever she needed one.

The Jaguar had an automatic gear change, she noticed. So had the car which her father had driven. But as most of the less expensive cars on the road in England had a manual gear change, she had learnt to drive on one of those.

'What are the plans you mentioned?' she asked coldly, as the car glided forward.

'I'll go into that in a moment. First you tell me something. Why do you want to get home early tonight? Are you going out?'

She didn't have a reason ready, nor could she improvise one.

'That was a lie, wasn't it?' he accused her. 'Like the one about Renfrew disapproving of more than a few books being removed from the library. It was obvious to me that Emily had never heard of that embargo—you invented it. It was an excuse to get you out of the schoolroom.'

When she said nothing, he continued, 'Don't ever try lying to me again, Miss Roberts. I dislike attempts to bamboozle me. If the reason you didn't want a lift was because you thought a double whisky might top up my alcohol level to the point of making me unsafe behind a wheel, you should have said so, point-blank. I never prevaricate myself, and I don't like people who do.'

Again there seemed nothing she could say, unless he expected her to apologise. If he did, he would have a long wait.

'Why are you nervous about drinking and driving? Is that how you lost your parents?—in an accident with a tanked-up driver?'

'No, they were drowned in a sailing accident—a freak squall hit them. They were both keen, experienced sailors. Unfortunately, I used to feel seasick if the water was the least bit choppy. It was the only thing we didn't do together.'

It was no longer an effort for her to speak unemotionally. Twelve years didn't make that kind of memory painless, but it transformed passionate grief into forlorn acceptance.

To give the devil his due, James Gardiner didn't produce any of the meaningless clichés which most people felt obliged to utter.

He said, 'What was your father's occupation? Did he leave you comfortably provided for?'

'He was an artist. No, he didn't,' she said briskly. 'But my mother's sister took me in.'

'How much have Emily's parents been paying you to teach her?'

She told him.

They had almost reached the end of the long tall tunnel of trees, their branches beating in the wind. At other seasons of the year they did offer some protection from lighter showers, but not now their leaves were gone and the rain was falling in a torrent, drumming on the roof of the car and blurring the windscreen even though the wipers were fanning back and forth at full speed.

He said, 'That's not much salary for a responsible job. They were taking advantage of your situation.'

She had sometimes thought the same thing, and wondered if she ought to press for a higher salary than the one proposed by Lord Edgedale when she changed from part-time to full-time.

However, as she hadn't any proper qualifications, and working at Cranmere was both convenient and congenial, she had said nothing. But she couldn't have

managed on her salary if Miss Ewing had not left a
small income. Being unearned, it was heavily taxed,
but it paid the rates on the cottage and the electricity
bills. As she never spent money on the usual pleasures
of her age-group—food was her only self-
indulgence—she had been able to manage.

They had come to the pair of lodges which flanked
the main gateway and housed the head gardener and
his wife in one, and a gamekeeper in the other.

The great gates, supported by stone piers topped
with finials in the form of swagged urns, stood open.
Beyond was the minor road which, after hugging the
brick wall which marked the boundary of the estate
for a few hundred yards, converged with the main
road.

From the junction to the outskirts of the village, her
companion was silent, peering through the veil of rain
on a winding stretch of road where each bend might
reveal a hazard.

When, further on, she began to explain the position
of Miss Ewing's cottage—her cottage now—he said,
'You forget—I've lived here longer than you have.
Your aunt was here in my time. An old dragon, from
what I remember of her.'

Outside the cottage he pulled the Jaguar on to the
grass verge where it wouldn't impede passing traffic.
She had thought that whatever he wanted to talk
about could be discussed in the car, but he said, 'I'll
come in for ten minutes.'

She could hardly refuse to admit him, but she was
simmering again at his arbitrary invasion of her home
as she ran down the path ahead of him.

Like most small, old houses in England this one
lacked an entrance hall, the door opening directly into
what was known as 'the front room'. Summer's cottage, which was at one end of a terrace of ten, had
had a small glazed porch added. Modern in style, it
was an eyesore to look at but an improvement in
practical terms. They were able to shelter inside
it while she fumbled for the front door key instead

of the one she usually used.

As she always did, she had left the fire ready to be lit. As soon as she had switched on some lamps and taken off her outer clothing, she struck a match and held it to the kindling in the grate.

She straightened to find that James Gardiner had removed his cap but not his coat, and was taking in the details of her sitting room. The ceiling was low and seemed lower with him standing there. She watched him glance at her bookshelves, at the water-colour painting—bought with pocket money at a jumble sale—which she had brought down from her bedroom to hang above the fireplace, and at the needle-point cushions, or pillows as her mother would have called them, she had stitched as a change from always reading in the evenings.

'You're very tidy,' he said. 'Do you do your own housework?'

'People in houses of this size usually do, if you remember. Did you expect me to live in chaos?'

Her grey eyes, always friendly and gentle when she looked at Emily, met his with a steelier expression.

'What is it you want to discuss with me, Mr Gardiner?' Deliberately, she refrained from offering to take his coat.

He took it off anyway, folded the wet side innermost, and threw it across an upright chair.

'Maybe discuss is the wrong word. I've decided on a course of action, now it's up to you to decide if you're willing to go along with it. Shall we sit down?'

To ask that had been her prerogative. But the only prerogatives he would respect were his own, she thought crossly as she sat down.

Having suggested they sit, he chose to remain on his feet, casting his eye along the titles on the bookshelves in the alcove on the far side of the chimney-breast.

'I've a house on the west coast of Florida—the Gulf of Mexico side,' he told her. 'I'm going to send Emily there for the rest of the winter, and I'd like you to go over with her. There's a large swimming pool in the grounds. I'm told that running is the worst exercise for asthmatics, and swimming is the best. It has to do with the weight of the body being supported by the water so that the total amount of energy used is less than in most other exercises.'

Not for the first time that evening she was silent after he stopped speaking. But not from annoyance or discomfiture.

For some moments Summer was overwhelmed. To return, at long last, to her homeland . . . to escape from an English winter to a climate where swimming was possible . . .

Although not a good small-boat sailor, she had always loved being in the water and had swum from an early age until her departure from America. It had been her favourite activity.

'I'd be happy to go there with Emily,' she told him, her enthusiasm for his plan tempered by her detestation of its author.

He didn't appear to be gratified by this reaction. Clearly he would have been surprised and put out if she hadn't acceded to it.

'Is your passport in order?'

'No, it expired some years ago.'

'That can be remedied. Call the Embassy first thing tomorrow and find out the drill. Do you rent this place, or do you own it?'

'It belongs to me.'

Now he did sit down—in the armchair opposite hers.

'What are the chances of finding a tenant for it?'

'I have no idea. But I don't think there would be much point in attempting to let it. I'd prefer to leave it standing empty and arrange for someone to keep an eye on it. It's not a damp cottage—I shan't come back in the spring to find it full of mildew.'

'In the spring I shall probably move Emily up to Cape Cod. She won't be coming back here.'

'I see. When will she come back?'

'Maybe in five or six years if she wants to revisit old

haunts. Certainly not before then, and maybe never if she finds America as much to her liking as I do.'

'I . . . I don't understand what you mean.'

'Emily is in the same situation that you were, Miss Roberts. The only person willing and able to take care of her lives in another country. Therefore she must adapt to a different way of life in a new place. Had she been at a boarding school, she could have continued her education in England and spent the vacations in America. As things are, she has you to be a link between her old life and her new one. I think she'll find the transition considerably less painful than it was for you.'

Summer stared at him for a moment; her own feelings forgotten. Her only concern for the child.

'But her situation isn't the same as mine was. I was left with nothing . . . and I did have some English blood in me. My mother had talked about England, and I knew a great deal about it. Emily is *totally* English, and while I'd travelled all over the States, she has never even been to London.'

'Then we'll make sure she has a day there before flying to Miami. It's unfortunate you don't drive. You'll have to learn—a car is a necessity where you're going.''

'I do drive. I'm a complete beginner, but I have a licence. I just can't afford to run a car at present.'

'Not on what you've been paid up to now, but from tomorrow that changes. I shan't be in Florida with you—or not very often. You'll be able to call me at all times, and there'll be staff to run the house for you. But you will be fully responsible for my niece's welfare, and I'll pay you a salary commensurate with that responsibility. If all goes well, you'll have job-security until Emily is sixteen or seventeen. But we'll have to see how it works out. For the present, I suggest a contract reviewable after six months.'

And then he suggested a salary, first in dollars and then in its current sterling equivalent, which made her gape in astonishment.

'But that's going to the other extreme. I don't need all that,' she protested.

His lion's eyes narrowed, watching her with an expression she couldn't interpret.

After a pause, he said, 'Learn from your father's improvidence, Miss Roberts. Enjoy the present, by all means, but give some thought to the future. You may not be aware of it yet, but we're living in the dawn of the Computer Age. In the next two or three decades, all our lives will be changed more radically than by the Industrial Revolution of the last century. It's hoped that new technology will create as many jobs as it destroys; but at this stage nothing is certain. Unemployment is already high—it could go higher. So make the most of your opportunities.'

She was struck by his tone of voice as he spoke of the changes ahead. The only person to whom she had talked about computers had been old Mr Renfrew. In recent years the facilities at the nearest large public library had been greatly improved by the introduction of microfiche to replace the old-fashioned card indexes. Other modernisations had taken place in the reference section.

She would have expected an archivist to welcome the new information storage and retrieval systems. Mr Renfrew had been against them; perhaps because deteriorating eyesight had made it difficult for him to read small print shown on a screen.

It was clear that James Gardiner's reaction to the Computer Age was one of excitement and enthusiasm.

She said, 'I shall try to, certainly. But when you speak of the transition to America being less painful for Emily than coming to Europe was for me, you're ignoring the fact that she has a home here. We were living in a rented apartment at the time of my parents' accident. I had no roots anywhere, and certainly not the deep tap-root which Emily has here. I don't understand why she has to be moved to America . . . why she can't continue as she is, in the place where she belongs.'

He didn't reply to that immediately, and Summer had the curious sensation of having her innermost thoughts probed by a penetrating intelligence, a kind of mental laser beam.

He said, 'Don't *you* want to go to America?'

'Yes, very much. There's nothing I should like better. But it's Emily's life we're discussing. Her place is here, at Cranmere. If you don't care about your heritage, then she is the last of the Lancasters. It may even be possible that the Queen will grant her the title of Marchioness, in the same way that Lord Mountbatten's elder daughter was made Countess Mountbatten after he was killed in Ireland.'

'I think you overrate the importance of a title,' he answered. 'I've never regretted dropping mine; and, as long as she's under my aegis in America, Emily will be known as plain Emily Lancaster. If she chooses to revive her title later, that's up to her. But a title with nothing to back it is like a crown without a kingdom. If it were possible to keep the estate going until she's grown up, maybe she could find a rich husband who would change his name to Lancaster. But that's talking of six years from now, and my guess is she won't be that kind of girl anyway. Right now the sane course of action is to put the house on the market and auction the contents.'

'You mean . . . *sell* Cranmere?' she expostulated.

'Correct,' he said crisply.

'But you can't do that! You can't throw away her birthright because she's thirteen . . . and a girl. It isn't fair. I think it's . . . damnable!'

'Life rarely is fair, Miss Roberts. Although I don't personally see this an outstanding example of its unfairness.'

'Naturally not. It doesn't affect you,' Summer said hotly. 'No doubt it will be to your benefit.'

The lines of his sun-tanned face tightened, the firm lips compressing for a moment before he said, 'What do you mean?'

What had she meant? She had flung the after-thought at him without choosing her words or considering their implication.

Now, as he looked coldly at her, waiting for her to explain herself, she had an uneasy feeling that she was skating on thin ice. It could be that what she had meant was defamation of character; and James Gardiner wouldn't like that any more than he liked disobedience.

On the other hand, they were alone. There was no one to hear her accuse him of using his niece's misfortune to feather his own nest.

She said recklessly, 'You're not dense, Mr Gardiner. I think you're extremely astute. As it stands, Emily's inheritance is no use to you. But converted into funds—very substantial funds—of which you, as her administrator, would have control for some years . . .' She finished the sentence with an expressive shrug.

There was a long-drawn-out silence. James Gardiner leaned back in his chair and watched her, his gaze as intent as that of a cat watching a mouse. Or a lion watching a springbok.

At length, he said softly, 'That's a very unpleasant suggestion, Miss Roberts. Are you prepared to stand by it?'

Her mouth felt dry, but her clear grey eyes didn't waver.

She said evenly, 'I'm prepared to do anything necessary to defend Emily's rights, and her happiness. Someone has to.'

'And you don't trust me to do it?'

'Why should I trust you, Mr Gardiner? You're a stranger to me. All I know is that you left here under a cloud, and as far as I'm aware, you never made contact with your family until the only one left was a little girl of thirteen. You've repudiated your title. Perhaps you've repudiated a great deal more than that. Things like honesty and decency. All the civilised values.'

His reaction to this was to smile. 'Dr Dyer told me you had a lot of guts—he was right. You're prepared to risk losing a good job to stand up for Emily.'

Her pale cheeks flooded with colour. Not because of the praise implicit in what he had said, but because of his gall in referring to a conversation in which he— damn his eyes!—had been as insulting about her as it was possible to be.

She never swore out loud, and only rarely in her mind, but right now there was only one word to apply to James Gardiner.

She looked at him, smiling at her, and she thought: You shit!

Did he read the message in her eyes? She couldn't be sure.

He said, 'Okay, I'll explain to you why your fears are unfounded. In my teens, when I wasn't poaching or doing various other illicit things, of which you've probably heard exaggerated rumours, I was interested in transistors. Later on, when I went to America, I became a computer buff.'

His body flexed. He stood up and began to pace about the room, as he had in the course of their first talk.

'Six years ago,' he went on, 'I founded a company to manufacture personal computers and some software. In case you don't know, software refers to video games and programmes for use with computers. The giant of the computer industry is IBM—International Business Machines. Everybody's heard of them. For a long time they concentrated on mainframe business computers and ignored the personal computer—that market was left to a number of much smaller companies, of which the most successful were Apple and my company. Our stock has a market value of two billion dollars, and as chairman of the board, I have shares worth two hundred and fifty million dollars. I have no designs on Emily's fortune, Miss Roberts. I'm a rich man, and getting richer. But I made my money the hard way, and I'm not going to use it to shore up a tottering tradition which means nothing to me.'

Was he speaking the truth? Was he really the head of a booming billion-dollar company? Or was that a spiel which he didn't think she would check out?

'Neither Emily's father nor her grandfather were men of foresight,' he continued. 'They made bad investments . . . bad decisions. The estate is heavily in debt. If I had nothing else to do, and I wanted to come back to England, I might, by careful management, be able to pull it out of the red. Might is the operative word. However, I have things to do, and no wish to come back. Two weeks is the most I can spare from my own affairs.'

He glanced at his watch. 'I'd better get back—that sandwich will be beginning to curl at the edges.'

As he put on the waterproof coat, she said, 'When are you going to tell Emily? Tonight?'

'I thought so—yes. Unless you'd prefer to tell her?'

'Whoever tells her, it's going to be a terrible shock. Cranmere has been her whole world.'

'A very small world,' he said shortly. 'Almost as confined as a convent.'

He picked up the cap, his glance running over her. She flushed. She felt sure he was thinking that, with her lack of sex appeal, she might just as well be a nun.

She said, 'Perhaps it would be better not to tell her yet. When we're in Florida, particularly if she's happy there, it won't come as such a blow.' Then she shook her head. 'No, on second thoughts, I couldn't deceive her like that. She has to be told, however much it upsets her. I think you should break it to her—she's taken an immediate liking to you.'

'Unlike her tutor,' he said mockingly. 'You don't like me or trust me, do you, Miss Roberts?'

She ignored that. 'Thank you for driving me home,' she said, with frigid politeness. 'Goodnight, Mr Gardiner.'

After he had gone, she made herself a pot of tea and sat by the fire, wondering about the influences which

had transformed the seventeen-year-old Etonian,
Lord James Lancaster, into Mr James Gardiner, a
naturalised American computer tycoon.

She couldn't understand his indifference to his
ancestral home. If he only occasionally visited the
house in Florida, where did he live? And who was the
woman in his life?

There had to be one. He might think she was
well-suited to a convent, but no one would ever suspect him of monastic leanings—not with that sensual
mouth.

What kind of woman would be James Gardiner's
girl-friend, she wondered. A beauty: that went without saying. Would she have brains as well? Or was he
one of those men who didn't require his woman to be
intelligent as long as she had a lovely face and an
alluring body?

It would do him a great deal of good, thought
Summer, sipping her tea, if one day he were to encounter the female equivalent of himself; a girl with
good looks, brains, panache, a successful career—and
an impregnable indifference to the charms of Mr James
Gardiner.

Her eyes on the play of the flames, all thought of
supper forgotten, she began to visualise the scene at
an elegant black tie dinner party. It was taking place in
a luxurious apartment on the fashionable East Side of
Manhattan. The host and hostess and seven, or possibly nine, guests, one of them him, were drinking
cocktails and waiting for the last to arrive: the most
sought-after girl in New York; talented, beautiful,
always exquisitely dressed and—no one knew why—
still single.

As if from the front row of the stalls, her mind's eye
surveyed the details of the *mise en scène*.

*A spacious, softly lit, split-level living room with large
windows, the curtains still open to show the glittering lights
of the city by night.*

*Everywhere there were beautiful flowers. The women were
expensively coiffed and dressed by America's top designers,*

their jewels catching the light as they turned their heads and moved their hands.

On the upper level, reached by three or four wide shallow steps, was a parquet-floored lobby and the entrance to the apartment.

When the sound of the buzzer penetrated the hum of witty conversation, a manservant moved swiftly to answer it, and the hostess detached herself from a group by the window in order to greet the last-comer.

As the door opened and she crossed the threshold, the murmur of voices died away. Everyone turned to look at the willowy blonde in the black silk taffeta evening coat.

There was a hush as the manservant helped her to remove it; revealing a skirt of matt black silk, a blouse of white crêpe de Chine and, at her throat, a pearl choker with an antique emerald centrepiece.

Suddenly all the other women were conscious of being overdressed, over-made-up and over-jewelled.

The hostess mounted the steps, hands outstretched, smiling a welcome.

'My dear . . . how lovely to see you again. It's been much too long since the last time, but I know how busy you are.'

Together they moved to the steps, the rest of those present still watching, entranced, the graceful carriage and radiant looks of someone they had all read or heard about.

The hostess began the introductions, and to each person there the girl gave her slender hand and her lovely smile.

Finally, the hostess presented a tall man whose white tuxedo emphasised the deep tan of his skin.

'And this, my dear, is James Gardiner, who is an American now but was born in England.'

As she gave him her hand, he turned it palm downwards and bowed, his lips brushing her knuckles.

'I've been wanting to meet you for months, Miss Roberts.' The look in his eyes told her she was everything he had expected, and more; the most captivating woman he had ever met.

She had heard about him, and most of what she had heard she hadn't liked. She had no time for arrogant men. His admiration meant nothing to her. She was waiting for the man to whom her essential being, her soul, would be more important than her beauty.

When, for politeness' sake, she had let James Gardiner engage her in small-talk for a minute or two, she was able to catch the eye of another man and send him a mute appeal for rescue. He was a distinguished professor whom she had met before and liked; a middle-aged widower, neither good-looking nor rich, but kind and with a great sense of humour. As, with alacrity, he joined them and she started to ask about his latest research project, she was aware of vibrations of annoyance from the other man. He wasn't accustomed to being gently cold-shouldered.

A lump of smokeless fuel fell into the hearth, making Summer start and bringing her back to reality.

When she started to pour a second cup of tea, she found it had gone cold while she was lost in her day-dream of giving James Gardiner his come-uppance.

Not physically, but in other ways, he had changed since his father threw him out. Was it possible, if she really put her mind to it, that she could one day become the *alter ego* of her day-dream?

Could she lose weight and keep it off? Could she learn to dress well and, with make-up, create an illusion of beauty? Was there, lurking inside her, as yet undiscovered, a talent she could build into a career?

Teaching Emily was enjoyable because the child was unusually bright and their personalities meshed. But she had no vocation for training the minds of other children. It didn't appeal to her at all; it had been her aunt's career choice for her. When her time with Emily was over, she wanted to do something different. But as yet she didn't know what.

Perhaps in Florida there would be evening classes where she could try her hand at pottery, or wood-work, or some other craft which would satisfy her urge to use her hands as well as her brain.

However, the personal excitement she felt at the

prospect of going there was overshadowed by her deep concern for Emily's welfare.

By next morning the rain had cleared. Half an hour earlier than usual, Summer set out on foot. She wasn't accustomed to walking and it seemed a long, tiring way.

Entering the house by the main door, she met Conway coming down the staircase.

'Lady Emily was up early this morning,' he told her. 'You'll find her in the library with his Lordship.'

She wondered if the butler knew the house would soon be for sale.

Evidently he did, and knew she did, because he said, 'It's a sad business . . . a sad business, Miss Roberts. His Lordship has asked me to assemble the staff at eleven. He's going to make an announcement.

In the library, James Gardiner was on the telephone while, at the far end of the room, Emily was seated at a table, a large volume open in front of her.

She waved and beckoned. When Summer came near, she said, 'Good morning. I'm studying Florida. Shall I show you where James has his house?'

Summer moved round the table and looked over her shoulder at the atlas, open at a map of the south-eastern corner of the United States.

'Just about there,' said Emily, indicating a spot some way south of a large inlet marked Tampa Bay. 'James says there are two ways we can get there from Miami. We can drive across the Everglades, by this road called Alligator Alley, and have lunch with some friends of his at Naples. Or we can drive up the Atlantic side and cross over further north by this big lake, Lake Okeechobee. But you can't see much of it, he says. I think Alligator Alley sounds more fun.'

'As long as we aren't likely to see too much of the alligators.'

The child's cheerful manner and her giggle at the joke made Summer suspect that she couldn't yet know the worst.

However, it seemed that she did. Her next remark was, 'After he's explained about everything to the others, James is going to take us to have our passport photographs taken. Aren't you excited? I am. He says he has pelicans in his garden instead of peacocks, and there are beaches close by where the sand is like talcum powder, with all sorts of interesting shells we can collect. How long do you think it will take me to learn to swim?'

Before Summer could answer, James joined them.

'Good morning,' he said to her. 'No lessons today. There are too many other things to be done.' He rumpled Emily's red curls. 'You can start the Christmas vacation earlier than usual this year. No more school until January—in Florida.'

At eleven they listened to him addressing the indoor and outdoor staffs whom Conway had marshalled in the Great Hall. Not everyone who worked at Cranmere was there. Nowadays many of the female staff were part-timers; women from the village who came in to dust and vacuum, working for half a day instead of the long, hard hours worked by housemaids in former times.

James stood a short way up the staircase, relaxed and wholly at ease, explaining the situation to them with the easy fluency of an experienced public speaker.

Today he was wearing a navy blue blazer with grey flannel trousers and a candy-striped shirt, grey on white, with a plain navy tie. Perhaps it had to do with being brown, but he looked much cleaner than most people. His skin had a slight healthy sheen in contrast to the dulled winter pallor of his audience, several of whom had the reddened nostrils of people suffering from colds.

He concluded his short speech by saying, 'Those of you who have served Lady Emily's family for many years may be sure that your loyalty won't go unregarded. For those close to retirement, the usual provisions will be made; and younger members of the staff will receive all possible help in finding suitable employment elsewhere. That's all I have to tell you at present. I'll talk to you all, individually, during the next week or so.'

They began to disperse, discussing the news he had broken to them in subdued voices.

As he left his place on the staircase, the cook approached him. 'Is there nothing to be done, Lord James . . . your Lordship, I should say.'

Summer heard him reply, 'I'm afraid there isn't, Mrs Briars.'

'But if *you* were to come home, your Lordship, and open the house to the public—'

'I can't shelve my responsibility to the people who work for me in America, Mrs Briars. A much larger work force than here.' He patted her shoulder. 'I understand how you feel, but—'

Summer moved away, out of earshot. He might understand the cook's feelings, but he didn't share them.

I made my money the hard way, and I'm not going to use it to shore up a tottering tradition which means nothing to me.

Less than an hour later she was sitting in a cubicle in Woolworth's having passport photographs taken by a coin-operated camera. Emily had gone in first and when the machine had ejected four almost identical photographs of her, they did justice to her thin little face with its straight nose and broad, clever forehead.

Summer's photographs were not nearly as flattering.

'They look like mug shots,' she said, torn between laughter and despair at the hideousness of them.

Emily peered over her arm. 'What are mug shots?'

'The photographs they take of criminals when they're being admitted to prison.'

'They're not a bit like you,' said Emily comfortingly. 'Why don't you have some more taken? Smiley ones.'

'There isn't time. We have to meet your uncle at one.'

They had parted from him in the car park of the

town's best hotel, once a coaching inn. He had gone off to consult a travel agent about flights to Florida, leaving them to organise the photographs. On the way to Woolworth's Emily had wanted to look in shop windows and to browse in a book shop. Window-shopping was a rare treat for her. Now, unless they went straight back to the hotel, they would be late for their rendezvous with him, and Summer suspected that unpunctuality was another thing he wouldn't tolerate.

They found him in the lounge bar, drinking lager. He had already ordered a glass of dry sherry for Summer and an orange juice for his niece.

'I've booked you on a flight next Wednesday,' he told them.

'*Wednesday!*' she exclaimed. That was only eight days away. It didn't seem very much time for all the arrangements which had to be made. 'Will our passports be ready by then?' she asked doubtfully.

'No problem. I have some strings I can pull—have already pulled on the telephone this morning. It's surprising how quickly these things can be organised if they have to be. After lunch we'll see a realtor about your cottage. An estate agent,' he translated for his niece's benefit.

As usual, Summer had had no breakfast that morning. It was the one time of day when she never felt hungry. They had missed elevenses because of his speech to the staff, and in any case she would have only had black coffee.

By the time she had drunk half the sherry, she could feel it going to her head, and she decided to leave the remainder.

When the others had finished their drinks and they rose to go to the restaurant, James Gardiner noticed the pale golden liquid still in her glass.

'Too dry for you?' Without waiting for her answer, he added, 'I'm sorry; it should have occurred to me that you'd probably prefer an oloroso sherry.' He stood back for her to precede him.

Flushing, she walked out of the lounge, resenting
the jibe at her sweet tooth and its visible effect on her
body.

In the restaurant, they were shown to a corner table.
Was it deliberate unkindness which made him offer
the chair in the corner to her? A slim person could have
slipped into it without the table being moved. For her,
the head waiter and another waiter had to move two
chairs and pull the table out of position to make room
for her to seat herself. It was done with swift, practised
skill, but nevertheless it made her acutely conscious of
her bulk. She knew her face was scarlet as she
sat down and the table was pushed back, but not
as far as before. Her fingers were trembling with
mortification as she unfolded the starched damask
napkin.

'Madame.' The head waiter, a foreigner, handed her
a red leather folder.

Thankfully she opened it and bent her head, pre-
tending to pore over the menus; printed *à la carte*
dishes on one side, the typed *table d'hôte* on the other.
But the words were a meaningless jumble. The sherry
had weakened her control and there were tears in her
eyes as she stared unseeingly at the letters.

Although physically undeveloped, in some ways
Emily was mature for her age. She was not in the habit
of making embarrassing gaffes. But nor was she used
to eating in public places and perhaps she was nervous.

She said, in an amused undertone, 'He called you
Madame. He thinks you're James's wife.'

'I doubt that,' Summer said shortly.

She could guess what *he* must be thinking. Eliza
Doolittle's comment—*Not bloody likely*.

To her dismay, the child said, 'Why not? You could
be.'

'Miss Roberts is too young to be married to someone
of my age,' her uncle said smoothly.

'Summer is twenty-two. That's only thirteen years
younger than you are.'

'Would you want to marry someone who was born this year?' he asked her.

Emily shook her head. 'No, because then I should be old when he was still young. But it's all right the other way round.'

'Where did you pick up that piece of worldly wisdom?'

'I heard Mummy talking to Lady Draycott about someone they know who is quite old but has a young husband. They said it couldn't possibly last. Lady Draycott said—'

'I'm sure Lady Draycott didn't realise you were listening, Emily,' Summer cut in. 'She was talking to your mother in confidence and wouldn't like the conversation to be repeated.'

She spoke more severely than usual and Emily looked hurt by the reproof.

'They knew I was there. I wasn't eavesdropping,' she said defensively.

The reminder of her own inadvertent eavesdropping, and how it had borne out the adage that listeners never hear good of themselves, renewed Summer's embarrassed flush.

An uncontrollable glutton . . . she must weigh as much as I do and most of her weight is blubber . . .

The shaming memory held her silent while Emily went on, 'Lady Draycott was only saying that her daughter and her son-in-law, who are both twenty-three, are always having quarrels and treading on each other's toes, and she wished Arabella had married somebody older—like Prince Charles and the Princess of Wales.'

She paused before adding, 'Then Mummy said that sometimes an age gap was the cause of the trouble, as it had been with Granpa and Granny. Did they have a lot of quarrels, James?'

He ignored the question. 'Have you decided what you'd like to eat? If not, I suggest you stop chattering and read the menu.'

Quelled by this even sterner rebuke from her new

idol, Emily hung her head and looked as if, like her tutor a few minutes earlier, she might be blinking back tears.

The head waiter returned to take their orders.

'Are you going to try one of our specialities, sir? The steak and kidney pudding is excellent, or you might like to try the jugged pigeons, an old Worcestershire recipe which the chef has revived. We are famous for our traditional English dishes.'

'But you're not English?'

'No, sir. I come from Italy. My wife is English. I've lived here for fifteen years, and I know English cooking, when it's well done, is as good as anything to be found on the Continent. We also have fish, if you prefer. The baked white fish with bacon is very good . . .'

He went on suggesting alternatives till James Gardiner silenced him with, 'I'll have the steak and kidney pudding. What about you two?'

While the head waiter was talking, Summer had been searching the menu for something which wasn't fattening. But there didn't seem to be anything. No doubt most people who lunched at the hotel were bent on feasting rather than fasting.

She chose the baked fish, with chicken soup for her first course, while the others had cream of celery. For her main course Emily asked if she might have roast duck.

There was already a roll on their bread and butter plates. To avoid drawing attention to herself, Summer broke hers when the others did.

'This is always a promising sign in an unknown restaurant,' said James Gardiner, as he passed her a dish of butter curls. 'When the butter is in foil-wrapped portions I don't expect to eat well.'

She took only one curl of butter and put it on the side of her plate. Then she spread a little on a small piece of bread. But she didn't put it in her mouth. Although she had eaten nothing since the night before—and then only eggs and oranges—in his presence her

appetite deserted her. Even chocolate mousse or pro-
fiteroles wouldn't tempt her while he was beside her.

'Did you never come here before . . . when you
lived here?' she asked.

'Yes, but it was under different management then.'

The wine waiter brought Perrier for her and Emily,
and another glass of Carlsberg for him. He had asked if
she would like to share a bottle of wine with him.
When she demurred, he had said, 'In that case I'll stick
to lager.'

After sitting in silence for some time, Emily ventured a question. 'How long will it take to fly to
Florida, James?'

'About eight hours. There'll be a movie to help pass
the time, and I'll try to arrange for you to visit the
flight-deck.'

He glanced at Summer. She felt sure he was
wondering if there would be room for her on the
flight-deck. She wanted to cry out: I'm not as enormous as all that. You make me feel like a freak.

At that moment she would have given anything
to have Emily's skinny wrists instead of her plump
ones, Emily's bony knuckles instead of the dimpled
depressions which showed where her own knuckles
were.

The conversation throughout lunch consisted mainly of Emily asking questions about Florida and James
answering them. Summer took little part in it.

She wondered why he had squashed Emily when
she asked if her grandparents had had frequent dis-
agreements. It might have been for the reason he had
given, or perhaps he disapproved of discussing family
matters in front of outsiders, or perhaps his parents
and his upbringing were a sore point with him, one he
preferred to ignore.

When the baked fish was placed in front of her, she
was dismayed to see that as well as being flanked by
rolls of bacon it had a crust of buttery breadcrumbs.

The vegetables were fresh and well-cooked. She
was able, discreetly, to decline the potatoes. She

would have liked to eat the fish and the Brussels
sprouts and creamed spinach, and to leave the bacon
and the crumb topping. But in a restaurant, with her
new employer sitting beside her, noticing, she hadn't
the courage.

It was the first time in her life she had ever had to
force herself to eat something. Each time she swallowed a piece of bacon, she was dismally conscious
that it would soon be undoing whatever improvement
she had wrought by several days' semi-starvation.

Yet, before the end of the meal, she was to suffer a
revulsion of feeling.

In place of the usual gâteaux and sugary confec-
tions, the restaurant offered a Victorian sherry trifle,
apple pie, treacle tart, an old-fashioned steamed
suet pudding stuffed with dates and sultanas and
served with egg custard and, to Summer's relief, a
fruit salad.

'Cream for you, *madame*?' The waiter stood at her
elbow, holding a silver jug of fresh double cream.

And it was then, as if being obliged to eat something
taboo during the previous course had somehow
sapped the self-discipline she had exerted for nearly
three days, that she almost said mentally, Oh, to hell
with it—why not? and aloud, 'Yes, please.'

Only the presence of the man who had called her a
glutton made Summer shake her head and say, 'No,
thank you.'

She watched the waiter pour some cream over
Emily's apple pie and then move round the table to
repeat the process with James Gardiner's treacle tart.

She had always adored treacle tart; the pastry case
filled with a deliciously glutinous mixture of course
crumbs and grated lemon peel enveloped in golden
syrup. Forcing herself not to look at the thick wedge of
hot, sticky tart on James Gardiner's plate, she admitted to herself that, if she were shut in a room with his
tart and Emily's pie, she would never be able to resist
eating both in addition to her fruit.

Much as she longed to be slim, she was as addicted

to food as a smoker to nicotine, a dipsomaniac to alcohol, or a junkie to dope.

Could she ever break free of her addiction, or would she always be tormented by pangs of longing when she saw other people eating the sweet things her mind rejected but her body craved?

Her dessert, an imaginative combination of fresh and dried fruit with a liqueur, possibly kirsch, added to the juices, was excellent. But it didn't satisfy her palate in the way which the pastry and cream which James Gardiner was eating would have done.

And he wouldn't put on an ounce, Summer thought enviously. Whereas her waistline was a fissure between her spare tyre and her tummy, the black leather belt slotted through the loops on his waistband encircled a muscular torso with no superfluous flesh, not even in the area where most men of his age had at least some padding, if not an incipient paunch. Before he had told her he was a company chairman, she had thought that whatever he did for a living must involve a lot of exercise.

'I wish you were flying to Florida with us, James,' said Emily, while the two adults were having coffee and she was nibbling the sweetmeats which the waiter had brought to accompany the coffee.

Her uncle said, 'You'll have my housekeeper, Mrs Hardy, to help you settle in, and I've no doubt Miss Roberts will quickly revert to her native language, even after a long break.'

Emily looked puzzled. 'I thought they spoke English in Florida?'

'American-English which is not always the same as British-English. For instance, what does the word mall mean to you?'

Although she had never been to London, Emily said instantly, 'The drive from Buckingham Palace to Admiralty Arch where you get a good view of the coaches on special occasions like the opening of Parliament or the Royal Wedding.'

'Yes, or possibly Pall Mall, where some of the surviving men's clubs are, or even Chiswick Mall where people who have friends living there get an excellent view of the Oxford and Cambridge Boat Race. But in Florida, you'll find that mall refers to large shopping arcades where people can do most of their shopping under cover and, in summer, out of the heat.'

'Is it *very* hot in the hot months?' Summer asked.

'Intensely hot . . . uncomfortably so. Florida is a winter place. Some people have to live there the year round, the way others have to endure the winters in New England. The hot months in Florida are fine for people who don't mind staying in an air-conditioned atmosphere. Houses and automobiles are air-conditioned, so are the malls and the supermarkets and restaurants. Unless there's a major power failure, no one has to sit around sweating. But I don't happen to like being indoors all the time, and so I only go there between October and April . . . when I want to unwind.'

'What does unwind mean?' asked Emily. 'Is that American-English?'

He laughed. Unwillingly, Summer had to admit he had an attractive laugh; both the sound, and the momentary glimpse of strong white American teeth.

'No, it's international office jargon meaning getting away from the pressures of business for a while,' he explained.

Summer was pondering the fact that she had thought of his teeth as American teeth.

She had still been wearing orthodontic bands on her teeth when she came to live with her aunt, and remembered being surprised that few English children seemed to wear them. Some of the English had excellent teeth; but, as a nation, they consumed enormous quantities of what she had once called candies and now knew as sweets, and this resulted in much decay. Upper- and middle-class people generally had good teeth, but not often as well-spaced and straight as her own and James Gardiner's teeth. In fact she had never before met an Englishman with what she called American teeth—he was the first one.

'Will you come to Florida for Christmas?' Emily asked.

Her face fell when he answered, 'No, but I'll probably fly down there some time in January or February.'

Summer had been worrying about Christmas before his arrival. Even if Emily's relationship with her parents had not been close, Christmas at Cranmere had been celebrated in a style she was bound to miss, especially this first year.

The house had always been filled with guests, all of whom had brought presents for her. Not only would she be denied the excitement of opening a large number of presents, but, at a deeper level, she could not fail to be conscious of her aloneness; of having no family any more.

When her uncle had paid the bill, Emily said, 'Instead of coming with you to the estate agent, Summer, could I go back to the bookshop, and have another browse?'

'I don't see why not. You've got your puffer with you?'

Emily nodded and produced the small aerosol inhaler from which, if she started to wheeze or thought she might start, she could give herself a puff of bronchodilator.

'Have you any money?' her uncle asked.

'No, but I don't want to buy anything, only to look.'

'Buy yourself two or three paperbacks for the journey.' He gave her a crisp new banknote.

Her eyes widened. 'Golly! Ten pounds.'

He said, 'If you get tired, come back here and sit in the lounge till we come. If we haven't turned up by four, order some tea.'

The offices of the town's oldest-established estate agent were a short walk from the hotel. As she hurried along beside him, Summer seized the opportunity presented by Emily's absence to bring up the subject of Christmas.

She began by saying, 'Where will you be spending Christmas, Mr Gardiner?'

'Skiing at Gstaad.'

His reply shocked her. She had assumed he must have an important reason for not coming to Florida, but that she might be able to convince him that nothing was more important than that Emily should not feel bereft and miserable.

His casual announcement that he would be enjoying himself in Switzerland took her breath away. Was this how he meant to discharge his responsibility? By being lavish with pin-money, but niggardly with the love and attention his niece needed far more?

'Oh, a white Christmas in the Alps—how nice. Emily would love that. As it's her first Christmas as an orphan'—she used the emotive word deliberately—'couldn't she spend it there, with you? She wouldn't interfere with your skiing. She's always perfectly happy as long as she has something to read.'

'If I were staying in an hotel it might be possible, although difficult, to get them to squeeze her in somewhere,' he agreed. 'But I'm staying at a private ski lodge and my hosts wouldn't take kindly to having a child foisted on them.'

'Are you sure? I should have thought most people would stretch a point in these special circumstances. After all, loving kindness is what Christmas is all about.'

'Not to most people, Miss Roberts,' he said dryly. 'In general, it's an excuse for eating and drinking and that unwinding I was talking about earlier.'

His cynicism repelled her. She had never believed the people—Miss Ewing among them—who claimed that the true spirit of Christmas was lost nowadays, swamped by commercialism. The Christmases of her childhood had been magic festivals. Her parents had always included one or two old or lonely people in their celebrations, and many of the gifts she had helped her mother to wrap had been for recipients who otherwise might not have shared in the annual upsurge of loving and giving.

'You could explain to them and ask them?' she persisted.

He shook his head, starting to frown. 'I shouldn't dream of putting them in the awkward position of having to refuse; not only on their own account but in the interests of their other guests. It won't be the kind of house party where a child wouldn't be noticed. They would find her presence intrusive, and she wouldn't feel comfortable either.'

Without stopping to think, she said curtly, 'What on earth do they do when not skiing? Smoke hash and go in for group sex?'

His grasp on her arm made her stop short. As he scowled down into her face, she found several new and alarming ideas flashing through her mind.

He was looking furious. Was it because she had hit on something? Could it be that his father had thrown him out and disowned him because he had been caught taking drugs or, worse, pushing them? At one time there had been a wave of expulsions at England's so-called public schools, which were actually very expensive fee-paying schools, for such crimes. Obviously, a man as fit-looking as James Gardiner couldn't be on drugs himself; but it could be that the huge income he claimed to be making from computers came from a more sinister trade.

The thought that Emily might now be dependent on a man who lived on the proceeds of other people's degradation filled Summer with horror and rage.

'No, they do not,' he said tersely. 'They're merely a group of people who don't happen to want children underfoot—or yapping lap dogs, or chain-smokers, or any of the various other nuisances which people are perfectly entitled to exclude from their lives if they wish to.'

'They sound a fun crowd,' she retorted, equally tersely.

His black look lightened a little. 'I wouldn't say that

precisely. They're all interesting, distinguished people whom I count it a privilege to mix with. If you must know, they include a couple of older people who haven't yet got over a particularly horrible tragedy. Their son and his wife and their two grandchildren were involved in an accident with a car driven by youngsters who were high on drugs. The parents and one child were killed outright. The other child—a girl the same age as Emily—is now a permanent hospital case. Now do you see why I can't ask my hosts to include her?'

'Yes,' she conceded. 'Yes, I do. But what I don't understand is why your concern for Emily doesn't outweigh your concern for them. Would it be such an intolerable sacrifice to give up your Christmas plans to make her Christmas less forlorn?'

'It won't be forlorn. She'll be in an interesting new environment and she'll have you with her. Until a few days ago, she barely knew I existed. You're a much more important figure in her life than I am—and at this stage, she's more important to you than to me,' he added. 'She seems a nice enough child, but I'm afraid my affections are not so easily engaged that I'm ready to prefer her company to that of my friends.'

Now that her flare of anger and suspicion had subsided, she could see the force of his argument. Emily had taken to him because she was an impressionable teenager whose father had never quite fulfilled her longing for someone to love, admire and depend on, and whose uncle seemed, on first acquaintance, as if he might fulfil all those needs.

He, on the other hand, was a mature, sophisticated male who, if he needed affection and admiration, would seek it from girls much older than Emily. Sex, perhaps pride of possession, and possibly intellectual stimulus would be what he required of the female sex. Not the innocent hero-worship of a flat-chested child of thirteen.

They walked the rest of the way without speaking. At the entrance to the building, as he pushed open the

heavy swing door for her, she was aware of the
pleasure of being treated with chivalrous courtesy by a
member of the opposite sex. Yet at the same time she
knew that, on this occasion, he had performed the
action as an automatic reflex, not because she aroused
his protective instincts. He didn't see her as a woman;
only as the grotesque outsize frump who was tutor to
his niece.

She didn't want to be, but she was glad of his
support in the discussion with the estate agent. If he
hadn't been with her, she knew she would have been
dealt with by a junior clerk at the front desk, not
ushered into the office of one of the partners.

And it wasn't because, in making the appointment
by telephone, he had given his title or said he was
ringing from Cranmere—they knew him only as Mr
Gardiner. But he was the kind of man—she couldn't
deny it—who, by something in his air and manner,
commanded respectful attention. He might repudiate
his heritage, but he could never rid himself of the
innate authority bred from generations of power and
influence.

Mr Watts, the partner who attended to them, was a
bald man who tried to disguise this by carefully
smarming his hair sideways. His manner was professionally genial.

'As it happens, we have a very nice elderly couple
who are looking for somewhere to rent in your area,'
the agent told her. 'They spent their working life in
Africa. For the past seven years, they've been living in
retirement in Spain, but they feel that now, in their
seventies, they should come back to England. They're
planning to build a small house, but it may take some
time. If you're agreeable to a year's lease, they could be
ideal tenants for you, Miss Roberts.'

The idea of renting, rather than selling in haste, was
more appealing to her. She felt the cottage was a
sheet-anchor which, if the worst came to the worst—
and she had no specific calamity in mind, only a vague
unease—she and Emily would have in reserve.

Although if there were tenants living in it, they themselves wouldn't be able to live there until the lease had expired.

'I think you had better come and look at the place, and then advise Miss Roberts about an appropriate rent and the price she could expect if she sold it, Mr Watts,' said James Gardiner.

Summer felt sure that, had she been on her own, Mr Watts would have agreed to do this—when he had time. It was only a two-bedroomed cottage from which, if he did sell it for her, he wouldn't derive much commission.

But with James Gardiner as her spokesman, the agent said, 'Yes, by all means. In fact I can come over later this afternoon, if that would suit you.'

'That would be splendid,' she said gratefully, giving him one of the smiles only seen by people who didn't make her feel self-conscious.

As he rose to show them out, he said, 'How long have you had your cottage, Miss Roberts?'

'It was left to me a year ago, but I've lived there for twelve years.'

'Ah, then you know the village well. Have you heard any rumours about Cranmere?'

'Rumours?' she echoed guardedly.

'About what's going to happen to it. There's no male heir, I understand, only an invalid daughter.'

She said, 'I don't have much to do with the village people. If there are rumours going about, I haven't heard them.'

'Let's hope it doesn't go the same way as Mentmore, the Rothschild mansion,' he said. 'That's now the headquarters of some strange religious cult, you know. The Government should have bought it for the nation. A sad loss to our heritage . . . a very sad loss.'

'Crocodile tears!' was James Gardiner's caustic comment a few minutes later, when they were outside in the street. 'If I asked Watts to handle the sale of Cranmere, he'd be only too delighted. Agents don't worry about other people's reverses if they can benefit from them.'

'Isn't that rather unfair? He provides a service which people need.'

He glanced sideways at her. 'That's the second time you've accused me of unfairness. I think if we're going to have dealings for a number of years, you'd better accept from the start that I'm not and never was a model of the English public school ethic of fair play and a stiff lip at all times.'

For the third time that afternoon she spoke without thinking.

'*That* was clear from the outset,' she informed him tartly. And then gave a smothered gasp as she realised she was speaking to her employer.

Far from looking annoyed, he laughed. 'I like you better when you speak your mind than when you're being pious, Miss Roberts.'

But I don't like you, and never shall, she retorted silently.

'On the other hand, I applaud your discretion when Watts was trying to pump you just now. Your answer was evasive but not untruthful. In spite of your lapse the other night, normally you disapprove of untruths as strongly as of unfairness, I expect?'

'Yes, I do. Don't you, Mr Gardiner?'

'I daresay I'm as truthful as the next man,' was his casual reply. 'As we're both Americans, don't you think it's time we stopped being formal. Even the British get on first-name terms pretty quickly these days, I noticed while I was in London. You've no objection to my using yours, have you?'

'No . . . not at all.' But she didn't want to call him by his.

'I've never met or even heard of a woman named after one of the seasons before,' he went on. 'But why not? Most of the names of the months have been used. April . . . May . . . June . . . Julia . . . Augusta. You were born in summer-time presumably?'

'Yes: on Midsummer Eve—June twenty-third.'

She could guess what he was thinking; that, for the person she had turned out to be, no name could be more ill-chosen. A girl called Summer should be a fairy-like creature, not a great galumphing 'hulk'.

She said, 'Last night, when you told her Cranmere had to be sold, what was Emily's reaction?'

'She accepted that if I said it was necessary, it was. I believe she has an adventurous streak which perhaps, up to this point in her life, hasn't been recognised because she's been sublimating it, reading other people's adventures. Have you ever looked closely at the portrait miniature of Maria Lancaster, painted in 1810, the year before she took off on her travels?'

The Castle contained many of the small portraits, painted on vellum or ivory, which in previous centuries had taken the place of family photographs.

'I don't think I have? Which room is it in?'

'It always used to be in the Yellow Bedroom, unless it's been moved, which I doubt. It was hung rather high, and surrounded by other paintings, so it didn't catch the eye; particularly as, in her thirties, Maria wasn't a beauty. Later on she published her *Memoirs*. Maybe you've read them?'

Summer shook her head.

'No? She was the eccentric spinster sister of the fourth Marquess. After Lady Hester Stanhope had gone off to live on Mount Lebanon in Syria, and become uncrowned queen of the local Arabs, Maria also left home for foreign parts. I may be wrong—it's a long time since I saw her portrait—but I think Emily's like her. The first time I saw her, I knew she reminded me of someone but I couldn't place the likeness. It came to me today, during lunch. When we get back I'll check it out with the miniature.'

'You say Lady Maria wasn't a beauty. I think, when she's older, Emily is going to be lovely.'

'Maybe—it's too early to tell. The Lancaster females have never been renowned for their looks. Some of the wives have been pretty women, but the daughters have usually been on the plain side.'

And the men haven't been notably handsome, she thought, mentally reviewing the many large and small portraits of the Marquesses and their sons and brothers.

Where had the last of the Lancasters come by his arresting looks? Not from his mother. Judging by her portrait, she had been one of the pretty wives he had mentioned. Blue-eyed with small, regular features. It was not from her genes that his looks had sprung. Perhaps his dark colouring and tawny eyes came from his maternal grandfather.

They found Emily in the hotel lounge, already engrossed in one of her new paperbacks.

'Summer has to hurry home—the estate agent is coming to look at her cottage. So we'll have tea when we get back,' her uncle told her, after she had handed over the change from the ten-pound note.

They dropped Summer at the cottage gate and she didn't expect to see them again till next day.

After the estate agent's visit, she felt deeply unsettled and in need of someone to talk to. But there was no one in whom to confide her uncertainties. Her aunt had prevented her from being on close terms with anyone in the village, and she had gradually lost touch with the friends she had made at University.

She had written letters to them, but they had been too involved in all the extra-curricular and social activities which the University offered to have time to reply regularly. Postcards, during the vacations, were the most she received from them now. She understood. Had she stayed up at Oxford herself, she would have been similarly involved—not with male undergraduates, but in other ways.

As she wandered restlessly from sitting room to kitchen and back again, needing company, needing comfort, a vision of the treacle tart which James had eaten at lunch came into her mind. She felt an overpowering craving for something to munch. A candy bar. Ginger biscuits. A tin of air-roasted peanuts.

Suddenly the need was so overpowering that she

flung on her raincoat, grabbed her purse, and rushed down the street to the village shop, a small general store which didn't close until six.

She arrived seconds too late. The shopkeeper was turning the sign on the door from OPEN to CLOSED before pulling down the roller blind.

She still bought all her groceries from him, and not many of his customers did now—a lot of his trade had been lost to the supermarkets in town. If she tapped on the glass, he would unlock the door and be pleased to serve her. But she couldn't bring herself to do it. The voracious longing for the foodstuffs she hadn't tasted for what seemed like three weeks, not three days, egged her on; self-respect held her back.

While mind and body were in battle, the proprietor switched off the lights and disappeared into his living quarters behind the shop. Still tormented by the longing for something sugary and crunchy, but thankful to have temptation removed until the shop opened tomorrow, she walked slowly back to the cottage.

There, fortunately, she had only two crispbreads left and one orange. When they were eaten, the larder was bare. If it hadn't been, she knew she wouldn't have had a hope of resisting temptation all evening. She *was* what James Gardiner had called her—an uncontrollable glutton. And if she didn't do something about it, it was going to ruin her life. Not quickly and horribly, like an addiction to a drug, but just as surely. For what man would love her as she was?

She was letting the fire die down, thinking about going to bed early, when there was a loud rap on the front door.

She rarely had any callers, and never in the evening. Before opening the door, she called out, 'Who is it?'

'James . . . James Gardiner.'

What could he want at this hour? Perplexed, she opened the door.

'Did Watts turn up as he promised?' he asked, as he entered the house.

'Yes, he did. I have to telephone him tomorrow morning to find out when those people from Spain, the Seatons, are coming to see me.'

He was carrying something wrapped in brown paper. It looked like a bottle. He handed it to her and began to take off his coat.

'As you don't seem to keep any liquor in the house—or at least you didn't offer me any when I ran you home last night—I brought some with me. Your fire's getting low. Shall I make it up while you get the glasses?'

Clearly he was intending to stay for some time. Flustered, she said, 'Yes . . . perhaps you'd better,' and went to the kitchen to fetch two glasses.

She didn't know yet what kind of liquor he had brought, and she had never drunk spirits. But, if he meant to stay a while, she could do with a little Dutch courage.

He had built up the fire and was relaxing in an armchair when she came back with two large tumblers.

'I'm afraid I haven't any ice.' She remembered her father had always had ice in his drinks.

'Don't you have a fridge?'

'Yes, but the ice tray is empty. I only use it in hot weather.'

The lion's eyes mocked her. 'You don't indulge in a Manhattan at the end of a long day at Cranmere?'

'I enjoy my days at Cranmere. I don't need to unwind.'

He put his hand inside his blazer. 'The portrait miniature of Maria was still in the same place. I brought it to show you.' He held it out to her.

It was in a narrow gilt frame; a portrait of a woman in a high-waisted white dress with most of her hair concealed by a satin bandeau and there was a string of pearls round her neck.

Lady Maria Lancaster. Not a beauty, but not so ugly that no one would have offered for her. Her level, imperious gaze, the forceful line of her chin, suggested an early feminist.

'I see what you mean. There is a likeness,' she said slowly. 'And probably more pronounced when Lady Maria was younger. Are her *Memoirs* in the library? We must read them. Things like this won't be auctioned, surely?'

'No, no—nothing which Emily wants to keep, or which she might want, later on, has to be sold. But such things as the Rubens *Lion Hunt* are more suited to an art gallery than a private house, wouldn't you agree?'

The painting he referred to was one she had always disliked, a huge canvas depicting two lions in combat with several horsemen. The horses looked terrified. It was a masterpiece, but at the same time a painting which no one could look at without a shudder of disgust. One of the lions had the face of a fiend—a human fiend.

'How did you come to notice this miniature, and to know about her *Memoirs*?' she asked. It seemed unlike a schoolboy, as he had been then, to be much interested in his forbears, particularly the females.

'When I was at school I used to go skiing every winter with the family of my closest friend. One year I shared a ski-lift with a woman who painted miniatures and had a collection of early examples. She got me interested. I learnt to recognise the good ones. I used to make myself some money buying them in country antique shops and selling them to dealers in London. In those days you could sometimes pick up a very good quality miniature for five to ten pounds. Now they'd fetch hundreds of pounds.'

His chance encounter with the woman on the ski-lift must have developed into more than a holiday acquaintance if she had had time to teach him the finer points of an art which, as Summer had discovered for herself, were only recognisable with the aid of a magnifying glass.

'Did your friend the artist paint one of you?' she asked.

'Yes, she did, as a matter of fact.'

The enquiry appeared to surprise him, as indeed it had her. She didn't know why she had asked that.

But when his reply was affirmative, it confirmed her strong suspicion that the artist had taught him more than how to know a valuable miniature.

He said, 'I discovered Maria by going round the house, trying to identify the painters of all the Lancaster miniatures. That one was easy. It's initialled G.E. and dated. The puzzle was: who was the subject? Fortunately, George Engleheart kept a fee book. He kept it for thirty-nine years and he entered the names of 4,853 sitters and what they paid him for his work. Among the people he painted in 1810 was Lady Maria Lancaster. She probably had it done as a parting gift to her brother, in case she didn't return. It's the only portrait of her there is.'

He unwrapped the bottle, a new one, uncapped it with a twist of his muscular wrist, and poured some of the late Lord Cranmere's favourite Johnnie Walker Black Label into the glasses.

'Have you any branch water or tonic in the house?'

She knew that by branch water he meant bottled spring water. 'I'm afraid not—only tap water.'

'That won't do. It's full of chlorine and God knows what other chemicals. We'll have to drink it neat.'

He handed one of the glasses to her. 'What shall we drink to? A new start in the New World?'

'To a happy future for Emily.'

Without waiting for his concurrence, she raised her glass to that toast and took a cautious sip of the de luxe blended whisky responsible for the old Marquess's purple complexion and bloodshot eyes. It wasn't as strong as she had feared. Remembering a sip of bourbon which had made her choke and splutter as a child, she had been prepared to find her mouth on fire. But taken in the small amount she had sipped, the whisky didn't taste unpleasantly fiery.

'A happy future for Emily,' he repeated.

They sat down.

'And the *Memoirs*; how did you find them?' she prompted.

'I was told about them by my history master. No one in the family seemed aware of their existence. The Lancasters have never been noted for their intellectual powers,' he said sardonically. 'Field-sports have been their main interest for generations. The *Memoirs* is a small thin volume. Like her portrait, the book was squeezed in among some larger, more impressive-looking ones. It took me some time to find it, but once I knew what to look for there were several copies.'

'I wish you had brought one of them with you. I'd like to have read it tonight.'

'Yes, I should have done. I didn't think of it. I shouldn't have thought of the miniature if I hadn't passed the Yellow Bedroom on my way from my own room. I actually came over to hear what Watts had to say. What rent did he suggest? And how much does he think the cottage might sell for?'

She told him. She thought it was typically high-handed of him to demand the information rather than waiting for her to volunteer it. But it would have been hypocritical to deny that she wanted to talk it over with someone.

From another inside pocket he produced a small calculator and a fountain pen. He used the rounded tip of the pen to touch the keys. After making calculations for some moments, he said, 'It's your decision, but my advice is—sell. The only strong reason for keeping the property would be if you were definitely going to return to this country. I should say that's extremely unlikely. Once you've been back to America, I'm sure you won't want to leave it again, except for vacations maybe.'

She took another sip of whisky. The first one had sent a warm feeling coursing downwards from her throat to her stomach.

'You may be right. On the other hand, I've spent more than half my life in this country. There are many things about England which I love and shall miss when I leave here. Legally I'm an American citizen; but I sound and think like an English person. I could be more home-sick for England than I used to be for America when I first came here.'

'Nothing is impossible,' he agreed. 'But if that were so, would you want to return to this village? How would you support yourself in this area if it weren't for your job at Cranmere?'

'No, probably I shouldn't want to come back here,' she conceded. 'But as long as one owns a place to live, one can always sell it and buy another. If I were to sell the cottage, and then property values rocketed, I could find in, say, three years' time, that the smallest, most badly-built bungalow was beyond my means.'

'That's been a well-founded theory at certain times and in certain conditions. There are also times when money works better in investments than in bricks and mortar. You have to bear in mind that any property, especially when it's old, as this is, requires some maintenance. And that's not the only expense to take into account. Your agent will require his cut for acting for you, and there'll be tax to pay.'

He paused, swirling the last of his whisky round the bottom of his glass.

'No doubt you're wondering if my advice is reliable. Before you come up to the house tomorrow, I'll put some figures down on paper for you. You can then get your bank to check them for you. They can check me out, too, if you ask them. You don't have to take my word for it that I know more about handling money than Emily's father and grandfather.'

Again that strange distant way of referring to his brother and father, she thought, as she watched him drain his tumbler and rise to replenish it.

'Can I refresh yours?' he asked her.

'No, thanks. Not at the moment.' She was becoming aware of the same slightly hazy feeling the sherry had induced before lunch.

Undoubtedly he and Emily would have had a more substantial evening meal than hers had been. Two

crispbreads and an orange wasn't much of a lining on
which to drink strong liquor.

'You may think it's none of my business, but I'd like
to know where Emily stands financially. Has she
means of her own now, or is she dependent on
you?'

'She'll have some funds when she's older. At
present she has none.'

'It seems so extraordinary that her parents made no
proper provision for her . . . just in case something
happened to them.'

'I agree. But it's not unusual for people to ignore
life's less pleasant eventualities. Your own parents
did.'

'Yes, but my father had practically nothing to leave.
Hers had a great deal.'

'Not really. I don't think you understand the
realities of owning an historic house. A few of
Britain's aristocratic families are rich. The Duke of
Buccleuch is said to be one of the richest men in the
country. But in terms of income, many owners are
actually quite poor. They may have paintings worth a
fortune on their walls, but amazingly little cash at the
bank.'

He leaned forward to poke the fire.

'Most of what Emily's father owned wasn't his in the
way my holdings are mine,' he went on. 'He was
merely a trustee, keeping things going for the next
generation or, as he had no sons, for the next in line.
Both he and the old man knew that, as much as they
might dislike it, there was no way they could prevent
my inheriting everything if they died.'

'But if they both disapproved of you—'

He cut her short with a harsh laugh. 'They hated my
guts.'

She longed to ask, Why did they hate you? What
had you done? But she hadn't drunk enough whisky
to overcome her very British inhibition about asking
intimate questions of anyone but a close friend.

Instead, she said, 'In that case, one would think

they would have taken particular care to protect Emily from being left in your charge.'

He shrugged. 'Emily, being a girl, was of little consequence in their scheme of things. The Lancasters have always been strongly sexist in outlook. The portrait of Maria proves that. She was a woman of achievements, but did they give her a place of honour? Certainly not. She was relegated to the Yellow Bedroom. You see, she hadn't fulfilled either of the functions for which your sex was created. She hadn't given a man pleasure in bed, and she hadn't given birth to sons.'

Summer knew it was foolish to flush after he said 'pleasure in bed'. At her age most girls had experienced that pleasure many times, sometimes with a variety of partners. She not only hadn't experienced it, she had seldom heard it discussed.

The circumstances of her life—no television, schoolfriends who were serious rather than frivolous, no money to buy magazines which dealt with feminist issues and sexual relationships and, perhaps the most important factor, her own appearance—had kept her as far behind the times as someone of her mother's generation.

Since her aunt's death she had bought a book about sex which had enlarged her theoretical knowledge. But her experience was as limited as that of one of Jane Austen's heroines. She had never been embraced or kissed except in her imagination.

Hoping he hadn't noticed her heightened colour, she said, 'How did you come by your more enlightened views?'

'What makes you think I am more enlightened?'

'Aren't you?'

'Not much. I'll allow women equality of opportunity, if that's what they want. But as far as I'm personally concerned, they have only one useful function—the first of the two I just mentioned. The second doesn't interest me, and for all my other needs from cooking to conversation I would always choose a man in preference to one of your sex. That isn't to say I've never had a good meal cooked by a woman, or an interesting conversation with a woman. But the best meals I've eaten have been prepared by chefs, and the memorable conversations have been with men.'

As a put-down it was masterly. It made her furious, yet she couldn't see how to rebut it.

'If your views have become widely known, I daresay the women who could give you memorable conversation try to avoid you,' she answered, striving to match the blandness of his tone.

'No man with my income is ever avoided by women, no matter what his views,' he said dryly. 'If a man has money and power, he can be the biggest bastard ever born; there'll always be plenty of women prepared to overlook his defects.'

His cynicism chilled and repelled her. She couldn't bear to think of Emily's most sensitive years being spent under the aegis of someone who saw women in those terms.

She said, with a sparkle in her eyes, 'Are *you* a bastard, Mr Gardiner?'

For a long tense moment his eyes narrowed almost to slits, making her wish she had kept her mouth shut and ignored his jibes about her sex. She felt he was going to annihilate her, and she realised precisely what it would mean if he ever chose to stop her from staying on with Emily. Which he could, if she riled him enough. He might claim to like plain speaking, but—

'James,' he reminded her quietly. 'We agreed to dispense with formality. And to answer your question—no, I don't think you'll find me an objectionable person to deal with. As long as you're always frank with me, and you don't waste my time arguing about decisions which I've already thought through and have no intention of changing. On those terms, we should get along splendidly.'

With these last words he rose, placed his empty

glass on the ledge along the top of the ugly ceramic-tiled fireplace, and moved to pick up his coat.

'You've forgotten the whisky,' she said, as he went towards the door.

'I'll leave it here. We may have other things to discuss over a dram. Goodnight, Summer.'

She had not heard his car drawing up outside the cottage but she heard it moving off. When the sound of the engine had died away down the road, she decided to try a drop more of the whisky.

He had also neglected to take the portrait miniature of Lady Maria. It was still on the low table beside her chair. She fetched Miss Ewing's magnifying glass in order to study the painting in all its exquisitely fine detail.

Thinking about the woman who had kindled his interest in the tiny pictures, she wondered what kind of youth he had been to arouse her interest in him.

Probably nearly as tall as he was now, and almost as powerfully built. But without the hard, ruthless look which, except when he smiled or laughed, characterised his dark face and made it difficult for her to trust him.

Who had formed his derogatory view of women? Not that first one, the painter of miniatures. His expression when he spoke of her had suggested that he remembered her with affection.

Did he have the portrait she had painted of him, or had she kept it? A memento of an amorous friendship between a gifted older woman and a virile youth on the brink of manhood.

It was said to be the kind of apprenticeship every man needed if he were to become an accomplished lover. She had learned that from reading French novels of the eighteenth and nineteenth centuries. But how could any man be a good lover if, at heart, he despised his bed-fellow, feeling lust for her body but only disdain for her mind?

Surely making love to perfection was not just a

matter of technique; the skilful performance of the
actions described in the manual. There had to be
affection . . . poetry . . . tenderness.

When she was undressing for bed, she was surprised and puzzled to find a dark mark on her arm,
above the elbow. Then she realised it was a bruise
caused when James had grabbed her in the street,
forcing her to a standstill after she had asked if his
friends indulged in marijuana and orgies.

She had always bruised easily and his fingers had
been painfully strong. It annoyed her to have the mark
of them there, like a brand. His brother would never
have dreamt of gripping her arm in that rough way.
But then, to be fair, she would never have suggested
that Lord Edgedale might be mixed up with those kind
of people.

She woke up with a headache, which was something
which had never happened to her before. She came to
the conclusion it must be caused by the whisky. She
ought to have chased the alcohol with a glass or two of
water.

As her bicycle was still at the Castle, she had to walk
there. By the time she arrived the exercise and fresh air
had cleared the headache and she felt equal to the
demands of the day. She had also come to a decision
about the cottage. She was going to burn her boats and
sell it.

The days which followed were very busy ones.
Suddenly the house was full of experts making inven-
tories. There were two or three people from Christie's
fine art department making lists of the paintings;
someone else valuing porcelain and china; a representative from Maggs, the London antiquarian
booksellers, was at work in the library, selecting the
most valuable works; and elsewhere experts on silver,
furniture, clocks and Oriental rugs all making their
separate assessments of the Castle's treasures.

James himself was in charge of the list of things
which were not to be sold but retained, in storage, for

the day when Emily was ready to furnish her own
house.

One day Summer had an opportunity to speak to
Conway alone. Inevitably the elderly butler was one of
the busiest members of the household, and she had
almost despaired of a chance to consult him in private,
without fear of interruption.

When the opportunity did arise, she almost had
second thoughts about tackling him on a matter which
he might regard as a gross breach of propriety.

'Mr Conway, I can't help being worried about this
tremendous disturbance in Lady Emily's life,' she
began. 'First the loss of her parents, then of her
grandfather, then all this upheaval and, next week, a
long tiring journey to a completely strange environment. It would put a great strain on an adult, let alone
a rather delicate child of her age.'

The butler regarded her with his grave stare for
some moments.

'I understand your concern, Miss Roberts, but I
think your presence throughout this calamitous
period in Cranmere's history has been Lady Emily's
bulwark, if I may say so.'

Lurking under her outward seriousness, Summer
had a sense of humour which often bubbled to the
surface when she and Emily were alone. There had
been little to make her laugh since James's arrival at
the Castle, and her size was not usually a matter which
she found amusing, although she had sometimes
forced herself to make jokes about it at school and at
Oxford.

'Perhaps not the kindest choice of metaphor, Mr
Conway, but I'm glad you think so and I hope you're
right,' she said, with a twinkle in her eye.

It was the first time she had ever seen Conway's
dignity disturbed. For a moment he actually looked
abashed.

She laughed. 'I was only joking—and what I want to
ask you is anything but a joking matter,' she went on,
her expression becoming serious. 'In fact I'm very

hesitant to consult you about it, in case you misunderstand my motives. It's not a matter of idle curiosity on my part—please believe that. But everything has happened so rapidly, and now we're about to fly to America under the aegis of someone who is virtually a stranger to us. You knew his Lordship as a boy, Mr Conway. What sort of boy was he? And why was he sent packing?'

He said nothing for so long that she thought he might be intending to remain silent until she muttered an apology for her breach of decorum and fled.

But at last, to her relief, he said, 'Lord James, as he was at that time, was never sent packing, Miss Roberts. He ran away. He and his late Lordship had never seen eye to eye; nor was Lord James on close terms with his brother, Lord Edgedale.'

'Was he fond of his mother?'

Again the butler pondered the question for some time.

At length, he said, 'Lady Cranmere was very beautiful and very gracious in her manner to everyone, high and low alike. When she first came here as a bride—we had a much larger staff and I was then the senior footman—everyone was charmed by her. The year before, the newspapers had called her the Débutante of the Year. However, as time went on, she became . . . less animated. Perhaps the fact that his Lordship was twenty years her senior had the effect of subduing her youthful high spirits. In those days his late Lordship was Master of the Cranmere Hunt, and they entertained a great deal. Lady Cranmere's social duties made it difficult for her to spend as much time with her sons as perhaps she could have wished. It was thought by the female staff, and from my own observations I have to agree, that both Lord and Lady Cranmere had a marked preference for their elder son.'

'Why was that, d'you think?' Summer asked.

Another long pause. She sensed he was choosing his words with great care.

'Lord James was a very mischievous child, always into some scrape or other,' he said eventually. 'Lord Edgedale was of a more law-abiding disposition. He liked riding and hunting which naturally found favour with his father. Lord James was an excellent shot from an early age, but he once made his father very angry by saying that he would prefer to run with the fox rather than hunt with the pack. The activities of the anti-blood-sports factions used to enrage his late Lordship. To have his younger son taking their part was more than he could stand.'

'His Lordship told me himself that he used to go poaching with an old man called Barty Hicks. But were any of his youthful misdeeds of a more serious nature, Mr Conway?'

'Not to my knowledge, Miss Roberts.'

Was he telling her the truth? She was, after all, an outsider, whereas he was part of the household, part of the family. She remembered the nom-de-plume used by the author of the Chevalier Bayard's biography. *Le Loyal Serviteur*. The Loyal Servant. Conway was an equally loyal servant of the Cranmeres'. Would he, like Bayard's servant, tend to gloss over the defects of members of the family he had served all his life?

She decided to press him. 'He never smoked pot, or . . . or misbehaved with the local girls?'

'No, no, I'm certain he never had anything to do with drugs, even the so-called soft drugs,' the butler answered firmly.

'There were young men of good family who were implicated in the drug scandals at certain public schools at that period.'

He gave a disapproving sniff. 'Mrs Briars reads a daily newspaper which delights in regaling its readers with any breath of scandal involving the upper classes. I regret to say that several of Lord James's contemporaries were involved in that "scene" as the papers called it. But he had too much respect for his body to abuse it with drugs or any other forms of dissipation. Quite the reverse. He was interested in physical fitness. He had a trapeze fitted up in one of the attics and he used to spend hours exercising. When he disappeared, it was thought by some of the female staff that he might have joined a circus as an acrobat. It was not a theory to which I attached any credence, I may add.'

He gave her an oblique glance before adding, 'I feel sure that, however his Lordship has occupied himself in the interim, he has had no connection with a circus.'

She repressed a smile at the smoothness with which he suggested the quid pro quo.

'I understand he's one of the leaders of the computer revolution,' she told him. 'He owns a company which makes them. So you think Lady Emily's future is in good hands, Mr Conway?'

'Based on my knowledge of his Lordship's character up to the age of seventeen, I would say yes, Miss Roberts.'

'In spite of the crippling death duties, I'm sure he has the drive and energy to keep the Castle going if he wanted to,' she said regretfully. 'You must feel very sad to see it about to be stripped of all its treasures.'

'The end of an era is always an occasion for some sadness,' he agreed. 'But perhaps it has come as less of a shock to me and Mrs Briars and other long-serving members of the staff than to you, Miss Roberts. When Lady Edgedale was very ill giving birth to Lady Emily, and several years passed without the birth of other children, it was clear that the family was likely to die with Lord Edgedale.'

'You never expected Lord James to reappear?'

For an instant, before he looked away, there was an expression in his eyes which convinced her he was concealing something.

'No,' he said. 'No, we didn't. Would you excuse me, Miss Roberts?'

With a slight inclination of the head, he left her.

Forty-eight hours before their flight to Miami, James drove them to London.

With her suitcase beside her, Summer was waiting for them outside the front gate of the cottage when, punctually at nine, the car came into view. Emily was sitting in the back. Her face wasn't woebegone, nor were there any signs that she had shed tears on leaving her ancestral home, never to live there again.

'I didn't sleep a wink,' she announced, after saying good morning. 'I was too excited. Only two more hours and we'll be in London!'

Summer hadn't slept much either, but her excitement had been tinged with sadness for the death of the beautiful house she had grown to love.

When James had stowed her case in the boot—in a few days' time she would have to revert to thinking of it as the trunk, and the bonnet as the hood—he slid behind the wheel and re-fastened his safety-belt.

Since the last time she had been a passenger with him, the adjustment of the nearside belt had been altered, perhaps to secure Emily's slight form. As she fumbled to loosen the straps to enclose her much larger body, he leaned over to help her.

For a moment before she withdrew them, her pale hands were entangled with his strong brown ones. His were warm but hers were cold, a fact he remarked on as he dealt with the belt.

Mortifyingly conscious that he was loosening it to its fullest extent, she said, 'My hands usually are cold, even when the rest of me feels warm.'

'That's poor circulation,' he told her. 'The cure for it is regular exercise. In Florida you should try swimming laps every day, morning and evening, gradually increasing the number.'

'Yes, perhaps I will.'

It was a relief when he had finished adjusting the belt and sat back in his own seat.

On the way through town, he parked outside Mr Watts' office while she hurried inside and left her labelled keys at the front desk. The cottage was to be sold furnished, there being very few possessions which she wanted to keep.

One or two things she was fond of were in her suitcase. Fitting them in had been no problem. She possessed few clothes suitable for a winter in Florida. Although he had told her there were sometimes 'killer frosts' which did much damage to the orange groves and subtropical shrubs, these were infrequent and short-lived. She would need a light coat for going out after dark, but by day the most she would require would be one warm sweater or cardigan. In general, she and his niece could expect to spend much of their time in bathing-suits and sun-dresses.

Like most overweight people, Summer had never been eager to strip off at the first sign of hot weather. Heatwaves were times of mental and physical discomfort for her. She disliked exposing her bulges to public view, and the insides of her thighs rubbed against each other and quickly became red and sore.

Large-size sun-dresses always had wide straps to conceal the straps of their wearers' no-nonsense bras. She knew that, as did most big women, she had nice shoulders. Yet she could never display them under ribbon ties and pretty halters because nobody made a strapless bra which worked, and wasn't torture to wear, for busts larger than thirty-eight inches. And she naturally couldn't go without a bra as girls with small breasts could.

If it hadn't been for her determination to lose weight, she wouldn't have been looking forward to the warmth awaiting them in Florida. However, already her clothes seemed fractionally looser. Not much, but a little; and she hoped it wouldn't be long before she could buy some new American clothes, a size smaller than last year's summer dresses.

They were travelling in the fast lane of the motorway when she realised that it had been some time since Emily had spoken. Twisting to peer over her shoulder, she found that her pupil was now curled in an embryo position on the back seat, catching up some lost sleep. 'Emily's dozing,' she murmured quietly. 'Were there tears when she said goodbye to Conway?'

To avoid a formal leave-taking, Emily had been encouraged to make her farewells to the staff over a period of several days. This morning, only the butler would have been present to see her off.

'Conway looked as if he might shed a few later. She gave him a hug and a kiss which pleased the old boy, but she didn't cry. Did you expect her to?'

'Perhaps not then, but I thought she might be upset when she had her last sight of the house.'

'I don't think she was. Were you, when you saw it for the last time yesterday?'

'Yes, I was a bit. As Conway said the other day, it's the end of an era. Doesn't it cause you the slightest pang to think of it standing empty, after hundreds of years in one family's possession?'

'Some men are content to rest on their ancestors' laurels, and others are driven to found their own dynasties,' he answered. 'I'm one of the latter.'

She fell silent.

He was sweeping along the fast lane, at the maximum speed, and all his attention was focussed on the road ahead, with a periodic glance in his rear-view mirror. He didn't grip the wheel tightly, like Mr Renfrew when once she had driven with him. James held the wheel lightly, almost casually, the bones of his long, blunt-tipped fingers clearly defined under the taut brown skin.

After a while she asked, 'Is your house in Florida very modern?'

'On the contrary, it's old compared with most houses there. It was built in 1929. My apartment in New York is modern, and I have a weekend place in Nantucket which is only a year or two old but designed to blend with the whaling-days' atmosphere there. At present I'm rarely in any of them for long. I spend a lot of time travelling from campus to campus, preaching the computer gospel to students.'

'Why is that necessary?'

'Because today's students are tomorrow's important

customers, and I want to have the edge on my competitors.'

She said, 'I see.' But she didn't. What was the point of having three places to live and not enough time to enjoy them.

It was mid-morning when they reached London. As they drove along Park Lane, he pointed out the Dorchester and Grosvenor House Hotels and, further on, a high-railinged mansion standing in splendid isolation between the green acres of Hyde Park and a whirlpool of traffic swirling round an impressive monument.

'That house is No 1, London—the home of the Iron Duke,' he told them. 'And the monument is the Wellington Arch.'

'How do you know which way to go?' Emily asked, as he steered the car through the converging and diverging streams of vehicles, many of them the distinctively high-built London taxis.

'I've been to London a number of times in the past ten years. Now we're going down Constitution Hill. Inside that high wall on your right is the garden of Buckingham Palace. You'll see it in a minute. If the Queen is in residence, her standard will be flying from the flagpole.'

As Emily and Summer gazed at the imposing façade of the Royal Family's London home, she wondered what had brought him here before. Business perhaps. Or could it be that he had renewed his connection with the portrait painter, and she would be one of the 'interesting, distinguished people' with whom he was to spend Christmas.

From the Palace it was not far to the flat which Emily's parents had kept as their London *pied-à-terre*. The block had a porter who took charge of the luggage while James drove away to return the car to the nearest office of the company which owned it.

On the way to London, he had told her that the flat had two double bedrooms and a single one. She and Emily were to share the room with twin beds.

Unlike Cranmere, where much of the décor remained as it had been when the great house was new, with some changes superimposed by each succeeding generation of Lancasters, Summer could see that the London flat had been decorated by a professional designer, and one whose style she recognised because Lady Edgedale had commissioned him to do up her bedroom at Cranmere.

The geometric-patterned carpets, the use of colour, the 'tablescapes' of carefully chosen collections of objects were all the hall-marks of David Hicks, the husband of Lady Pamela Hicks, younger daughter of the late Lord Mountbatten.

By the time James reappeared, Summer had unpacked their overnight things and Emily, exploring, had found a saucepan of vegetable soup on the kitchen stove and an attractively arranged platter of smoked salmon salad in the refrigerator.

'I rang up an organisation which does rather civilised catering and asked them to lay on a light lunch,' her uncle said, when she told him about these discoveries. 'Tonight we're going to sample the flesh-pots so we don't want to spoil our appetites.'

Summer wasn't sure whether this plan included her. If it did, she had nothing to wear and she knew a meal in a restaurant was sure to present the temptations she was trying to avoid.

She said, 'Emily has outgrown the dress she had for special occasions last winter. Perhaps, after lunch, we could go shopping for a new one.'

'I was joking about the flesh-pots,' said James. 'Neither of you needs to dress up for the place I'm taking you to tonight.'

'It's kind of you to include me, but I'd be quite happy to spend the evening here. I can watch television—it's a novelty for me.'

'Don't be silly, of course you must come. We shan't enjoy it without you,' Emily insisted.

'No, you can't spend your first night in London watching TV,' James agreed.

She felt sure that, had Emily not butted in, he wouldn't have objected to her suggestion. Even if where they were going was not an elegant place, he couldn't want to be seen with a fat frump.

After lunch they took a taxi to Grosvenor Square to collect her passport from the American Embassy. Another taxi took them to the British Passport Office in Petty France where Emily's document was waiting for her. From there it was a short walk to see the Houses of Parliament and, close by, Westminster Abbey.

It wouldn't have surprised Summer if the excitement of sight-seeing combined with the unaccustomed fumes of heavy traffic had brought on one of Emily's bouts of wheezing. Throughout the afternoon she kept a discreet look-out for the first hint of difficult breathing. However, Emily's enjoyment of the wonders of London was far from flagging when James announced, 'Time for tea,' and hailed another cruising taxi.

Back at the flat they took off their outdoor clothes and Emily switched on the television and started to curl herself comfortably on the sofa.

A programme appeared. And disappeared, as James touched the OFF button.

'Why have you switched it off?' she asked him.

'Because you didn't ask Summer if you might switch it on, and because you have work to do.'

Her forehead wrinkled. 'What work?'

'Making some tea for her. She's tired.'

Emily turned to her tutor. 'Are you? Oh, Summer, I'm sorry. I didn't know that.'

Summer was about to deny her weariness when, over the top of Emily's head, James gave her a look which silenced her.

He said to his niece, 'Your packing was done for you. She had no one to do hers. This morning she had to get up much earlier than we did, cook her own breakfast and leave the cottage clean and neat. People don't always say when they're feeling bushed, Emily. You have to notice it. Come on, I'll show you how to make tea.' He swept her off to the kitchen.

Left alone, Summer collapsed on the sofa with a thankful sigh. It had not only been a long day—it had been a long, weary week with a good deal of mental stress on top of the extra physical exertion; and the drastic cut in her calorie intake was another drain on her energy.

Presently he returned, by himself.

'She has to learn that from now on she won't always be waited on,' he said. 'That was quite a hard lesson for me, and I was a lot more self-sufficient than Emily. Don't spoil her, Summer. You'll get short-shrift from me if I catch you over-indulging her.'

The peremptory tone in which he said this swiftly dispelled her gratitude for his uncharacteristic show of consideration a few minutes earlier.

She said defensively, 'Emily has never been spoilt, certainly not by me. She's very unselfish for her age. But she's not an angel. Who is? Everyone has moments of thoughtlessness.'

'Which they may get away with later, but not at thirteen,' he said dryly.

'Are you sure she can handle the kettle? It's a large one and she has such thin wrists. It would be awful if she scalded herself,' Summer said anxiously.

'She can manage. Don't fuss. A girl of thirteen can still have her character shaped, but she's old enough to cope with boiling water and sharp knives. For God's sake, in the old West girls her age dressed wounds and helped deliver babies. The young do whatever's required of them.'

'Yes . . . they do.'

She was thinking of herself, spending the summer evenings on the extra home-work set by her aunt instead of playing tennis like the vicar's teenage children, or flirting with boys on street corners like the milkman's daughter.

The place where he took them for supper was in a basement off Hanover Square.

'A foretaste of America,' he said, as they entered the

restaurant, its walls hung with old posters and street signs.

The busboys and waitresses were young people, informally dressed with friendly manners. The list of drinks included American beer and a St Valentine's Day Massacre cocktail. Before Summer could demur, James had ordered Coca Cola for Emily and a bottle of red wine for them.

The menu, as Emily soon discovered, was a souvenir she could take away with her.

'The Chicago Pizza Pie Factory—Purveyors of Chicago pizza to London, Bath and the World,' she read out. 'Deep-dish Chicago pizza was first served in Chicago about 40 years ago; since then it has been duplicated by scores of restaurants in and out of Chicago. Our very own recipe has been created to capitalise on the best of the Chicago versions but with special attention to the taste of our London patrons. Radio tapes from Chicago's best station, WFYR, arrive regularly.'

Summer had already noticed that as well as an inexpensive side salad, the menu offered a more elaborate chef's salad. She wondered if she could ask to have that by itself without incurring sardonic comments from James.

Emily had discovered another section of the menu.

'Please allow us 20-30 minutes to prepare your pizza,' she read out. 'It takes a bit longer to make this wonderfulness'— here she paused for a giggle—'but we think you will agree it's worth waiting for. A regular pizza serves up to two people. A large serves three to four people. Don't worry if you can't finish it all, we'll give you a doggie bag to take home.'

Summer said, 'I think I'd like to try the stuffed mushrooms and the chef's salad while you two share a regular pizza.'

The stuffed mushrooms—We stuff 'em with butter, breadcrumbs, sherry, parsley, grated Italian cheese and more than a hint of garlic. You won't soon forget them—weren't slimming food, but they sounded less fattening than the cheese-laden pizzas.

It was Emily who argued that she couldn't come to a pizza pie factory and not have pizza.

James said, 'Why don't you and I share a half and half pizza, Emily? I like the cheese and pepperoni. Which filling do you fancy? How about the speciality—cheese and sausage?' When she had agreed, he added, 'If Summer is going to have garlic in her mushrooms, you and I'd better have some as well. I'll order some hot garlic bread to eat while we're waiting for the pizza.'

'Garlic is the thing the French use which makes your breath smell, isn't it?' asked Emily. 'That was the thing Daddy didn't like about French food.'

'More fool him,' James said shortly. 'Garlic is one of the reasons French food is so delicious, and if everyone eats it the smell isn't noticeable.'

Summer felt it was bad form for him to speak scathingly of his dead brother. But probably bad form or good form were not matters of great moment to him. That he had given her a homily about Emily's character-training didn't mean he applied the same principles to his own conduct.

'You must try a teeny bit, Summer,' said Emily, when the half and half pizza arrived, the cheese bubbling gently and giving off a savoury aroma.

'I'm quite happy with my mushrooms, thank you.'

'Just a taste,' Emily persisted.

A glass of what the menu called *Chateau Chicago*, while they were waiting, and the sight and smell of other diners' pizzas being carried past, had undermined Summer's resolve. If James hadn't been there, she would have said, 'All right—a small piece.' But he was there, watching her, a hint of a derisive smile lurking at the corner of his mouth.

It was that which made her say firmly, 'I don't wish for any, thank you. I have tasted pizza, when I was little. You mustn't press people to eat things, Emily. They may have refused because they're allergic to it, or it gives them indigestion.'

The child, unused to being spoken to in that

governessy tone, looked so crushed that Summer
couldn't help smiling and saying, in her normal voice,
'But it was nice of you to offer to share some with me.
Would you like a little of my salad?'

'No, thank you.' Emily gave her a look which reminded Summer of a puppy which has been punished
but is now back in favour.

She felt a rush of protective tenderness towards her.
Poor little thing: it was rotten for her, having no one
but an uncle and a tutor, neither of whom could take
the place of loving parents. Not that her parents had
been particularly loving, but merely by their existence
they must have given her a greater sense of security
than she had now.

When, some time later, their waiter returned to their
table, he asked, 'Would you care for some dessert?
Cheesecake . . . or ice cream?'

He sounded Australian and looked about seventeen—the age when James had left home.

'Not for me, thank you,' she said.

'I'm not sure if I have room,' said Emily.

'They serve two forks with each order of cheesecake. How about sharing one?' James suggested. 'It
says here that their cheesecakes are '*a little bit of heaven,
made with cream cheese, sour cream, other fresh goodies and
lots of love. All served with honeyed whipped cream and
almonds.*'

Was he suggesting she and Emily should share one?
Deliberately tempting her? Or had he meant he and
Emily?

The child decided she still did have a corner to
fill.

'Two coffees and one cheesecake, please,' James
said to the waiter.

When her dessert was placed in front of Emily, she
said, 'Who's going to have the other fork?'

'Not I,' said Summer firmly.

But, oh, how she longed for a taste of the delicious
sweet goo into which Emily was dipping her fork.

James shared the last of the wine between her glass

and his, then he picked up the second fork and sampled the cheesecake.

'Mm . . . not bad . . . in fact good,' was his verdict. He had another forkful.

Summer forced herself to ignore them and to concentrate on reading the posters on the walls and studying the other diners. But a part of her mind was conscious that it would be years before she could share the pleasure which they could enjoy with impunity.

It might be that, like an alcoholic, she would *never* be able to eat pizza or cheesecake. It was a dreary prospect.

From the restaurant, they walked the short distance to Bond Street and turned in the direction of Piccadilly. Yves St Laurent . . . Hermes . . . Ted Lapidus . . . Gucci . . . Ferragamo . . . Loewe . . . Chanel. The internationally famous names, the glimpses of elegant clothes and expensive leather goods turned her thoughts from a lingering longing for the taste of cheesecake to the unknown pleasure of wearing beautiful clothes.

Emily was disappointed that the windows of the great jewellers—Cartier, Kutchinsky, Boucheron, Philip Antrobus—were denuded of the glittering jewels she had expected to see.

'A sign of the times,' said James. 'They put them away before they close. You have to ring a bell on the door before you can walk inside most London jewellers' shops nowadays.'

The remark made Summer wonder if he knew this by hearsay or experience. And, if the latter, what he had bought and for whom?

In Piccadilly, they walked past the Ritz Hotel and along the edge of Green Park until James hailed a taxi to take them the rest of the way.

At the flat, Emily needed no urging to have a hot bath and go to bed. By the time Summer had finished in the bathroom, the child was asleep with Cyprian tucked in beside her.

Knowing she felt sheepish about her attachment to

him, but would be profoundly upset if he were packed in the luggage and it became lost or misrouted, Summer had given her a tote bag in which, safely curled at the bottom, under books, he could travel in the cabin with her.

Not long after switching out Emily's light, she turned out her own and was soon asleep.

Much of their last day in England was spent looking round Harrods, the greatest department store in Europe, where the Queen did her Christmas shopping and where they found hundreds of her subjects crowding certain departments in search of presents.

Wandering wide-eyed round the Food Halls and the white marble Perfumery where girls, their eyes and lips painted in the style advocated by whichever of the great cosmetic houses they represented, were spraying scent on customers' wrists or demonstrating make-up colours on the backs of their own manicured hands, Summer and Emily were conscious of being country bumpkins.

'What is a bumpkin in America?' asked Emily, as they glided to a higher floor.

Summer dredged her memory. 'A hick.'

'We're a couple of hicks who've just come up from the sticks . . .' Emily sang, to the tune of *We're A Couple Of Swells*.

Her pale little face was aglow with the thrill of seeing London decked for Christmas, all the great stores vying with each other to have the most enticing windows, the most spectacular façades.

Having left them to their own devices during the day, that night James took them to the theatre. He had chosen a musical show and both this and the theatre itself were perfect for the occasion.

The small, intimate, old-fashioned theatre, still with its gilded decorations and two tiers of private boxes on either side of the proscenium arch, was a much nicer introduction to London's theatres than a large, modern auditorium.

And the show, with its light-hearted theme and catchy melodies, was an ideal choice for the eve of a transatlantic journey about which, even though she had done it before, Summer was beginning to have tremors. It wasn't the flight which caused the butterflies. It was going from the known to the unknown—with no way of coming back if they didn't like it there.

Next morning James said, 'I won't come to the airport with you. I have an appointment at the time you need to arrive there, and I'm sure you can manage to get from the taxi to the check-in without any assistance. There'll be luggage trolleys available. You won't have to carry your bags.'

'Yes, of course we can manage,' said Summer. 'There would be no point in your coming.'

'When you land at Miami, a car will be waiting to take you to an hotel for the night. Tomorrow it will pick you up and take you back to the airport to fly to Sarasota. I've decided that, as you've only just passed your driving test—having learnt to drive on the left—it will be better for you to have some practice on quiet roads before going on any main highways.'

'When shall we see you again?' his niece asked him.

'I don't know, but I'll call you regularly to hear how things are going.'

'I wish you were coming with us.'

He answered that with, 'When I do come, I'm expecting to find you a pretty good swimmer. Maybe you can get the boy who cleans the pool to give you some coaching.'

Which means he doesn't have much confidence in my coaching, thought Summer. Perhaps he was right. There were twelve years and many pounds of flesh between her and the slim ten-year-old of whom she remembered her father saying proudly to someone, 'My daughter must have a mermaid in her ancestry. She's the best little swimmer you ever saw.'

They said goodbye to him in the street, beside the taxi which was taking them to Heathrow.

'Take care not to let the sun burn you, the first two weeks,' was his parting advice to Emily. 'Enjoy yourself.' He stooped to kiss her on the cheek and received in return a swift but enthusiastic hug.

To Summer, he said, 'You'll have to be careful, too. Your skin is even fairer than Emily's. The midday sun can be fierce, even at this time of year. Slap on plenty of sun cream. Goodbye.'

'Goodbye.' They shook hands.

Then she turned and stepped inside the taxi.

Emily waved to him through the rear window till she could no longer see him. Summer didn't look back.

As the child turned to settle herself for the first lap of their long journey, she said, 'I hope it isn't *very* long before we see him again.'

Summer was having a final check through her bag to make sure she had the airline tickets, their passports and the American money which James had given her to cover incidental expenses until they reached his home. She gave a non-committal murmur.

Her personal hope was that it would be as long as possible before their next encounter with him. And when they did meet again, she intended to be a different person.

PART TWO
FLORIDA

'It's beautiful! *Oh . . . isn't it beautiful!*'

Emily's face was close to the pane and she was craning, enraptured, at the sight of Miami by night; hundreds . . . thousands . . . *millions* of lights, some of them in static rows and clusters, some of them moving in streams.

It reminded Summer, peering over her shoulder, of the jewellers' windows in Bond Street. Here were the jewels which had been missing from them; here were the diamond necklaces, the sparkling bracelets, the brooches; all flung down in lavish confusion on a bed of black velvet.

'If this is America—' breathed Emily.

Summer found her throat tight with emotion. She was thinking of some lines by Housman.

> That is the land of lost content,
> I see it shining plain,
> The happy highways where I went
> And cannot come again.

But she had come again. There it was below her, glittering Welcome. Welcome back.

As she fumbled in her pocket for a tissue, her eyes brimmed and overflowed. Emily, turning to exchange a delighted glance, saw two tears rolling down the older girl's cheeks.

'You're crying,' she exclaimed, in dismay.

'I know. Isn't it silly of me.' Summer was smiling and crying at the same time.

Suddenly Emily's eyes filled with tears of sympathy. She flung her arms round her tutor.

'Don't cry,' she said, in a choked voice. And then: 'Oh, Summer—I do love you.'

'I love you, too,' Summer answered shakily, hugging her.

Their embrace was the first demonstration of the close, sisterly affection which had been building up between them for more than a year. But neither of them was used to displaying their feelings and, drawing apart, both felt a little self-conscious.

'Can you see the airport yet?' Summer asked, to give Emily an excuse to turn back to the window while she herself wiped her eyes and recovered her composure.

'No . . . not yet. But it can't be far away. We're getting lower every minute.'

As, shading their faces from the light within the aircraft's cabin, they peered at their destination, Summer saw that the dazzle of downtown lights had given place to straight rows of dimmer street lamps illuminating a chequer-board pattern of residential blocks.

All the houses she could see were detached with unfenced gardens round them. Even from the air, the suburbs surrounding Miami looked different from those surrounding London where most of the houses were either built in pairs or in terraces.

After touchdown, the next excitement—instead of having a long walk from arrival point to baggage reclaim—was to ride in a vehicle like the London Underground train they had been on yesterday, which glided slowly up a sloping rail to the main part of the airport.

'It's more like a disco than an airport,' said Summer, surprised by the purple carpets and the brilliant pools of light shed by downlighters in the ceiling. She had never been to a disco, but she had heard about them.

They had had a taste of racial intermingling during their brief time in London, the home of large numbers of Indians and West Indians, and smaller communities from most of the world's nations.

Here in Miami there seemed to be an even more striking mixture of races and nationalities. As many travellers seemed to be speaking Spanish as English, and fair-headed people like Summer were outnumbered by dark-haired ones.

The American Immigration officer studied her passport without comment. After looking at Emily's, he fixed her with an expressionless stare, and said, 'So you're Lady Emily Lancaster. How about that?'

If he had said it with a smile, she would have beamed back at him. But Summer could see that she found him alarming.

Before Summer could reassure her, the Immigration officer said, 'Cat got your tongue, Lady Emily Lancaster?'

Emily shook her head. With a glimmer of a nervous smile, she said, 'James says I should call myself Miss Lancaster in America. It's more democratic.'

Regardless of the people waiting in line behind them, the officer leaned his elbows on the desk and gazed into her eyes. 'Does he now? And who might James be?'

'He's my American uncle. We're going to spend the winter at his house in Sarasota.'

'Is that so?' Suddenly his face creased in a grin. 'You know something? That sure is a cute British accent.' He straightened again. 'But I guess some of these people'—with a nod at the queue—'would rather go where they're going than stand around listening to you and me having a talk. So'—he tapped her on the head with her passport—'on your way, *Miss* Emily. Enjoy your trip.'

'Thank you. Goodbye.'

For an instant, as the child gave him her most radiant smile, Summer caught another glimpse of the charmer she was going to be . . . one day.

'Wasn't he nice?' said Emily, as they moved on to have their luggage checked by Customs.

Soon after emerging into the public concourse, fol-

lowed by a porter with their luggage, they saw a man
in chauffeur's uniform holding a placard with Roberts/
Lancaster written in large letters on it.

A few minutes later they were in the back of a large
limousine, sweeping luxuriously past the travellers
who were lining up for taxis or climbing aboard buses.

'Did you have a good flight, ma'am?' the driver
asked.

'Very good, thank you—but we shan't be sorry to
have a bath and stretch our legs. Where are you taking
us?' Summer asked.

'To the Fontainebleau Hilton, ma'am. You'll find it a
very good hotel, right on Miami Beach overlooking the
ocean.'

'Will you be taking us back to the airport tomorrow?'

'Yes, ma'am. Your flight to Sarasota is scheduled for
four o'clock. I'll be there to pick you up at three.'

After driving for a time on an expressway, they
came to a long causeway crossing a stretch of water
which the driver said was Biscayne Bay.

Summer had caught sight of a sign: *Julia Tuttle
Causeway.*

'Who is Julia Tuttle?' she asked him, expecting
to hear the causeway had been named after a local
benefactor.

'Mrs Tuttle lived here when there was just a small
settlement on the Miami River, ma'am. She wanted to
have the railroad come down here, but Henry Flagler
who built the East Coast Railroad didn't want to bring
it further south than Palm Beach. In those days the
Gold Coast, as it's called now, was a real wilderness.
Nothing but forest and swamp. Back in 1895, the year
when most of the state's crops were destroyed in a
freeze, Mrs Tuttle sent Flagler some orange blossoms
which hadn't been touched by frost. That made him
decide not only to bring the railroad down, but to build
a town here. That's the story anyway.'

They were almost across the causeway when he
added, 'Most people think Miami and Miami Beach
are the same place. That's not so. Miami is the town

we just left, in back of the Bay. Miami Beach is this strip of land up ahead. Seven and a half square miles, that's all there is, but I guess you won't find more or better hotels anywhere in the world.'

Certainly neither Summer nor Emily had seen anything like the view from the parlour of their suite, to which they had been conducted by a friendly young man from the reception desk.

It was Emily who discovered the view while Summer was tipping the bell-boy who had brought their baggage up to the seventh floor in a separate elevator.

'Summer, you'll never believe . . .' she breathed, in an awed voice, from the window.

Summer crossed the deep-pile green carpet which toned with the green and white wallpaper which matched the curtains and covers on the two long sofas.

'Oh . . . my goodness!' she exclaimed.

As the driver had told them, the hotel was close to the ocean, and their window looked out on a moonlit sea lapping a beach of pale sand.

In the foreground were the hotel gardens with palm-fringed walkways winding among well-kept lawns. And at the heart of the gardens was a huge flood-lit, free-form swimming pool, roughly the shape of an oak leaf. In the centre of the pool was an island with several palm trees growing on it, and in the place where a leaf would have its stem, there was a great crag of rocks with several cascades streaming from it like shining veils. All around the pool was a spacious deck with many sun-beds. A number of people were still swimming.

'Can we swim tomorrow morning?' Emily asked. 'It's not deep everywhere. Look, those people over there are only up to their waists.'

'We haven't any bathing-suits,' said Summer. 'But perhaps we could buy some. Right now I'm going to take a shower. How about you?'

Each of the two luxuriously furnished bedrooms had its own bathroom. They wouldn't have to take

turns. While Summer was unpacking, she heard
Emily give a shriek of excitement. A moment later she
rushed in and seized Summer's arm.

'You must come. I've found something specially for
you.'

Wondering what it could be, Summer allowed herself to be hustled back to the parlour.

She had noticed the large television, the table
lamps, the round dining table on which a meal could
be served, and the large indoor plant growing in a
jardinière. She had also noticed a beautiful arrangement of cut flowers in a vase on the coffee table, but
not the small envelope tucked among the blossoms.

'It's addressed to you,' Emily told her.

Puzzled, Summer looked at her name for a moment
before she opened it. Inside was a card.

Welcome back to America. James.

'Who is it from?' asked Emily.

Summer showed the card to her.

'How could he send you flowers from England?'

'He must have ordered them by telephone and
dictated this message. This must be the florist's hand-
writing,' Summer explained.

'Isn't he kind to us,' said Emily. 'Arranging for us to
stay in this super hotel, and sending you flowers and
everything. I think he's the kindest person I've ever
known.'

'Yes, very kind,' said Summer. And very unkind
sometimes, she added mentally. Cruelly unkind.

For a moment or two the flowers and the message
accompanying them had pierced her implacable dislike of the man for whom, but for Emily, she wouldn't
have worked if he'd offered her twice her present
salary.

But as she resumed her unpacking, she thought it
more than likely that all the arrangements for their
arrival in America had been handled by James's secretary or personal assistant, including the ordering of
the flowers and the message with them. Yet how could
his secretary have known Summer was returning to

America. She couldn't. He must have dictated the words on the card. Well, it was a flattering attention to detail on his part, but it didn't wipe out—nothing could—the memory of those brutal words spoken on the Grand Staircase at Cranmere.

In her bathroom she found not only an abundance of thick fluffy towels ranging in size from a bath sheet to a face cloth, but also a disposable shower cap and phials of shampoo and body lotion.

She undressed and hung up her clothes. Here, unlike the bathroom at the cottage, there were large mirrors everywhere, making it impossible to avoid seeing her naked body. It was a depressing sight, increasing her guilt at her lapse from grace on the aeroplane.

They had travelled first class and she hadn't been able to resist the lavish lunch or, later, the afternoon tea served by attentive stewardesses. She hadn't refused anything, not even the chocolate-covered mints brought round with the post-luncheon coffee, or a second slice of fruit cake at tea.

With champagne before lunch, and different wines with each course, she must have consumed enough calories to undo all the good of several days' self-denial.

Why had she weakened? Why couldn't she control her appetite? What was the matter with her that she had this compulsive urge to gorge foods which she knew would add flesh to her heavy hips and bulging tummy?

She woke with the sun on her face and the sound of music coming from somewhere nearby.

At first, dazzled by the bright golden light, she couldn't think where she could be. Blinking, she pushed herself up on her elbows and peered at her surroundings.

The vast bed in which she was lying settled her confusion. She was back in America . . . home.

The night before she had opened both pairs of

curtains; the pink ones which matched the wallpaper, with their sun-proof linings, and the filmy net glass curtains. Then the sea had been dark except for the silver moonglade stretching from the beach to the horizon. Now, as far as she could see in both directions, the Atlantic Ocean shimmered and sparkled in the brilliant sunlight of a cloudless December morning.

The music had stopped and now there were voices coming from the next room. Summer put her head round the door and found her charge watching television.

'I thought you were never going to wake up,' said Emily, bouncing off the sofa. 'I've been awake for *ages* . . . since five o'clock. It's a good thing I saved some biscuits from tea yesterday—I'd have starved without them. Can we have breakfast soon?'

'What time is it?'

'A quarter to eight but that's quarter to one in England . . . almost lunchtime.'

'We didn't go to bed until the small hours—by our body clocks,' Summer reminded her.

They had been too keyed-up after the journey, and it had seemed a good idea to stay awake as long as possible. So although they had gone to bed early by local time, in England it would have been three in the morning when they said goodnight.

'I'm going to wash and get dressed. You can ring Room Service and order breakfast,' she continued. 'I'm not very hungry. I'll have grapefruit, if they have it, and coffee.'

As she brushed her teeth, she made herself a solemn promise that yesterday's lapse would be the last one—ever. Today was the beginning of a new life; a fresh start. From now on, before she put anything in her mouth, she would think: Do I really want to eat this? Or do I want to be slim and elegant and desirable?

By the time she was dressed, a waiter was laying the table in the other room. His 'Good morning' was said with a strong foreign accent. He looked as if he might be Cuban, certainly Latin-American.

Determined to eat her grapefruit without sugar, Summer was agreeably surprised to find it naturally sweet, and much juicier than the grapefruit sold at the village shop. Both the flesh and skin had a rosy tinge.

Emily had ordered a full American breakfast, starting with orange juice and ham and eggs with hashed brown potatoes, followed—because she had never had them—by waffles with maple syrup.

They were wondering if there were any shops nearby where they could buy bathing-suits, when the telephone rang. When Summer answered it, a switchboard operator said, 'I have a call for Miss Emily Lancaster.'

'One moment please.' Summer beckoned Emily. 'It's for you,' she mouthed.

'For me?' Emily looked baffled. She took over the receiver. 'Hello? Yes . . . speaking. Oh—James! Good morning.' A pause. 'Yes, super, thank you. Yes, we both did. The Captain was nice. So was the other pilot.' Another pause. 'We're just finishing breakfast. If we can buy some bathing-suits, we're going to swim in the fabulous pool they have here. Have you seen it? Have you stayed here?' A third, longer pause. 'Yes, hold on a minute.' She covered the mouthpiece with her hand. 'He'd like to speak to you.'

Conscious of a tiny stab of nervousness, Summer took back the receiver. 'Good morning. Thank you for the flowers.'

'My pleasure. I gather you had a smooth trip. Are you feeling jet-lagged?'

His voice sounded deeper on the telephone, but his American accent was less pronounced than when they first met. The longer he stayed in England, the more he reverted to the long a's and the British emphases of his youth.

'Not at the moment,' she answered.

'You will. It takes a few days to adjust to a five-hour time slip. I heard you want to buy bathing-suits. There may be swimwear on sale in the hotel. I've never

explored the shopping facilities. If not, go to the Bal
Harbor Shopping Center. Neiman-Marcus have a
store there, and there's also a Saks and a Burdines. I'll
call you tomorrow.' He rang off.

When they went down to the lobby, a girl at the
hospitality desk suggested that, as they were leaving
the hotel soon after lunch, rather than going to Bal
Harbor they should try a swimwear boutique a few
blocks away. She gave them a card showing the shop's
location on the back. Summer wondered if she had
some connection with it, perhaps receiving a small
commission for sending people to it.

The boutique proved to have a vast range of styles
and sizes and Emily was soon the pleased owner of
a vivid lime green bikini which suited her auburn
colouring and would look even better with a tan.

Summer had braced herself for the embarrassment
of not being able to squeeze into anything. She didn't
know what her size was in America, but the colours
she saw on the rails suggested that they didn't cater to
heavyweights, only to sylphs.

'Do you have anything which might fit me? Something plain and dark?' she asked doubtfully.

'Sure we have, honey. These along here are your
size.' The saleswoman spread her arms to indicate an
extensive selection. 'Two pieces on the top rail, one-
piece suits on the bottom. Pick out a few and try them
on. With your lovely blonde hair, I'd think this blue
and white would be good. It's a very slimming style.
You see, it has this cute little skirt which is great if you
have a problem here'—patting the top of her thigh—
'as I used to.' She gave a reminiscent laugh. 'Before I
slimmed down, my big thighs were the bane of my
life. Talk about flub-rub! How about this turquoise
suit?'—selecting another.

'What's a flub-rub?' Emily asked her.

The saleswoman grinned. 'Oh, that's a Weight
Watchers joke. The girl who took my class, Betty, she
was a natural comedienne. It was worth going to
meetings for the laughs. She had us falling off our

chairs. She'd been heavy herself—all the lecturers have. She weighed over two hundred pounds before she joined, but you'd never guess it to look at her. She has a great figure now. How d'you like this black and white?'

Summer felt none of the suits was going to do anything for her, or she for them. However, as Emily had to be taught to swim, it was impossible to shirk the ordeal of appearing in public with all her bulges on show.

In the fitting room there was a notice asking customers to wear their panties while fitting garments. She had sometimes looked longingly at the bright-coloured micro-briefs worn by her contemporaries, but she had always needed the control of a waist-high stretch panty.

As she struggled in and out of the suits, she could hear Emily telling the saleswoman about their flight and where they were going.

When she emerged, she had decided that the suit with the black bottom half and a white top, these colours separated by a diagonal band of deep pink, was the least conspicuous of the three.

'Do you need a wrap?' the woman asked. 'You do? These pareus are nice.' She took out a piece of fabric like an enormous scarf and showed them how it was worn, wrapped round the body with two of the corners knotted. 'Or these terry robes are useful because they can double as a beach towel.'

Summer chose an emerald-green robe, knee-length with loose sleeves and patch pockets, and Emily a shorter bright blue one.

'And how about thongs?' The saleswoman pointed out a bin of inexpensive rubber flip-flops.

While she was writing out the bill, Summer said, 'Was going to Weight Watchers classes really helpful when you were slimming?'

'Oh, sure—it made all the difference. I'd been yo-yo dieting for years. You know how it goes . . . up and down . . . up and down. Starving one week, stuffing

the next. Weight Watchers was the big breakthrough
for me. I've never looked back. You should try it.
Don't they have classes in Britain? I thought it was
world-wide now.'

'Yes, they do have classes in Britain, but not near
where I lived.'

'Here there's a class almost everywhere. The little
girl says you're going over to the Gulf coast. Sarasota
. . . Bradenton . . . round there. Look it up in the
Yellow Pages. I'm sure there'll be a class near you.'

'Yes . . . perhaps I will,' Summer agreed.

The saleswoman, who was about forty-five and
wearing a lot of make-up which made her face look
harder than it really was, said kindly, 'You do that,
honey. You're young, you're pretty, and if you were to
lose forty pounds you'd be really something. But
dieting by yourself is too difficult. I know I needed
help, and maybe you do. If you join Weight Watchers,
the next time you're in Miami you'll be shopping for
size eight.'

'Americans are very outspoken, aren't they?' said
Emily, as they walked back to the hotel. 'I don't think
an assistant in an English shop would have told you to
join a slimming class, would she?'

'She might—if she'd had a weight problem and
could see that I had one,' said Summer.

You're young, you're pretty . . .

The saleswoman's words had been balm on the
still-raw wounds inflicted by James Gardiner. But
forty pounds had been a tactful understatement—
sixty was nearer the mark!

'You are pretty, Summer,' the child said. 'I was
looking at you this morning, before you woke up. I
tiptoed into your bedroom to see if you might be *nearly*
awake. When you're asleep, your eyelashes are like
little dark feathery fans. And your face is like petals on
roses . . . all sort of velvety and lovely. But I don't like
your hair,' she added bluntly.

'Now who's being outspoken?' Summer asked,
laughing. At the same time she was deeply touched by

her pupil's compliments.

'I don't mean I don't like the colour. It's your pigtail which isn't nice. At least not all wound round and pinned. Why don't you wear your hair loose?'

'It would be too long and untidy.'

'Then why not have some cut off. It would look nice the way the girl at the hospitality desk had her hair.'

'It costs quite a lot of money to have one's hair cut every few weeks. But perhaps now I have no household expenses I'll be able to afford it.'

There were quite a number of people round and in the pool when, wearing their new beach outfits, they approached the inviting expanse of shining blue-green water.

Mindful of James's warning, Summer had bought a tube of sun cream and applied plenty of it to Emily's shoulders and arms and to her own.

Most of the people round the pool were tanned in varying degrees. Nobody else was as pallid as they were. As, reluctantly, she shed her robe, she felt that anyone looking in their direction must be thinking: Ugh! What a horrible sight that great white whale of a girl is. She could only have felt more ashamed of her obese body if James had been there to watch her follow Emily to the pool's edge.

Sitting down on the rim and dangling her feet in the water, Emily said, 'It's beautifully warm.'

Summer lost no time in immersing as much of herself as the water in that part of the pool would cover. It came to just above her waist and she felt less noticeable with her lower half, if not hidden, at least partially camouflaged.

But presently, demonstrating the arm and leg movements of the breast stroke, and then supporting the child while she practised them, she became less self-conscious.

'If you want to go and swim in the deep part, I'll be all right. I won't go out of my depth,' Emily assured her, some time later.

'Okay, but I shan't be long.'

Using the stroke she had been teaching, Summer
swam slowly towards another area of the pool. Then,
drawing a deep breath and burying her face in the
water, she changed to the crawl, her arms slowly
rising and falling while her legs performed a rapid
scissor-motion in the way her father had taught her,
long ago.

She couldn't keep it up for long. Panting from the
unaccustomed exertion, she rolled on to her back and
lay floating, watching a seagull gliding in the sky
above her, the outline of its wings gilded by the
sunlight.

'Ah . . . lovely!' she murmured aloud, at the almost
forgotten pleasure of drifting under a blue sky, in
lukewarm water which flowed like silk against her
skin and made her feel light and free, like the soaring
gull.

They had a light raw-food lunch in the cavernlike
setting of the Lagoon Saloon, one of the hotel's many
restaurants, which was inside the rocks by the pool.
They sipped their fruit juice cocktails looking out
through one of the cascades at the island in the centre
of the pool. Various kinds of seafood were set out in
giant clam shells. Summer knew, from diets she had
tried in the past, that seafood was high in protein and
low in calories.

'When I asked James if he had stayed here,' said
Emily, 'he said yes, he had, but it wasn't one of his
favourite hotels although he thought it would amuse
us. I wonder why he doesn't like it? I think it's super.
Don't you?'

'Yes, but I expect his experience of hotels is much
wider than ours is. If he's always travelling, he must
be a connoisseur. The pool and the grounds here are
lovely, but the hotel itself isn't what one would call a
beautiful building; and the lobby and the public rooms
are perhaps a bit flashy. Not in the cheap and nasty
sense,' Summer qualified her last remark. 'All those
chandeliers and statues obviously cost a small fortune.
But I think they'd have more appeal to a sheik and his

wives than to a man like your uncle.'

'I wonder what his house is like?'

'I've no idea. The only thing he told me about it was that it was built in 1929,' Summer answered.

She found herself intensely curious to see the house; not only because it was where they had to live until he chose to move them elsewhere, but also for what it might reveal about her employer's somewhat enigmatic character.

They were met at Sarasota-Bradenton airport by a small, neat, grey-haired woman in her late fifties who introduced herself as Mary Hardy, James's house-keeper.

She was driving a Cadillac with room for them both to sit beside her.

'It's just a few minutes' drive to the house,' she told them. 'You'll be glad to get settled after being in transit two days.'

They joined a stream of fast traffic on a main high-way.

'We're beginning to feel sleepy,' said Summer. 'Although it's still afternoon here, we feel it's much later.'

'Yes, you'll feel that for a day or two. If you want to go to bed right away, you can. We thought you might be tuckered out so Mrs Antonio turned your beds down, all ready for you. Mrs Antonio cleans and her husband looks after the garden,' she explained. 'They live in the apartment over the garage. I have my bedroom and sitting room in the main house.'

As they stopped at traffic lights, she waved her hands towards some modern buildings on the far side of the road.

'That's the University of South Florida campus. Caples Hall, the house next door to Mr Gardiner's, belongs to the University. It was left to them by Mrs Ralph Caples who was the *grande dame* of Sarasota until she died, age ninety-eight, in 1971.'

A short distance beyond the intersection Mrs Hardy

turned off the highway into a quiet side road bordered
by wide stretches of grass and with a large older
building visible at the far end.

'Surely that isn't Mr Gardiner's house, is it?' Summer asked.

Mrs Hardy laughed. 'No, no—that's the Ringling
Museum of Art. Have you heard of John Ringling, the
circus magnate?'

'No, I haven't.'

'They used to call him the Circus King of America.
Way back in the 1920s, he put Sarasota on the map
when he had the winter quarters of the circus moved
here from Bridgeport, Connecticut. You can't see his
mansion from the road—it's built right on the edge of
the bay. It's called Ca'd'Zan which is Venetian dialect
for House of John.'

'What is my uncle's house called?' asked Emily.

'In a minute you'll see,' said Mrs Hardy, turning left
at the T-junction in front of the museum. 'This is Bay
Shore Road where most of the rich people who came
here in the early days built their winter houses. And
here we are!'

She braked to drive under an arch capped with
Roman tiles beneath which, inset in the terracotta-
coloured wall, was a row of white ceramic tiles with
the words *Baile del Sol* written on them in elegant dark
blue script.

'What does it mean?' asked Emily.

'It's Spanish for Dance of the Sun,' the housekeeper
told her. 'People who don't speak Spanish say the first
word like bail, but it should be pronounced ba-ee-lay,
Mr Gardiner told me.'

'Does he speak Spanish?'

'He speaks several languages. The last time he was
down here, the computer was teaching him Chinese.'

The car was moving up a drive bordered by two
rows of towering palm trees with smooth grey trunks
and long, graceful, feathery fronds growing at the top.

'These are Royal Palms,' said Mrs Hardy. 'There are
all kinds of palms in the garden, including the Christ-

mas palm which has clusters of bright red fruit at this time of year. If you're interested, Mr Antonio will tell you the names of them all.'

As she spoke, a curve in the drive brought the house into view.

Like the high, tile-capped wall round the garden, it was painted pale terracotta which, in the afternoon light, gave it a soft, welcoming glow. The roofs—there were many of them for the house was irregular in shape—were clad with more Roman tiles in age-speckled colours ranging from dark brown to pink. A creeper with a profusion of white flowers smothered parts of the façade between the tall downstairs windows, each topped with a group of three onion-shaped panes, giving a Moorish effect. All the paint-work was white, and the bedroom windows had white balconies, many with the foliage of pot plants cascading between the railings. These upper windows also had louvred shutters, all at present standing open. The shutters were painted a soft bluish-green. Either they had been faded by the sun, or the colour had been chosen to give that effect.

The instant she saw it, Summer knew that *Baile del Sol* was the kind of house her parents had loved. Whoever had built it had not done so with the object of displaying his wealth in the ostentatious grandeur of the *nouveau riche*. This house—one could see at a glance—had been the realisation of a different, more romantic ambition. Beauty and timeless serenity had been the inspiration here.

'Here comes Mr Antonio to carry your bags up,' said Mrs Hardy, as they climbed out of the Cadillac.

The short, thick-set man approaching them had a tan even deeper than James Gardiner's. Although his thick hair was white, his active-looking body wasn't that of an old man. His very dark, smiling eyes would have suggested a Mediterranean origin if they hadn't been told his name. He seemed to go with the house.

However, his accent, when he said hello and en-quired about their trip, was American, and a form of

American which Summer remembered from her childhood although she could no longer place it.

Her first impression of the interior of the house was
of high, bleached-beam ceilings, pale colour-washed
walls, vases of white flowers reflected in antique gilt
mirrors and clay-tiled floors, with the patina of decades of polishing, spread with needlework rugs.

Noticing her looking at one of them, Mrs Hardy
said, 'All the rugs in the house were hand-made in a
place called Arraiolos in Portugal. Some of the patterns were brought back from the Orient by Portuguese mariners, centuries ago. The Portuguese were
responsible for charting most of the world's sea
routes, you know. Other patterns are from ceramic
tiles made by the Moors when they ruled the whole
Iberian peninsula for hundreds of years.'

As she led the way up the staircase, she went on,
'Once a year Mr Gardiner opens the house to the
public in aid of the National Trust for Historic Pres-
ervation, and I have to be able to answer visitors'
questions about everything. I thought Emily would
like to sleep in the Octagon Room. It's quite small, but
it's pretty and I'm sure she'll like it.'

They had reached the landing by now, a long sunny
corridor with windows all along one side. These over-
looked a large patio between two projecting wings of
the house. On the outer side of the patio was a loggia;
two lines of slender pillars forming arches to support
the tiled roof.

Beyond this was a large garden, the lawn shaded by
groups of palms and sloping gently towards a huge
stretch of water bounded, in the distance, by a long
line of low-lying land.

'That's Longboat Key out there,' said the housekeeper. 'Beyond that is the Gulf. There are Keys all the
way along this coast. Lido Key . . . Siesta Key . . .
Casey Key. On the Gulf side they all have fine beaches
for swimming and shelling, but only a few hardy souls
go swimming this time of year. In winter, the ocean is
usually much warmer on the east coast of Florida.'

She opened the door of a small room with eight
walls and three french windows, each of them opening on to a balcony. A four-poster bed, smaller than
Emily's bed in England, and more lightly draped
with airy folds of white batiste, had its back to one
wall.

'Oh . . . !' Emily's gasp expressed more than liking
for her new quarters. She was visibly enchanted by the
room.

Mr Antonio lifted her suitcase on to a luggage rack
and went away, taking Summer's case with him.

'Just before sunset the computer turns on the heating,' said Mrs Hardy, indicating a radiator. 'The computer almost runs this house. At dusk it switches
on the pool lighting and the other outdoor lighting. It answers the telephone when no one's here.
If you want to wake up specially early, you don't have
to set an alarm. The computer wakes you with
Tchaikovsky's violin concerto. I tell Mr Gardiner
that if the computer gets any more efficient, I'll be
redundant! Your bathroom is right here, Emily.'

Summer was about to follow them into an adjoining
bathroom when she realised that what she had
thought was an alcove of books built into the wall
between two of the windows was not.

It was a *trompe-l'oeil* like the jib-door in the library of
Cranmere.

So were the shelves with china dogs—pugs and
King Charles spaniels—arranged on them. So was the
wide-brimmed straw hat, wreathed with rosebuds
and forget-me-nots, which appeared to be hanging
from a hook by long pale blue silk ribbons.

Suddenly, out of the past, came the echo of her
father's voice.

*They have more money than they know what to do with,
but it won't buy the one thing they want—their daughter's
health. She's fifteen years old, and she has less than a year to
live, Laura. They're doing everything they can to amuse her
and make her happy. They want me to paint her bedroom in
their winter house as a surprise for her birthday . . . her last*

*birthday, poor little kid. It's her favourite of all their houses
and they're going down there in November. But right now it
will be much too hot for you and Summer and the baby. It
won't be a long commission if I work at it all hours. I'll be back
before you know it.*

Even though they had not come to Florida with him,
Laura Roberts had lost the baby she had been expecting. Summer's parents had wanted a large family, but
after having her first one, Laura had never managed to
carry another child to term.

Summer remembered the times when her mother
had had to rest a great deal, but till this moment she
had forgotten the tragedy of the millionaire whose
youngest daughter had contracted an incurable dis-
ease.

The others came out of the bathroom.

'Miss Roberts . . . are you feeling unwell?' Mrs
Hardy asked, seeing Summer's face.

'No . . . I'm fine, really,' she assured her. 'It just
came as rather a shock to see these paintings here.'

'Aren't they clever? They fool everyone. They're
Thomas Roberts' work. He was—oh, goodness me,
Roberts. Was he a relation of yours?'

'Yes, he was,' Summer answered huskily.

And then, because she knew she was going to cry,
and she didn't want Emily to see her in floods for the
second time in two days, she added quickly, 'Emily,
would you unpack your night things while Mrs Hardy
shows me my room. I—I want to use the bathroom,
but I'll be right back.' She walked quickly out of the
room.

In silence the housekeeper accompanied her along
the landing, moving ahead to open a door at the other
end.

By this time tears were pouring down Summer's
cheeks. She felt acutely embarrassed because, if she
hadn't been jet-lagged, she would have been able to
control her reaction till later.

'My dear—' Mrs Hardy began, looking concernedly
at her.

'P-please come in. Close the door.' Summer's voice was ragged with emotion.

Inside the room, which she saw through a blur of tears, she gasped, 'Where's the bathroom?'

'Over there in the corner.'

'Th-thank you.'

In the bathroom, she grabbed a towel and buried her face in it while several deep shuddering sobs forced their way from her heaving chest.

Being able to break down completely, where no one could see her, was a great relief. For a minute or two she let herself weep unrestrainedly. Then, remembering poor Mrs Hardy, hovering in perturbation in the outer room, she pulled herself together and ran the tap to splash her face quickly with cold water.

When she returned to the bedroom, she said, 'I'm so sorry, Mrs Hardy. You must wonder if I'm round the bend. The thing is that Thomas Roberts was my father. Those paintings in the Octagon Room are the first time I've seen his work since I was a little girl, younger than Emily.'

'Oh, I see . . . no wonder you were upset. But isn't that lovely . . . to find your father's work here, in the house where you're going to live.'

'Yes, it is. It makes him seem . . . close,' Summer agreed, her voice still unsteady. 'But the reason he came here was very sad. Do you know the story behind those paintings?'

The housekeeper nodded. 'They were done for the Melroses' youngest daughter . . . the one who died at sixteen.'

'Did she die here, at *Baile del Sol*?'

'No, no—not here. She died at their other house in Maine. Afterwards they couldn't stand to come here any more. They sold it to Mrs Charles Rathbone and she lived here till five years ago. Then she moved across to Palm Beach where most of her friends have their winter houses, and Mr Gardiner bought it from her. She sometimes comes back to stay with him. Now I'm going to make you some tea and bread and butter, and then I'll come help you unpack.'

'Tea would be marvellous, but no bread and butter, please.' Summer decided to take Mrs Hardy into her confidence. 'I'm trying very hard to lose weight. In fact, if there is one near here, as soon as we've settled in I want to join a Weight Watchers class.'

'That's a good idea. I have a friend whose daughter went to those classes in Bradenton. That's in Manatee County, north of here—although nowadays Bradenton and Sarasota have both expanded so much, with all the retirement and holiday condominiums which have been built, that the two towns more or less merge. There's also a Weight Watchers class right here in Sarasota. I don't know where the meetings are held, but it's easy enough to find out.'

Outside on the landing a bell rang. Mrs Hardy crossed to the telephone on one of the two night-tables flanking the king-size bed.

'Hello? Oh, Mr Gardiner. Yes, they've arrived. I'm with Miss Roberts in her bedroom. I'll put her on.' She held out the receiver.

He had said he would call tomorrow. Summer wondered why he was calling again today.

'Hello.'

'So—you've arrived.' The line was good. He sounded as if he were speaking from another room. 'Do you think you'll like living in my house?'

'I'm sure we shall. From what we've seen of it since we arrived, about a quarter of an hour ago, it's a lovely house. Emily is enraptured by the Octagon Room.'

'Good. Your voice sounds throaty. Have you picked up a cold?'

'I hope not. Shall I fetch Emily?'

'No, no. I only wanted to be sure you'd arrived in good order. It may be some days, even a week, before I call again. Meanwhile, you're in good hands with Mrs Hardy and the Antonios.'

Without saying goodbye, or sending any message to his niece, he rang off.

*   *   *

By the time they had been at *Baile del Sol* for a week,
their systems had adjusted to local time, their skins
were beginning to change colour, and Summer had
found out where and when she could become a
Weight Watcher.

She was given a lift to her first class by Mr and Mrs
Antonio who were going to spend the evening shopping at a nearby mall. The class she had chosen to join
took place in a smaller shopping centre to which they
would return to pick her up.

A number of women were converging on the
Weight Watchers premises when she arrived. On
either side of it were shops, and the place where the
meetings were held had been built to be a shop.
Instead, the plate glass window was curtained. But
through the glass door could be seen a long room with
rows of chairs facing the inner end.

Immediately inside the door was a section made into
an office. Here, two women clerks were seated behind
a table, taking the weekly meeting fees and registering
newcomers.

'You're lucky. There's a five-dollar reduction on
membership this month,' said one of the clerks, when
Summer had filled in a form, giving her name and
address and telephone number. 'Do you have bathroom scales at home, or do you want to buy Weight
Watchers scales? They're on sale right now.'

As she wasn't sure if Mrs Hardy had scales, she
decided to buy them, and also the current issue of the
organisation's monthly magazine. With these, and her
Attendance Book in its plastic wallet, she joined the
line of women waiting to be weighed.

Some had already been on the scales and were
sitting down, discussing their progress since the previous week's meeting. Some were jubilant at having
lost more than they had expected. Others were complaining of having been hungry all week without
losing an ounce.

There were women from every age group, and of
every size. Several were as huge and shapeless as the

manatees from which a nearby river and the neighbouring county took their names. A few were slim and shapely. Their presence surprised her till she realised they must be reformed foodaholics with only a few pounds left to lose.

As the line in front of her moved forward, she noticed that the pointer on the weighing machine was hidden. It could only be seen by the lecturer, a pleasant-looking woman in her forties, her blue linen suit matching her friendly eyes.

After weighing each person in the line—which included one or two men—she would mark their weight on their card and have a short conversation with them.

When Summer's turn came to step, without shoes, on the weighing platform, the lecturer said, 'Hi! I'm Eleanor. How are you this evening?'

'I'm fine, thank you.'

Although she would have been embarrassed to step on a public weighing machine where other people might read her weight from behind her, here Summer felt no such awkwardness. The people in the queue all had the same problems as she did. They would sympathise, not deride her. Also, she was by no means the heaviest there. Compared with some, she was a lightweight.

'How tall are you, Summer?' asked Eleanor. 'That's an unusual name. Pretty, too.'

'Thank you.' She gave her height.

'How much do you think you weigh right now?'

Summer told her. Before leaving the hotel in Miami, she had checked her weight on the bathroom scales. But she knew that such scales were seldom completely accurate.

'You're a couple of pounds above that. I'm going to give you a temporary goal of one hundred and thirtynine pounds. If, later on, you want to go lower, we'll discuss it. Okay?'

When everyone had been weighed, Eleanor read out the number of Members present, the number of new Members, and the number of Lifetime Members.

She also announced the weight lost by the class as a whole since the last meeting. It totalled more than one hundred pounds.

Next, she called each member by name and asked for their individual weight loss. When it was two pounds or more, she praised them and called for applause. If they hadn't lost any or—more disheartening—had put some on, she didn't reprove them but asked how much they had lost since starting their 16-week course. This was usually a substantial amount, meriting another round of applause. Nobody was made to feel uncomfortable or guilty. They were encouraged to persevere.

When she came to Summer, and other newcomers, she said, 'Welcome', and smiled as if she meant it.

Next she talked for a while about bingeing; the uncontrollable orgies of eating, usually between meals and often in secret, which were some overweight people's way of coping with problems and worries, and their own shaky self-esteem.

She said she herself had been a binger till becoming a Weight Watcher had cured her. She compared a binger's compulsion with that of an alcoholic.

When she added that most people at the meeting had probably had a little too much to drink at some time in their lives, a male voice called out, 'Speak for yourself, ma'am.'

There was an outburst of laughter and Summer leaned forward to see the author of this interruption.

He was seated at the end of her row, a burly man with brown hair, a beer-drinker's belly and a neck too thick for his age, which was probably twenty-six or -seven. But he had a nice, humorous face, and eyes of an even deeper blue than the lecturer's.

Eleanor was laughing as much as everyone else. Afterwards, Summer thought that good humour and rueful self-mockery had been the keynotes of the meeting.

The new members stayed after the others had gone home. Each was given a Personal Program book and

Eleanor went through it with them, explaining and answering questions.

The book contained three different diet plans—Full Choice, Limited Choice and No Choice. They were all to begin with the Full Choice. Reading the sample menus, Summer was surprised at how much she would be allowed to eat. Even such things as popcorn and bagels, wine, beer and peanut butter were allowed, in limited quantities.

When the meeting finally broke up, she was surprised to notice that, although he was not a new member, the brown-haired man was still sitting at the back of the room near the diet soda dispenser.

He intercepted her on her way to the door. 'Hi! Where are you from? You're not an American, are you?'

'Yes, I am, but I've spent the past twelve years in England.'

'Oh, really? My grandparents came from England. A place called Southport. Do you know it?'

Because America was so unimaginably vast, and England looked so small on the map, she had already found that a lot of Americans who had never been to Europe were under the impression that all English people must know their little country like the back of their hands.

'I know *of* it. It's up north, near Liverpool.'

'Why is it called Southport if it's in the north?'

'I've no idea. I've never been there. It's a long way from where I lived.'

By now he was pulling open the door for her. She thanked him and looked around the parking lot. The Antonios had said they would be back by nine, but at present there was no sign of them.

'Are you living in Florida now?' he asked her.

'Yes, for the winter, at any rate.'

'I'm Hal Cochran.' He held out his hand.

'I'm Summer Roberts.'

They shook hands, and his grip was painfully firm. The last man to shake her hand like that had been

James—she remembered his hands very clearly. Well-kept and more shapely than Hal's, but with the same latent power. Hands which could crush an apple. What her employer did to maintain his strength, she didn't know. Worked out in a health club perhaps. Judging by the calloused roughness of his palm, Hal did some kind of manual work.

'Is someone picking you up?' he asked.

'Yes, some friends. They're shopping, but they won't be long.'

'If you don't mind, I'll stick around until they show. Sometimes there are young guys around here who might get fresh if they saw you waiting alone.'

She smiled at him. 'That's very nice of you. Have you been a Weight Watcher long?'

'A couple of months. Since my mother went into hospital. She lost her leg, and they're teaching her to use an artificial one.'

'How terrible. Was it a road accident?'

'No, nothing like that. It was her own fault, I guess. She weighed over two hundred pounds and she had bad varicose veins. My sisters and I tried to make her see a doctor, but she kept putting it off. By the time she went, it was too late to save the leg. While she was away seemed a good time for me to do something about my weight. I've lost thirty pounds in eight weeks. Men seem to take it off faster than women do.'

'Have you found it hard to stick to the diet?'

'Not too bad. Giving up beer was the hardest. I'm allowed three small beers a week, but that only makes me want more, so I stay off beer altogether.'

'I've never drunk beer so I shan't miss that. Bread will be my problem, I expect.'

It seemed a peculiar subject to be discussing with a man. Or perhaps it was talking to a man at all which felt peculiar. Hal was the first man who had ever made friendly overtures to her without being obliged to. From his reference to his mother's absence, she concluded that he was still single and living at home.

'Who cooks for you?' she asked.

'I do. Frozen stuff mostly. Tonight I'm having Weight Watchers chili con carne with beans, and a serving of Frozen Dessert. Have you tried them? They're good. I know you only just joined, but you don't have to belong to Weight Watchers to use the food made for them by their licensees. They're on sale in most supermarkets.'

Summer saw the Antonios' car approaching.

'Here come my friends. Thank you for keeping me company.'

'You're welcome. I'll look forward to talking to you again next week.'

He stepped off the sidewalk where they had been standing to open the back door of the car for her.

'I'm sorry we kept you waiting, Miss Roberts,' said Mrs Antonio, turning round in her seat. 'Was that young man trying to pick you up?'

The idea of anyone attempting such a thing made Summer laugh.

'He's a member of my class, Mrs Antonio. He was keeping me company until you arrived.'

'Good. That was nice of him. You have to be careful at night. There are bad people around. Next week, when you come by yourself, be sure to keep the doors locked or someone might try to jump in when you stop at traffic lights.'

'Really?' said Summer, astonished.

From the little she had seen of it so far, Sarasota seemed a most peaceful locality, the indigenous population swollen by large numbers of sun-seekers from colder parts of the United States, most of them elderly.

'It's not as bad as New York, thank goodness,' said the gardener's wife. 'But there's crime everywhere nowadays. Bag snatchers in the mall parking lots. Thieves breaking into people's houses.'

By this time Summer had learned that the Antonios were second-generation Americans who had lived all their lives in New York where Mr Antonio had inherited a small greengrocery business from his father. At

fifty, he had handed this over to his son, and come to
Florida to enjoy an early retirement. But as he was not
a golfer, and had bought a house on a condominium
where the gardens were communal and kept in order
by professional landscapers, he and his wife had soon
become bored with unlimited leisure.

Their present employment was disapproved of by
their children who couldn't understand them engag-
ing in what the younger Antonios considered to be
menial tasks, beneath their parents' dignity.

But the older Antonios were happy. Mrs Antonio
was a woman who couldn't sit still, and who found it
no trouble to keep her apartment over the garage
immaculate and help Mrs Hardy in the big house. The
hard work—windows and floors—was done once a
month by contractors. The two women had only to
dust and attend to the bathrooms.

In spite of his lack of previous experience, Mr
Antonio had become a knowledgeable gardener; and
even though the garden was large, the fact that there
were no flower-beds, only shrubs and creepers to tend
and grass to cut, meant that he was not overworked.

The maintenance of the swimming pool was not his
responsibility. It was handled by a company specialis-
ing in pool-care. Someone came every other day to
skim it and check the chemical balance of the water,
and also to look after the jacuzzi close by the swimming pool. But up to now the pool-minder had been a
young woman, not the boy whom James had suggested might give Emily coaching.

Skip Newman entered their lives the following morning.

At Mr Antonio's suggestion, Summer had bought
Emily a pair of inflatable arm-bands which supported
her weight in the water and enabled her to practise
swimming while her tutor was doing her exercise laps.

A great deal of their first week at *Baile del Sol* had
been spent in the pool, or lying on two of the pale
green cushioned chaise-longues on a shady part of the

paved deck. By this time Summer was able to swim several lengths without tiring, and the stiffness she had suffered from at first was also wearing off.

She had swum four lengths and was leaning against the side at the shallow end, breathing hard but not panting, when a young man as blond as she, but with a deep golden tan, came whistling along the path through the shrubbery which surrounded the pool.

Seeing the two girls, he grinned and said, 'Hi!'

'Hi!' they both echoed.

She wished she were standing in deeper water which would conceal her size from him. Because, like James Gardiner but in a different way, the young man was one of the beautiful people; those exceptional human beings who, whether by nature or self-discipline, had lithe, graceful, fat-free bodies which made them appear like gods compared with lesser mortals.

This young man was a Norse god. His Scandinavian ancestry was as clear to see as Mr Antonio's Italian extraction. Long ago, in the dawn of history, Vikings with his hair and eyes had ravaged the northern coasts of Europe. But ten centuries had transmuted the ferocious energy of his sea-roving ancestors into the smiling friendliness of an all-American college boy who looked as if he worked off his aggression in athletics.

'I'm Skip Newman. And you're Emily and Summer, but which is which?' he asked, probably having been told their names by Mrs Hardy.

'I'm Emily.'

She climbed out of the water by the steps at the deep end. Because of her tutor's insistence that she must only sunbathe for short periods in the early morning and late afternoon, never—at least at this stage—in the hot middle hours of the day, her thin body was now the very palest shade of toast, with darker patches which, close to, could be seen to be freckles.

'Glad to know you, Emily.' He offered a hand which, compared with her bony little paw, looked as large as a baseball catcher's mitt. 'I hear you want to be drown-proofed.'

'Drown-proofed?'

'That's what it's called. Even kids too young to swim properly can be drown-proofed. It means teaching them how to stay afloat if they fall in or maybe get pushed in. I'll show you.'

He stripped off his sweat-shirt, untied and toed off his sneakers and finally unzipped and shed his chinos. Under them, he was wearing a pair of long-length stretch trunks, patterned with once-vivid flowers, which outlined his powerfully-developed thigh muscles.

There was also a lot of muscle on his upper body. The area round his navel was flat and hard. Summer, who wasn't accustomed to seeing semi-nude males, couldn't help but notice the bulge at his crotch. She wondered how old he was. James had called him 'the boy'. There was nothing boyish about Skip Newman's body, but his face had a youthful openness which suggested he wasn't more than nineteen or twenty. A little younger than herself, but probably light years ahead in his knowledge of the opposite sex.

While he and Emily were holding their faces under water at the shallow end, she seized the opportunity to leave the pool and put on her beach wrap.

Suddenly he looked up and noticed her sitting on a chaise, watching them.

'Hey, how about you, Summer?' he called. 'Are you drown-proof?'

'Oh, Summer's a super swimmer. She can dive, too,' Emily informed him.

'So will you, pretty soon . . . Freckles.' As he tacked on the nickname, he feinted a punch at her chin.

It was the kind of big-brother playfulness which neither of the girls had ever experienced. Summer could tell that Emily liked it very much. If she were to see a lot of Skip, it could lead to a serious attack of real-life hero-worship. She was at the age for a passionate yet asexual crush.

And I'm at the age—past it!—for a real love affair,
Summer thought wistfully. She wondered how many
pounds she would have to lose before men began to
see her as a woman, not a neuter.

Yet, come to think of it, Hal Cochran hadn't treated
her as if she were completely unattractive. She could
almost believe he had stayed on after the main meeting in order to make her acquaintance.

No, that was deluding herself. The real reason he
had hung about while the three new members were
being briefed was probably that he didn't want to go
home to an empty house and couldn't go to a bar for
fear of being tempted to have a beer.

If they knew he was dieting, his friends would rib
him, try to make him weaken. Non-dieters and those
without weight problems were seldom helpful towards fat people. They said things like, 'Oh, come on,
one won't hurt you,' not understanding that a fat
person couldn't stop at one beer, one cookie, one
chocolate.

Presently she heard Skip say, 'Okay, that's enough
for today. We'll do some more tomorrow: right?'

'Right!' The child's enthusiastic assent carried
clearly to where Summer was sitting.

'I think you should come out now, Emily,' she called
to her.

'Oh, must I? Already?'

Skip said, 'Yeah, out you go. I'm going to have a
quick swim and then I have work to do.' He gave her a
gentle shove in the direction of the steps before prop-
elling himself, with a lazy back-stroke, in the direction
of the spring-board.

Emily pattered along the deck, leaving a trail of wet
footprints, to fetch her towel and drape it round her
like a shawl. She watched admiringly as Skip grasped
the board and pulled himself out of the water with
effortless ease, his muscles bunching and rippling
under the amber-satin skin. He stood on the end of
the board, bouncing lightly for a moment or two
before launching himself in an arc which took him

down into the crystalline depths.

They watched him swimming along the bottom to surface at the shallow end and then surge back the way he had come with a fast racing crawl.

Emily's curls were plastered to her skull in a sleek dark red cap. Her wet lashes were sticking together. Her eyes were wide with admiration.

'Wow!' she murmured reverently.

Mrs Antonio appeared, bringing orange juice for Emily, diet soda for Summer and beer for Skip. Also on the tray were two apples and a small Chinese bowl containing carrot sticks, pieces of celery and sprigs of cauliflower. These were Summer's mid-morning nibbles, prepared for her by Mrs Hardy who had studied the Personal Program book and was doing her best to help her to abide by its directions.

'So how d'you like living in America?' Skip asked, as he joined them.

'We love it,' said Emily. 'What is Skip short for?'

'My real name is Ames. But that's also my father's name and his father's name, so I've always been called Skip. How come you never learned to swim before?'

'We didn't have a swimming pool in England.'

'Not everyone has a pool here. They don't teach you to swim at school in Britain?'

'I've never been to school because I have asthma. Summer teaches me.'

He glanced at the older girl. She could see he was puzzled by this arrangement.

'Is pool-care your regular work, or are you a student doing it part-time?' she asked him.

'I'm at USF. During term I only look after a few pools. In the vacations, when my married sister has her kids home from school, I take over the pools she normally looks after. It's a family business, run by Dad and my elder brother. We all help out, including Mom. It was my sister who was here last week.'

'What are you studying at college?'

'American history. Are you a graduate?'

She shook her head. 'I had two terms at college but

then I had to leave for family reasons.'

'That's tough . . . or maybe not so tough,' he amended. 'I guess there are a lot of graduates who wouldn't mind teaching Freckles here, in this set-up.' His nod at Emily was followed by a movement of the head which included the house and the pool.

'I'm sure there are,' she agreed. 'I'm very lucky to have a nice pupil and these splendid working conditions.'

The only fly in the ointment is my employer, she thought to herself.

Skip's thoughts must have turned in the same direction as the next thing he said was, 'There's an article about Mr Gardiner in *Newsweek* this week. Have you seen it?'

'No, we haven't.'

'It's about him and Steven Jobs, the guy behind Apple computers. *Newsweek* calls them "The Young Lions of Electronics". It's really a comparison of their business methods and their life-styles.'

When he had finished his beer, Skip said, 'See you tomorrow,' and walked off towards the pool-house which, screened by a hedge of oleanders, housed the heating plant which kept the pool at eighty degrees and that in the jacuzzi at over a hundred degrees.

Mindful of James's disapproval of late rising, Summer had taken advantage of the time change to institute a new regime. They now had breakfast at seven forty-five and, from eight-fifteen, spent the next two hours out of doors, either in the pool or beside it. After their mid-morning snack, at eleven, they went to the library, there to work until lunch at one o'clock.

The library at *Baile del Sol* was quite different from that at Cranmere. It was much smaller in size, and most of the books on the shelves had been published within the past fifteen years. They reflected the wide-ranging interests of the man who now owned the house. Every aspect of science was represented, as was art, history and philosophy. Serious biographies and memoirs filled two long shelves, and few parts of

the world were not covered by the travel books.
Even—and this had surprised her—poetry had a
place. But the only novelists to be found were two
writers of detection stories; an Englishwoman, Ruth
Rendell, and an American, Lawrence Sanders.

Every afternoon they took the car and went exploring. Not the Cadillac, because that belonged to Mary
Hardy. It had been her husband's and, after selling
their house, it had pleased her to keep it as a memento
of their life together.

She had confided to Summer that, like the Antonios, she was not obliged to work for her living but had
found being a widow of leisure less satisfactory than
her life as James's housekeeper. When he was absent,
her duties were light. When he was there, she enjoyed
the short spasms of greater activity.

The car for Summer's use was a small Ford Fiesta
and the large six-car garage also contained a Lincoln
Convertible which James drove when in Florida.

The afternoon after meeting Skip, they set out for
Lido Key, first heading south on US41 and then,
before reaching downtown Sarasota, turning right at
the road to the causeway which led to the Keys.

Mrs Hardy had come with them. As they passed the
entrance to Bird Key, she told them it was an enclave
of expensive houses. A little farther on, the wide
straight John Ringling Boulevard crossed tiny Coon
Key before arriving at St Armand's Key.

This was Mrs Hardy's favourite shopping place and
they dropped her off before driving on to Lido Key
where Summer parked the car and they went for a
walk on the beach.

Many other people were walking there, including
an Amish family whose old-fashioned costumes con-
trasted oddly with the scanty resort clothes worn by
other strollers and shell-hunters.

Summer was impatient to get hold of a copy of
Newsweek and read the piece about James. It might
hold the answer to some of her queries about him.

Indeed, she would have preferred to spend the

afternoon looking round the shops with Mrs Hardy.
But she knew that both she and Emily would benefit
more from a walk beside the sunlit ocean.

The beach was a long one, with most of the people
on it congregated on the central stretch. As they
walked north, the people thinned out and the drifts of
shells thickened and yielded more interesting speci-
mens.

'If there isn't one at home, we must get ourselves a
book on shells which will help us to identify them,'
said Emily.

After less than a fortnight in Florida, already she
spoke of *Baile del Sol* as home, Summer noticed. It was
amazing how quickly and easily she had adapted to a
dramatic change in her environment.

Summer felt equally at home in the beautiful house
on Bay Shore Road. In every room, she felt that her
father might have stood where she was standing,
looking out at the views she was seeing. She had a
strong, comforting sense of his presence.

At the same time she was continually and *un*comfortably aware of the man to whom the house belonged. This did not make for peace of mind.

It was not long before the shops closed when they
returned to collect Mrs Hardy. They had no trouble
finding a parking place close to St Armand's Circle, a
ring of speciality shops in an attractively landscaped
setting. They had arranged to meet her outside Jacob-
son's, one of the larger stores. On the way there,
Summer found a drug store where she bought a copy
of *Newsweek* and *Vogue*. It might be a long time before
she could buy herself some nicer clothes. Meanwhile,
there was no harm in starting to study the unknown
worlds of beauty and fashion. Looking at pictures of
well-dressed women would be an added incentive to
slim.

Mrs Hardy's major purchase that afternoon had
been a painted canvas and wools. It turned out that
she was a keen needlepointer.

'There's an excellent shop here called Fleece &

Floss,' she said, when she discovered that Summer had also done needlepoint.

'Who was St Armand?' asked the ever-curious Emily, as they returned to the car together.

'He was the Frenchman who was the first person to live here,' the housekeeper told her. 'He bought the Key in 1893. They say he paid twenty-one dollars and seventy-one cents for it. Can you imagine what it must be worth today? Millions! Then, in 1917, John Ringling bought it for development. He's said to have had circus elephants hauling timbers to build the causeway. But after the stock-market crash and the depression of the 'Twenties and 'Thirties, the construction stopped and didn't resume until the 'Fifties.'

Back at the house, Emily wanted to swim with her arm-bands before the sun left the pool. Mrs Hardy joined her. Twice a week, she went to an aerobic dance class at the YMCA. For her age, she had a trim figure.

Summer did not swim that evening. She lay on a chaise-longue, reading the article about 'The Young Lions of Electronics'.

Steven Jobs was of little interest to her. She skimmed the parts about him, scanning the paragraphs for every reference to James.

Jobs is the adopted son of Paul and Clara Jobs. Gardiner's origins are unknown, she read. *He has always shunned personal publicity. Nothing is known of his life before he graduated from Massachusetts Institute of Technology. Next came Harvard Business School where his dean predicted an outstanding future for him.*

Jobs lives in Los Gatos, California, not far from Cupertino, a small town transformed by the company he founded, the article continued.

Gardiner is known to have three houses: a Spanish-style house in Florida, a weekend cottage in Nantucket, and a penthouse in St James's Tower, an élite block of apartments between Manhattan's exclusive Beekman Place and Sutton Place.

An ex-vegetarian, Jobs has been quoted as saying that shopping for, preparing and eating food takes more energy than the resulting meal generates. Gardiner is a gourmet who delights in fine wines and culinary delicacies. He is rumored to fuel his phenomenal mental and physical energy with Royal Beluga fresh caviare and Dom Ruinart champagne.

Further on, after a résumé of Jobs' private life, she read: *Not long ago, Gardiner paid the London coin dealers, Spink & Son Ltd., £13,000 for a silver head of Tetradrachm from Rhodes dating from about 360 B.C. He then commissioned a leading New York City jeweler, Nicola Bulgari, to design a pendant setting for the coin. Who was or will be the recipient of this costly bauble is a well-guarded secret.*

Although both men have the looks and charisma to be successful with women without the added attraction of their wealth and power, neither has playboy inclinations.

In James Gardiner's private life the keyword is private. Some acquaintances—his close friends are as close-mouthed about him as intimates of Britain's Royal Family are about Queen Elizabeth II—claim that he is a workaholic with no time for personal relationships. Also, Gardiner is on record as despising the permissive manners and morals of the 'Seventies, both sexually and in other spheres.

Close observers of his life over the past five years claim that he has twice been involved in serious if not permanent relationships with women. At one time he was frequently seen at the theater in parties which included Sofia Damaskinos, the six-foot-tall, elegant, Greek-born journalist who was sent to interview him by Paris Match. The interview was never filed and soon after Damaskinos moved to Manhattan, saying she had fallen in love with the city.

Another name linked with his—

At this point her concentration on the article was broken by the arrival of the Antonios, coming for their evening dip in the jacuzzi and pausing on the way to talk to her.

At her second Weight Watchers meeting, Summer weighed five pounds less than the week before. When her loss was applauded by the other members, she felt

a glow of achievement she had never experienced
before.

After the meeting, Hal Cochran walked to her car
with her.

'Did you find it difficult to stay on programme?' he
asked her.

'No, not at all. In fact, I've been eating more this
week than when I was dieting on my own. I haven't
had breakfast in years—I was never hungry in the
morning. But now that I *have* to eat one of the choices
on the programme, I don't feel as hungry later.'

'That's exactly my experience. I used to go to work
on a few cups of coffee and not eat till mid-morning
when I'd have a hamburger or something. Eleanor
says that most overweight people skip breakfast. It's
half their trouble.'

'What kind of work do you do, Hal?'

'I'm in the construction business . . . building
condos for all the people who want a place in the sun.
Say, instead of standing around, why don't we have
coffee someplace? You don't have to be home right
away, do you?'

'I shouldn't be too late. If I'm not back when they
expect me, they may start to worry.'

'Why not call them? Say you're having coffee with
another Weight Watcher and you'll be half an hour
later?'

'Yes, I could do that,' she agreed.

The fact that he had suggested it, and added a time
limit, allayed her qualms about accepting his invitation. After all, she didn't know anything about him
except that he had a pleasant manner and a sense of
humour. But some very unpleasant people could
possess those attributes.

'Which way do you go when you leave here?' he
asked her.

She told him.

'That's my way,' said Hal. 'You know where
McDonald's is? The fast-food place with the big
yellow M sign? Let's go there.'

A little while later, when she joined him at a table in
McDonald's after making her call, he said, 'Who are
the people who would worry if you were late home?
Your family?'

'No—Mrs Hardy and Emily. Mrs Hardy is my employer's housekeeper, and Emily is his thirteen-year-
old niece whom I teach. She has health problems
which have prevented her going to school.'

Hal stirred his coffee, although he hadn't put sugar
in it, or saccharine.

He said, 'When I told you I was in construction,
maybe you thought I was one of the bosses. I'm not.
I'm strictly blue collar. My job is laying tiles on roofs.'

It was obvious to her that, in his mind, a tiler was
someone a teacher might not want to know. It was an
unexpected attitude to find in a country where social
divisions were supposed to be looser than in Europe.
It made her wonder if, at some time in the past, he had
been given the brush off by a girl with snobbish ideas.

She said, 'It must be hot work in summer when, so
everyone tells me, the heat here is really broiling.'

'Yeah, I guess so, but you get used to it. Most jobs
have some drawback. I'd sooner fry than freeze the
way they do up in New England and places like that.'

'How is your mother getting on? Where is she in
hospital?'

Hearing about his mother's progress and explaining
her own lack of relations took up the rest of their half
an hour together. In the parking lot they said goodnight, and for about half a mile he drove behind her
until their ways home diverged.

'It's nice that you've made a friend,' said Mrs Hardy,
when she got home.

The housekeeper was keeping Emily company in
the little upstairs sitting room which at night was
a cosier place to sit than the large living room
downstairs.

Summer agreed. She guessed that Mrs Hardy
assumed her friend was another woman, and she
didn't correct this misapprehension. She had a feeling

Mary Hardy might not approve of her making friends with a man.

The next time Eleanor weighed her, Summer had lost another four pounds. It was the last meeting before Christmas and the lecturer's talk to the members was about ways to withstand the temptations of the festive season.

At the end of the meeting, Hal said, 'How about a coffee, Summer?'

She hadn't been sure he would ask her and had hoped he wouldn't because there was a programme on TV which she wanted to watch. But when he did ask her, she didn't like to refuse in case he thought it was because of his blue-collar job.

At McDonald's, he produced a small package in Christmas wrapping paper.

'It's not much,' he said, when she thanked him.

It hadn't occurred to her to bring him a present, even a small one, and she was embarrassed by his gift.

'Shall I open it now, or keep it till Christmas Day?'

'You can open it now if you like.' Clearly he wanted her to.

She read the message on the gift tag—*To Summer: Merry Christmas: Hal*—before she undid the wrapping. Inside was a small cardboard box papered to look like an old-fashioned well with a roof and a bucket dangling on a chain.

'It's a wishing well, made in England,' he told her.

Inside the box was a pottery thimble, shaped and painted like a well.

'It's . . . darling,' she said. 'Useful, too. I do quite a lot of needlework. Thank you very much, Hal.'

When she got home, she put it away in a drawer. She was grateful for the kindness of Hal's thought while disliking the object he had chosen. It was an ugly little thing which didn't fit her thimble finger and was too clumsily made to be of practical use. When she sewed on a button, or did needlepoint, she wore an antique silver thimble bought for twenty-five pence at a village jumble sale.

She and Emily had already bought Christmas presents for Mrs Hardy, the Antonios and Skip, and the next day they spent the morning in one of the big shopping malls where they separated to hunt for a surprise present for each other.

Lord and Lady Edgedale had stopped filling a Christmas stocking for Emily several years earlier. Summer felt that, this year, it would be fun to revive the custom. The shops were full of delightful stocking stuffers and she had more money to spend on the person dearest to her.

Going to bed on Christmas Eve, she tapped 0630 on the miniature keyboard fitted to the wall by her bed. She wanted to be up early to swim extra laps in the pool to work off the one glass of Mrs Hardy's egg nogg she had allowed herself during the evening. She had resisted the mince pies.

She didn't expect to lose any weight this week, but she was determined to maintain the loss made so far; and somehow the thought of all the members of her class facing the same temptations had made it easier to say no to the hot, fragrant pies the rest of the household had eaten during the evening.

Promptly at six-thirty next morning the first quiet notes of the violin concerto which James Gardiner liked to be woken by broke the silence of her spacious bedroom.

She was lying with her eyes closed, listening to a glorious cadenza played by a single violin, when she became aware of someone else in the room. Opening her eyes she found Emily standing by the bed, holding the scarlet felt stocking which Summer had bought to contain a selection of little presents.

'I did knock, but you didn't hear because of the music,' Emily said. 'Happy Christmas!' She sat down on the bed and, as her tutor sat up, leaned forward to kiss her cheek.

Summer gave her a hug. 'Happy Christmas, darling.' Unconsciously, she used the Christmas morning greeting her mother had always given her. 'Haven't you opened your stocking yet?'

'Yes, I opened it the minute I woke up. This is yours,' said Emily. 'Mrs Hardy made me promise not to creep in a minute before half past six. I thought you'd still be asleep.'

'A stocking for me? Emily, what a lovely surprise.'

The child beamed. 'And there's nothing in it you mustn't have—no chocolate money or sugar mice,' she assured her.

It was the beginning of the most convivial Christmas Day since Summer's childhood. The Antonios were away for a week, spending Christmas with their son and his family and New Year with their daughter and her husband. But Mrs Hardy's son was in the Navy, overseas, and she would have been on her own but for Emily's and her tutor's arrival.

'Which I shouldn't have minded, but it's nicer to have you two here,' she said, smiling, as they ate pink grapefruit in the sunny breakfast room on the inland side of the house.

'If only James were here, instead of in Switzerland,' said Emily. 'Do you think he'll ring up this morning?'

'He may,' said Summer. 'But don't be too disappointed if he doesn't. He's a guest in someone else's house and that could make it difficult.'

For her own part, she felt the day would be more enjoyable for his absence. She couldn't have relaxed had he been with them. And she felt sure he would be bored out of his mind by a Christmas Day spent with three females, unless they were of the calibre of Sofia Damaskinos, or the other woman mentioned in the *Newsweek* article.

After helping Mary Hardy to clear the table and put the dishes in the dishwasher, they went to the living room to open the parcels piled beneath the Christmas tree.

To their surprise, these included a number of presents from James. He hadn't bought them himself; that would have been impossible. But he had sent his housekeeper a list of suggested gifts, and some cards on which, in a bold and legible hand, he had written appropriate messages.

On the card attached to the parcel for Summer, the message was a conventional *With good wishes for an enjoyable Christmas*, and the present he had chosen was a recent non-fiction bestseller.

For his niece there were many presents, but none of them unduly extravagant. In addition to several books, there was a Frisbee, a pocket calculator, a Garfield tee-shirt, a special pen for italic calligraphy and an inexpensive camera.

During the morning, to Emily's delight, Skip came by. She hadn't expected to see him on Christmas Day, and certainly not to receive a present from him. It was a belt clasp in the form of two gilt turtles, nose to nose.

Grinning at her ecstatic thanks, he turned to Mary Hardy to say, 'If you need any help with anything while Mr Antonio is away, be sure to call me.'

'That's a very nice, thoughtful young man,' said the housekeeper, when he had gone.

Summer agreed. She hoped the child's other hero, her uncle, would be equally thoughtful and telephone her. In spite of what she had said to Emily at breakfast, she thought it unlikely that being a member of a house party would prevent James from telephoning. If he didn't call, it would be for selfish reasons, not because he couldn't. He was the kind of man who would always find a way to do anything he really wanted to do.

When, at noon, the telephone rang, Emily dashed to answer it, her face alight with expectation. Almost at once her expression changed to disappointment.

'It's for you, Summer. Someone called Hal.'

Summer took the receiver. She said, perhaps a little too briskly, 'Hello, Hal. Merry Christmas.'

'Merry Christmas. Have I picked a bad time to call you?'

'No, not at all. Where are you? At your sister's house?'

'Yeah. Drinking beer with my brother-in-law. I'm darned if I'm going to diet on Christmas Day.'

'I'm going to try to. I haven't sinned up to now. But I'm further from my target than you are. I can't afford to.'

'You know something? You're a lovely girl whatever you weigh. See you.' As abruptly as James, he rang off.

'Who is Hal?' asked Emily, after Summer had replaced the receiver.

'He belongs to my Weight Watchers class.'

'I didn't know *men* went to Weight Watchers.'

'Why not? They have weight problems, too.'

'Is he the person you've been having coffee with after meetings?' Mrs Hardy asked her.

'Yes, he is.' She tried to sound casual.

At that moment the telephone rang again. Thinking it was Hal calling back, she picked up the receiver. 'Hello?'

'Merry Christmas,' said James Gardiner's voice.

'Oh . . . Merry Christmas to you. Thank you very much for my present. I'll put Emily on.'

'I'll speak to her in a moment. How are you liking Christmas Day in the sun?'

'Very much. We've just come in from the pool. In a little while we're going to help Mrs Hardy with the final preparations for lunch.'

'I'm dressing for dinner. Here, we've been skiing all day.'

'Well . . . Christmas is a moveable feast.' She didn't know why she had said that; except that it was the only answer which came to mind.

The last response she expected was to hear him say, 'If you are lucky enough to have lived in Paris as a young man, then wherever you go for the rest of your life, it stays with you, for Paris is a moveable feast.'

She had bought Ernest Hemingway's book *The Moveable Feast* in a second-hand bookshop in Oxford. She had an indistinct memory of her father speaking admiringly of Hemingway's contribution to American

literature. The lines which James had just quoted were
from a letter Hemingway had written to a friend before
she was born. They had fired her with a longing to see
Paris, even though she knew the city as he had described it had gone forever, the Paris of the 'Twenties.

One of her teenage pipe-dreams—more down to
earth than the fantasies woven around the Chevalier
Bayard and Lion Gardiner—had been of meeting
someone who had read all her favourite books and
with whom she could spend hours discussing them.

Before she went up to Oxford, she had day-dreamed
that she would meet him in a bookshop. He would be a
fellow undergraduate, or perhaps one of the younger
dons. They would both reach for the same volume . . .

But of course it had never happened like that.
Initially, even intellectual men were drawn to a girl by
her appearance, not her mind.

That the first man ever to quote to her a passage
which had the magic of poetry to her should turn out
to be someone she actively disliked was a most disconcerting shock.

'Have you ever spent Christmas in Paris?' She was
thinking of Sofia Damaskinos who, if she had worked
for *Paris Match*, must have had an apartment in Paris.

'No, I haven't. I don't think any large city is an ideal
place to spend Christmas. It's a small town festival.'

Summer agreed, although a sophisticated ski resort
like Gstaad, where many of the chalets belonged to
royalty, movie stars and other international cel-
ebrities, wasn't her idea of a small town.

However, she didn't say this. 'Emily is dying to
speak to you. I'll put her on.'

She went back to where she had been sitting before
Hal's call.

Only half-listening to her pupil's excited babble, she
told herself that it wasn't really remarkable that James
should know that piece by heart. Probably all Americans who had been to college would know it. Hal
Cochran wouldn't, but Skip might.

What should bother her more than James's famili-

arity with Hemingway was that parting remark of
Hal's. Perhaps, after a period of abstinence, a few
beers had had more effect than in his pre-Weight
Watchers days. Maybe that remark about her being a
lovely girl had been the beer talking. She hoped so.
Hal was a pleasant person, but apart from watching
their weight they had little else in common.

By the end of January, Summer's Attendance Book
showed a loss of twenty pounds.

She had never repeated the five pound loss after her
first week on the programme. One week, not because
of any backsliding, she had lost only three-quarters of
a pound. But in general her weekly losses had ranged
between two and four pounds. Now, with an aggre-
gate of twenty, she was still a fat girl, a long way from
being a slim one, but a shape was beginning to
emerge.

As she spent so much time in a bathing-suit, instead
of attempting to alter the one she had bought in
Miami, she had bought another. She hoped it
wouldn't be long before she was fit to be seen in a
two-piece and could tan her midriff to match the rest of
her.

For that was the second great change which living in
Florida had wrought; she was now on the way to
becoming as golden brown as Skip.

The third change in her appearance was her hair. No
longer confined in the unbecoming coil of braid, it now
swung loose on her shoulders, re-styled by Mrs
Hardy's hairdresser. But the hightlights had come
about naturally. She had not had to sit with some of
her hair pulled through holes in a plastic cap, in the
way she had seen other women achieving their high-
lights. Hers had been bleached by the sun. The
wonderful, warm, day after day winter sun which
they continued to enjoy while most of the rest of
America endured months of penetrating cold.

Early in January she had been handed details of the
Pepstep Program, a choice of two exercise regimes

designed to promote loss of fat. However, as she was
already swimming an increasing number of laps in the
pool, taking long daily walks on the beaches in search
of shells and, twice a week, attending aerobic dancing
classes with Mrs Hardy, she felt that it wasn't necessary for her to do Pepstep. But this was the only way in
which she failed to conform to a Weight Watcher's
life-style. In every other respect, she adhered to the
programme rigidly.

During March she lost another thirteen pounds,
making the second bathing-suit start to fit loosely. She
went to Edlyn, a shop in St Armand's Circle, and
bought herself some new clothes; an emerald-green
wraparound skirt which would adjust as her hips
deflated, and a green and white shirt. At another shop
she bought some green canvas espadrilles, the rope-
covered wedges equivalent to medium high heels.
When she tried her new outfit on, with a new, smaller
bra, the full-length mirror in her bedroom reflected a
girl who seemed to be a different person from the
plodding, double-chinned frump she had glimpsed in
the mirrors in Harrods.

Emily had also changed, although not as visibly as
Summer. She had begun to menstruate and her flat
chest was starting to show some signs of feminine
shape. When she wasn't in her bikini, she lived in
white shorts and sun-tops, and a belt clasped by Skip's
gilt turtles.

She had long weekly chats on the telephone with
her uncle who called her from wherever he was—
Manhattan, the west coast, Chicago. But when, at the
end of their conversations, she asked when he was
coming to Florida, he was always too busy.

Summer was glad that he called Emily regularly, but
she doubted that he would exert himself to visit her
until he felt like a vacation, which might not be till the
spring, if then.

From time to time, during this period, she would
dream that she had broken her diet, or that she was
back in England, still 'an uncontrollable glutton' and

'as fat as a pig'. She would wake up sweating with horror, as from a nightmare.

One night she had a particularly horrible dream in which it was she who was partially paralysed, and her aunt who was caring for her. She was propped up in bed at the cottage and Miss Ewing was forcing her to eat a mountain of stodgy suet dumplings. She was being spoon-fed, and each mouthful of the soggy white dough made her gag. But her aunt wouldn't listen to her pleas that she wasn't hungry.

'Nonsense, Summer. You must eat to keep up your strength. Dr Dyer gave me strict instructions that you were to have at least five dumplings at every meal. Come along—open your mouth.'

'I can't eat any more, Aunt Margaret. I'll throw up. I—'

At this point she woke up, trembling, filled with rage and despair at her helplessness and the torture of being forced to eat those horrible white lumps of glob.

Even after she had switched on the light and could see that she was thousands of miles from the cottage, and fully mobile, not a bedridden hulk of blubber, she still felt upset.

Presently she was able to see the absurdity of Dr Dyer prescribing dumplings. It was strange how the subconscious mind twisted facts into fantasies. Her aunt had liked one or two dumplings as an accompaniment to meat and gravy, and Summer had taught herself to make excellent dumplings, as light in texture and weight as those in the dream had been heavy.

It was now half past one in the morning, but she felt wide awake and disinclined to lie down again. Perhaps she would read for a while. On impulse, she flung back the bedclothes and swung her feet to the floor. The room was warm. There was no need to put on a robe to go to the window and stand looking out at the garden. Not that she would see it with the light on. She turned off the bedside lamp and immediately the warm light was replaced by the silver radiance of moonlight.

From her window, she could see the pool which, although not illuminated by underwater lights at this hour, was clearly visible under the full moon. But for the vapour rising from the surface of the water, it might have been a summer night. The sky was full of stars, and the garden was full of flowers—hibiscus, poinsettia, cassia, solandra, plumbago and a dozen others.

The motionless, vaporous surface of the pool had a fairy-tale air. It reminded her of the setting of a ballet which she and Emily had watched on television recently. She half expected to see a troop of sylphides emerge from the shadows of the Madagascar palms and begin to dance round the pool deck. It was that kind of magical night.

Suddenly she wanted to be out there, floating in the water, star-gazing.

Her bathing-suit was in the shower where she had hung it to dry after her final swim of the day. As she was about to put it on, she thought: Why do I need a bathing-suit? Nobody's going to see me. I can swim in my skin.

The house had more than one staircase. There were the main stairs which they had first used on the day of their arrival, and two other flights, one leading from the entrance hall to the master bedroom and her room, and a staircase, originally for servants' use, from the kitchen to Mrs Hardy's quarters.

She padded downstairs with bare feet and only slipped on her thongs when she reached the door to the patio. Although she was wrapped in her terry-cloth robe, the outside air made her shiver as she crossed the patio, passed through the shadowy loggia and followed the path to the pool.

Arriving at the shallow end, she noticed that, beyond and to one side of the deep end, the hot water in the jacuzzi was wreathed in denser clouds of vapour than the main pool. But as she tossed her robe over a sun-bed, she was in too much of a hurry to immerse herself to look closely in that direction.

She walked down the submerged steps with their central handrail and, when the water was up to her thighs, bent and launched herself forward as quietly as a water-bird gliding away from the bank of a pond.

Slowly she swam two lengths and then, in the centre of the pool, rolled on to her back and lay with her arms outstretched, looking up at the canopy of stars. As always, beauty evoked fragments of poetry.

Longfellow's

Silently one by one, in the infinite meadows of
  heaven
Blossomed the lovely stars, the forget-me-nots
  of the angels

Rossetti's

The blessed damozel leaned out
From the gold bar of Heaven;
Her eyes were deeper than the depth
Of waters stilled at even;
She had three lilies in her hand,
And the stars in her hair were seven.

The night air was cool on her face and on her still pale-skinned breasts which, when she lay with her spine straight, also floated clear of the surface, the nipples dilated by the chill. She adjusted her spine to immerse them, enjoying the freedom of being naked, wishing she could always swim like this.

'Do you make a habit of skinny-dipping in the small hours?'

The mocking male voice rang out from somewhere behind her, making her slack body jerk in a convulsive and panic-stricken movement to bring herself upright and turn to see who had spoken.

He was by the side of the pool, wearing a long white robe with a hood hanging from the shoulders. Just for an instant, with his arms crossed inside the wide sleeves, he looked like a tall monk standing there.

Then she recognised him. Emily's uncle.

*   *   *

When after a few moments she had failed to utter any sound but a horrified gasp, he said what the Immigration officer had said to Emily.

'Cat got your tongue?'

Still petrified with dismay at her appalling predicament—confronted, stark naked, by the last man on earth she would have wished to catch her in that condition—she longed for the pool to become a bottomless lake in which she could sink and never surface. Instead of which it seemed, all at once, to have shrunk to the size and transparency of a small goldfish bowl.

'Young women who trespass on private property at night have to take the consequences,' he told her.

Before her paralysed wits had grasped what he meant to do, he had stripped off his robe and plunged in. Seconds later he surfaced, beside her.

'Which in this case is—this.'

As he spoke, he pulled her against him. As he finished speaking, he kissed her.

It was not a prolonged or passionate kiss; merely a vigorous buss on her startled lips. But it was her first kiss and coming from him, of all people, a shattering experience.

She felt her bare breasts pressed against his muscular chest. She felt his powerful arms round her. She felt the warmth and unexpected softness of his mouth.

They were all sensations which shocked her; like violent jolts of electricity. The most shocking of all was when, as he raised his head but continued to hold her against him—where they were was within his depth and his feet were firmly planted on the bottom—she felt a change in his body which, inexperienced as she was, she recognised as a sign that holding her was beginning to arouse him.

That panicked her, and she struggled to free herself. When he wouldn't release her, she pounded his chest with her clenched fists.

'Let me go . . . *let me go!*' she demanded furiously. Then, hearing the note of hysteria in her voice, she forced herself to stop fighting him and said, very clearly and coldly, 'If you don't let me go, I'll scream for help, Mr Gardiner.'

This was more effective. He didn't let her go, but he did stop the unequal wrestling match during which he had not only kept her his unwilling captive but contrived to caress a good deal of her squirming body. Holding her by the upper arms with the same steely grip she had undergone once before, he stared into her face.

'Do I know you?'

'Of course you know me, you oaf! I'm Summer Roberts . . . Emily's tutor. Who else would you expect to find here?'

'Well, I'll be damned,' he said blankly. 'I thought you'd sneaked over from the campus.' He began to laugh.

'You're bruising my arms,' she said icily.

His fingers slackened. At last she was free to retreat to the side of the pool where the shape of her body would be hidden from him. Was he also naked? His sudden plunge into the water had been so swift and unexpected that she wasn't sure if she had seen a very brief bathing slip, or if it had been his body hair which had made a dark triangle at the top of his thighs.

The thought of being in a swimming pool with a naked man in a state of semi-arousal was intensely disturbing. That, having no idea who she was, he could feel an incipient desire for her, exacerbated her dislike of the man. She didn't think him capable of rape but, as he had already demonstrated, he was capable of almost every outrage short of rape. The sooner she was out of his way, her bedroom door securely locked, the better she would like it. But she wasn't going to leave the pool while he was watching her, thus giving him as good a view of her backside as he had already had of the front of her.

He said, 'You haven't answered my question. Do you make a habit of skinny-dipping at night?' Before she could answer, he went on with mock severity,

'I'm not sure I approve. It isn't the behaviour I expected when I entrusted my niece to you. You
appeared, at that time, to be rather a prudish young
woman. Not the sort to get up to these antics.'

Ignoring this raillery, she said, 'I've never swum at
night before, and I wish very much I hadn't tried it
tonight. Now I'd like to go back to the house, but not
with you gawking at me. If you have any decency at
all—'

'I'll avert my eyes or, better still, make myself
scarce.'

He turned away from her. A couple of strokes took
him across to the far side. She watched him grasp the
tiled rim and pull himself upwards. He wasn't wearing a bathing-suit! She could see the paler skin of his
buttocks as he swung himself on to the deck and bent
to pick up his robe. He put it on with his back to her.
Then, tying the white rope-like sash, he stepped into a
pair of slides and began to walk round the pool in the
direction of the house.

She let out a breath of relief. He was going. The
ordeal was over.

But no—it wasn't. When he came to her robe, he
checked. Taking it from the chair where she had left it,
he turned to face her.

'But you didn't avert your eyes, did you?' he said
derisively.

He shook out the robe and held it, like a man
holding a woman's coat for her.

'Out you come. There's no need to be embarrassed.
From what I've seen of it already, you now have an
excellent figure. *You can't be too rich or too thin* is okay as
a motto for men, but a woman needs curves here and
there.'

Summer knew that what she should have done was
to rush for her robe at the same time he went for his.
Fool that she was, by delaying she had played into his
hands. Now, enveloped in his ankle-length robe, he
was probably as warm as she was and certainly a great
deal better covered. She was as naked as Eve except for

the cover afforded by the moonlit water.

'Yes, you're right,' he said, reading her mind. 'I can stand here for longer than you can remain cowering there.'

'What a swine you are,' she said bitterly, goaded past caring that tomorrow he might sack her.

He clicked his tongue disapprovingly. 'Not the way to speak to your employer, but I daresay I'll overlook it—if you don't keep me waiting too much longer.'

At that moment, she hated him more than she had at Cranmere. Her loathing and detestation reached the point where she thought: Oh, sod him! And, on that note of defiance, swam into the shallows and walked briskly up the steps. Let him see her naked. Let him look—if it gave him any satisfaction.

Thrusting her arms into the sleeves of her robe, she drew it around her and fastened the terry-cloth belt. Winding a towel round her head and stepping into her thongs, she would have marched swiftly away had his hand not fallen on her shoulder.

'I want to talk to you,' he said.

'Can't it wait until the morning?'

'No. If you go to bed now, you won't sleep. You're too wound up,' he said calmly. 'You can make me some coffee.'

'When did you arrive? Why didn't you let us know you were coming?' she asked coldly, as they walked to the house.

'I prefer to arrive unannounced. It keeps my staff on their toes. As I have a key, and my bed here is always made up, it wasn't necessary to disturb Mrs Hardy. I flew into Tampa two hours ago. A taxi brought me to the gate. I thought fifteen minutes in the jacuzzi would relax me and help me to sleep. Then a magnificent Amazon—with both breasts intact—appeared on the scene, and I didn't feel tired any more,' he told her, with laughter in his voice.

Summer was not amused. She said, 'Your voice will wake Mrs Hardy and possibly alarm her.'

He said nothing more until they were inside the

house. Then, when she would have attempted to bolt
up the stairs, he blocked her escape, saying softly, 'I
didn't eat on the plane. You can scramble some eggs
for me—if you know how.'

She was tempted to answer, 'No, I don't. Scramble
them yourself.' But she guessed he was sure to find
out she was a competent cook, and would make her
pay for the lie.

Seething, she said, 'Very well, but first I'd like to get
dressed.'

'You're respectably covered as you are. Don't worry: the knowledge that you're naked under that robe
won't drive me to do anything you wouldn't like,' he
said dryly.

She glowered at him, hating his complete self-
assurance, longing to defy him. He might have discarded his title, but he still had the *droit de seigneur*
attitude which had been making life hell for women
through the centuries from Norman serving wenches
to Victorian housemaids.

Straight-backed, but inwardly quivering with reaction to what she had been through, she stalked to the
kitchen.

'How many eggs do you want scrambled?' she
asked him frigidly.

'Four, please. I'll make the coffee.'

Obviously he knew his way around the kitchen. He
didn't have to ask her where to find the paper filters
for the automatic coffee maker, or how to use the
machine. As the water began to drip into the jug, he
leaned his hips against a worktop, folded his arms
across his chest, and watched her performing her task.

Summer found it unnerving to be under such close
surveillance. Her hair, only roughly dried and finger-
combed, was hanging in damp rat's-tails. Never having had the figure to go without a bra—a style which
she didn't intend to ape when she was slim—she
was acutely conscious of her unconstricted breasts.
Fortunately her beach robe was now too big for her,
forming folds which were some help in concealing

her still too ample curves from him.

'How long are you staying?' she asked, hoping it would be a fleeting visit.

'I'm not sure. A week, I hope. It's some while since I had a break down here. Three months in Florida has certainly done wonders for you. As you just found out, you're unrecognisable.'

She flushed. She would have liked to say cuttingly, 'You mean you wouldn't describe me as "as fat as a pig" now?'

But dearly as she would have liked to discomfit him, she knew she would never be able to fling his brutal words back at him. There might be other ways of revenging herself for that terrible humiliation, but the things he had said about her were sealed away in her mind; words she would never forget, but would never repeat to anyone. Not if she lived to be ninety!

'Has Emily undergone a similar sea-change?' he asked.

'She's looking healthier, yes. But then everyone looks healthier when they're tanned—even chronic invalids,' she said, thinking of some of the old people she had seen around.

He himself was as deeply tanned as when they had parted from him in London. Skiing at Gstaad and, since then, spending some time in California, had maintained his Indian-dark colouring.

'Yes, it can be illusory,' he agreed. 'But obviously not in your case. There's a sparkle in your eye and an air of vitality about you which you didn't have in England.'

She wanted to snap 'Save your compliments', but she said nothing, silently hating him.

She had already laid a place at the breakfast counter for him. Now she warmed a plate by placing it upside down over one of the hobs, buttered the toast ejected by the toaster and piled on the fluffy, moist eggs.

At one time preparing the food for him would have made her feel ravenous. But tonight, perhaps because of the vivid dream she had had earlier, it didn't.

'Thank you. That looks good,' he said, as she set the dish on the place-mat.

She poured coffee into a pottery mug and put it beside him, with a jug of the milk she had heated while cooking the eggs.

'So tonight was your first experience of one of the more harmless American teenage escapades—midnight skinny-dipping,' he remarked, apparently determined not to let her forget it.

'And my last. If you don't mind, I'll go to bed now. I have to be up early.'

'You're going somewhere tomorrow?'

'No, I always get up early. I have a swim before breakfast—or I have been doing so up to now. But if that's the time you like to use the pool, I'll alter my swimming times.'

'Or take care to have a chaperone,' he suggested, with an amused glance. 'I'm not likely to make a pass at you if there's someone else around, am I?'

A flush brought an apricot tinge to her golden skin. She glared at him, grey eyes stormy.

'I hope you won't make another in any circumstances, *Mr Gardiner*'—emphasising her reversion to formality.

'I can't guarantee that I won't. It depends how much provocation you offer me,' he said, cutting into the toast and beginning to eat.

She hadn't noticed before that, in spite of his admiration for and commitment to the American way of life, he still ate in the English way, keeping the fork in the left hand instead of transferring it to the right hand as Mrs Hardy and the Antonios did. Perhaps by the age of seventeen such habits were too deeply ingrained to be changed.

'I shan't offer any, I assure you,' she informed him vehemently.

'What does that mean?' he asked. 'That you don't fancy me, or that you've found yourself a boy-friend?'

She lifted her chin which her loss of weight was revealing as a firmly-shaped feature with more than a hint of determination, even obstinacy, in its form.

'It means that if you want me to remain Emily's tutor, you won't subject me to harassment,' she said, with a level look. 'I won't put up with it, Mr Gardiner. I shall leave.'

'Don't you think you're making a mountain out of a molehill? I mistook you for an attractive trespasser and imposed a penalty—one kiss. That hardly constitutes sexual harassment of an employee.'

He had been speaking seriously, with a trace of impatience. Now the laughter returned to his eyes. 'I've never found it necessary to harass women to satisfy my sexual needs. It tends to be the other way round. They harass me. Not because they desire me,' he added sardonically. 'It's my financial position which lights the lust in their eyes.'

She was not used to such plain-speaking. Sex was a subject never mentioned by her aunt except in the form of warnings about never talking to strange men. Fortunately, Summer's fundamental attitude to sex had been formed by growing up with parents who adored each other. With a father like Tom Roberts, no one subsequently could have convinced her that men as a sex were aggressive, predatory or basically hostile to women. She knew that not all were as generously, tenderly loving as her father. But he was her standard; not the threatening male figure projected by Miss Ewing's warnings.

Nevertheless, she had lived under her aunt's influence for too long not to be embarrassed by her employer's frank reference to his sexual needs. He spoke as if, for him, sex had no emotional connotation but was a physical appetite like hunger and thirst which, when it occurred, he would satisfy as straightforwardly as he had asked her to cook him some eggs.

She noticed that the front of his robe had loosened, showing the hard bronzed chest she had beaten with her fists with as little effect as if she had been pummelling rock. Like Skip's, his chest wasn't hairy. In contrast to the fleecy white terry, it had the slight sheen of polished hide. She averted her eyes.

'No coffee for you?' he asked.

'No. I'm going up to dry my hair. Goodnight,' she said tersely.

'Goodnight, Summer. Sleep well.'

She had a feeling he smiled at her as she passed him, but she kept her own gaze averted.

A few minutes later, in her bathroom, the sight of her naked body as she took off the robe was a mortifying reminder of the way his lean hands had both restrained and caressed her while she fought to free herself. Quickly she put on her nightdress and used her dryer which, luckily, wasn't a noisy one. As soon as her hair was dry, she turned off the light and returned to the moonlit bedroom.

An hour later she was still awake, unable to switch off her troubled thoughts.

A few days before, when she and Emily had gone to the Selby Library to use the reference section, she had picked up a leaflet issued by the American National Red Cross and headed HURRICANE SAFETY RULES.

The leaflet had given advice on what to do during the months from June to November if the National Weather Service gave warning of an approaching hurricane.

Among the instructions had been a paragraph about the eye of the hurricane. She could remember it word for word.

If the calm storm center passes directly overhead, there will be a lull in the wind lasting from a few minutes to half an hour or more. Stay in a safe place unless emergency repairs are absolutely necessary. But remember, at the other side of the eye, the winds rise very rapidly to hurricane force, and come from the opposite direction.

As she lay on her side, looking at the motionless fronds of the tall palm not far from her window, it seemed to her that paragraph expressed precisely the effect James Gardiner had had on her life.

He had borne down on Cranmere with all the disruptive force of a major hurricane. There had followed a lull, until tonight, without any advance warning, he had burst upon her a second time. And whereas before he had been totally, crushingly indifferent to her as a woman, this time it was the reverse. Now, because of the unfortunate circumstances in which he had caught her, he was too much aware of her femininity. And in spite of her ultimatum, from him, if he chose to be difficult, there was no safe refuge.

Next morning she overslept and was woken by Emily.

'What time is it?' Summer asked.

'Ten o'clock.'

'Oh, my goodness! Why didn't you wake me earlier?'

'James wouldn't let me. He said you'd had a disturbed night . . . that you'd heard him arrive and cooked something for him.'

She had certainly had a disturbed night, thought Summer, as she rolled out of bed.

'We're going out to dinner and then to the theatre,' Emily told her.

'The Asolo Theater? How exciting. You can wear your new dress.'

Mrs Hardy, a talented dressmaker who made many of her own clothes, had recently made a charming dress for Emily.

'What'll you wear? You haven't a dress. All your English clothes are too big now.'

'I think your uncle intends this to be an evening *à deux* . . . just the two of you.'

'No, he doesn't. Everyone's going. Mrs Hardy as well. He wasn't going to include her, but I said it would be unkind to leave her on her own. Why don't you buy a dress, Summer? The red one you liked in the window of the shop near the traffic lights.'

This was a dress which had caught Summer's eye on their way home from an afternoon's shelling. She had stopped the car to have a look at it, but it hadn't been her intention to buy any expensive clothes until she had reached her target weight, and the red dress had been made of silk, not a synthetic imitation.

'It probably wasn't my size. I'm not sure how much people dress up for the theatre here. Perhaps my green things will do. I'll have to ask Mrs Hardy. I'll be down in about fifteen minutes,' she added, on her way to the shower.

They were by the pool, James stretched on a chaise-longue with Emily seated on the foot of it, when she joined them.

Seeing her approaching, he stood up. 'Good morning.' His tawny eyes took in her bathing-suit; the navy blue halter-tied one piece she had bought in Sarasota.

'Good morning.' She was willing herself not to blush at the memory of last night's encounter.

This morning he was wearing a pair of faded Madras cotton boxer swim trunks.

'I applaud the new hairdo,' he said. 'Much more becoming.'

'Thank you,' she said, without smiling. 'As Emily had only a short break from lessons at Christmas, she can take a few days off now if you'd like to spend some time together.'

He let the suggestion ride, saying, 'Among other things you've been studying the Gulf Stream, I hear?'

'Yes, and the history of Florida. But Emily's curriculum is something I'd like to discuss with you.'

'Providing you're teaching her to think for herself, I don't feel it matters what means you use. The history of Florida or the history of France . . . the aim is the same. To equip her mind to take off on its own adventures. You know what Sam Johnson said about knowledge. There are two kinds. *We know a subject ourselves, or we know where we can find information upon it*. I don't give a damn if today Emily has never heard of Jacques Cartier as long as she can produce a file on him this time next week. Could you do that, Emily?'

'Oh, yes—easily,' she answered confidently. 'We hadn't been here five minutes before Summer discovered a terrific library down near that strange-shaped, lilac-coloured building.'

'The Van Wezel Hall. I don't care for that colour either, but the auditorium is impressive and they put on some excellent concerts. You haven't been to one yet, I gather?'

The child shook her head.

He turned to Summer. 'Why not? Don't you care for music?'

He asked the question with an uplifted eyebrow and an expression which suggested that if the answer were negative it would be received with displeasure.

For her age, Emily was very sensitive to nuances. Before her tutor could reply, she said defensively, 'Summer loves music. She adores the violin concerto your computer plays. She must have played it a hundred times.'

Summer smiled at her, touched by her loyalty. To James, she said, 'It doesn't damage the mechanism to play that music for pleasure sometimes, I hope?'

'Not at all. But the computer only plays the first movement. The second and third are on tape in the library, as perhaps you've discovered.'

'No, we haven't liked to use your music library for fear of doing some damage,' she answered. 'The equipment looks rather complicated, and I know that records can be spoiled if they're not handled properly.'

'So can books. You had the run of the library at Cranmere. I'm sure you won't do any harm to my records and tapes. Later on today I'll show you how the music centre operates. Mrs Hardy has her own record-player so I've never shown her how mine works. It should have occurred to me to send you instructions.'

At this point Skip Newman appeared, considerably later than usual for reasons which, after shaking hands with James, he explained.

When Emily had followed him to the pool-house, her uncle said, 'Why haven't you been to the Van

Wezel yet? Surely you realised that I would be happy
to pay for you to take Emily there as often as you cared
to go? You have *carte blanche* as far as expenses of that
sort are concerned.'

'Thank you, but if we had thought of going I should
have been glad to pay for the tickets out of my salary,'
she answered. 'I suppose the reasons we haven't been
to the Van Wezel yet are three-fold. Neither of us is
used to going out at night; we've found quite a lot to
interest us on television; and leading a more energetic,
outdoor life, we tend to go to bed earlier now.'

'I see. Well, we have to pass the Hall on our way to
dinner tonight so I'll pick up the current programme
and from now on I suggest you go at least once a week,
certainly to all the ballets and operas they put
on. Because her father only knew *John Peel* is no
reason why Emily should grow up a musical
philistine. You've taken her to the Ringling Museums,
presumably?'

'Oh, yes. Once to the Circus Museum, once to the
Ringlings' mansion, and several times to the Art
Museum.'

'John Ringling was an interesting man. Not the
brash vulgarian you might expect of the boss of "The
Greatest Show on Earth". At the peak of his career he
was one of the twenty richest men in the United
States. In the 1920s, before the stock market crash
which contributed to his downfall, he used to go to
Europe every year, looking for new circus acts and also
going round the art galleries. I don't share his passion
for huge Baroque paintings like the four Rubens, and
one can't applaud Mabel Ringling's taste in designing
and furnishing their house, but nevertheless they
were a remarkable pair who did a great deal to enrich
the lives of people living here now.'

'Their mansion is rather hideous compared with
Cranmere,' said Summer. 'The paintings I like best in
the Art Museum are the Boucher of a girl reading a
letter, and the Duplessis portraits of French kings
given by Mrs Caples. What has happened to

Cranmere? Has it been sold yet?'

'Not yet. Have you had any news of the cottage?'

'Yes, Mr Watts wrote to me recently. The property market has been very slow this winter, but it seems to be picking up now. He thinks it will sell in the spring. Living here, one tends to forget the weather is still cold in England.'

Only later did she realise how skilfully he had deflected her curiosity about Cranmere.

Mrs Hardy, when consulted about what to wear for their outing that evening, said, 'Burdines have a sale this week. After lunch, why don't we go see if they've any good bargains. I love your new emerald outfit, but maybe it's a little casual for tonight.

At lunchtime, Summer said to James, 'We usually go to the beach for a couple of hours in the afternoon. But perhaps you have other plans.'

'Yes, I'm going to introduce Emily to the secret of the inner sanctum,' he said, with a teasing smile at his niece.

'Really? Where's the inner sanctum?' she asked, agog.

'Upstairs. It's time you and Oz got together.'

'Oh, you mean the computer?'

Because Skip had mentioned it in her hearing, Summer had been unable to prevent Emily reading the *Newsweek* piece about her uncle; but even if she had not learnt the name of his computer and his company from the article, the computer was widely advertised in all the media.

'Presumably you named it after the Wizard of Oz?' she said to him.

'Yes, it seemed an appropriate name for a machine with the powers of a wizard. Originally I intended to call it Merlin, after Merlin the Enchanter.'

'That would have been a nicer name,' said Emily.

Among her favourite books in the library at Cranmere had been Geoffrey of Monmouth's *History of the Kings of Britain* and the stories which it had inspired, Malory's *Le Morte d'Arthur* and Tennyson's *The Idylls of the King*.

'I agree,' said James. 'But I was advised that Oz would have greater impact here in America, and since then Merlin has been used by British Telecom.' He turned to Summer. 'Would you care to meet Oz?'

'Very much—some other time. This afternoon I'd like to go out with Mrs Hardy, if that's all right?'

'By all means. Curtain time at the Asolo is eight-fifteen so we have to dine early, at a quarter to seven. I'd like to leave here not later than six-fifteen. As long as you're ready by then, do whatever you like this afternoon. You should have some regular time off, anyway. You can't be expected to spend every hour of your life in this child's company . . . a fearful fate,' he added, making Emily giggle.

'I can think of worse,' Summer said lightly. 'I do leave Emily with Mrs Hardy from time to time.'

'Only for your Weight Watchers meetings,' said Emily.

'So that's the secret of your transformation,' said James. 'What or who made you decide to join Weight Watchers?'

She hesitated, wishing Emily hadn't raised the subject. It was not a topic she wanted to discuss with him.

To her vexation, his niece answered for her. 'A woman in a bathing-suit shop in Miami advised her to join.'

'With impressive results,' was his comment. 'I've heard of Weight Watchers, but I don't know what their methods are. What's the secret of their success?'

To her relief, at that moment the telephone rang. After a brief conversation he asked whoever was calling to hold the line while he went upstairs to take the rest of the call on the extension in his bedroom.

Burdines store, which she and Mrs Hardy entered about an hour later, was part of a shopping complex on the southern outskirts of Sarasota. The most striking feature of the store was a glass elevator which, as it glided upwards to the second floor, gave an interesting view of the lay-out of the first floor. The style of Burdines reminded Summer of Harvey Nichols, a store near Harrods in London—smaller but in many ways more elegant—which she and Emily had looked round.

One of the books which she had borrowed from Selby Library was *Working Wardrobe* by Janet Wallach, Fashion Director of Garfinckel's store in Washington, DC. The book explained Mrs Wallach's Capsule Concept, a way of avoiding expensive mistakes and always looking well-dressed.

Impressed by the author's theories, Summer wandered through Burdines' women's departments, not looking for one special dress, but with an eye for separates adaptable to many occasions.

A spectacular drop-dead dress was in her mind for the future when—if!—she achieved her target weight. Meanwhile, she was content to buy inexpensive, quiet clothes which she could discard without a qualm when she dropped to a smaller size.

So when Mrs Hardy, who had good taste, plucked from the rails dresses which Summer liked but which were too distinctive to be worn again and again, she shook her head and continued searching.

What she chose, in the end, was a black skirt of fine wool crêpe and a Liz Claiborne blouse which looked like ivory crêpe de Chine but was in fact polyester.

'Now I need some black pumps, and ear-rings and perhaps some beads,' she said, her major purchases completed.

A pair of black Chanel sling-backs were easy to find in the store's shoe department. Looking for ear-rings, she discovered that the ones she liked best were all made for pierced ears. She bought a pair of small pearls with clip fastenings, and resolved to have her ears pierced at the first opportunity.

It was while she was looking for a necklace that, for the first time in her life, she fell in love with an object far beyond her means.

It was a dramatic necklace made of sprigs of coral,

river pearls, little chunks of gold and, as a pendant, the strangest and most beautiful shell.

'What is this lovely shell?' she asked the girl behind the counter.

'It's a lion's paw. Isn't it beautiful? Would you like to try it on?' the salesgirl asked.

'Oh, no—thank you. I couldn't afford it, but it is lovely,' Summer said longingly.

The shape was that of a half-open fan, with striations which reminded her of the bark-like pleats of the Mary McFadden dresses she had seen in *Vogue* magazine.

It was the perfect accessory for her ivory blouse, and she had enough in her bank account to pay for it. Yet the idea of spending so much money on herself was completely at variance with her upbringing.

She wanted it more than she had ever wanted anything. But it was a shell; fragile, breakable, as insubstantial as a bubble. The kind of amusing novelty bought by millionairesses, not ordinary people like herself.

She turned away from the show-case and found a strand of imitation ivory beads. But all the way back to *Baile del Sol* she was haunted by the lion's paw necklace.

The Café l'Europe on St Armand's Key, where James took them for dinner, was a more formal restaurant than the one he had chosen in London.

Round tables spread with pink cloths and surrounded by dark bentwood chairs were arranged in a series of rooms separated by archways.

When they entered the restaurant, they seemed to attract a good deal of attention from the diners already present. In Florida, quarter to seven was not an unduly early hour to dine. Summer and Emily had been puzzled to see long lines of elderly people waiting outside some of the restaurants on the Tamiami Trail—another name for US41 which ran all the way from Tampa to Miami—as early as five o'clock. Mrs Hardy had explained that these were retired people living on pensions and attracted by the reduced prices at early sittings.

However, the Café l'Europe's clientele were not elderly people on tight budgets. They were younger and richer looking, and Summer noticed the women's eyes resting with interest on James's tall figure. She wondered what conclusions they were drawing about his entourage of females.

Mrs Hardy was old enough to be his mother and Emily could, at a pinch, be his daughter by a youthful marriage. But nobody was likely to mistake her for his second wife. Even though her figure could now be described as plump rather than obese, she didn't have the eye-catching presence which any woman of his—wife or mistress—would be sure to have.

Would she ever?

Yes . . . yes, I will, she thought fiercely. I've managed to reach the point where I can walk into a restaurant without feeling self-conscious or being stared at for unflattering reasons. I can progress further. I can make myself anything I want to be—and I want to be strikingly elegant with gorgeous clothes and unusual accessories, like that lion's paw necklace.

Nobody glancing at her would have guessed from her expression that her mind was full of plans and ambitions for a much greater transformation than the one she had achieved to date.

In fact no one was looking at her; or even at Emily, in her new dress, or Mrs Hardy in her stylish dark shirt-dress with a coral scarf tied in a bow at the neck.

Those people who hadn't by now had the good manners to stop eyeing the new arrivals were still watching the man of the party. Their continued attention made Summer realise that it wasn't only because he was tall and personable, with an air of distinction which had nothing to do with the cut of his clothes.

They recognised him.

Forgetting that thousands of people besides herself would have read the piece in *Newsweek*, and that he had probably been the subject of articles in other periodicals and newspapers, she hadn't realised until now that, although not famous in England, in this country he must be a nationally-known celebrity.

If he were aware of being the cynosure of some of the restaurant's other patrons, he gave no sign of it. He was scanning the menu with the speed of a connoisseur who will listen to the maître d's suggestions but make his own decisions.

He had mentioned on the way there that the restaurant had won various awards for the excellence of its Continental and American cuisine, but Summer studied the *carte* with a view to staying on her programme.

She would be able to drink one glass of wine—she was allowed three a week, to be drunk on different days—and by omitting bread at lunchtime and ignoring the rolls and breadsticks this evening, she could eat a potato or some rice or a little pasta. At home, Mrs Hardy was punctilious about weighing portions for her. By now she had become a good judge, by eye, of a three-ounce serving of meat, fish or poultry or a six-ounce serving of *légumes*.

Also, in addition to their programme, Weight Watchers were issued with modules which were leaflets about the management of situations—such as going out to dinner—which were hazardous for reforming food junkies.

'How did you get on with Oz, Emily?' asked Mrs Hardy, when they had chosen what to eat.

It had been quite late by the time she and Summer had returned from their shopping expedition and she had gone straight to her room to change.

'He's fabulous!' said Emily rapturously. 'You wouldn't believe all the things he can do, Summer. He can sing *Gentlemen Prefer Blondes* in the funniest, buzzy sort of voice. He can translate anything you type on his keyboard into other languages. If you can speak *his* language, you can make him do amost anything you want.'

'The computer I have is not our best-selling microcomputer,' said James. 'It's what's known as a professional work station with a much wider range of possibilities than our less expensive models. Generally speaking, children—even those much younger than Emily—find it easier to work with computers than many adults.'

'Will you give me another lesson tomorrow?' she asked him.

'Possibly, but you didn't come to Florida to spend too much time shut indoors with Oz. I think we'll have to make a rule that one hour a day, preferably after sundown, is long enough.'

Thinking about his reasons for coming to Florida—to relax from the stresses of controlling a billion-dollar company plus constantly travelling and talking to audiences of students—she felt that most men in his position would have brought a girl-friend along to aid the unwinding process.

Mrs Hardy never gossiped about their employer to her, but Summer had formed the impression that neither of the women with whom his name had been linked had ever been to *Baile del Sol*.

Perhaps he confined his discreet amours to New York.

Just as she was thinking this, a woman's voice said, 'Good evening, James. When did you arrive in Sarasota? I hadn't heard you were here.'

He rose to his feet and shook hands with the woman standing by his chair.

'Good evening, Anita. I arrived in the early hours of this morning. You know Mrs Hardy. This is Miss Roberts . . . Miss Adams.'

With the width of the table between them, they did not shake hands but smiled and said how do you do. Miss Adams smiled with her lips but her eyes remained cool. They were brown eyes and her eyebrows were dark, suggesting that she was by nature a brunette who had chosen to be a silver-beige blonde.

'And this is Emily, my niece.'

Emily rose to shake hands.

'I had no idea you had a niece . . . and such a pretty
one, too,' said Miss Adams charmingly. 'You're very
brown, Emily. You must have been in Florida longer
than your uncle. Or do you come from a warm place?'

'I came from England before Christmas.'

'I see.' Anita Adams laid red-lacquered fingertips
lightly on the child's shoulder and on James's forearm.
'Please sit down again, both of you. I only came over to
say hello. I must get back to our party. I hope we'll
meet again very soon, Emily. Goodbye for the moment.' This parting remark included the other two
women.

As she returned to a table in another section of the
restaurant, James said, 'Miss Adams and her father
have an apartment at 888, Boulevard of the Arts—
those large blocks you see as you're crossing the
causeway from this side of the Bay.'

Then he changed the subject by saying, 'As you'll
see in a little while, Emily, the Asolo Theater is quite
unusual. It was opened in 1798.'

'But I thought there was nothing here then but
swamps and mangroves and mosquitoes?'

'There wasn't. But in the little town of Asolo in Italy,
not far from Venice, life was a lot more sophisticated.
That's where the theatre was built and where it stayed
till in 1930 it was dismantled to make way for a modern
movie theatre. Fortunately an antique dealer bought
all the parts of the old theatre and stored them for
almost twenty years. Soon after the Second World
War, the then director of the Ringling Museums heard
about them and recommended the State of Florida to
buy them. Which they did. Now, in Asolo, they'd like
to have the theatre back. As they can't, they're building a replica of it.'

The play which the Asolo company were presenting
that night was a revival of *The Second Mrs Tanqueray* by
the Victorian dramatist, Sir Arthur Wing Pinero. It was
beautifully costumed, and the actors' voices carried
clearly to the second floor box at the back of the
horseshoe-shaped theatre where James and Summer

sat behind Mrs Hardy and Emily.

Above them was another tier of boxes; below them the orchestra stalls divided by a central aisle with a splendid chandelier hanging above it. The seating was not very comfortable and some of the people in the side boxes had to crane to get a good view, but the charm of the little theatre, with its original lamps and painted decorations, compensated for its defects.

The night James had taken them to the theatre in London, Emily had sat between them. Here, with a curtain drawn across the entrance to the box, and little or no space around them, she was very much aware of his shoulder and arm close to hers.

There wasn't room for his long thighs behind Mrs Hardy's seat. He had to sit with them splayed, which brought his right knee within an inch or two of Summer's knee. She found this proximity disturbing, reminding her as it did of what had occurred in the swimming pool the night before.

The following day James said that after lunch he would take Emily shelling and Summer could again have the afternoon free for her own pursuits.

This suited her because she had finished a needle-point belt she had been working for her pupil, and wanted to go to Fleece & Floss to buy another canvas.

The needlework shop was hidden away in an arcade off one of the four streets which converged on St Armand's Circle. It was a small shop, its walls bright with hanks of crewel wool in a wonderful range of colours and its ceiling covered with designs for needle-point rugs. She spent a long time browsing through a revolving rack of designs, mainly for pillows and many of them with sea shell motifs.

As she was leaving the shop, a woman stepped out of the clothes shop opposite. Summer recognised her instantly. But for a moment it seemed that Anita Adams had no recollection of seeing her before.

Then she said, 'Oh, Miss . . . Roberts. Hello. How are you?'

Summer smiled at her. 'Good afternoon, Miss Adams.'

'What have you been buying in Fleece & Floss?' asked the older woman, eyeing Summer's parcel. 'Aren't their designs enchanting? I'm on my way to have coffee at The French Hearth. Will you join me?'

For some indefinable reason Summer didn't take to Miss Adams. However, having no ready excuse to refuse the invitation, she said, 'Thank you.'

As they left the arcade, Miss Adams said, 'Are you here on vacation?'

'No, I'm Emily's tutor.'

'Why doesn't she go to school?'

'She used to have quite severe asthma, but she seems to be growing out of it.'

'How long are you staying at her uncle's house?'

'I'm not sure.'

'Are Emily's parents coming over?'

'Her parents are dead. She's in Mr Gardiner's care now.'

They crossed the street and turned towards the shops on the North West Quadrant of the Circle.

'Is she his brother's child, or his sister's?'

'His brother's.' Summer was beginning to be irked by this catechism. She decided it was her turn to ask a question. 'Have you known Mr Gardiner long, Miss Adams?'

'Since he bought his house from Cordelia Rathbone . . . Mrs Charles Rathbone. She and my mother were close friends. I expect you've heard of the Rathbones—they're one of our most prominent families. They can trace their ancestry back to before the war—the War of Independence,' she added impressively. 'Mrs Rathbone was one of the great beauties of her day. Her first husband was an English aristocrat, Lord Cranmere, and she lived in England for several years. What part of England do you come from?'

'I'm an American. I was born in Baltimore. Have you always lived in Florida?'

'Certainly not!' said Miss Adams, as if the suggestion had something offensive about it. 'We have a winter place here, but we lived in Connecticut.'

She then added that her father was president of what Summer knew to be one of the largest corporations in the United States.

'And what is your work?' Summer asked her.

'Since my mother died, I've acted as my father's hostess. We do a great deal of entertaining. I have very little leisure except when we're here in Sarasota.'

By this time they had reached the café she had mentioned. It was reached through a bakery shop where people were buying croissants and long French-style loaves. The premises were pervaded by a delicious smell of *pâtisserie* which, at one time, would have titillated Summer's taste-buds. Up to a point it still did, but not to the extent that she felt herself tempted to order a sugary confection to eat with her coffee; not even if she had come to the café on her own, and certainly not in the company of Anita Adams who was slender to the point of being emaciated.

'You must have spent a long time over there to have acquired an English accent,' she remarked, when they were sitting down.

'Twelve years. But my mother was English so I think I always had an Anglo-American accent.'

'Were there no other relations who could have taken charge of Emily?' the other woman asked. 'The care of a girl of her age—What is she? Thirteen?—is somewhat of an onerous responsibility for a bachelor with the commitments which James has.'

'She's almost fourteen and extremely bright. I think he enjoys her company. They've gone off together this afternoon.'

Summer wished she had not agreed to have coffee. It was increasingly clear that Anita Adams was being sociable only in order to pump her. Summer was beginning to suspect that Miss Adams, still unmarried in her late twenties, had ambitions to put a period to James Gardiner's bachelorhood.

'James has never talked about his English connections. We assumed there had been some estrangement between him and the rest of his family,' was her next remark.

Summer parried this by saying, 'Perhaps if you had asked him he would have talked about his family. The English often don't volunteer information about themselves unless someone shows an interest.'

'How long have you been Emily's tutor?'

'About eighteen months. Her parents were killed in a car crash in France last summer.'

'What a tragedy! Poor little thing. She has no brothers or sisters?'

'No.'

'Her father must have been a successful man to have her educated privately. What was his occupation?'

'He had a farm,' Summer answered, not untruthfully.

It was a relief when she was able to make her escape and continue shopping, alone. In spite of the much greater age gap between them, she found Mrs Hardy a more congenial companion than Miss Adams whose manner veered from patronising to ingratiating.

She was waiting to cross the street between the South East and South West Quadrant when she noticed, farther along the street, a palm tree with yards of brilliantly coloured fabric wound round its trunk like the binding on the frame of a lampshade.

It was outside a shop called Lilly Pulitzer, and the interior of the shop was a bower of wonderful suncolours—lime-green, banana-yellow, shocking-pink, turquoise, azure.

These vivid colours gave her the same inner thrill she had felt when she looked at the softer, more subtle shades of the needlepoint wools in Fleece & Floss.

She bought a cute top for Emily to wear with her white shorts. The saleswoman packed it in a bag to which she clipped ringlets of coloured ribbon to match the colours of Summer's purchase. It was a touch which delighted her and she walked out of the shop feeling, for several reasons, on top of the world.

In the first place she was discovering how much she liked shopping; not necessarily buying anything, but just looking, comparing, admiring, learning what she liked and didn't like. At the same time it was good to know that she *could* buy anything she particularly liked, unless it was wildly expensive, like the lion's paw necklace.

Another good feeling was the freedom of having a car to run around in, by herself, while knowing that she wasn't going back to an empty house and a lonely evening.

Yet another pleasure was the mellow warmth of the afternoon. In an hour or two there would be a spectacular sunset over the Gulf, but at present the light was still bright, the air temperature was warm as if it were June or July instead of early March.

Best of all was her new, shapelier self. Unexpected reflections in shop windows no longer made her miserable; an outcast from the world of attractive women. And as well as being slimmer, she seemed to have more zest for life, more mental and physical energy.

As she drove back across the causeway she was humming the principal theme from the Tchaikovsky violin concerto. She was still humming when she had to stop at the traffic lights at the junction with 41.

An elderly man in the car in the lane next to hers leaned out of his window. 'You sound very happy, young lady.'

She smiled at him. 'I guess I am.'

'Got a big date tonight, huh?' He winked at her.

The lights changed. The cars moved forward. Still smiling, Summer turned north while the other car headed downtown. Three months ago no one would have said that to her. Admittedly he had only been able to see her from the elbows up, but even that limited view would have been enough, last December, to indicate that she wasn't a girl who had dates.

I ought to write to that woman in the shop in Miami, she thought. I should thank her for changing my life.

Yet, deep in her heart, she knew it hadn't been the

saleswoman who had done that. It had been James Gardiner's caustic indictment of her as a glutton which had jolted her out of her apathetic acceptance of her condition. The woman in Miami had pointed her in the right direction to find help. But the impetus to seek it had been the scathing male voice overheard from the Gallery at Cranmere.

For that impetus she would stand in his debt for the rest of her life; and, at the same time, she would never forgive him. What he had said about her to Dr Dyer had been an expression of contempt as unpardonably humiliating as if he had struck her, or spat on her.

She knew there was only one way she could purge her mind of that shaming memory, and that was by turning the tables on him, by making him fall in love with her, and rejecting him.

Which was such a wild, crazy idea that it made her blush to have thought it. James Gardiner in love with Summer Roberts? Impossible.

At Indian Beach Drive she turned off, wondering which beach the others had chosen for their walk. For some time Emily had wanted to see Midnight Pass, a break in the Keys farther south. Perhaps he had taken her there. If so, Summer hoped the place had lived up to its romantic name.

Thinking about the top she had bought for Emily and about its designer, Lilly Pulitzer, and the striking originality of her colours and patterns, she found herself wondering if perhaps she herself had a vocation which she hadn't yet discovered; something to do with colour and design.

Her aunt had decided for her that she was going to be a teacher, and she did enjoy teaching Emily. But every time she looked at her father's *trompe-l'oeil* paintings on the walls of the Octagon Room, she was filled with a longing to be able to create something beautiful, as he had. She knew her ability to draw was better than average, but nothing like good enough for her ever to become a professional artist. What about the fringes of the art world? Interior design . . .

fashion designing. Might she find her *métier* somewhere there?

Instead of going shelling, James had taken his niece across the Sunshine Skyway, the fifteen-mile-long bridge and causeway which spanned Tampa Bay, north of Sarasota. In St Petersburg, on the other side of the Bay, they had gone to a famous bookshop, Haslam's, to buy, among other things, an illustrated guide to shells.

'And I thought you'd like this, Summer,' said Emily, presenting her with a large book about embroidery. 'James says the author, Erica Wilson, has a summer house in Nantucket like he has.'

'This looks lovely, Emily. Thank you very much, darling,' she said, looking through the pages of needlework projects. 'I bought a present for you.'

The child was delighted with the top and rushed upstairs to try it on. But when Summer would have settled down to study her present more thoroughly, James said, 'Come into the library and I'll show you how the music centre functions.'

It turned out to be less complicated than it looked and, having shown her how it worked, he said, 'I hadn't realised that Weight Watchers included men in their classes. I thought they were only for women.'

'No, there are several men in my class.'

'And one who takes you for a drink after class, I hear.'

Had Emily volunteered that information, or had he extracted it from her?

'For a coffee, yes—sometimes,' she agreed.

Twice she had made an excuse not to have coffee with Hal, and once she had invited another class member to join them.

'What kind of guy is he?'

'A very nice one. You don't object to my having some friends of the opposite sex, do you?'

'In principle—certainly not. I'd prefer, for your own security, that you had some guarantee of their bona fides. Such as an introduction. Presumably anyone who can pay the fees can enrol for these classes. What's his name and what does he do?'

'His name is Hal Cochran and he's in the construction business.'

'I don't know any Cochrans,' said James. 'And "the construction business" covers a pretty wide field. Is that all you know about his job?'

'Hal lays roof tiles. He's twenty-eight, he lives with his widowed mother who's in hospital at the moment, and he spends a lot of his evenings baby-sitting for his married sister. He couldn't be more respectable and harmless.'

'A description which could probably be applied to a lot of unpleasant characters before they went berserk,' James said sardonically. 'Why isn't he married?'

'I have no idea. Why aren't you married?' she retorted.

'Because I agree with Sam Johnson that marriage is an unnatural state, and because I'm too involved in my work which, I imagine, is rather more satisfying and absorbing than your friend's occupation. An artisan of twenty-eight, still living at home, with a weight problem which impels him to join a predominantly female slimming class, strikes me as a pretty odd fish.'

'Well, he isn't. He's entirely normal.'

'How d'you know?'

'By instinct.'

'I think your instincts about men may not be as highly developed as those of most girls your age,' he told her. 'If I'm not mistaken, when I kissed you in the pool the night before last, it was the first time it had happened to you.'

Her clear golden skin was suffused by a wave of warmer colour. Had he no sensitivity that he didn't know what it did to her to be told, with unsparing bluntness, that no one had kissed her until she was twenty-two?

'I think, after the next meeting, you should bring him back here for coffee and let me be the judge of whether he's harmless or not,' James went on. 'But even if he is, I shouldn't have thought you had much in common.'

Before she could reply, Emily reappeared in her new top, which was probably just as well because she had been on the brink of losing her temper, Summer realised.

After dinner, James went out to visit some friends. Emily was disappointed—she had been hoping he would take her up to his room and put the computer through some more of its paces.

'But actually the one upstairs is obsolete now,' she told Summer. 'His newest one has a mouse, which is a gadget which makes it much easier to use a computer. James says it will take people forty minutes to learn what used to take forty hours with the first generation of computers.'

Presently, finding her enthusiasm for computers a little hard to share, Summer asked her to look up the lion's paw shell in her new book.

Emily consulted the index and turned to the page indicated.

'It doesn't say much about it. *The Lion's Paw*. Lyropecten nodosus. *Found in Florida and the West Indies. It belongs to the group known as Eastern American Scallops. A strong heavy shell, 3–5 inches. A collector's favourite.* Why are you interested in it, Summer?'

'Because I saw a beautiful necklace with a lion's paw as the pendant in Burdines yesterday. But it cost a great deal of money. Too much, considering that even a strong shell is still quite fragile.'

'Oh, I see.' Emily began to read the descriptions of other shells and soon was deeply absorbed.

Summer would have liked to become equally absorbed in her embroidery book. But James's remarks about Hal interfered with her concentration.

The annoying thing was that, in one particular, he had been right; she had little in common with Hal other than their need to lose weight. She had long since discovered that books, her refuge and solace, had no place in his life. Similarly none of his interests—baseball, bowling, clay pigeon shooting—had any appeal to her.

Realising their lack of rapport, she had tried to avoid always leaving the meetings with him and had been at pains to make friends with other women in the class. But it had been difficult to shake him off without being actively unkind. He was lonely and he liked her. How could she brush him off when, at the beginning, his friendliness had done so much for her morale?

'Hi, Summer. How did you do?' a friend asked her at the next meeting.

'Two pounds down. How did you do?'

The other girl groaned. 'Up half a pound. It must be water retention. I've been *starving* all week.'

As they chatted, Summer was aware of Hal at the back of the class. When it was over, he was waiting for her by the door. They walked to her car together, discussing Eleanor's lecture and the fortnightly module.

'Friday's my birthday,' he said suddenly. 'I'd like to take you out to dinner. I thought you'd enjoy the dinner cruise on the paddle-wheel steamer berthed down on Bayfront Drive?'

How could she refuse when he looked at her so hopefully?

'Thank you, Hal. That sounds fun,' she answered.

'I'll pick you up at a quarter of seven—okay?'

'Fine. I'll be looking forward to it.'

'Coming for a coffee?'

'Not tonight—I have to get back. I'll see you on Friday.'

Next day, although he knew she had been to a meeting the night before, James didn't ask why she hadn't carried out his instruction to bring Hal to the house.

On Friday morning, she told Mrs Hardy she would be out for dinner that night. But she didn't say anything to Emily until she was going up to change.

'Where are you going?' Emily asked.

'I've been invited to a birthday dinner on board the paddle-boat. By a Weight Watchers friend,' she added casually.

'Lucky you. I wish I were coming.'

'If it's fun, perhaps we'll go on a lunch cruise for your next birthday treat,' said Summer.

She was ready and waiting on the doorstep when Hal drove up in his Ford Escort.

'That's some house!' he said admiringly, taking in its balconied façade and blossoming creepers.

She felt relieved when he had installed her in the passenger seat and they were moving down the drive. Her employer's bedroom was on the bay side of the building. It was unlikely he had seen her departure. She wondered how he would react when he learnt she was out on a date with the man who had sounded to him 'a pretty odd fish'. Anyway, it was none of his business what she did in her free time, she told herself firmly.

Hal was in high spirits. But, considering it was her first time out with a man—apart from the two disastrous foursome dates at Oxford—her own mood was not buoyant. James, damn him, had succeeded in making her feel like a rebellious teenager sneaking out on an illicit date with a boy her family disapproved of.

She could tell that Hal had had some beer before he picked her up, but that didn't mean he was going to be drunk by the end of the evening. One can was enough to make a man's breath smell beery. If it hadn't been for her employer's homily, probably she wouldn't have noticed it.

Midway along Sarasota's curving, palm-treed waterfront was Island Park, a man-made islet dredged from the bay bottom to provide berths for game-fishing charter boats, excursion craft and private yachts.

As they left the car on the parking lot and walked past a row of gift shops towards the Marina Jack restaurant and, moored alongside, Marina Jack II, the floating restaurant, she was glad of the black crochet shawl Mrs Hardy had lent her as a wrap.

Not that the evening was cold. A slight breeze had sprung up since sunset and was rustling the palm fronds, and the temperature had dropped a few degrees. But the other women she saw were only wearing blazers or showercoats over their dresses. She felt chilly because she was nervous.

They were a little early. The steamer hadn't started taking on passengers.

'She was built here in Florida as an authentic reproduction of a pool boat,' said Hal, as they waited to go on board. 'When dams were built along the Upper Mississippi and Ohio Rivers, they reduced the bridge clearance in the pools above them. So this kind of boat developed, with the pilot house forward and short or folding smoke stacks. Boats like this pushed fleets of wood and coal barges. She had two independent paddle-wheels at the other end. Now she runs on diesel but she would have run on coal in the old days.'

'You seem very knowledgeable,' Summer said. 'Are you interested in American river history?'

He grinned and shook his head. 'I read all that on the souvenir menu. I've been on this cruise before—on my sister's birthday.'

She was disappointed. Listening to his explanation, she had hoped that it indicated a serious interest which she could use to confute James's snobbish assumption that, because Hal laid tiles and she taught, he was an unsuitable companion for her.

She glanced at her watch. There was some time to wait before the steamer was due to embark. Emily knew about the dinner cruise—supposing she told her uncle and he took it into his head to come down here and make her go home with him?

No, no—of course he wouldn't. He might read the riot act tomorrow, but he wouldn't go to the lengths of behaving like a tyrannical Victorian paterfamilias. If—and the idea was absurd—he did attempt to break up her date, she would refuse to go with him and Hal

would support her refusal. He wasn't as tall as James,
but he was a big, burly man, not the kind to be bullied
or brushed aside by other men.

Yet, visualising a confrontation between them, she
doubted that Hal would stand up to James.

Hal was born to take orders; James to give them. For
almost six hundred years, since one of his forbears had
helped King Henry V to win the Battle of Agincourt,
the pedigree of his family was scattered with the
names of leaders, either military men or influential
statesmen. It was only during the twentieth century
that the Lancasters had failed to produce any outstanding men until he, using another name, had become a leading figure in the revolutionary field of
computer science.

James would only have to display the autocratic
manner of which she had seen a few glimpses, and
take an authoritative tone, and Hal would defer to him
as instinctively as a private soldier to his commanding
officer.

It was not until they were on board, seated at one of
the tables in the dining saloon, with the steamer free
of her moorings and beginning to move into Little
Sarasota Bay, that she was able to relax.

'Oh, I almost forgot,' she exclaimed. 'I have a
present for you.'

It had been difficult to know what to give him. He
didn't read and wasn't a lover of music, so she had
settled for a bottle of aftershave lotion.

'Many happy returns of the day, Hal,' she said, as
she handed him the gift-wrapped package.

He was almost embarrassingly pleased with the
uninspired gift; so much so that she was made to feel
she had given him something very personal whereas
her intention had been to choose something as imper-
sonal as possible.

The head waiter—or perhaps in a floating restaurant
he was called the chief steward—presented them with
menus written in a curious mixture of English and
French. Reading hers, she found herself imagining

the amused curl of the lips which would be James's reaction to it.

'I don't know how you feel, but I'm sure not dieting tonight—not on this special occasion,' said Hal, giving her a look which made her feel sure he meant it was dining with her rather than celebrating his birthday which made it special. 'I'm going to start with the seafood crêpe followed by the prime ribs of beef,' he decided. 'How about you, honey?'

The endearment increased her unease. 'I'd like to try the French onion soup and the filet of Florida grouper, please.'

He wanted her to have a cocktail beforehand. When she asked if she might have a glass of wine, he ordered a bottle for them to share, although she felt sure he would have preferred to drink beer.

Searching for a tactful way to keep the conversation on a safe track, she said, 'I wonder if there's a Weight Watchers class in Nantucket? I hope so. I don't want to miss any classes before I've completed my sixteen consecutive weeks and got my first award.'

'You're going to Nantucket? When?' he asked, looking surprised.

'I don't know for certain. Probably some time next month. It sounds a very interesting place.'

'Hell, I didn't realise you'd be leaving as soon as that. When'll you be back?'

'I've no idea, Hal. We're entirely dependent on Emily's uncle's decisions.'

'What kind of guy is he?'

'A very high-powered, dynamic businessman. You must have heard of Oz computers.'

'Oh, sure. Who hasn't? With a big house on Bay Shore Road I guess he has to be a vice-president.'

'He's higher than that. He's the king-pin.'

'Is that so?' He gave a low whistle. 'You must have a pretty good job, working for someone like that. I guess you wouldn't want to give it up . . . living in style . . . travelling around, and everything.'

'Not only for those reasons. I'm very attached to

Emily. I hope to stay with her till she's at least seventeen, which is just over three years.'

'How about if some guy comes along you like more than you like her?'

'I shouldn't want to get married before I was twenty-five anyway. I think marrying young is a mistake. Afterwards people regret all the things they didn't have time to do before they settled down. In my case, being overweight, I've missed a lot of the fun most girls have from eighteen to my age. I'm twenty-two and this is my first dinner date!'

'It won't be your last, that's for sure. You get prettier every time I see you. By the time you get your award, you're going to have guys standing in line for a date with you,' he told her.

She laughed. 'Somehow I doubt that. I suppose when you hit your target, you'll stop going to classes?'

'Not if you're still around.'

'I shall be in Nantucket,' she reminded him, although she knew he had only a few pounds more to lose before he was ready to change to the Maintenance Program. 'Oh, look—we're going through the causeway.'

They stopped talking to look at the lines of cars waiting for the steamer to pass into the wider expanse of water north of the causeway. Soon, on the mainland, they could see the lights of the blocks of apartments where Anita Adams lived, and the floodlights illuminating the armadillo-shape of the Van Wezel hall.

'If we're taking this route you'll be able to see your place,' said Hal. 'Sometimes they go around Bird Key and sometimes down into Roberts Bay by Siesta Key. But tonight they're going north and the turnaround point should be near the Ringling Mansion. Have you been in there?'

'Yes, soon after we arrived here.'

'Did you ever see anywhere like it? Your boss has a fancy house, but not like the Ringling Mansion. That's really something.'

'Yes . . . extraordinary,' she agreed, her inward ear hearing the echo of James saying, *Let me be the judge of whether he's harmless or not, but even if he is I shouldn't have thought you had much in common*.

Reluctant as she was to admit that he had been right, she knew that the kind, lonely man on the other side of the table would, if she were to live with him, bore her to tears in three months.

It wasn't his fault that he had never heard of Petra, the 'rose-red city "half as old as Time"', or the water-lily pool in Monet's garden at Giverny, or 'many-tower'd Camelot'; but it was a barrier between them of which he wasn't even aware.

To him the Ringling Mansion was one of the wonders of the world. To her it didn't compare with *Baile del Sol* which had probably cost a fraction as much to build but had been inspired by the houses of Spanish grandees, while Ca'd'Zan was a hybrid of Mabel Ringling's two favourite buildings, the Doge's palace in Venice and the old Madison Square Garden in New York City.

Her preference for James Gardiner's house was reinforced later in the cruise when they saw both houses from the Bay. The Ringling Mansion was set close to the water's edge, its ornate façade constructed from shiploads of arches and windows brought to Florida from Europe, and dominated by a great tower from which, when the Ringlings were in residence, a bright light had beamed like a beacon.

Baile del Sol was partially screened from the Bay by the tall palms which shadowed its lawns. The soft glow of shaded table-lamps outlined the windows of the living room and, upstairs, of the landing and James's room.

Had she known nothing about either building, it would have been the smaller, less showy house which would have intrigued her, but she doubted if Hal would agree.

He finished his meal with a piece of Florida lime pie and tried to persuade her to join him. But Summer resisted and, later, wouldn't let him coax her to have one of what the menu described as Speciality Coffees with Assorted Liquors and Whipped Cream.

Considering what their dinner was going to cost him, she wasn't impressed by the food. However, as he had dined on board before, he must find it satisfactory.

It wasn't late when the steamer returned to her berth.

'Would you like to go dancing?' he asked.

It made her feel guilty to admit it, even to herself, but the truth was that by now she was longing to be in bed, reading. Listening to Hal describing the wonders of Walt Disney World which, regarding it as Florida's principal attraction, he was amazed they hadn't visited yet, had made the past hour rather boring.

They were planning to go and see Disney World, but it was the house on Key West where Ernest Hemingway had written *For Whom The Bell Tolls* and *A Farewell To Arms* which was at the top of her personal sightseeing list.

'I don't think I should be out late tonight, Hal. Mr Gardiner is down here at the moment, and I don't want to give the impression that I'm turning into a social butterfly. I'd like to go home now, if you don't mind.'

He didn't argue but clearly he was disappointed. She felt mean for curtailing his birthday celebration. At the same time she couldn't face spending another hour or two with him in a dark smoky disco.

Hal turned off at Indian Beach Drive, as Summer usually did to get home, and reduced speed to a slow glide through the quiet residential area. Summer began to wonder if he meant to kiss her goodnight.

From reading Ann Landers' advice column in the *Sarasota Herald-Tribune*, she knew that a lot of men expected more than a kiss in return for dining and wining a girl, but she didn't think Hal was the type to make a heavy pass on the strength of one date. After her efforts to keep the evening on a friendly basis, he might not expect even to kiss her.

A week ago it was possible she could have acquiesced to being kissed out of sheer curiosity to know what it felt like to have a man's lips pressed to hers. Since then she had learnt what it felt like. James had not only filled that gap in her education but taken it considerably further, holding her close in his arms, making her feel his reaction to the contact with her naked flesh.

As she thought of those moments in the pool, she was conscious that now, days later, in a car with another man, her own body was belatedly responding to that reaction. She could feel her thighs tingling and throbbing and, inside her, a softening as, against her will, her senses were stirred by the memory of that powerful embrace in the water, and the strength and virility of the man who had held her.

Sometimes, in her night-time fantasies of being Barbara dei Trechi in the arms of Bayard, or Mary Wilemson on her wedding night with Lion Gardiner, she had experienced similar reactions.

But this was the first time a living man had aroused those strange, secret feelings. She felt outraged and disgusted that it should be James Gardiner, a man she actively disliked.

Hal was talking about the Busch Gardens at Tampa where his sister and her husband were taking their children on Sunday. She forced herself to concentrate.

'Why don't we join them? Me, you and Emily?' he suggested. 'She'd love it. It's a great place for kids. There are tigers and dolphins and all kinds of fun.'

'It's a nice idea, Hal, but I think her uncle's planning to take her to see Thomas Edison's house at Fort Myers.'

'I've been there. It's okay, but kinda dull for kids, especially girls. She'd like Busch Gardens better.'

Summer felt slightly irritated that, never having met Emily, he considered himself able to judge what she would or wouldn't enjoy.

But she said only, 'She adores her uncle. She'd

enjoy anywhere he took her.'

He swung the car under the arch and cruised slowly up the drive. When the house came into view, the only lights showing were in the Antonios' apartment above the garage.

There were no outside lights on. When the full moon was shining they weren't necessary, but from time to time the moon was obscured by a cloud.

Hal turned the car in a loop until the beam of his headlights was pointing towards the drive, then he switched off both engine and lights, and climbed out.

As he came round to open her door, she felt that he wouldn't have done this if it were not in his mind to kiss her in the shadow of the porch. But she didn't want to be kissed and *her* mind searched frantically for a way to avoid the embrace without hurting his feelings. The trouble was she had as little experience of handling this kind of situation as a girl in her middle-teens.

'It's been a very nice evening, Hal,' she said, as she stepped from the car. 'Seeing this house from the Bay was most interesting. Thank you very much for taking me.'

'Why don't we do it again next week?' As they walked towards the house, he put his hand lightly on the small of her back.

'Well . . . I'm not sure. I—I may be busy,' she temporised awkwardly.

'You won't be busy every night, will you?' he persisted.

She had never realised what a difficult business it was to back out of a relationship with a man, even at this early stage when it was hardly more than an acquaintance.

'It depends,' she said vaguely. 'Anyway, we'll be seeing each other at class.'

Outside the front door his hand drew her round to face him and his other hand moved to her shoulder.

'Oh, Hal—' she began.

Before she could add, '—please don't!' the lantern

above them was switched on from inside the house, and the front door opened.

'Oh, it's you, Summer,' said her employer. 'I heard a car arriving, but I didn't expect you back for some time yet.' He turned to her companion. 'You must be Hal Cochran. My name is Gardiner.' He offered his hand to the younger man. 'Come in and have a drink, won't you?'

Hal's expressions were easy to read. Surprise, frustration, then annoyance showed on his square, open face; quickly followed by gratification at being invited to enter the home of the head of a big company.

'That's very kind of you, sir,' he said deferentially.

'Not at all. I've been wanting to meet you.'

'Oh, really?' Hal looked somewhat startled.

James closed the front door behind them and led the way to the living room.

'Yes,' he said, speaking over his shoulder. 'Summer has led a sheltered life. She's new to America and I feel responsible for her welfare. Till she's somewhat older and wiser, I don't like her going out with people I haven't met. Does that strike you as unreasonable?'

'No—no, I think you're right, sir. Nice girls do have to be careful. Hell, these days even old ladies have to watch out.'

'Precisely. But I don't think Summer accepts her vulnerability. Perhaps you can convince her that I'm not fussing unnecessarily.'

By this time they had reached the living room where Hal turned to her and said earnestly, 'Mr Gardiner is right about that, honey. There are a lot of bad people around. Not like in Miami or New York City or those places, maybe, but—'

'I'm aware of the hazards,' she interrupted. 'Only recently someone not far from here had an exceedingly unpleasant experience while she was using the swimming pool.'

'In her own backyard? That's terrible. What happened?'

'Nothing much,' James put in blandly. 'The girl was

swimming in the nude and someone dived in with
her. She knew him. It was harmless horse-play. What
would you like to drink, Summer? Your usual Perrier
and lemon, or something stronger?'

'Perrier, please,' she said stiffly, taking off Mrs
Hardy's shawl. 'I think what a man might call horse-
play could be very objectionable to a woman.'

'If she was swimming in the raw, I'd say she was
asking for it,' said Hal.

She gave him a sparkling look. 'Have you never
swum without clothes when you thought there was no
one around?'

'Sure I have, but that's different.'

'Only because you know that if a girl came along
when you were like that she'd be most unlikely to
embarrass you. She certainly wouldn't alarm you—as
this man we're talking about did with the girl in
question.'

'Oh, come now, don't tell me she thought she was
about to be raped?' said James. 'In that case why didn't
she yell for help. There were plenty of people within
earshot. What about you, Cochran? Beer . . . bourbon
. . . Scotch?'

'A little Scotch for me, please.' Hal began to glance
round the room, taking in its unusual shape, an
elongated octagon, and the high vaulted ceiling.

The lofty proportions and the monochromatic
colour scheme—the walls curtains and the upholstery
were all in shades of pale raw umber—was a restful
background   for   an   eclectic   collection   of
beautiful objects.

Above the French marble fireplace hung a large
gilded baroque mirror with its original time-misted
mysterious glass. This was surrounded by six gilded
Florentine brackets forming perches for porcelain
birds of vivid plumage.

The object which Summer liked best stood by itself
on a black and gold lacquer tray-table at one end of the
comfortable sofa. It was a bronze sculpture of Pegasus,
the winged horse ridden by Bellerophon who, in

Greek legend, after spurning the advances of his queen, was set many dangerous tasks such as killing the Chimaera, a fire-breathing monster with a lion's head, the body of a goat and a dragon's tail.

She had immediately recognised the horse as Pegasus, but hadn't realised, till Mary Hardy showed her, that the sculpture had hidden hinges which enabled its shape to be changed. It was by a sculptor called Francisco Baron, and James had bought it on a visit to Spain. The house contained many paintings and *objets d'art* bought on his travels.

However, although she could not deny his excellent taste, at this moment she was too furious with his hypocritical pretence of avuncular concern for her welfare to allow him any good points.

She wished Hal were less visibly awed, and wouldn't keep calling James 'sir' as if he were a much older man, or someone entitled to special deference. She was ready, at the first hint of condescension in James's manner towards him, to spring to Hal's defence.

But during the following half an hour there was nothing patronising in her employer's attitude to the younger man. He was very pleasant to him; and apparently genuinely interested in the subjects which she had found tedious.

At length, breaking off a conversation about the Chicago White Sox, he said, 'I think we're boring Summer. May I get you another drink, Cochran?'

'No, thanks. I'd better be going.' Hal put down his glass and stood up. 'It's been very nice meeting you, sir. I hope now you'll have no objection to us maybe going dancing next week?'

'If Summer is here, that's up to her. But my niece needs her teeth checked, and the two of them may have to go to New York next week.'

'Oh . . . I see.' Hal looked downcast.

If he had hoped to say goodnight to her in private when she showed him to the door, another disappointment was in store for him. James came with them. He kept the door open till Hal had climbed into his car, then he closed and locked it, and fastened the chain and the bolts.

'Come back to the living room,' he said. 'I want to talk to you,' and Summer found herself starting to quake. Since the episode in the swimming pool, she could never feel at ease alone with him, and especially not late at night with the others upstairs in their bedrooms.

Following her into the living room, he closed the door quietly behind him.

'Tell me something,' he said conversationally. 'If you knew Emily meant to do something I disapproved of, how would you react? Would you let her go ahead?'

'Naturally not. I'd try to persuade her against it.'

'How can I rely on that when you yourself don't respect my wishes?'

'In general, I do,' she answered. 'But because I have a living-in job I don't think it gives you the right to vet all my friends and acquaintances as if I were a Victorian governess. Now that you have met Hal, you might have the fairness to admit that my judgment about him was sound. There's nothing "odd fish" about him.'

'There wouldn't appear to be—no. If I hadn't opened the door when I did, he was going to kiss you. Did you want him to?'

She began to flush. 'No, I didn't.'

'How were you going to prevent it?'

'I—I don't know. It didn't arise.'

'Thanks to my intervention. Otherwise the way to avoid that situation was to politely refuse the invitation in the first place. If I don't send you to New York, how are you planning to slide out of another date with him?'

'Because I didn't want him to kiss me, doesn't mean I don't like him,' she prevaricated.

Her glass still contained some Perrier. His, like Hal's, was empty. He picked it up and crossed the

room to the antique black lacquer cabinet which
served as a drinks cupboard.

'As I said, you've led a sheltered life. The mating
dance is no longer a courtly minuet,' he told her dryly.
'It's a fast fandango into bed. If Cochran's been fat
since his teens, he's probably a slow worker. But once
he gets started he may try to make up lost time. You
could find him hard to fend off.'

She said coldly, 'You obviously see every relationship in terms of sex. It isn't everyone's outlook.
There are people who want to be friends before they
. . . go any further.'

'There are indeed.'

He strolled back to the main group of seating where
she perched on the edge of a giltwood bergère and
where now he stretched his long frame on a blond
linen sofa.

'And it'll surprise you to know that I'm among
them,' he went on. 'At my age, unless he's a fool, a
man wants more from a woman than her body.'

'But you don't give Hal the credit for being equally
discriminating?'

'I think he's probably like you—several years behind his contemporaries in experience with the opposite sex. I also think he's a simple soul with simple
needs. What he wants is a wife. You're not ready to be
anyone's wife—certainly not his. The man has no
conversation other than sport. If he's not out, he'll
spend his evenings in front of the television. When
he's older, midway through the evening he'll go to
sleep in front of the television.'

She couldn't argue with him on that score.

When she didn't answer, he said, 'Where did he
take you this evening?'

'We had dinner on Marina Jack II.'

He arched an expressive dark eyebrow.

'Have you ever been on it?' she asked, annoyed by
the supercilious gesture.

'No. It's popular with the tourists, I believe. What
was the food like?'

'I don't think you'd have been impressed. I would have enjoyed it just for the view from the Bay. We came past this house and Ca'd'Zan.'

He said, 'Mabel Ringling used to have a Venetian gondola moored on a small island near their terrace. The gondola and the island were swept away by a hurricane in 1926.'

Relieved to be on a safe subject, she said, 'How frequent are serious hurricanes?'

'In the last fifty years, there've been thirteen; the worst in 1944 when eighteen people were killed. But shortly before that period, in 1928, nearly two thousand people were killed. You're in no danger here. The Keys are the vulnerable areas, and there could be evacuation problems with hundreds of mobile homes, towed by elderly drivers, choking the main exit routes. But September is the most hazardous month, and you and Emily won't be here then.'

'*Are* you sending us to New York next week?'

'I think so—yes. If you've no objection?' he said suavely, the tawny eyes mocking her.

He knew she would be glad to escape the difficult situation into which her inexperience had led her.

She rose from the bergère. 'If that's all, I'll go to bed now.'

'There's one more thing.' He put aside his drink and stood up.

She expected him to say what it was on his way to open the door for her. When he didn't move in that direction, she said interrogatively, 'Yes?'

He crooked a finger, beckoning her to come closer.

Puzzled, uncertain, she obeyed.

'Perhaps I should have left you to cope with Cochran,' he said reflectively. 'It might have made you less uptight about being kissed in the pool. Were you really as frightened as you made out the girl was to him? Or would flustered be more accurate?'

'I was both,' she said stiffly. 'What else would you expect? Did you really suppose I should enjoy it?'

His eyes glinted, laughing at her. 'I did,' he

answered softly.

Before she realised his intention, he put his hands on her shoulders and drew her firmly towards him.

'Maybe you'll like this better,' he said, as he bent his head.

Summer recoiled and attempted to turn her face away, but his right hand came up from her shoulder and his palm turned her face back to his. She had a last glimpse of the amusement in his eyes before his mouth touched down on hers and, instinctively, she closed her eyes.

There was nothing boisterous about this kiss. He put his mouth lightly on hers and for a few moments he didn't even move his lips but just kept them warmly in place while his palm cradled her cheek and the tips of his fingers caressed the soft places behind her ear.

When his lips did begin to move it was with the utmost gentleness, like the feather-light circling of his fingertips at the back of her ear and down the side of her neck.

Gradually, with such subtlety that she was hardly aware of the transition, the persuasive pressure increased, coaxing her closed, still lips to respond to the movements of his. Without consciously ceasing to resist, she found she was no longer being subjected to a kiss. Somehow she was participating.

How long it lasted, she never knew. It seemed to go on for ever . . . but also to end far too soon.

When James took his mouth away from hers, she was in a daze of pleasure such as she had often imagined but never experienced. Slowly she opened her eyes and came down to earth.

'That wasn't unpleasant, was it?' he asked, his hand still on her neck.

She shook her head, still half-entranced by the magical feelings induced by his skilful kissing.

He looked down at her, no longer smiling. While his right hand fondled her neck, his left stroked and smoothed her shoulder. She had the impression he was debating whether to kiss her again. At that moment there was nothing she wanted more than to repeat the experience.

He confirmed her intuition by saying, 'No, I think not.' And then, after a slight pause, 'But I hope that's erased the experience you didn't enjoy, and that now you'll accept that it wasn't my intention to scare you the other night.'

After a demonstration which she knew in her bones had been far beyond Hal's capacity to send shivers of delight coursing through her, she could only give a small nod.

'Good.' He took his hands away and thrust them into the pockets of his pants. 'We can't do what's best for Emily if we're not *en rapport*. I hope from now on we'll have a more relaxed relationship. Goodnight, Summer.'

Turning, he strode to the door and held it open for her.

It was in the grounds of Thomas Edison's winter home that, a few days later, Emily had her first serious recurrence of asthma.

They had left Sarasota early in order to stop at Fort Myers en route to a lunch party at Naples. The home of the great inventor, the father of electric light, the cinema and the gramophone, was in itself quite remarkable. It was one of the first prefabricated buildings in America. Constructed to Edison's design and built in Fairfield, Maine, in 1885, the house had been transported to Florida by four schooners, and was still furnished as he had left it at his death in 1931.

After touring the house and museum, they were taken round the garden of which the most outstanding feature was an enormous banyan tree, brought as a present from India in 1925 and now three hundred and ninety feet around the trunk.

The garden had been Edison's hobby. It was full of rare trees and plants which he had begun to plant almost a hundred years earlier. Suddenly, while they were part of a guided tour, Emily began to have breathing difficulties.

If she had had her aerosol with her, she wouldn't have panicked. But the long interval since her last attack had made her feel she was cured. The puffer was in her bedroom at *Baile de Sol* and she was in Edison's garden, beginning to wheeze and terrified that, without it, her airways would cease to function.

Afterwards Summer wondered if, by herself, she could have pulled Emily through the horrible bout of dyspnoea. The child was pale, with beads of sweat on her forehead. All at once, on a warm sunny morning, her skin was both cold and clammy. She was gasping for air, the skin round her neck sucked in with the effort of breathing.

It was James who convinced her she could survive the attack. Completely calm, he emanated quiet confidence.

Because it was evidently something in the garden which had triggered the attack, the first thing to do was to get her away from the irritant. As she couldn't walk when she was wheezing without increasing her distress, James picked her up and carried her back to the car, talking reassuringly as he did so.

'You drive, will you, Summer? The keys are in my right-hand pocket. I'll sit behind with Emily. There'll be a pharmacy in town where we can get an inhaler.'

At the wheel of an unfamiliar car, with Emily gasping for breath behind her, Summer forced herself to be, outwardly, as calm as James. To drive too fast, she realised, would only increase Emily's fear. They had to get to a pharmacy as quickly as possible but not with a reckless haste which might cause an accident.

Fortunately, the Edison house was only a mile out of town, and it wasn't hard to find a pharmacy.

She jumped out and went swiftly in. Interrupting a customer who was talking to the pharmacist, she said, 'Excuse me, there's a child having a bad attack of asthma in the car outside. We need a bronchodilator in a pressurised inhaler—quickly.'

A few minutes later the worst was over.

Her eyes closed, her lips pursed round the mouth-piece of an inhaler similar to her English one, Emily was beginning to relax, her terror subsiding as the drug opened her narrowed airways.

'She may like a glass of water—asthmatics often feel thirsty after an attack,' the pharmacist said to Summer, as they re-entered his premises.

When, having paid for the inhaler, she returned to the car with the water, Emily was lying back with her head on her uncle's shoulder.

It was obvious that, but for her tan, her face would have been ashen. She looked exhausted. But when Summer offered her the water she sat up and drank it thirstily.

'Thank you.' She gave back the glass, her voice a hoarse croak. Suddenly her lower lip trembled. 'I was so frightened,' she whispered, and began to cry.

James drew her into his arms, looking down at her curly head—she was hiding her face against his chest—with a strange expression on his face.

'Poor old Freckles . . . it wasn't very nice for you. Never mind: it's all over now, and whatever it was which set you off is probably something quite rare which you won't come across very often.'

Her throat tight with tears of sympathy, Summer watched him comforting the child, his voice unexpectedly tender, his long fingers gently stroking her mop of red curls.

It was then that her mind acknowledged what her heart had known since his second kiss. She had fallen in love with him; and that complex process had not begun a few nights ago in the library at *Baile del Sol*, but months ago in the library at Cranmere.

From the moment when he had swept open the double doors and their eyes had met for the first time, she had known that here was the personification of the man of her day-dreams. No longer a figment of make-believe, he had become real flesh and blood. That was why it had wounded her so terribly to overhear his derogatory comments about her to Dr Dyer.

Since then almost everything she had learnt about him had affirmed that it wasn't merely a physical attraction but that, in many other ways, he matched up to her ideal.

Deep down, she had even accepted those lacerating remarks he had made on the Grand Staircase. He had been speaking the truth. Why should a man who respected his body have felt anything but contempt for a girl who was wrecking hers? How would she have felt about him had he turned out to be an alcoholic or a drug addict? Exactly the same as he had felt about her then.

Even her furious indignation at being kissed in the swimming pool she could see now for what it had been—a piece of self-deception. What had *really* upset her that night had been that he had reappeared before she was ready for him; before she had completed the programme of self-improvement at the end of which she had hoped to stun him with her glamour.

Now, watching him wipe the tears from his niece's cheeks with a clean white handkerchief, she was pierced by a sharp pang of longing to change places with Emily and feel his strong arm round her own shoulders.

When Emily was feeling better, he said, 'We'll go back to Sarasota and have a quiet lunch at home. The Hamiltons will understand if I call and explain. We can go see them some other time.'

Although she had been looking forward to the lunch party at Naples, Emily didn't protest at this change of plan. Clearly the unexpected and severe attack of her former malady had taken a great deal out of her.

Later in the day Summer seized the first opportunity to speak to him privately to say, 'I know what you must be thinking—that it was incredibly careless of me to let Emily go out for the day without her puffer. You don't have to reprimand me—I already feel terrible about it.

'I wasn't intending to reprimand you,' he answered.

'Emily isn't a small child, too young to be responsible for her own welfare. From now on it will be up to her to make sure she always has an inhaler with her. But as it's so long since she had an attack, and she's clearly much fitter and healthier than she was in England, it was natural for both of you to feel she had probably outgrown her asthma.'

His leniency surprised her. She had expected a blistering dressing-down, even the threat of dismissal. She had been worrying about it all the way back from Fort Myers.

'I think we should try to find out the cause of today's attack,' he went on. 'It's possible now, by means of blood tests, to check people's sensitivity to a much wider range of allergens than by the old skin-prick test. Today's experience suggests that Emily's atopic. About ten per cent of people are severely atopic and have the kind of immediate reaction she had at the Edison place this morning. As soon as we get to New York we'll get an allergy specialist to look at her. We'll fly from Tampa tomorrow. You won't need to pack much, but you'll want warmer clothes in New York. You can buy them at Altman's on Thursday.'

With these casual instructions, he uprooted them for the second time.

But this time she didn't mind. She had been happier in Florida than at any time since the loss of her parents. But she was looking forward to experiencing what was said to be one of the most exciting cities in the world, and she hoped that in New York they might see more of him than they had during their time in Sarasota.

It was strange to remember that only a short while ago she had felt she could never forgive him for those scathing things he had said about her, and that she would derive great satisfaction from having him want her, and rejecting him.

But hurt pride and vengeful feelings had no place in her heart now that she knew she loved him. To win his love—and it still seemed about as unlikely as going to the moon—had suddenly become her dearest wish.

PART THREE

MANHATTAN
NANTUCKET ISLAND

SUMMER and Emily were lying on the floor in Emily's bedroom, their pointed toes touching the carpet behind their heads in a position called The Plough, when there was a tap at the door.

Assuming it must be Victoria, and wondering why the Spanish maid was interrupting their pre-dinner work-out, Summer left it to Emily to call out, 'Come in.'

When an amused male voice said, 'A very neat pair of backsides,' her feet swept in a rapid arc from the floor behind her to the floor in front of her.

It wasn't Victoria. It was James. How typical of him to catch her with her bottom stuck up in the air and a hole in her exercise tights.

'James!' With a shout of delight, Emily sprang up from the floor and rushed to embrace him.

In her two years in America, she had grown several inches but not filled out very much. Now almost sixteen years old, she looked, in her pale blue leotard and darker blue leg warmers, like a young, gracile ballerina.

As his niece flung her arms round his neck, Summer rose and went to the music centre to switch off the tape of the half-hour exercise programme they did together most evenings when in New York.

It was now more than a year since she had reached her permanent goal weight and, after eight weeks on Maintenance, achieved Lifetime Membership of Weight Watchers. As long as she stayed within two pounds of her goal weight, and attended one meeting a month, that meeting was free of charge.

But although she was now a slim girl with a small waist and slender legs, she was never quite convinced that this would always be her shape. The fear of regressing lurked at the back of her mind. She knew that many reformed fat people did revert. Their own cells conspired against them to replace the lost flesh.

Whenever James re-entered their lives the spectre of her obesity came with him. He remembered her as she had been and perhaps he always would.

Although since their first trip to New York they had made a number of journeys about the world with him, they hadn't seen anything like as much of him as she had once hoped. He was absent from their lives far more often than he was present. Long-distance telephone calls, amusing postcards and unexpected presents kept Emily happy when he was not there. But by checking through her pocket diary, Summer had once worked out that in the six months preceding the date of her check he had spent only sixteen days with them.

Although, inwardly, she was delighted to see him, her greeting was cooler than Emily's.

'Hello, James. How are you?' she said politely, shaking hands with him.

His brown hand closed over hers and his tawny eyes made a comprehensive assessment of the figure inside the black leotard and black footless exercise tights.

The disappearance of her superfluous flesh had revealed an unexpectedly fine-boned and well-proportioned frame. As his swift up and down scrutiny included her small, round breasts clearly outlined by the clinging stretch-fabric of the leotard, and the contours of her hips and thighs, she felt her pulse quicken and found herself imagining what it would be like if he stretched out his hand and ran it slowly down her body from shoulder to hip. But her face revealed nothing of the sensual reactions he stirred in her.

'I'm well—and you are five pounds too thin,' he informed her.

'In your opinion,' she said equably.

'Why are you back a week sooner than you thought you would be, James?' Emily broke in.

For the past twelve months she had been growing her red hair which was now shoulder-length, although at the moment it was tied back with a ribbon in a curly pony-tail.

'Aren't you pleased to see me?' he asked teasingly.

Still standing close to him, she linked her arm with his and beamed lovingly up at him. 'Of course. Everything's twice as much fun when you're with us.'

'I was going to spend this week in San Francisco on my way back from Japan, but I changed my plans,' he explained, looking down at his niece with an expression reserved for her.

More than one person, observing the affection between them, had mistaken them for father and daughter. It was a bond strengthened by Emily's passionate interest in computers. When they were alone together, or with only Summer present, much of their conversation was in the esoteric jargon of computer buffs. Sometimes, at the end of a meal, they would apologise to her for spending the whole time engrossed in a discussion in which she couldn't take part. But they knew that she didn't mind being excluded from these conversations because she had an absorbing interest of her own. Often, thinking about it, she would become oblivious to her surroundings.

'Summer's in one of her trances,' Emily would say, passing a hand back and forth in front of her tutor's face to rouse her from her abstraction.

Wherever he travelled, James invariably returned with a present for his niece and something which Summer could use in what was at present a hobby but she hoped might become a profession.

'While I was in Japan I was given some beads. They're in my briefcase. Come and have a look at them,' he said to her.

They went with him down the hall to his bedroom where Victoria's husband, José, who combined the duties of butler and valet, was unpacking his employer's suitcase.

James unlocked his black leather briefcase and took out a box like a small-ish cigar box. He put it on top of a chest of drawers with a lamp on it, opened the hinged lid and removed a piece of protective wadding.

Arranged in rows on another piece of wadding—and clearly the box contained several similar layers under the top one—an array of small pearls gleamed in the light from the lamp. They were not ordinary pearls. All were irregular in shape, and their colours ranged from pale bronze to the iridescent grey of a pigeon's neck feathers.

'D'you think you can incorporate these in one of your designs?' he asked.

Before Summer could answer, Emily said, 'Why are they such funny shapes and colours? Are they rejects?'

'No, they're a special kind of pearl. They're called Biwa pearls after Lake Biwa which is where they were first made. They're cultured in mussels, not oysters, and at first they weren't popular because of their odd shapes.'

'But now they're in fashion,' said Summer, who had seen twisted skeins of the pearls in the windows of fashionable jewellers on Fifth Avenue. 'They're too valuable for me to use. Why don't you have them made into a necklace for Emily to wear when she's older?'

'She'll have all the Lancaster jewels. These were a gift which I have no use for. You're welcome to them. But you may not find them inspiring,' he said, closing the box and handing it to her.

'I'm sure I shall. They're beautiful. Thank you.'

'And a little something for you, Freckles,' he said, producing a much smaller box.

'Oh . . . what a darling little thing,' his niece exclaimed, when she found that his present for her was a tiny curly-tailed pug dog carved out of ivory. 'But why has he got this hole in him?'

'Because it's a *netsuke* which, in the days before

Japanese dress became Westernised, was a toggle which helped to secure an *inro* to the girdle of a kimono. A kimono has no pockets. Anything a Japanese wanted to carry about with him, such as tobacco or medicine, was kept in a pouch called an *inro*. I thought if you put a cord through that *netsuke* you could wear it as a pendant or a belt.'

'You find the most super presents. I love him. Thank you.' She reached up to kiss his lean cheek.

He said, 'I'm going to take a shower now. Are you both eating at home tonight?'

'Yes, and I've a splendid idea which I'm dying to discuss with you.'

'I'll be all ears, as soon as I've changed.' He glanced at Summer. 'No date tonight?'

'Not tonight.'

Once again he appraised her slim figure, reminding her of his arbitrary remark that she was now underweight.

Conscious that however long she worked for him, she would never be at ease with him, she returned to the hall.

Emily, following her, said, 'Hold my little dog in your hand. Doesn't he have a nice smooth feel?'

Summer turned the *netsuke* in her palm, deriving the same tactile pleasure from it which the younger girl had felt. Outside Emily's door she handed it back and went on to her own room.

As she put the box of pearls on her desk, she wondered why James had said he had no use for them. Did that mean that his long-running affair with Loretta Fox, a divorcee of his own age who ran a contemporary art gallery, had come to an end? Was he, for the time being, without a woman in his life? Or was it merely that Loretta wasn't the type to wear Biwa pearls?

Summer had never seen her, but she had been coming across allusions to their association in newspapers and magazines for the past eighteen months. Even Emily was aware of her existence, although

James kept his domestic life and his amorous life in strictly separate compartments.

His relationship with Ms Fox, as she styled herself, was not unlike that of a nineteenth-century man and his mistress. Obviously he saw her frequently when he was in New York, but in his household her name was never mentioned; she might not have existed.

Summer felt that, had she been Ms Fox, she would have resented being treated like a courtesan; never invited to his apartment, never introduced to his niece. But although one columnist had referred to her as an ardent feminist, apparently she accepted her exclusion from the other side of James's private life. Perhaps she was in love with him and her principles weren't proof against her feelings for him.

Summer's own love-life was as negative as it had been two years earlier. She had dated a number of men but none of them had succeeded in kindling a response to compare with her feelings towards James.

Feeling sure those emotions would never be requited, she had done her best to succumb to other men's charm but so far without success. To some extent this was because of the interrupted nature of her friendships with the opposite sex. No sooner had they begun to flourish than she was whisked away to live somewhere else. Two or three months later she would return to find her date now involved with someone else.

In the course of these abortive relationships she had learnt how to handle men who tried to rush her into bed. Not all of them did. After two decades of increasing permissiveness, the 'Eighties were seeing a swing away from hedonistic attitudes.

Most of the men she had dated—intelligent men in their late twenties—were not solely bent on a roll in the hay. They would have liked to make love to her. However, if she were not willing they weren't going to drop her on that account. She had other things to offer her men-friends. She had always been capable of talking and listening intelligently. Now, after two years of dedicated self-improvement, she was a girl who turned heads wherever she went. Not only because of her shapely size eight figure, but because of the style she had acquired.

She dressed well, but without much regard for being in vogue unless she happened to like whatever was currently the mode. Inexpensive copies of fad fashions didn't appeal to her. She preferred one luxurious silk shirt to several polyester dresses. There were not many clothes in her wardrobe, but they were all carefully chosen and kept in meticulous order so that she was never panicked by James's sudden decisions to take them to Florence or Montreal.

As she peeled off her leotard and tights, she wondered how long he meant to remain with them this time.

Everything is twice as much fun when you're with us, Emily had told him. Asked to second that opinion, Summer would have had to amend it. James's presence wasn't fun for her; it was a kind of blissful torment during which she felt twice as alive—and twice as vulnerable to pain.

Emily's splendid idea was for a computer programme and she and James spent much of dinner discussing it while Summer thought about the Biwa pearls and how she might use them.

After dinner she left the others talking and went to her room to work on her latest design. It was a needlepoint evening bag, a simple envelope style with the flap embellished with beads, shells and twists of ribbon secured by gold metal threads.

She had been bending over her embroidery frame for some time when there was a knock at the door which made her straighten.

'Come in.' She knew before the door opened who it would be.

'Am I disturbing you?' asked James, pausing on the threshold. 'Emily is watching television for half an hour, and I'd like to talk to you about her.'

Taking her assent for granted, he came in and closed the door.

Her bedroom had a sofa and a comfortable armchair, but at the moment she was seated on the dressing stool which allowed her to pull the frame close to her.

'Won't you sit down?' She indicated the sofa on the far side of the room.

As he did so it occurred to her that her puritanical aunt would have thought that he should have asked her to go to his study rather than coming to her bedroom. Victoria might think the same if she came in to draw the curtains and turn down the bed. Summer herself, although she saw nothing improper in his presence in her room, found herself peculiarly conscious that conversation would not usually be what James had in mind when he entered a woman's bedroom.

Her boxes of threads and trimmings were set out on the bed with their lids off. With them, in its own small box which she took everywhere with her, was the object she regarded as her talisman—a perfect lion's paw shell, bought from a shell dealer during her second winter in Sarasota. She felt now that seeing and wanting the lion's paw necklace in Burdines had woken the designer in her.

Hitch your wagon to a star, had been the advice of her favourite philosopher, Ralph Waldo Emerson.

The rare shell had been her star, guiding her to her *métier*.

Before sitting down James noticed the boxes of bits and pieces on the bed and went to look at them. She had several old beaded evening bags, discovered in thrift shops, too delapidated to be usable but yielding unusual metal sequins and glass bugle beads of a kind no longer to be had. Sometimes she bought junk jewellery from dime stores because it had beads or gilt spacers which she could take apart and re-use in a different way.

'What's this?' he asked, picking up the box containing the shell.

'It's *Lyropecten nodosus*, the lion's paw. Please be careful how you handle it. It's quite fragile.'

'Shells usually are. What makes you think I might damage it?'

'I didn't think that.'

'You must have done, or you wouldn't have warned me to take care. I'm aware that, in your eyes, I'm a reprehensible character, but my faults don't include careless handling of other people's treasures,' he said dryly.

It was always like this whenever they were alone together; he would say something disconcerting—often deliberately, she suspected—and watch her reaction, his tawny eyes narrowed and mocking.

Now, to avoid meeting that sardonic gaze, she resumed her embroidery. Fortunately, she was working on a piece of background, filling it in with plain tent stitch which didn't require the concentration of some of the more complicated stitches she had learnt at Erica Wilson's five-day needlework seminar on Nantucket, the summer before last.

Emily had known that Summer longed to attend the seminar. She had told James who had booked one of the forty places, paid the fee and arranged for them to be in Nantucket at that time. He had told Summer to regard it as a birthday present.

For her twenty-fourth birthday he had given her a shagreen case containing a mother-of-pearl thimble, scissors with mother-of-pearl handles, an eighteenth-century sewing tool called a tambour hook and two snowflake-shaped pieces of nacre on which to wind off lengths of thread. He had seen it in an antique shop in Paris and thought it would please her. It had.

'How could I think you reprehensible when you've been very kind to us both?' she answered.

He replaced the box on the bed and moved to sit down on the sofa.

'I don't think you've ever forgiven me for not wanting Cranmere.'

'But you didn't sell it after all. I understand you're

having it converted into a kind of very grand condominium.'

'How did you find that out?'

'I hear from old Mr Renfrew, the archivist, occasionally.'

'If you had asked me, I'd have told you what was happening there. Rather than sell the place outright to a sheik or a pop star, I decided to make it available to people more likely to have heard of Vanbrugh and who would appreciate his genius. I've had it divided into eighteen apartments. The conversions and the legal arrangements have taken some time, the first buyers are moving in shortly. One apartment is being leased for four years. The lease will expire shortly before Emily's twentieth birthday. From then on it will be hers, if she wants to stay there sometimes or even to live there. But she doesn't seem nostalgic for Cranmere.'

'No, she isn't—she loves America. But perhaps if she goes back to England later on, her feelings for Cranmere may revive. What is it about her that you want to discuss?'

'At present she's set on becoming a software engineer . . . a professional programmer,' he added.

Emily's future was safer ground; she put down her needle and looked up.

'Although I don't share your mutual passion for computers, I can speak some of the language. I do know the difference between hardware and software and RAM and ROM. I'm not totally bletcherous,' she told him, using a pejorative term she had picked up from *The Hacker's Dictionary*, a printout of computerese compiled by computer buffs at Massachusetts Institute of Technology and other computer science centres.

James laughed. 'I'm sure you're not. I'm glad you don't share our mutual passion, as you call it. I agree with Professor Weizenbaum of MIT that computer enthusiasts are always in danger of thinking that everything in life is, or should be, computable. I don't want Emily developing that kind of tunnel vision. So far she hasn't because you've been opening other horizons for her. However, I do wonder if we should start thinking of getting her into Vassar or one of the other women's colleges in a year's time. What do you think?'

Summer said, 'I feel she should go to college. Apart from the academic advantages, I think people make valuable friendships during their college years. But Emily's very resistant to the idea. She says she would rather spend the time in Italy or France, learning to speak the language really well.'

'That's another possibility which I don't dismiss,' he replied. 'I wonder if her resistance to college is because she's afraid of losing you? I'd like to be able to assure her that, if she does go to college, you'll still be with us to keep her company in the vacations. Obviously you can't commit yourself too far ahead. But, providing you don't want to get married, are you prepared to stay with us as long as Emily needs you?'

'I should think, if she went to college, she would find pretty soon that she didn't need me,' she answered. 'If things go as I hope, I shall have my career launched about the same time that she's ready to try her wings. I've sold some embroidered belts to an accessories shop on Madison Avenue. It's a long way from earning my living as a designer, but it's a start.'

'How much did they pay you for them?'

She told him, adding, 'And they'll probably sell them for ten times as much. But at this stage the money is less important than getting my name known. I had some labels woven to sew on everything I make. I'm hoping whoever buys the belts—if anyone buys them—will ask if I make other things.'

She pushed the frame aside and rose to show him the labels. They were slips of cream satin ribbon with *a Summer Roberts design* written in black.

'I hope you don't think I'm spending more time on this than on Emily. I'm not, I assure you. I only do it in the evening or when she's busy with written work.'

'It may not be mutual, but I have a high regard for your integrity,' he said. 'If it isn't Cranmere which makes you doubtful of mine, perhaps you still hold it against me that I once caught you skinny-dipping and kissed you.'

She was standing near him, and she forced herself not to move away too rapidly.

'That was a long time ago. I'd forgotten it,' she said untruthfully, returning to the dressing stool.

He said, 'I'm told that a woman never forgets her first kiss . . . or first lover. But although you've un-doubtedly been kissed many times since I introduced you to the pastime, I have the impression you haven't had a lover.'

She tried not to blush, unsuccessfully. 'I—I think that's my business.'

'It makes you a *rara avis*, which is always better than being one of the herd. Does Emily discuss sex with you?'

'She discusses love. At present she's very rom-antic.'

'As you're her principal influence, I imagine she would be.'

'I don't know that I'm particularly romantic,' she said coolly. 'I think I'm more of a realist.'

'Then you don't recognise your own nature. That piece of embroidery you're working on is a romantic concept. The swirling lines. The colours. The jewelled effect.'

He glanced round her bedroom at the personal details which weren't part of the basic décor. Post-cards from the city's art museums; a pen-and-wash drawing she had bought from a students' stall near Columbia University over on the West Side; a single, exquisite spray of white lilac from Trousselier on the Boulevard Haussmann in Paris where they had spent a few days last autumn. Flowers from Trousselier were said to be so realistic that they would deceive a bee, and the spray beside Summer's bed looked as if it had just been cut from a bush.

'Everything in this room indicates a romantic temperament. Let's hope neither you nor Emily is ever disillusioned,' he said. 'In my opinion, love is very overrated. I agree with Thomas Carlyle. *Blessed is he who has found his work; let him ask no other blessedness.*' He stood up. 'It's time I left you in peace to get on with yours. Goodnight, Summer.'

'Goodnight.'

She watched the door close behind him, then slowly resumed her embroidery. Her mind was never at peace after a *tête-à-tête* with him. He was right; she hadn't forgotten the night he had kissed her in the pool, but she was surprised he remembered it.

Why did he think love was overrated? Had he ever been in love?

She found it difficult to imagine James in the grip of an overwhelming emotion which made everything else in his life seem relatively unimportant. He was not a cold man; if he had been she wouldn't have loved him. Many times, in his treatment of Emily, he had shown his capacity for tender loving care. He had even, on that one occasion in the library at *Baile del Sol*, shown tenderness towards Summer. But although, for some time afterwards, she had hoped for a repetition of that sweet, soft, sensuous kiss, he had never repeated it.

Occasionally he had looked at her mouth or her body in a way which had sent a tremor of excitement through her, but on the few occasions when she had tried to make it clear that she found him attractive, there had been no response to her tentative overtures. Tentative because, with him, she lacked the confidence she had gained in her relationships with other men. Not only that but it was manifestly obvious that he wasn't the type who would have any doubts about his ability to make a woman want him if he wanted her. He was the least diffident person she had ever met. His assurance was part of his charm, and she knew she could never be comfortable with a man who lacked self-assurance. She didn't want to be bossed,

but she did want to feel protected; and James was a
man who, if ever he loved a woman, would never try
to dominate her, except in the bedroom.

But how could you hope to win the heart of a man
who didn't believe in love? she thought forlornly. And
who had proved that he didn't by still being unmarried at an age when most men were not only husbands
but fathers.

Why did he think love overrated? Because he had
never met a woman who stirred him to the depths of
his being? Or because he had, but she hadn't felt the
same way?

To her it was almost inconceivable that any member
of her sex could resist him if he exerted the full force of
his charm. Unless he had fallen for someone who was
already married. The thought of a younger, more
vulnerable James loving someone who could never be
his filled her with a strange pain.

She couldn't bear to think of him being hurt
although, of the two possibilities, that one was the
more hopeful, from her own point of view.

If he had once been in love, there might come a time
when he would experience again the need to share his
life with someone else. If he had never loved at all, it
might be that life's best gift would always be the one
thing which was withheld from him.

Later, when she closed her boxes and put them
away, she spent a few minutes gazing at the lion's paw
shell. For some time she had had it in mind to make the
shell the centrepiece of an embroidered choker to wear
with a very plain dress.

She had noticed in portraits of beauties of the eighteenth century that they sometimes wore ruffles round
their necks with revealingly low-cut bodices. She also
admired the Edwardian-style dog-collars of pearls
brought back into fashion by the Princess of Wales.
Some day, she was going to create a wonderful,
dramatic collar to wear with a deep *décolletage*.

Her room had a bath with a hand-shower for
washing her hair. As she lay in the warm, scented

water looking down at her firm, flat stomach and her breasts which now fitted into pretty, airy lace bras, she wondered who her first lover would be, and where he was at this moment.

She wanted to believe he was here, in the apartment; that the first man ever to kiss her would also be the first to take her to bed with him.

She wondered how James would react if, after her bath, she went to his room and said, 'May I spend the night with you?'

Would he look startled . . . amused . . . intrigued? It probably wouldn't be the first time a woman had offered herself to him, but perhaps never so directly. How would he handle a situation like that? Would he send her away? Or invite her in?

Only the sudden realisation that the water in which she was lying had lost its heat roused her from her pipe-dream; one of the many fantasies about James in which she indulged when alone.

As she rose to her feet and reached for a shell-pink bath towel, its thick pile luxuriously warm from the heated rail, she wondered how much longer she would have to go on repressing the restless longings which only he could fulfil.

But although she yearned to feel his lips on her mouth and his long lean hands caressing her naked body, she knew she would never have the courage to put her fantasy into practice.

One evening, the following week, James took them to the Metropolitan Museum of Art to hear a lecture by an Anglo-American woman who was widely known as Madame Bernier because, at one time, she had been married to a Frenchman.

She was no longer a young woman, but her elegance, her charm, her erudition and her brilliance as a speaker made her lectures notable events which were sold out months in advance and attracted very distinguished audiences.

At one time she had been features editor in Europe

for *Vogue* and, in that capacity, had met many world-renowned artists including Picasso, Matisse, Braque and Miró.

One of her most famous friends was Jacqueline Onassis, and she was known and admired by art lovers throughout America. She was also a dealer from whom James had recently bought a painting, and he and Summer had been invited to the reception after the lecture.

This took place in the museum's Grace Rainey Rogers Auditorium. Emily sat between them and, shortly after their arrival, the seat on Summer's left was taken by a man on his own.

He was in his early thirties with wheat-blond hair like Skip Newman's. As he took his place beside her, Summer felt sure he wasn't an American. He struck her as somewhat Slavic-looking, if only facially. He was tall, although not as tall as James, and she had the idea that Slavs were inclined to be stocky.

There were still some minutes to wait before the lecture began, and Emily was having a murmured conversation with her uncle. Summer looked at the heads of the three rows of people in front of them and wondered who they were. She had no doubt that everyone in the audience, with the exception of herself, had some claim to distinction. Even Emily was the grandchild of a marquess and the niece of a millionaire.

Perhaps in a few years' time I shall be a well-known designer.

The thought made her glance at her wrist on which she was wearing a bracelet of turkey wing shells attached to a cuff of very fine *petit point* canvas and surrounded by beads and embroidery.

'Do you mind if I ask you if that delightful ornament you're wearing is by a designer called Summer Roberts?' the man sitting next to her asked.

She raised startled eyes to his face.

'Yes . . . it is. But how did you know?'

'A few days ago my sister bought one of her belts. I

could see the resemblance between them . . . the combination of shells, beads and needlework, and also the subtlety of the colouring. A good designer, like a good artist, has a recognisable style . . . an unwritten signature. I'm a designer myself so I have an eye for these things.'

'Oh, really? What do you design?'

'Jewels. My name is Santerre . . . Raoul Santerre.'

She was momentarily dumbfounded. Santerre was a name as well known to New Yorkers as Tiffany, Van Cleef & Arpels, Bulgari, David Webb or Harry Winston. That one of her belts should have been bought by a member of the Santerre family, and another should recognise her style and compliment her on it, sent her spirits soaring.

Suddenly radiant, she said, 'How do you do, Monsieur Santerre. My name is Roberts . . . Summer Roberts.'

It was his turn to stare. 'This is *your* work?' with a gesture at the bracelet.

She nodded, her cheeks pink with pleasure.

'But what a marvellous piece of luck to find myself next to you tonight,' he exclaimed. 'Do you believe in destiny, Miss Roberts?'

Before she could answer it became apparent that the lecture was about to begin.

Raoul Santerre leaned closer. 'We must talk afterwards.'

As she nodded and settled back to give her attention to Madame Bernier, she became aware of Emily watching her. Turning to give a quick smile to her pupil, she encountered a glance from James which sent a thrust of irritation through her. Obviously he thought that Raoul Santerre didn't realise she was with them and had been trying to pick her up.

Trust him always to take the cynical view, she thought vexedly.

The lecture—mainly about Catherine the Great of Russia's art collection, but also about her as a woman—was riveting.

As befitted a former *Vogue* editor, Rosamund Bernier came onstage in a dress which Summer recognised as a Mary McFadden. She had one of those rare speaking voices which, once heard, is forever recognisable; and the even rarer ability to make each member of her audience feel that she was talking to them alone. Illustrating her talk with slides shown by not one but two projectors, she made Catherine II, Empress of Russia for almost thirty-five years, come alive with extraordinary vividness.

By the time the lecture was over, Summer had forgotten her new acquaintance on her left, and her annoyance with James. As the applause died away, she leaned towards him, saying warmly, 'That was unforgettable! Thank you for bringing us. What fascinating women—Catherine *and* Madame Bernier.'

'I'm glad you enjoyed it. I hope you'll meet her later on—although everyone here wants to do that.'

But later they were introduced to her and, in close conversation, she was as warm, witty and delightful as she had seemed during her virtuoso performance in the auditorium. Glancing at James while Rosamund Bernier was talking to them, Summer had a feeling it would take a woman of this quality to capture his heart, and in spite of the transformation she had achieved since leaving England she knew she wasn't in Madame Bernier's class.

Probably no young woman could compete with the vivacious lecturer any more than a man in his twenties could vie with a man like James, still physically magnificent but with the suavity and humour which younger men lacked.

Wishing she had the wit to contribute an amusing remark which would make him look as warmly at her as at the ravishing Rosamund, she listened and smiled and longed to be five years older with a broader experience of life and some of the relaxed charm of this entrancing older woman.

Summer hadn't spoken to Raoul Santerre after the

lecture because someone in the row behind had touched him on the shoulder and engaged him in conversation. He had had his back to James's party as they left their seats. She wondered if he would seek her out during the reception, and what he had meant by the remark about destiny.

James knew many of the people there and he introduced his niece and her tutor to some of them. As she had in the presence of the lecturer, Summer played a minor part in the conversation which followed these introductions.

It was while she was standing quietly on the fringe of an animated discussion of the lecture that a voice said, 'If we can find a mutual friend to introduce us, I can ask you to have lunch with me tomorrow.'

She turned to find Raoul Santerre standing beside her.

'Or, better yet, if you haven't already dined this evening, to eat with me tonight after the reception,' he added.

She smiled at him. 'You don't need an introduction, Mr Santerre.' Because he spoke perfect English with only the faintest trace of Frenchness underlying his American accent, she decided not to continue addressing him as a Frenchman.

'Everyone in New York who is at all interested in jewels must have pressed their noses to the windows of Santerre et Cie.'

'Are you interested in jewels, Miss Roberts?'

She laughed. 'Isn't every woman?'

'Yes, but for many different reasons. To some women jewels are status symbols. To others they are fashion accents. They may also be collectors' pieces, or even investments.'

'I suppose I see them just as beautiful objects . . . feasts for the eye. I can't say I long to possess them—or not the very valuable jewels which you show in your windows. I'd be frightened of losing them, or having them stolen. This is my kind of jewellery.'

She lifted her lightly clenched hand to show him the

ring she was wearing on her little finger. It was an intaglio, the design hollowed out of the stone so that, if it were applied to a soft material such as sealing wax, it would leave an impression in relief. The design was the crest of a coat of arms; a mailed arm emerging from a coronet.

He took hold of her wrist to look closely at the carving. 'Rose quartz, but not in its original setting. Is this your family's crest?'

She shook her head. 'I found the stone in a box of cheap beads from a thrift shop in Florida.'

'The setting isn't worthy of the stone.'

'I know. It should be gold, not silver. But at the time—'

'Won't you introduce us, Summer?'

Intent on the ring, she hadn't noticed that the group beside them had broken up and now only Emily and James were standing near them. Until his sardonic voice interrupted her explanation of why she had economised on the setting, Raoul Santerre's hold on her wrist hadn't seemed an undue familiarity. But now, with James's attention turned on them, she felt like snatching her hand away. At the same moment the jeweller released it and smiled at the others.

'I recognise you, Mr Gardiner. I am Raoul Santerre. How do you do?'

When the two men had shaken hands, Summer said, 'This is Mr Gardiner's niece, Emily Lancaster. I am her tutor.'

'A pleasure to meet you, Miss Lancaster.' As he took her thin hand in a gentler clasp, he gave a slight, courtly bow. Then he turned back to James.

'I'm impressed by Miss Roberts' talent as a designer. As I told her before the lecture, my sister has a belt embroidered in the same style as this ornament she is wearing tonight. In recent years a number of women have demonstrated a talent for designing jewels. Picasso's daughter, Paloma, designs for Tiffany, and many of their most beautiful pieces are the work of Angela Cummings whose husband is their gem-buyer. For some time we've been looking for a woman designer, but it's difficult to discover a truly original talent. I'd like to find out if Miss Roberts' originality with her needle can be applied to precious stones. May I take her away and discuss this with her?'

James looked at him thoughtfully for some seconds before he said, 'Why not come back to our apartment where you can see other examples of her work?'

'That would be even better.'

Raoul had come to the lecture by taxi. When they left the reception he joined them in the hired Lincoln Continental which James used when in New York. He sat beside the driver and Raoul sat next to Emily and talked mainly to her about other lectures by Madame Bernier which he had attended.

His irises were the same deep blue as Hal Cochran's, but his eyes held more shrewdness and intelligence. Summer hadn't seen Hal again after that first winter in Florida, and she wondered if he had managed to keep his weight down. Sometimes it was harder for men if their wives or whoever cooked for them wouldn't co-operate.

She herself now had no trouble in maintaining her weight at its present level. Not only was she much more active than in her fat days but, although it had taken a long time, the Weight Watchers programme *had* re-educated her palate as the lecturer had promised them it would. Now she genuinely preferred a carton of natural yogurt to a couple of chocolate-chip cookies, French beans to French fries, and a tangerine to a sugary, creamy dessert.

She knew that, if she had still been fat, this moment in her life would never have arisen. Probably James would not have included her in tonight's outing. Even if he had, she wouldn't have been dressed as she was in a shirt-dress of cream crêpe de Chine with the eye-catching band round her wrist. Raoul Santerre wouldn't have noticed her except for her obesity.

When they reached the apartment, James said, 'Help Summer to carry her embroidery frame to the living room, will you, Emily?'

'Wouldn't it be easier for Mr Santerre to come to my room?' Summer suggested.

'As you wish.' He had used his key to open the front door, but now he touched a bell to summon José.

The weather in New York was still cold and both men were wearing chesterfields over their suits. Emily had on her camel-hair coat, and Summer was wrapped in a black wool cloak with arm-slits. She had a small silver fox muff to keep her hands warm. She had bought it at a shop on 57th Street where rich women sold last year's furs. Even there it had been quite expensive. But now she had some private means as well as her salary. The cottage had been sold and James had advised her how best to invest the purchase price. The income from this capital wasn't enough to support her—in Manhattan it would barely pay the rent on a one-room, walk-up apartment in a seedy district—but it meant that if she lost her present job, she wouldn't be destitute.

Sometimes she had the feeling that, some day, she and James might have a difference of opinion which even their mutual concern for Emily's feelings wouldn't restrain from becoming a volcanic row.

While they were taking off their outer garments, the manservant appeared from the staff quarters and took charge of the two men's coats.

'My room is this way, Mr Santerre.' With her cloak folded over her arm, she led him along the hall, leaving James speaking to José.

However, a few moments later, he followed them. Evidently it was all right for him to visit her bedroom, but not for another man—however innocuous his purpose—to spend any time there alone with her.

Rather amused by James's sudden regard for the proprieties, she laid her cloak on the bed and removed the muslin dust-cover from the frame.

'This is an evening bag I'm making, and I've one or two other things in a drawer. A spectacle case . . . two small trinket boxes . . .'

He looked carefully at all her work, making no comments and showing no reaction.

'Where were you trained?' he asked her.

'I've never had any training . . . well, apart from an embroidery seminar in Nantucket taken by Erica Wilson. But it's not very difficult to learn embroidery techniques from books.'

'You've never been to art school?'

She shook her head.

'Summer is the daughter of a professional artist, Thomas Roberts,' said James who, by this time, knew that the *trompe-l'oeil* paintings at *Baile del Sol* had been done by her father.

'Ah, and he taught you about line and colour?' said the other man, looking at her.

'No, he died when I was a child. But although I can't draw at all well, I think I've inherited something from him.'

'A great deal, Miss Roberts. This isn't the work of an enthusiastic amateur. I can't pretend to be an expert on embroidery, but I take an interest in all the applied arts including the world of fashion. I think you're a natural innovator like the English dress designer, Zandra Rhodes or, here in New York, Norma Kamali. I'd like to find out if you can be equally innovative with diamonds and sapphires.'

Emily was hovering in the doorway. James said, 'Let's go and have a drink, shall we?'

Before he left it, the other man glanced round the bedroom and his eye was caught by the spray of white lilac.

'That looks like a flower from Trousselier.'

'It is,' said Summer.

'I thought so. The silk flowers imported from Hong Kong are attractive, but they aren't minor works of art. Have you spent much time in Paris, Miss Roberts?'

'Only a few days, but I loved it. Do you spend much time there?'

'I was born there and lived in Paris until I was twenty. Now I'm a New Yorker and only go back for

vacations. I like the American way of life, and I find
Manhattan a very stimulating place to live. Like Mr
Gardiner I have an apartment not far from here,
although my *pied-au-ciel* is smaller than this,' he
added, as they reached the large living room with its
spectacular views of the city by night.

'You say *pied-au-ciel* . . . does that mean you com-
mute to the country at weekends?' James asked him.

'Not often at this time of year, but in summer—yes,
most weekends. I've a house at Old Lyme near the
mouth of the Connecticut River. For a hundred miles
upstream, the river valley is one of the most beautiful
and historic parts of New England. Perhaps you know
it.'

'I do, but Emily and Summer have only been in
America for just over two years and most of their time
has been spent in Florida and Nantucket. They're only
here at the moment because my niece needed some
urgent dental treatment. Normally they stay in Florida
until the weather in the north is warmer. But now that
they're here, they'll probably stay until they can go to
Nantucket.'

While James was speaking, José had been uncorking
a bottle of champagne and filling three glasses. There
was a fourth glass on the tray but before he filled it he
murmured something in Spanish to which James replied in the same language.

Summer guessed what José had been asking when
he poured champagne into the fourth glass, although
not to the level in the other glasses.

He presented the tray to her first. She smiled and
thanked him, taking the smallest glass, and waited for
the others to take theirs. It didn't surprise her that
James had asked for champagne because he often
drank it.

But she was surprised when he raised his glass to
her, and said, 'It's a memorable occasion when a
creative artist receives his or her first recognition. I
think tonight is that occasion in your life, Summer.
We'll drink to your success as a designer. But I must

make it plain to you, Santerre, that for some time to come she is committed to her present career as Emily's tutor.' His keen gaze swung back to her. 'Success!'

The other two echoed the toast and drank to it.

'Thank you.' She sipped her champagne.

'I seem to remember reading that your family have some connection with Carl Fabergé, the goldsmith to the Imperial Court of Russia until the Revolution,' James said to the Frenchman.

'Yes, my maternal grandfather was one of Fabergé's workmasters. When the firm was closed down by the Bolsheviks in 1918, Fabergé escaped as a courier attached to the British Embassy. He was already an old man, and he died two years later in Switzerland. My grandfather was younger. His first wife had died, and after he settled in Paris, he married the daughter of a French jeweller whose fortunes he greatly enhanced. My father was their youngest son.'

Raoul paused to drink some champagne before he continued, 'Having escaped being shot by the Bolsheviks, my grandfather didn't intend to be victimised by the Nazis, so a few years before the Second World War, he came to America. But my father felt himself to be a Frenchman and he joined the Free French forces, and after the war he married a French girl. He was a man of action, never a craftsman. But I took after my grandfather.'

'I have a Fabergé elephant,' said Emily. 'He's red with tiny little diamond eyes. Daddy gave him to me for Christmas, a long time ago, but he isn't here. He's in Florida.'

'You must come and see the collection of Fabergé animals which we have at our shop on Fifth Avenue,' Raoul said to her. 'Why don't you both come . . . tomorrow. You, too, Mr Gardiner, if it would interest you.'

'Unfortunately I'm busy tomorrow, but I'm sure Summer and Emily would enjoy it,' said James.

'Come at half past eleven. After I've shown you round, we'll have lunch,' Raoul suggested.

*   *   *

A week later, when Summer was having dinner with him at Le Cirque, Raoul said, 'You know, it's crazy that you should have to waste time playing governess to Gardiner's niece. Every moment of your life should be devoted to developing your talent.'

'In that case, I shouldn't really be dining with you, Raoul. I should be at home, studying those books on jewellery you lent me,' she told him teasingly.

It was strange how comfortable she felt with him. He was an attractive, sophisticated, worldly man; but he didn't unnerve her as James did. Raoul was an open, outgoing personality. She felt that, behind a suave façade, her employer was a private person who never fully revealed himself to anyone. Not to Emily. Probably not to Loretta Fox.

The day they had visited Santerre et Cie, Raoul had insisted she must take off her rose quartz ring and let him re-set it for her.

'It offends my eye, that cheap setting. I'll make something more appropriate. I'm a qualified gold-smith, you know,' he had told her. 'Not that I have as much time for practical work as I should like.'

Now, having ordered the wine to accompany the dishes they had chosen, he produced from an inside pocket a small chamois bag.

'I hope you'll like what I've done to your ring.' He tipped it on to the damask cloth.

The new gold shank gleamed in the lamplight. Yet somehow it didn't look new. When she picked up the ring she saw that the bezel surrounding the stone was delicately engraved.

'It's perfect, Raoul. Is this an old setting which happened to be the right size for the stone?'

'No, no—I made it for the stone. Nowadays most gold alloys are produced by large refining companies. But a few manufacturing jewellers still alloy and melt their own gold. Santerre are among them. For your ring, I used the slightly redder gold which is popular in Europe; although not in England where they like a yellower gold. I've tried to make the setting look the

same age as the intaglio, but it's difficult to be sure
how old it is.'

He took the ring from her and slid it over her little
finger. Then he placed her hand on his palm, fanning
her fingers by sliding his own between them.

'You have good hands for rings. I don't care for
hands which are too small, with long sharp nails like
cats' claws. In fact you have all the features a woman
needs to wear jewels well,' he told her. 'A long neck,
pretty ears, a fine skin. Unfortunately, most of my
designs are destined to be worn by women whose skin
has long lost the bloom of youth, or who, if they are
young, have no elegance.'

Had James held her hand on his and discussed her
physical attributes, she would have found it disturbing. Raoul's touch and his compliments pleased her.
Her only unease had to do with the setting he had
made and how to deal gracefully with the question of
payment.

He seemed to read her mind. He said, with a smile,
'Now you're worried that I'm about to present you
with an exorbitant bill for my services. But I made the
new setting for my own pleasure.'

'It's terribly kind of you, Raoul. I never dreamt of
having a ring custom-made by one of the Santerres.
But apart from your skill there's the gold . . .'

He put her hand on the banquette between them
and gave it a friendly pat.

'The gold's an investment from which I may reap
rich dividends if you become a designer for us. But
first you have to learn something about the materials
we have at our disposal, and what can and can't be
done with them. For example, most rose quartz is full
of what we call inclusions, which are particles of
foreign matter. For that reason it's usually carved or
made into beads. Talking of your ring, when you go to
England it would be interesting to find out whose crest
you have there. There's a shop in London which
specialises in heraldic objects—crested silver and
porcelain and so on. They find lost heirlooms for

people. They would probably recognise that crest.'

'If it's English. It might be French, or Italian. I'd love to know how it found its way to a thrift shop.'

During dinner he told her about his mother's collection of antique cameos, most of them cut from agates unlike the nineteenth century and modern cameos which were almost all cut from shells.

The evening flew by as, prompted by her eager questions, he talked with knowledge and enthusiasm of the world's finest jewels from their origins in remote mines through the workshops of master craftsmen to vitrines in museums, or bank vaults, or the rich women's jewel-cases from which they were sometimes stolen to be broken down and refashioned.

'I'm afraid I've bored you,' he said, taking her home.

'Not for a second. You're as riveting as Madame Bernier.'

He laughed. 'That's carrying flattery too far.'

'No, I mean it,' she told him seriously. 'I enjoyed her lecture enormously, but I'm more interested in the things you've told me tonight. James and Emily spend hours talking about computers, and I can see that, to them, it's the most fascinating subject in life. But it leaves me cold. Well, no, that's an exaggeration. There are some aspects which interest me. But I could never be a programmer, and Emily is bored by needlework.'

The block where James had his apartment had a high level of security with two porters on duty round the clock so that it was impossible for any unauthorised person to sneak into the building while the porters' desk was unattended.

Raoul accompanied her to the elevators. She wondered if, as it wasn't late, he was hoping to be asked up for a nightcap. But having no sitting room of her own, it was impossible for her to entertain her dates. Up to now, she hadn't wanted to.

'Thank you again for an excellent evening,' she said, holding out her hand.

'Thank you for being such an excellent listener.' He

turned her hand palm uppermost and brushed it lightly with his lips. 'Goodnight, Summer.'

When, using her key, she let herself into the apartment, the double doors between the lobby and the living room were wide open. During the day they usually were, but at night they were more often closed.

She had intended to go straight to her room, but instead she found herself looking at James who was sitting in a chair facing the open doors. He was listening to someone on the telephone, but he beckoned her into the room and she couldn't ignore the signal.

Dropping her muff on a chair, she unclasped the collar of her cloak. There had been a beautiful cloak clasp in the collection of Fabergé objects at Santerre et Cie. It had consisted of two octagonal panels, linked by a chain. The centre of each panel had been set with a sherry-coloured citrine framed by rose diamonds surrounded by a diamond trellis on a ground of pale blue enamel. The panels had been bordered with green and red golds chased with laurel leaves. Raoul had taken the clasp out of its glass case to show them his grandfather's initials on the back of it.

As she took off her cloak, James said to the person on the telephone, 'Yes, very well. That suits me. Goodbye.' He replaced the receiver and stood up. 'You've been dining with Santerre, I believe?'

He had been out all day. Emily must have told him when he came in.

She said, 'Yes, and learning some fascinating things. Do you know about the Merensky Reef in South Africa?'

'It rings a bell. Is it a platinum mine?'

'Yes. How clever of you. I'd never heard of it.'

'I've been around longer than you have. I'm about to have a glass of Armagnac—will you join me?'

She didn't think he had beckoned her into the living room in order to have a drink with him, but she said, 'Thank you—yes. I've never been sure of the difference between Armagnac and Cognac.'

'They're both brandies, but made in different areas of France. Armagnac used to be the name of a province in the south-west. Have you read *The Three Musketeers*?'

'Yes.'

'D'Artagnan, the leader of the King's Musketeers, was a real person—Charles Castelmore, Seigneur D'Artagnan. He was a Gascon, and Gascony was part of the province of Armagnac. When I was a small boy I was a great admirer of the Musketeers' wrists of steel and iron thews. Perhaps that's why I've always preferred Armagnac to Cognac. Some people think it's an inferior brandy. It's not. It's just different and less widely advertised.'

Occasionally he would say something which would make her warm to him. Now, the picture of him as a child, losing himself in the adventures of Alexandre Dumas' dashing swordsmen, just as Emily used to lose herself in tales of knights and fair ladies, was unexpectedly touching.

He brought her a tulip-shaped glass, not very large but, she noticed, of very thin glass. Her glass and his own were only about a third full.

'Never trust a man who gives you brandy in a huge balloon,' he told her. 'He's an ostentatious fool who knows nothing about brandy and probably not much about anything. If the glass is too big, the fragrance of the brandy is thrown off before it reaches your nose. An even more heinous crime, which one sees in far too many restaurants where they should know better, is for the glass to be heated over a flame. It ruins a fine brandy. The makers of Remy Martin don't approve of warming the glass with one's palm, but most connoisseurs disagree with them on that point.'

She watched him hold the glass near his nose, give the liquid in it a slight swirl, and inhale the aroma as he was drinking. She followed suit.

'What else did you learn from Santerre?' he asked, some moments later.

'Oh, innumerable things. Apparently the finest

sapphires come from Kashmir. They were discovered in a valley fifteen thousand feet up in the Himalayas. There'd been an avalanche. When the snow melted, these wonderful blue crystals were lying on the earth. But sapphires come in other colours, too. Green . . . violet . . . purple . . . pink . . . yellow.'

'You seem to have had an instructive evening. Did he tell you much about himself?'

The question was casually put, but she sensed that now they were coming to the point of the conversation.

'A certain amount, yes,' she said warily.

'Is he married?'

There was a pause. Raoul's marital status was something which had never occurred to her.

She said, 'No, I'm sure he isn't. If he were, he wouldn't have asked me to have dinner with him.'

He gave a harsh laugh. 'For *naïveté*, there seems to be little to choose between you and Emily. I should think if a count could be taken of all the men in Manhattan who are spending this evening with women other than their wives, the total would be quite substantial. Santerre's not a boy. He's thirty at least, and engaged in a very successful family business. Isn't it likely he would be married?'

'He's never mentioned his wife.'

'There are circumstances in which men don't,' he said caustically. 'Girls with any sense ask, in an indirect way. It can save a lot of trouble later on.' He paused, looking down at her with frowning impatience. 'Would it upset you if I told you he was a married man?'

'Yes . . . yes, it would . . . very much. I—'

'You can relax. He isn't. I checked him out earlier this evening. But it's time you were more on your guard. The men you meet aren't to know how guileless you are. They're likely to assume that a good-looking girl of your age knows most if not all the answers.'

She said angrily, 'Raoul Santerre is interested in my

potential as a designer, not as a bed partner. You may view every woman in that light, but not all men do.'

'Which just goes to prove how little you know about men. *All* men—unless they're homosexual or exceptionally happily married—look at any attractive female with an eye to bedding her. It's a law of life,' he said dryly. 'Women do the same thing. Don't tell me you haven't noticed that Santerre's not a bad-looking guy. Would you have dined with him tonight if he'd been fifty and paunchy? No. You'd have found some excuse.'

'If he'd been fifty, I should have expected him to be married. What do you mean: you checked him out?'

'I talked to someone who knows him. Up to about a year ago he had a girl living with him, but apparently that's over now. He has no involvements.'

'I don't think Raoul's personal life is any of my business—or yours. I'm sure you'd be most annoyed if you found someone had been prying into your private life.'

'It would depend who was prying,' he answered. 'If I were dating a young girl, I'd expect her father to make enquiries about her. Don't tell me you're not a young girl and I'm not your father. You're a virgin, and I'm the only watch-dog you and Emily have. As long as you're under my roof, I'll keep the same eye on you that I shall on her later on.'

Summer said stiffly, 'Your enquiries about Raoul may have been made from excellent motives, but they weren't necessary. The fact that I—I haven't slept with anyone doesn't make me some kind of halfwit. I agree that two years ago I was glad to be extricated from a slightly tricky situation with Hal Cochran. Today I should never get into that kind of awkward corner.'

She paused, waiting for his comment. When he said nothing, she went on, 'As far as Raoul is concerned, whatever you may say about men's attitudes to women, he's interested in me as a prospective designer. Tonight's dinner wasn't a date. It was exactly like a business lunch . . . a pleasant way of discussing some of the technicalities of jewellery design. We had very little personal conversation.'

'Yet you've admitted that it would have upset you to find out he was married?'

'Yes, but not because it matters to me whether he's married or not. I just feel that, even in business relationships, there are certain things which aren't done. Had he been married, I should have expected him either to bring his wife with him, or to ask me to dinner at their apartment. I think an honourable man tries to avoid situations which could be misinterpreted. For a married man to have dinner with a single girl, however innocently, could cause malicious gossip which might reach his wife and make her unhappy.'

Again James received this in silence, his expression inscrutable.

After a moment, she added, 'When you say I *admitted* it would have upset me, you make me feel as if I were on the witness stand and you were the attorney for the prosecution. I hope you're not going to take that attitude with Emily when she's older. You'll be making a mistake if you do. If you badger her about the men she meets, you'll only make her secretive.'

They were standing in the centre of the room. As she finished speaking, he turned and strolled across to the expanse of uncurtained glass which always made her feel as if she were on the flight-deck of a space ship hovering above Manhattan's soaring towers of light.

He was dressed for an evening meal at home in a cashmere sweater over a Madras shirt. The soft canary-coloured cashmere seemed to emphasise the hardness and fitness of the body it clothed. His free hand was thrust into the pocket of his pants, pulling the fabric tighter across his muscular buttocks.

Watching him, wondering what he was thinking, she found herself thinking that d'Artagnan of the steely wrists and iron thews probably hadn't been any more powerful than her employer. In another age, he would have been a horseman and swordsman. Being a twentieth-century man, he played tennis, skied, sailed and windsurfed. But if the circumstances ever

arose that he had to fight for his life, she felt sure he
would be just as dangerous an adversary as the
Gascon aristocrat. She had felt his power in the pool at
Baile del Sol, and that had been only a fraction of his full
strength. And yet he was capable of gentleness. She
had a mental picture of his long fingers stroking
Emily's hair after her bout of asthma at Fort Myers.

He swung to face her. 'I shall never alienate Emily
because she trusts me,' he said. 'We have our dis-
agreements from time to time but they don't disturb
our basic liking for each other. With you, it's a different situation. You're always on the defensive.'

He came back to where she was standing. 'I can only
conclude it has to do with the first time I kissed you.
Although I should have thought that subsequent
kisses would have cured any lingering trauma caused
by mine. You have allowed your various men-friends
to kiss you, I assume?'

Her face, still golden from the Florida sun, became
peach-coloured as the blood burned in her cheeks
under his quizzical scrutiny.

'Naturally,' she said huskily.

'Did you enjoy it?'

As she opened her mouth to protest that it was none
of his business, he added swiftly, 'Don't flare up at
me. I'm asking a serious question. There has to be
some reason why you're always on edge when I'm
around. You are, aren't you?'

Made uneasy by his closeness, she turned away and
moved, as he had, to the windows. Attempting
casualness, she said, 'You needn't worry. You haven't
damaged my libido. I just happen to be reserving it for
someone I really care about.'

'That makes sense—provided the man you have in
mind isn't such a paragon that no flesh-and-blood guy
can ever match him. There aren't too many *sans peur et
sans reproche* types about, you know.'

The reference to Bayard, the knight without fear and
above reproach, brought her swinging round.

'If Emily has said that I'm waiting for a Bayard, she's

wrong. The man I'm waiting for isn't a paragon. He'll have his faults as I have. You don't believe in love. I do. I grew up with people who loved each other. Their kind of happiness is worth far more than all this'— with a gesture encompassing the beautiful room and its spectacular outlook. 'I'm not so idealistic that I think love can make even poverty bearable. But I do believe that a couple in fairly modest circumstances can be wonderfully happy if they love each other— happier than millionaires surrounded by every possibly luxury except love.'

He sat down on the arm of a sofa.

'Perhaps; but you can't be sure your parents would have continued to be happy had they lived. I agree with John Ciardi's definition of love as a label for the sexual excitement of the young, the habituation of the middle-aged and the mutual dependence of the old. I'd prefer to avoid the second phase and, when I'm old, I'd sooner have a pretty nurse than a querulous elderly wife.'

'What about your dynasty? How will you found that without a wife?'

'That's a problem I'm working on. Would you like some more brandy?'

'No, thank you. It's time I was in bed.'

As she placed her glass on a table near where he was sitting, he said, 'What's happened to your ring?'

Surprised that he had ever looked at it closely enough to notice the change, she said, 'It's been re-set.'

'May I see?'

Before she could slip it off and hand it to him, he reached out a long arm to take hold of her wrist and draw her closer.

'Mm . . . an improvement on the silver setting,' he remarked. 'Did Santerre have this done for you?'

'Yes, the other setting offended his jeweller's eye.'

He looked up at her. 'Is your pulse always this rapid?'

'You make me nervous,' she admitted, standing

beside his outstretched long legs, wishing he would let her go.

'I wonder why?'

There was no answer to that; she didn't know herself why he was the one man with whom she was never at ease unless someone else's presence ensured that he wouldn't do anything unpredictable.

His tawny glance slid from her face to the rounded contours of her breasts under the cream crêpe de Chine she had worn for Madame Bernier's lecture. His strong hand slipped from her wrist to imprison her fingers.

'Relax,' he said softly. 'I don't bite.'

She felt as if she were hypnotised; unable to speak or move—scarcely able to breathe—until he chose to release her from the powerful aura of his masculinity. She had never been more aware of a man's body; the wide, muscle-armoured shoulders stretching the soft yellow cashmere, the solid wall of his chest, the flat stomach, the long hard thighs.

Her own body was supple and firm now, but close to him she felt fragile, her muscles puny compared with his, her strength feeble if ever he chose to exert his against her.

As she was thinking how easily he could overpower her, he lifted his free hand and very gently brushed her cheek with the backs of his fingers.

'You have a beautiful skin.' He was looking into her eyes. She could see the gold flecks on his irises.

'Thank you,' she murmured on an uneven breath. Her heart seemed to have stopped beating.

His hand uncurled, sliding round to the back of her neck, there to caress her nape as softly and delicately as he had stroked her hot cheek. It was impossible to look away. She was trapped by his stare and his touch.

His long fingers spread and slid upwards to hold her head still while he leaned slowly closer and trailed his lips from the top of her cheekbone down to the curve of her jaw.

A shiver ran through her. Her eyes closed. In a

movement outside her control, her free hand rose to his shoulder. As his mouth hovered not far from hers, she felt her other hand released and his arm thrown round her, pulling her off balance, making her fall on to his thighs.

Although she was now more experienced than she had been the last time this happened, other men's kisses were no preparation for the arms and lips of the man she had loved in secret for almost two years.

Her mouth softened under his, her body yielded, she clung.

When, some time later, he stopped kissing her but continued to hold her in his arms, she opened her eyes and found him looking down at her flushed cheeks and parted lips with an intent, frowning expression.

After a moment or two he stood up, lifting her with him and putting her back on her feet.

'Much as I'd like to continue this, I think, with Emily to consider, it's better we don't complicate things, do you agree?' he asked briskly.

She had never wanted anything more than to resume their embrace, to press herself closely against him and feel those strong arms closing round her, that hard mouth softening on hers.

But she forced herself to say, 'Much better.'

Whatever wayward impulse had prompted him to kiss her, she knew it was not a kiss to be taken seriously. There was nothing she could do but pretend it had meant as little to her as it had to him.

The next morning he flew to Chicago, leaving Emily downcast and Summer free to continue seeing Raoul without their meetings being monitored.

Later that day she had a jubilant call from the owner of the shop on Madison Avenue to tell her that one of the belts had caught the eye of *Vogue*'s accessories editor and was going to be shown in a future issue of the glossy, with a credit for her and for the shop. All the other belts had sold. How soon could she deliver another consignment?

Summer would have liked to discuss this development with Raoul but she hesitated to call him. She didn't want him to think her pushy. She would wait for him to call her.

It was almost a week before she heard from him. Meanwhile she burned a good deal of midnight oil finishing the evening bag and beginning a wrist-band to match the belt bought by his sister. It was to be a gesture of appreciation for the setting he had made for her.

She was studying one of the books he had lent her when he called.

'I wondered, if you're free this evening, if you and Emily would like to come and see my apartment and try my speciality—kidneys *à la brochette*?' he suggested.

'We'd love to, Raoul.'

That the invitation included Emily increased her liking for him. Obviously he realised that she wouldn't have wanted to go to his apartment on her own till they had known each other longer; and perhaps he also discerned that by now she and the younger girl were virtually sisters.

He gave her his address and suggested they arrive at seven.

Although he had said that his apartment was smaller than James's, as soon as they stepped out of the cab at his address she could tell by the elegant canopy from the edge of the sidewalk to the entrance, and by the liveried doorman waiting to usher them inside, that the block where Raoul lived was as exclusive as theirs.

He had told them not to dress up and Emily was wearing her favourite pale blue corduroy pants embroidered with green frogs, and a blue Shetland sweater over a blue turtleneck. Summer was dressed in the same way except that her pants were plain cream corduroy worn with a boy's cream cable-knit tennis pullover and a shirt. The shirt was navy to match the stripe around the waist and cuffs of the pullover.

When Raoul opened the door he had a butcher's apron over jeans and a plaid shirt with the collar open and the cuffs turned back. The hair on his forearms was so fair as to be almost invisible. His skin seemed very white by comparison with James's teak tan or even with their lighter tans. But it was a time of year when most people in Manhattan were pale after months with little sunshine.

That he shook hands with them both, before taking their coats, was, she thought, the Frenchman surfacing. An American's greeting would have been more casual, and it was unlikely that an American would have kissed her hand with the accustomed ease with which he had performed that delightful gesture the last time she saw him.

'We're eating in the kitchen,' he told them. 'But we'll have a drink in here first'—showing them into his living room. 'What can I get you?'

Summer asked for a soda water, Emily for Coke. Then, while he was getting their drinks, they looked with interest at their surroundings.

The most striking feature of the room was a huge modern painting of a choppy sea flecked with white horses under a sky of broken clouds.

Although he was busy putting ice into tall glasses, and not watching them, Raoul said, 'The picture is by Bonade.'

Clearly all his visitors looked at the painting before anything else.

The white clouds and foam, and the blue sky reflected in the tossing water, had been used as a theme for the room's décor. Most of the furniture was white, but one sofa was covered in blue linen and the white curtains had blue borders.

The room was recognisably designer-decorated. As Summer was wondering who had done it, he said, 'I used to have a girl-friend who was an interior designer. She decorated the apartment for me.'

And lived in it with him for a while, Summer

concluded, remembering what James had told her about him. She wondered why they had split up.

While Emily made a bee-line for his bookshelves, Summer was drawn to the corner with a large sloped drawing table and a wall panelled with cork to which he had pinned numerous clippings, sketches, swatches of fabric and other references.

On the table was an intricate drawing of a necklace, obviously inspired by the photograph, pinned beside it, of a spider's web beaded with dew and glistening in sunlight.

Raoul took Emily's Coke to her, then brought Summer's drink and his own—a glass of red wine—to his working area.

'That's a design for platinum and diamonds,' he told her. 'Those very delicate links and claws wouldn't be feasible in gold. Platinum is the perfect setting for diamonds—if they're set in gold they pick up yellow from the metal—and also the most secure one because of its hardness and strength.'

'It's beautiful, Raoul. Will you make it yourself?'

'No, I don't have the time. Platinum takes longer to polish than gold. That's one of the reasons, apart from its rarity and purity, why it's so expensive. Eighteen carat gold is only about seventy per cent pure. Platinum is ninety-five per cent pure. I'd like to make this necklace, but I have too much administrative responsibility to be able to craft all my designs. Nor do I have the skills. I know the theory of diamond cutting, but I'm not capable of putting it into practice.'

They had supper sitting on tall stools round the breakfast bar in his pine-walled kitchen.

'How come you're such a good cook?' Summer asked, as they ate lambs' kidneys wrapped in bacon and broiled on skewers, with baked potatoes and sour cream, and a side salad redolent of garlic.

'I'm not. I can cook three things—a steak, an omelette and these. Do you like to cook?'

'Yes. I cook on Victoria's night off. You must come and try my chicken with apples and brandy.'

In place of dessert he served cheese and fruit. Summer had a thin sliver of Roquefort and a pear which she cut into pieces and ate very slowly. The eating habits of a slim person were becoming second nature to her.

For coffee, they returned to the sitting room where Emily was happy to continue looking at Raoul's books while her elders talked about jewellery.

At ten o'clock they went home after a relaxed, happy evening which was the forerunner of many pleasant threesomes.

In the following week or two, Raoul introduced them to many aspects of New York which they might not have discovered without him. He took them to a performance of the dance division of the Juillard School, a hot-bed for future stars in all the performing arts. He took them to the Amato Opera Theater down in the Bowery to hear singers who might one day be stars at the Metropolitan Opera Company; and he took them to the Met itself although, at the time, they had no idea that orchestra seats were hard to come by and very expensive.

The night José and Victoria went to visit his brother in Queens, and Summer cooked her *pièce de résistance*, was the night James reappeared.

Emily and Raoul were playing backgammon in the living room and she was busy in the kitchen when she was startled by a buzzer. Looking up at the indicator panel above the kitchen door, she saw that the summons came from the lobby and knew instantly that James had come home and was ringing for José.

Her immediate reaction was dismay that he should have chosen tonight to descend on them. Leaving her preparations, she went out of the kitchen and along the short passage beyond which was the lobby.

Mustering a polite smile, she greeted him with, 'You picked the wrong night to come home. Victoria's out and I'm deputising as cook.'

He smiled at her. 'Hello, Summer. How are you?'

'Fine, thanks. How are you?'

'In need of a shower and a pick-me-up. It's been one of those days.'

He was unbuttoning his coat. For the first time since she had known him, he looked tired and rather drawn.

'Let me take your coat.' She moved round behind him.

'Thanks.'

'I'm afraid we have a guest to supper. We weren't expecting you, and—'

'No need to apologise. Who is it?'

'Raoul Santerre. He took us to hear Placido Domingo at the Met last week and this is by way of a return.'

Whatever comment he might have made was forestalled by the doorbell, heralding the arrival of one of the porters with his baggage. This was a sound which could be heard in the living room even though tonight the double doors were closed. As Summer was putting his coat on a hanger in the closet and he was opening the outer door, Emily appeared.

'James!' Her face lit up.

She flung herself into his arms for a hug. As he looked down at her, Summer saw his hard, cynical face take on the softer expression and the look of indulgent affection which was his invariable reaction to the sight, after an absence, of his niece's fiery red mop and ear-to-ear beam.

'You're just in time for a gourmet dinner cooked by Summer,' she told him.

'So I hear.' He thanked the porter for bringing up his suitcase and hanging bag, closed the outer door and said to Summer, 'Am I going to ruin the soufflé if I take a quick shower first?'

She said, 'Dinner won't be ready for half an hour yet, and there's nothing to spoil if I have to hold it back longer. Why don't you have a hot tub with a whisky sour or a daiquiri?'

She knew there was a hot tub in his bathroom because sometimes, when he was away, she and Emily used it. The first time she had seen his Manhattan bathroom, she had been amazed. It had trees growing in it; and a wall of mirror-glass which reflected the fabulous view from the huge floor-to-ceiling window; and a trapeze like the one which the butler had told her James had rigged in an attic at Cranmere.

'I'll do that,' he agreed. 'I'll be exactly twenty-five minutes.'

She went back to the kitchen where she had been making the sauce for curried eggs. She had already shelled the lightly boiled eggs and chopped the chives to sprinkle over the curry sauce. The Chicken Normandy was cooking in a casserole in the stove and she was going to steam the vegetables while they were eating the first course.

As she was piping mashed potato on to a baking tray, Emily came in followed by Raoul.

'James wants champagne. Raoul is going to open it for us.'

She showed him the special insulated and temperature-controlled cupboard in which there was always a selection of the best champagnes, including the rare still champagne known as *vin nature*.

'Her uncle is a man who knows how to enjoy his fortune,' said Raoul when, after he had poured some champagne for Summer and himself, and half a glass for Emily, she had gone off to take the bottle and an empty glass to James. 'He's not, like many of our customers, a man with more money than taste.'

She was about to reply that James came from a family which had been rich for centuries when she thought better of it, and said only, 'No, he's very discriminating.'

He watched her finish piping the Duchess potatoes.

'I can see you enjoy doing that. You don't despise the domestic arts?'

'Oh, no—I like them. I'd love to have a place of my own, which I could furnish and where I could give dinner parties.'

'My friend, Louise, who decorated my apartment,

wasn't domesticated. She was very good at her profession and always beautifully dressed, but she couldn't cook and she didn't want to have children,' he said, contemplating his glass with a sombre expression.

'Are you still in love with her, Raoul?' she asked gently.

Somehow she felt it was all right to ask him a question she would never have dared to put to James, had it arisen.

He looked up. 'No—no, I'm not. I was in love with her, but not any more. It was mostly sex between us, and that isn't enough for a marriage which is going to last. My attitude to marriage is French, not American. I'm not a practising Catholic, but I don't believe in divorce. Marriage should be for life. Do you agree?'

'I'd like *my* marriage to be for life.' She put the tray of potato rosettes in the oven to set for a few minutes while she beat an egg to brush over them.

'Have you ever loved a man, Summer?'

Avoiding a direct answer, she said, 'I feel there's plenty of time. I'd like to achieve something on my own account before I settle down to being Mrs John Doe—although designing should mesh with marriage better than some careers.'

As she slipped her hands into the pockets of a double oven mitt, preparatory to taking out the baking tray after another minute or two, he came round to her side of the work-island and said, 'I think you're going to make someone a very happy man.'

And then he tipped up her chin and kissed her lightly on the lips.

'Oh . . . sorry!'

Sweeping through the swing door, Emily saw what was happening and hurriedly backed out.

Inwardly, Summer groaned. She didn't mind Emily seeing Raoul kissing her, but she didn't want James to be told and, sooner or later, Emily always told him everything.

She said, smiling, 'You're distracting me from my duties. I think you'd better go back to the living room or dinner may wind up a burnt offering.'

An answering smile in his blue eyes, he said, 'Okay, I'll get out of your way.'

James was in the living room with the others when she summoned them to the dining table. The worn look had gone. He looked refreshed and revitalised.

The dinner was a success. The curried eggs, which she served in white bowls on green cabbage-leaf saucers, looked attractive in their orange-coloured sauce with a sprinkling of dark green chives, and the yolks were just as they should be, still slightly fluid.

The Chicken Normandy, cooked with smoked bacon, apples and New England applejack in place of Calvados, the French apple brandy specified by the recipe, was eaten with relish by everyone.

To complete the meal she had assembled an interesting cheese board, the cheeses bought at Zabar's, a West Side delicatessen recommended by Raoul, which had also supplied the French bread.

'That was a splendid meal, Summer. I must make sure I always come home on Victoria's night off,' said James, leaning back in his chair at the head of the table.

'Thank you. I'm glad you enjoyed it.'

Emily helped her to clear the table and load the dishes in the dishwasher.

While Summer was making coffee, Emily said, 'I'm sorry I barged in at the wrong moment.'

'You didn't,' Summer said lightly.

She would have liked to add, *But I'd rather you didn't mention to James that Raoul kissed me.*

But then Emily would want to know why, and that was something she couldn't explain, except by saying that James might tease her, which was only one of the reasons she didn't want him to know she and Raoul were now on kissing terms.

The two men were drinking Armagnac and talking politics when they joined them.

'We haven't finished our game of backgammon, Emily,' said Raoul.

The two of them moved away to the backgammon

table, leaving Summer to pour out the coffee while
James went to choose some music.

The tape he selected began with Elisabeth Schwarz-
kopf singing *Sei Nicht Bos* from *Der Obersteiger*. As the
lovely soprano voice began the song of an ambitious
girl rejecting the courtship of a young fisherman—
'Don't be cross, it can never be. God bless you and
don't forget me'—he relaxed his long frame in a comfortable chair.

Taking a cup of coffee to him, she wondered what
kind of relationship he had with Loretta Fox that it
wasn't to her apartment that he went for relaxation at
the end of a gruelling trip.

Perhaps she was like Raoul's ex-girl-friend, primarily a careerist who had no use for traditional male and
female rôles. Maybe she never wanted to lean on his
shoulder, or sometimes to cosset him.

But what kind of woman never needed to feel taken
care of by a strong, protective, dominant male? And
what kind of man, however powerful in his public life,
never wanted, in private, to have an adoring female
waiting on him? It must be an arid relationship which
excluded those elements of human nature and
confined itself to sex, she reflected.

Having beaten Raoul at backgammon, Emily said,
'You haven't told James your most exciting news,
Summer.' She perched on the arm of his chair. 'One of
her belts is going to be featured in *Vogue*.'

'Really? Congratulations, Summer.'

He sounded genuinely impressed, but she was conscious that it must seem a trifling achievement to a
man who had made the name Oz a household word.

Later that night, lying awake, she wondered what,
if any, significance to attach to Raoul's kiss before
dinner. Had it, like James's kiss, been merely an
impulse? Or a sign Raoul felt they were two of a kind
who might one day become more than friends?

Another Frenchman, Antoine de Saint-Exupéry,
had written: *Love does not consist of gazing at each other
but in looking outward together in the same direction.*

With Raoul that would be possible. They had so much in common. Perhaps it had been destiny which had brought them together at the Bernier lecture. Perhaps he was the man who could cure her of her ill-advised love for James.

James's cottage on Nantucket was a spring and fall retreat rather than a summer place.

In winter not many people other than the hardy Nantucketers stayed on the flat, windswept island thirty miles south of Cape Cod. In high summer it swarmed with tourists. Only between those seasons was it at its best; and its peak of perfection were warm, cloudless days in late spring when all the fine old trees and well-kept gardens in the town surrounding the port were in fresh green leaf, and the white picket fences and the white window trims on the old grey-shingled houses built by whaling captains, and others who had prospered in the island's first heyday, were bright with fresh paint as the islanders prepared to receive the summer people.

On a sunny morning in May, before Memorial Day when the holiday season started, the quiet streets of Nantucket Town with their brick sidewalks and eighteenth- and nineteenth-century houses, ranging from the white-columned mansions of the whaling merchants to the more modest dwellings of the craftsmen who serviced the ships, were a delightful place to wander.

For a hundred years, Nantucket had been the world's premier whaling port. Because that historic time in the island's annals had been followed by disasters and depression, the town had escaped the modernisations which would have destroyed the original character of the place. Instead, it had survived its reverses to become one of the nation's architectural jewels; an unspoilt example of how a flourishing maritime community had lived and contributed an important chapter to the history of America.

In Nantucket, Summer and Emily lived in shorts

and sneakers and went everywhere on foot or by bicycle. If the weather was cool they wore Nantucket Reds—brick-coloured yachtsmen's trousers which gradually faded in the wash to a soft pink—and hand-knitted black sheep's-wool sweaters from the Irish imports shop on Main Street. If it rained, they wore foul-weather gear.

The cottage was reached by a cat-walk from the end of one of the old wharves. It was built on pilings and, at night, they could lie in their bunks and listen to the water lapping against the heavy timbers which supported *The Fo'c'sle*. The name was a seaman's abbreviation for the forecastle or crew's quarters.

The cottage was kept in order by an energetic, cheerful widow, Hetty O'Brien. It had a double bedroom where James slept, and two smaller bedrooms with bunks, one above the other. The kitchen was tiny, like a galley on a yacht, and the living room wasn't large. However, there was also a spacious roofed balcony outside the living room and this, when the weather was fine, was where they spent most of their time, surrounded by the comings and goings of the waterfront.

There were always two or three seagulls standing on the ridge of *The Fo'c'sle*'s shallow-pitched roof, and sometimes a gull would perch on the top of the flag-pole from which, when they were in residence, they flew the Stars and Stripes.

Their third spring sojourn in Nantucket was the best yet. Everywhere they went they were recognised and given friendly greetings by the local people, and by now they had a wide circle of friends among other people 'from off' who loved Nantucket and had weekend and vacation houses there. Even when James was not with them, they had many invitations to brunches, barbecues and beach picnics.

It was from Mrs O'Brien that Summer learnt that James's liaison with Loretta Fox had come to an end.

The caretaker let fall this piece of gossip one morning while Emily was at the Atheneum, changing her library books. Mrs O'Brien looked after two other houses for their owners, and had come upon the item about James in a gossip column in a discarded copy of the *New York Daily News*.

'It said Mr Gardiner's close friend, Ms Loretta Fox, was moving her art gallery to California,' she told Summer. 'I never heard of her before. She never came here. Did you know her?'

'No, I didn't, Hetty.'

'She can't have been that close a friend if you didn't know her.' It was a disingenuous remark for Mrs O'Brien was perfectly aware what the term close friend implied. She appeared to be more intrigued than shocked by the discovery that James had had a mistress.

'I don't think gossip columns are ever very reliable sources of information,' said Summer. 'Half the things they print are probably inventions.'

'There's no smoke without fire, they say. I think it's time he was married and starting a family. Maybe now he'll look round for a wife. There's no shortage of nice girls who'd have him, that's for sure.'

Summer remembered the night she had asked James how he was going to found his dynasty without a wife. And his reply: *That's a problem I'm working on.*

Had the break-up with Loretta been impending then?

If the stories about him had some substance, she had been only the third of his long-term close friends. Which, for a man of his age, was a comparatively sedate sexual history. Many men with his looks and his means would have had women galore.

The following Friday evening he arrived on the island.

Emily was at a friend's house on Pleasant Street, and Summer was alone on the deck sewing a button on a shirt cuff, when she heard a firm tread on the cat-walk and looked up to see him striding towards her, dressed for New York, with a raincoat over his arm and a briefcase in his other hand.

'Hi! How are you doing?' was his greeting.

As usual, he hadn't let them know he was coming. *The Fo'c'sle* was not on the telephone, but Mrs O'Brien's house, nearby, had a telephone and he could be contacted through her if anything urgent arose.

'We're fine. It was raining this morning, but the forecast for the weekend is good. Emily's visiting with Muffy, but she'll be back soon.'

'I'll go and get changed,' said James.

He disappeared into the cottage and she heard him starting to whistle as he crossed the living room. He didn't sound like a man left in low spirits by the departure of a woman who had been important to him.

When he reappeared he was wearing a pair of Nantucket Reds so bleached by the sun and many washings that they were paler than a strawberry ice. He was carrying a bottle of red wine and two glasses.

'Are you eating in or out tonight?' he asked.

'In. We were going to have sweetcorn and steaks, but I haven't been over to the A & P to buy them yet if you'd rather we had something else.'

'That sounds fine to me—I'll come shopping with you. There's no hurry. Let's have a glass of wine first.'

He poured out the wine, put one of the glasses beside her, and settled himself in a canvas director's chair which, like all the furniture on the deck, could be folded and stacked in a store room when the place was closed up.

'I heard on the plane coming over that a house on Orange Street may be coming on the market soon,' he told her.

Orange Street was famous for having, in the space of a century, been the home of one hundred and twenty-six sea captains. The old houses in the historic part of town didn't change hands often. When they did, they fetched high prices.

'Perhaps I might buy it,' he said thoughtfully. 'The cottage is fine for short stays, but it has its limitations.'

In the light of what she had learned from Mrs O'Brien, this remark had a significance which otherwise might not have struck her. It seemed to confirm that his mind was turning towards marriage. Certainly *The Fo'c'sle*, poised over the waters of the harbour, with railings through which a small child could easily fall, was a place where the mother of young children would never dare to leave them alone for a moment.

She was sipping her wine, and wondering how James would go about choosing a wife, when he stopped surveying the harbour and turned his head to look searchingly at her.

'What's the matter, Summer? Pining for your boy-friend?'

'If you mean Raoul, he isn't my boy-friend and, no, I'm not pining for him or pining at all. Why should I be? I like Nantucket.'

'I know you do. But even a favourite place can lose its charm if it's a long way from one's favourite person.'

'My favourite person is right here with me,' she answered.

His tawny eyes glinted. 'You overwhelm me. I had no idea you felt so warmly towards me. There've been times when I've felt I was almost your least favourite person.'

Determined not to be flustered by his mocking glance, she said, 'I meant Emily—as you very well know.'

'Ah, I see. How disappointing. I thought for a moment you were declaring a secret *tendresse* for me. It is Leap Year when, by tradition, your sex are allowed to take the initiative.'

She managed a rather forced smile and, attempting to match his banter, said, 'I should think declining a proposal might tax even your *savoir-faire*. Or, knowing how irresistible you are, did you take the precaution, at the beginning of the year, of preparing a gracious refusal in case that contingency arose?'

He laughed; and then, slowly, his expression

changed until he was watching her with an intent, narrowed gaze which she found even more unnerving than his previous badinage.

'What makes you think I would refuse?' he said. 'If you were to ask me to marry you, I might say yes. Why not try me?'

She searched for a flippant riposte with which to counter this strange joke. Thank God he had no idea it wasn't a joke to her! If he had been serious, it would have been a dream come true. But of course he couldn't be serious.

To her relief she saw his niece running along the cat-walk.

'Here comes Emily,' she said.

James rose to his feet. 'You think I'm kidding, don't you?' he said, looking down at her. 'I'm not. We'll talk about it later.' Then he turned away to greet the younger girl.

Half an hour later the two of them went off to the A & P supermarket to buy the ingredients for supper. Summer had made an excuse to opt out of this expedition. She needed some time alone to recover from being thrown off balance by those extraordinary remarks before Emily's arrival. The more she thought about them, the less sense they made. What could have possessed him to tease her on such a subject. At worst it was cruel and at best in very poor taste.

They were starting their supper that night with corn on the cob when Emily suddenly stopped nibbling the sweet yellow kernels to ask, 'What do you two think about people living together?'

'What makes you ask?' James enquired.

'Muffy's sister is living with someone and her father is furious and won't let them share a room when they come to stay. That makes the boy-friend furious and he won't come with her any more. Then she doesn't enjoy herself and cries, and her mother gets upset and cries too. Muffy says it's making life miserable for the whole family, and they always used to be so happy.'

James finished eating his first cob. They were all

wearing lobster bibs to stop drops of melted butter from falling on their clothes.

He wiped butter from his firm lips before he said, 'I think Muffy's sister's boy-friend needs straightening out. If he's serious about her, he ought to be able to stand a few nights in separate rooms to appease her father. If he isn't serious about her, she's going to cry a lot more when he ditches her for someone else. What do you think, Summer?'

She had wondered what he would say and was faintly surprised that his assessment of the situation matched her own.

'I agree,' she said. 'How old is Muffy's sister, Emily?'

'Nineteen.'

'In that case it's hardly surprising that her father doesn't approve. She's too young to commit herself to any one boy-friend . . . in so far as living with some-one is a commitment, which I don't think it is really. At nineteen a girl should be finding out what kind of person she is, not trying to meld her life with someone else's. That comes later, when *she* knows who she is.'

Emily looked thoughtfully at her. Recently she had had her hair cut short again—very short. The stylist had shown her how to blow-dry what was left of her curly mop into the kind of head-shaping cap seen on statues of ancient Greeks.

She had also had her ears pierced and now wore fine gold rings in her delicate lobes. Since hearing Rosamund Bernier's lecture, and seeing that she, too, had freckles, she had given up regretting her own. With every month that passed now, she left childhood further behind and showed more clearly the promise of lovely womanhood.

Tonight, wearing an off-white Nantucket black-smith's shirt from Bobbi Wade's shop on North Beach Street, with a green scarf which emphasised the green in her hazel eyes knotted round her slim neck, she was like a flower ready to bloom.

'Do you know who you are yet?' she asked.

'I think so . . . just about. I certainly know that if my father were alive and he didn't approve of unmarried people sleeping together under his roof, I'd feel he was entitled to make the rules in his own house.'

'But would you live with someone if you loved them?'

Summer would have found it easier to answer this question if James hadn't been with them. Although she talked frankly and freely to Emily when they were alone together, in his presence this was a topic she would have preferred to avoid.

'I don't know,' she admitted. 'I'd hope that, if I loved someone, he would love me enough to want to marry me. I feel that "Will you live with me?" is like saying "I think I love you, but I'm not sure. If I hang on, I may meet someone I like better than you."'

'How do people know for certain that they're really and truly in love?' Emily asked, looking first at Summer and then at her uncle for enlightenment.

'If they want to live happily ever after they marry for much sounder reasons than the heady state of being in love,' was his dry reply. 'That never lasts more than six months.'

His niece slowly twirled her corn holders, revolving the half-nibbled cob.

'Sometimes it does.'

Summer knew what she was thinking. Emily was in love with Skip Newman, and had been since the winter before last. Whether it was an emotion which would outlast her teens, who could say? That seemed to depend, in part, on whether he was still free when her budding looks burst into flower and he realised that she was no longer his little pal, Freckles.

'I've heard of people being in love all their lives and never being able to marry each other,' she added.

'Oh, yes—an unconsummated passion will burn indefinitely,' said James. 'But the flame soon dies down once they start sleeping together. It's like Christmas pudding; if you ate it all the time it would become as unexciting as bread.'

Summer felt this was being much too damping with a sensitive sixteen-year-old.

She said, 'That depends on the bread. You can eat lovely hot, home-baked brown bread every day of the year and not get tired of it. And that's what true love is like, Emily. Sir Walter Ralegh wrote a poem about it.

> But love is a durable fire
> In the mind ever burning;
> Never sick, never old, never dead,
> From itself never turning.'

She gave James a level look; willing him not to produce some cynical comment which would tarnish Emily's bright dreams.

At her age, romantic ideals were as right and proper as believing, at five, in Father Christmas. It was one thing to make her aware of the danger of mistaking infatuation for real love; but to make out that love never outlasted the fulfilment of desire was going too far.

Emily looked at her uncle. She said, 'I think married people can love each other all their lives. Muffy's grandmother was talking about a movie star whom she liked when she was a young girl. He was a Frenchman: Charles Boyer. Have you heard of him?'

His mouth full of corn, James nodded.

'He and his wife were married for forty-four years. A few days after she died, he killed himself. He couldn't bear to go on living without her. Forty-four years is a long time, and he was very handsome and charming and must have had lots of women throwing themselves at him. Next time we're at the apartment, or in Florida, I'm going to watch out for one of his movies being shown on late-night TV. I'd like to see what he was like.'

'And add him to your pantheon of heroes,' her uncle said teasingly.

'You have heroes, too,' she said equably. 'Washington . . . Dr Johnson . . . the Iron Duke. You even took the name of one of your heroes. Why did you change your name from Lancaster to Gardiner, James?'

Summer found herself holding her breath for fear that Emily had broached a subject better avoided. James never spoke of his pre-American life. As far as she knew, he hadn't set foot in England since the business of disclaiming his title and disposing of Cranmere had forced him to return to his birthplace.

'I thought if I ended on Skid Row it would spare my relations any further embarrassment.'

His tone was casual, but there was something about his expression which made Summer suspect that his niece's question had been an unwelcome reminder of things he preferred to forget.

From the days when she had accompanied her aunt to church every Sunday, a text from Proverbs came into her mind. *The spirit of a man will sustain his infirmity; but a wounded spirit who can bear?*

Once James had wounded her spirit but, eventually, she had got over it. What had happened to him as a boy that his wound still festered, she wondered.

With the steaks and the salad, they finished the bottle of wine he had opened earlier. For dessert they had apples and yogurt.

'I'll make the coffee,' said Emily.

She had brought the tray through to the living room—the nights were not warm enough yet to eat on the deck—when a computer nerd named Dave came by.

'If you've nothing better to do, Em, how about coming over to my place and helping me thrash out a problem.'

There was no computer at the cottage, but that didn't mean she was deprived of her favourite pastime in Nantucket.

'Sure, Dave, I'd like to. Is that okay with you two?' she asked them.

James said, 'As long as you're home by ten o'clock.'

While she went to her room to fetch a sweater, Dave began to explain his problem to James who cut him short, saying, 'Sorry to be unhelpful, Dave, but tell it

to Emily, will you? I have a problem of my own to work
out this weekend.'

When the two younger people had gone off to
Dave's parents' guesthouse, he said to Summer, 'Let's
have another bottle of wine, shall we?'

'I won't have any more, thanks. I've had three
glasses already.'

'Go wild! Have four. You can afford to put on half a
pound.'

It was odd that within a few minutes of believing
herself to be free of all rancour towards him, he should
test that belief by reminding her that he had known
her when she was enormous.

The reminder didn't make her flinch. She had been
slim for long enough now not to have any more
nightmares, not to worry about getting fat again.
Every morning she stepped on the scales. If her weight
was more than a pound up she ate less and exercised
harder till it was back to where it should be.

'All right,' she agreed, starting to pour out the
coffee.

He fetched another bottle. The table had already
been cleared and the dishes loaded in the machine.
They were now alone till Emily returned, and she
couldn't think of any reason to avoid spending the
evening sitting with him. She had washed her hair the
night before. She couldn't pretend to have a date
because, if she had, why wasn't he coming to collect
her? She could only hope that someone they knew
might stop by and prevent James from resuming the
conversation interrupted by his niece some hours
earlier.

'Does Emily spend a lot of time with Dave?' he
asked, filling their glasses.

'No more than with anyone else. Muffy is her closest
friend here. They have endless chats about life.'

The seating arrangements inside the cottage consisted of two long sofas placed in a corner at right
angles with a shared end table, and two armchairs
forming a compact conversation area for six to eight

people. Normally Summer occupied one sofa and Emily the other, both with their feet up on the squabs. Tonight she had purposely avoided sitting on a sofa in case James decided to join her there. She didn't know why he should, but she felt that he might. In fact she felt very uneasy altogether. She still hadn't worked out what he could possibly have meant by those strange remarks about marriage, and the rider that he hadn't been kidding.

'I flew down to see Cordelia Rathbone at Palm Beach last weekend,' he told her. 'I'd heard that she hadn't been well, but she denied it and she seemed as sprightly as ever. As you know, she's never been to *Baile del Sol* since you and Emily arrived there, and she's never suggested that I take Emily to see her. In fact, although I haven't mentioned this before, when I told her I'd taken charge of Emily, she said she wanted nothing more to do with any Lancasters.'

'That's rather a bigoted attitude, isn't it?' said Summer. 'She likes you. Why shouldn't she like Emily?'

'When I bought the house from Cordelia, she didn't know I had any connection with the man who gave her a bad time. That only emerged later on. Anyway, suddenly she's changed her mind. She's coming to New York soon—I suspect for a second opinion about her health—and she wants to meet Emily. She tells me, and she may be right, that after two decades out of fashion the débutante party is back. Girls are being introduced to society as they were way back in the 'Fifties, in white dresses with their fathers in white tie. What's your opinion? Do you think that kind of thing has any place in modern life?'

'I'm not sure. It might seem frivolous extravagance, but it must provide a lot of employment,' Summer said thoughtfully. 'The caterers, the florists, the bands, the dress shops, the hairdressers—all those people must benefit. As to whether Emily would enjoy being a deb, or hate it, I really don't know. But I foresee one problem,' she added.

'What's that?'

'I think by the time she's eighteen, perhaps even sooner, she's going to be a stunning girl. As an outstandingly lovely débutante, she might attract a lot of publicity and it might be found out who she really is. And once she was revealed as Lady Emily Lancaster, granddaughter of Lord Cranmere, it might blow your cover, so to speak.'

'That's where Cordelia comes in. She could present Emily. I shouldn't have to be involved. She feels that as Emily hasn't been to Miss Porter's or one of the other right schools, a débutante year would give her a chance to make friends with girls of the right sort. Cordelia, as you'll have gathered, is a tremendous snob.'

'Yes, but I thought you were a democrat; or, to be more precise, an autocrat with democratic views.'

'Above all, I'm a realist,' he answered. 'Emily isn't going to be happy married to anyone who can't keep her in the style she's used to. The right husband for her will probably be a brother of Cordelia's "right sort of girl".'

Summer said, 'Or a socially *un*prominent computer nerd like Dave, with whom she has much more in common than some of the Preppies around here.'

'Some hackers are Preppies,' he said dryly. 'But at the moment it's not Emily's matrimonial prospects which concern me.' He smiled at her. 'Have you thought over what I said earlier about this being Leap Year?'

She drained the last of her coffee. 'It didn't make sense to me.'

'Okay, I'll put it more plainly. I want to marry and have children. I think you and I get along together pretty well. I'm suggesting you change your rôle slightly—from being Emily's mentor to being my wife,' he said casually.

She had sensed this was in his mind, but she hadn't been able to believe it. She reached for her wine and, amazingly, her hand was steady as she picked up the glass and drank.

'Without your loving me or my loving you,' she said flatly.

'You know my views on that score. We have better qualifications for living in harmony than that. We've known each other for over two years. We have no foolish illusions that either of us is perfect. You know my faults. I know yours. As far as your career as a designer is concerned, I'm in a position to relieve you of all the domestic burdens which would interfere with your work. Those are the practical considerations. Looking at the other aspects, I see no reason to suppose that we shouldn't enjoy making love together. Do you have any doubts about that?'

'I—I've never considered it.'

'Think back to the times I've kissed you.'

'They're a long time ago. I don't really remember what I felt,' she said untruthfully.

'That's easily remedied.'

He made a movement towards her.

She jerked back, saying sharply, 'No!'

If it had been his intention—and undoubtedly it had—to draw her out of her chair and on to the sofa beside him, her recoil changed his mind.

He gave a slight shrug. 'Don't panic. I realise you may need time to get used to the idea. You can have time. It's taken me quite a while to make sure we have the makings of a workable marriage. I don't expect you to accept that premise without equally long and careful thought.'

She said stiffly, 'What does Oz think about it? I'm sure you haven't arrived at this life-changing decision without consulting your computer.'

Her sarcasm only amused him. 'A computer can't think,' he said mildly. 'You should know that by now.'

'If medical computers can make diagnoses, I'm amazed you can't programme Oz to select a wife. I feel sure you have. But I'm puzzled as to why my rating should be higher than the rest of the short list.' She hesitated, then added recklessly, 'In what way am I superior to your close friend Ms Fox, for instance?'

His mobile dark brows drew together in a sudden frown. She could see that she had annoyed him and it pleased her that, for once, she had managed to break through his guard.

He said curtly, 'Loretta and I split up some time ago—for the reason I was talking about earlier when we were discussing living together with Emily. Loretta and I didn't live together but, as you're obviously aware, we had a physical relationship. It suited us both for a time, and it ended by mutual consent because we'd grown bored with each other. But if you're afraid that I'd be an unfaithful husband, you needn't be. I've never been a stud, and illicit affairs aren't my style.'

It was her turn to shrug. 'I believe you, but it doesn't concern me what your habits are in that respect. I don't have to think it over. I can tell you right now that I'd never marry anyone for the reasons which you've put forward. I don't want a "workable marriage". I'd rather stay a single career-girl and hope that one day I'll be asked to marry someone because he loves me and can't live without me.'

She jumped up from her chair. 'Excuse me: I'm going for a walk.'

One of the nice things about Nantucket was that, unlike Manhattan, it was a safe place for people to wander about alone after dark. No menacing figure was likely to emerge from the tree-shadowed lanes which offered short-cuts between many of the main streets.

Not that she was in a mood for ambling. She stepped out briskly, feeling she needed exercise to work off the irritation induced by James's crazy proposal.

What a strange, unemotional, cold-hearted man he was to imagine that she or any woman, except possibly an outright gold-digger, would be willing to marry him on those terms.

Poor Emily if, having outgrown her calf-love for Skip, she fell in love with a young man who didn't

meet with her uncle's approval, or that of the snobbish
Mrs Rathbone. Between them, they would make her
life hell. Yet Mrs Rathbone's first marriage should
have proved to her the unwisdom of marrying a man
who was eligible but not lovable.

Had Summer had any money on her, she would
have gone somewhere for coffee or a drink, and stayed
away from the cottage till Emily's return defused the
tense atmosphere which would make it embarrassing
to be there alone with him.

But as she had left *The Fo'c'sle* without even a dollar
in her pocket, and she didn't want to go on walking
round town for another hour, she had no choice but to
go back and hope that, during her absence, James had
also gone out.

Seeing, from some distance away, that the place was
in darkness, she gave a sigh of relief, but her relaxation
was short-lived. When she reached the end of the
cat-walk she saw a tall figure sitting on the railings
surrounding the deck with his back against an upright.

She couldn't walk past him and go inside the cottage
without saying something—but what?

James solved the problem by turning to face her.
'Hello. Enjoy your walk?'

His tone was as affable as if her outspoken rejection
of his proposal had never happened.

'Yes, thank you. I'm going to make some more
coffee. Would you care for some?' she asked politely.

'Good idea. By the way, how's the designing going?
What have you been working on since you've been
here?' he asked, following her inside.

When she told him, he wanted to see her sketches
and with some reluctance, for she felt his interest was
assumed, she brought them for his inspection.

'I haven't had a satisfactory idea for the pearls which
you gave me after your trip to Japan,' she said.
'Perhaps if Emily does make her début, I can use them
on an evening bag for her, or even design one of her
dresses.'

'For the time being don't mention that to her. We'll see how she gets on with Cordelia. If they don't take to each other, the idea will fall through.'

'Wouldn't being a deb conflict with your plan to send her to college?'

'Apparently not. Most of the current crop of debs are either freshmen or sophomores. According to Cordelia, the revival of the début doesn't mean a rebirth of the social butterflies of her era. The contemporary deb has brains as well as breeding, and she wants a career as well as a husband.'

On the safe topic of Emily's future, she had become less conscious of the awkwardness of turning down one's employer, even when no feelings were involved. Now the word husband rekindled her discomfiture.

He said shrewdly, 'Don't look so worried. Nothing has changed. There's no need for you to feel uncomfortable.'

'I—I may have been rude to you . . . certainly ungracious,' she said, flushing. 'It was so very unexpected. I expressed myself too forcefully. I'm sorry.'

'Don't apologise for speaking your mind.'

His tawny gaze shifted to her mouth. She knew he was going to kiss her and this time she didn't recoil but stood still, hypnotised by the glinting smile in his eyes and the curling movement of his lips as they drew back from his white teeth. The certainty that, in a moment, she would feel those firm lips on her own made her insides clench with excitement. But she showed no visible reaction as he put his hands on her waist and drew her towards him.

She had discarded her sweater while she was fetching her sketches. His palms were warm through the thin Madras cotton of her pink and blue Ralph Lauren shirt. He slid his hands higher up her sides, making her sharply aware of their closeness to her breasts. In spite of her unisex clothes—the boyish plaid shirt and pale blue jeans—she had never been more conscious of her femininity and of the soft contours of her body compared with the hard planes of his.

Their bodies were not in contact when he bent to kiss her. But soon they were breast to chest, hip to hip and thigh to thigh, as they had been in the pool in Florida. Only this time she wasn't naked and she wouldn't have cared if she had been. Nothing mattered but being in his arms, clasped to his tall, strong body, her hands clutching his broad shoulders, her lips soft and yielding under the pressure of his.

This time he wasn't as gentle as he had been in New York. For a few mad moments, she thought he might pick her up and carry her to his bedroom. If he had, she wouldn't have resisted. Love and longing blazed up inside her and reached a flashpoint, consuming all her normal controls and leaving nothing but an aching need to respond to the urgent desire which she knew had flared up in him. She could feel his body's reaction to holding her and kissing her.

Once she would have struggled to break free, but tonight she had reached a pitch when her starved senses clamoured for fulfilment. The physical proof that he wanted her ignited a wild exultation. She flung one arm round his neck while her other hand travelled higher, delving into his dense dark hair and feeling the shape of his skull.

He lifted his head and said thickly, 'Now do you doubt that we should enjoy making love?'

Without waiting for her to answer, he tilted her head back and began kissing her neck, making her gasp and shudder as he found a place behind her ear where the heat and pressure of his mouth was almost unbearably pleasurable.

But that delicious sensation was abruptly terminated when the sound of footsteps on the cat-walk and the murmur of voices reminded them they were not alone at the cottage.

With a smothered exclamation of annoyance James straightened and slackened his hold on her. For three or four seconds they stared at each other, both with heightened colour and fever-bright eyes.

Then, knowing that in a few moments Emily and Dave would breeze in, she broke free from James's already loosened embrace and fled to the privacy of the bathroom.

At first light, after a restless night, Summer went for another walk. When she returned, James was doing press-ups on the deck. The sight of his muscular torso immediately reanimated the feelings she had been striving to suppress.

Annoyed with herself, she gave him a frigid good morning as he sprang lightly on to his feet.

'Wait a minute.' As she would have entered the cottage, he caught her by the wrist, forcing her to halt. 'Emily isn't up yet—which gives us a chance to finish our conversation.'

'I don't think there's anything more to say. What happened last night didn't prove anything . . . or change anything. I—I'd prefer to forget it,' she said stiffly.

He lifted an eyebrow. 'Can you?'

The answer to that was—No, never. Not if I live to a hundred.

While she was searching for a false answer, he said, 'Okay, we don't have to discuss it now if you don't want to. But I believe you'll change your mind eventually. Take your time . . . think it over carefully. It makes a lot of sense, Summer.'

He released her and reached for the sweat-shirt which was hanging over the rail. As he pulled it over his head, she had a last glimpse of the smooth brown chest and taut midriff which she longed to be able to touch.

'I'll go and fix breakfast,' she murmured, turning away.

In the kitchen she busied herself with the routine of making coffee, chopping up fruit and spooning out thick creamy yogurt. But her mind wasn't on the tasks which occupied her hands. She was thinking about his final words. They repeated in her head like a record replaying the same groove over and over.

It makes a lot of sense, Summer . . . a lot of sense . . . a lot of sense.

Perhaps it did make sense—to him. But how, loving him as she did, could she ever be satisfied with a marriage which, on his side, was purely practical? James himself had told her she had a romantic temperament, and he had been right.

She needed to be told she was loved with words as well as caresses . . . to be looked at with eyes which held adoration as well as desire.

In a way, his extraordinary proposal reminded her of a tempting dessert—lemon meringue pie or chocolate cake topped with frosting and sprinkled with nuts—offered to a fat person. The slogan to remember in that situation was: A moment on the lips, a lifetime on the hips.

This was a parallel situation. The temptation to experience his love-making was almost irresistible. She wanted to sleep with him even more than she had once craved fattening junk foods. But if she succumbed to her longing, she knew the price of her pleasure would be the pain of knowing that sooner or later he would tire of her. Without love—the durable fire—how could it be otherwise? All other flames burnt out.

Later that morning the mailman brought a letter from Raoul.

My dear Summer,

I miss you.

On the twentieth of this month I'm giving a party at Old Lyme. I hope you'll be able to come. I can't ask Emily to come with you because there is only one small guest bedroom at the cottage. My room will be occupied by Andrew and Nancy Sinclair, two close friends whom I see too seldom since they moved to Canada. I shall sleep in my workroom.

Could you come to New York on Friday and travel down to the cottage with me, returning on Monday

morning? I'm sure you can be spared for one
weekend. I'd like you to see the cottage and meet
my friends. My sister will be at the party. She wants
to thank you in person for the bracelet you made
her.

Do come. It's too long since we talked. Raoul.

She was alone when the letter arrived. James, who
also had a bicycle on Nantucket, had gone with Emily
to Siasconset, a village at the other end of the island
always called 'Sconset' by anyone who knew
Nantucket. They had taken a box lunch with them and
were planning to be out all day. Summer could have
gone with them, but she wanted to do some work, and
she thought it a good thing for them to spend time
together without her tagging along.

Raoul's letter pleased her. She had missed him, too.
He was such a comfortable person, and she was never
on edge with him. It was typical of his considerate
nature that he made it clear they wouldn't be alone at
the cottage, and to foresee that it would be difficult for
her to reach Old Lyme except by the method he
suggested.

She wondered if it would turn out to be a birthday
party. She had better take a present, just in case. In
New York choosing something for him would have
been no problem. Here it was more difficult. There
were some delightful shops on the island, notably
Nantucket Looms which always had covetable knitted
garments and beautiful hand-woven fabrics. But to
buy clothing for a man was tricky without knowing his
collar size and leg length. It would probably be wiser
to go to Mitchell's Book Corner and find a book for
him.

It was late in the afternoon when the others returned and found her busy at her embroidery frame on
the sunlit deck. She stopped work to make tea for
them and to hear about their expedition which had
included a ramble on foot to Gibbs Pond in the wild
area known as The Commons because it had once

been common pastureland shared by the island's early settlers.

It wasn't until later, when they had changed to go to a Saturday night barbecue at one of the large summer houses on the Cliff, that she said to James, 'Would you mind if I took a Friday-to-Monday holiday later this month? I'm sure Hetty would let Emily sleep at her house, or come and sleep here.'

'By all means,' he answered.

'Where are you going?' asked Emily.

'Raoul and his sister are giving a party at Old Lyme. They've asked me to spend the weekend there.' She wasn't quite sure why she included his sister in the invitation. 'You won't mind my being away for a few days, will you? I shall only be gone for three nights.'

'Of course not,' the younger girl said readily.

But it would be the first time they had spent a night apart since arriving in America, and Summer sensed that, inwardly, Emily was disappointed at being left behind.

'Perhaps you'll be able to come here that weekend,' she said to James.

'Possibly—or Emily might prefer to spend the weekend at the apartment.'

The next day he took them sailing on the sheltered waters of the huge inner harbour protected from the ocean by a barrier of sand and beach grass. Summer seemed to have outgrown her childhood tendency to feel queasy if a boat even rocked at her moorings. However, although she enjoyed harbour sailing now, she wasn't sure how she would fare in a large boat in rougher conditions.

Later, when they went ashore for a picnic lunch, she cut the sole of her foot on a broken bottle concealed in the sand. She had been running, and the sudden sharp stab of pain made her lose her balance and fall. When she didn't get back on her feet the others realised something was amiss and came over to find her looking with dismay at the bright red blood welling from a cut on the ball of her foot.

'The first thing to do with that is to wash off the sand and see what the damage is. I'm going to pick you up and carry you to the water,' said James.

He slid an arm under her knees and the other round her back and swung her up against his broad chest.

'Put an arm round my neck,' he instructed.

After the initial pain of the injury, her foot was now in the numb stage before the cut began to hurt. As he carried her down to the water's edge, she was conscious only of his strength and of the intimacy of being cradled against him, her arm round his powerful shoulders, her face close to his.

Although she now weighed a little under the recommended weight for her height, she was a tall girl and, as a result of daily workouts, quite strong herself even though her muscles didn't show the way his did. Not many men would have carried her as easily.

He walked into the water until it came up to his calves.

'Stand on your good foot and hang on to me for support.'

He lowered her legs towards the water and held her steady while he turned round and, like a blacksmith shoeing a horse, turned the sole of her injured foot upwards.

She steadied herself with a hand on the small of his back, feeling his left hand supporting her ankle while he rinsed away the sand.

He said, 'There should be some first aid stuff in the boat's locker, Emily. Go and check what there is, will you? We'll be there in a minute when I'm sure the cut's clean.'

Emily splashed off to do as he told her.

'Is it much of a cut?' Summer asked.

'Yes, quite a deep one, but don't worry. It won't stop you going to Santerre's party.'

He turned round and scooped her up, and carried her to the dinghy. There he gave her first aid and then made her put on her sweater and tuck his sweater round her bare legs, because although it was a hot day she had begun to feel chilly.

By the time they got back to the cottage her foot had begun to throb. Telling Emily to hurry ahead and start making a pot of tea, James helped Summer to mount the ladder to *The Fo'c'sle's* deck. When she would have hobbled indoors, using the heel of her cut foot, he picked her up for the third time and carried her inside.

'I think it's bleeding again. I don't want to get blood on the covers,' she said anxiously, when he laid her down on one of the sofas.

'The blood isn't coming through the dressing yet. Lie still with your foot raised like this'—he lifted her ankle on to the arm of the sofa—'and I'll take another look at it.'

So that she didn't have to prop herself up on her elbows, he took several squabs from the other sofa and made them into a backrest for her. When the arm of the sofa had been protected from seeping blood by a beach towel and a split-open plastic bag, he went off to scrub his hands.

Presently, sipping hot tea, she watched him remove the emergency dressing from her foot. His lean brown fingers with their well-kept nails were as deft and efficient as a doctor's.

'I think a couple of adhesive sutures should hold it together, but if it doesn't look good tomorrow we'll get some professional treatment,' he told her.

'Aren't you going back to New York tomorrow morning? I thought you'd be leaving on the seven o'clock plane.'

'In view of this accident I'll stay over until Tuesday.'

'I'm sorry to be a nuisance.'

He scowled and his answer was curt, but his annoyance was not directed at her.

'It's not your fault if some bloody fool leaves broken glass on the beach.'

Before they had left the place he had found the bottle which had cut her and hurled it far out into deep water where it wouldn't harm anyone else.

It was the strongest language she had ever known

him to use, and the irascible comment was typically
English. Several times she had heard old Lord
Cranmere and his son referring to someone as a
bloody fool. And yet, as she studied James's profile as
he finished attending to her foot, she could see no
resemblance at all between his strong, good-looking
face and the features of his father and brother.

He said, 'Have you a pair of socks? I've taped the
new dressing as firmly as possible, but a couple of
socks will help to keep it in place.'

'Yes, I wear socks with my running shoes. Emily
will get them when she comes back.'

His niece had gone to take the dinghy back to the
boat-house where it was kept.

'Can't I get them?'

'They're rolled up in the second drawer of my
chest.'

He went away for a few moments, returning with
the white sports socks.

As he drew one of them carefully over her foot, he
said, 'Are your drawers always in such immaculate
order?'

'I have plenty of time to be tidy. If I were rushing off
to work every morning . . .' She concluded the sentence with an expressive gesture.

He pulled the second sock over the first. 'Is your foot
aching?'

'A little,' she admitted.

'Would you like a couple of pain-killers?'

'Not unless it gets worse—I don't like taking pills.
I'd love some more tea.'

They had been intending to eat at a restaurant that
night and, later, she urged them to go without her,
saying she would be perfectly happy with bread,
cheese and fruit. But neither of them would hear of it,
and the supper they prepared, between them, was
certainly nicer than a solitary snack. Emily made the
French dressing for the avocado pears, and James
made the mushroom omelettes.

Afterwards they played rummy for an hour, and he

and Summer finished the bottle of wine he had opened the night before.

Whether his good-humoured acceptance of such a domestic evening masked inner boredom was impossible to tell. Perhaps in his high-pressured life an occasional interlude of this kind was not unacceptable.

It was Emily who helped her to hobble to their shared bathroom and, while Summer was there, removed the cover from her bunk and took her nightie from the hook behind the door.

She had been in bed for ten minutes, and was trying to concentrate on a book and ignore her aching foot, when there was a tap at the door and James walked in.

'I've brought you a couple of tablets and some water in case that cut keeps you awake.'

He put them on the shelf which served the upper bunk as a night table. Both she and Emily preferred to sleep in the upper bunks, although climbing up there tonight had not been as easy as usual.

'Thank you. It is a bit sore now.'

'I don't doubt it. It'll be a week before you can walk on it.'

'Oh, surely not as long as that!'

'Maybe not. You're in good shape so you ought to heal fast.' His glance drifted from her face to the silky skin under the ribbon-ties of her nightdress and the soft curves revealed by the thin flower-sprigged cotton voile. 'In excellent shape,' he added, the corner of his mouth lifting.

She resisted a desire to snatch the sheet and pull it higher.

'You're a little flushed. I wonder if you have a slight temperature.' He laid his palm against her forehead.

He knew why her colour had risen, damn him! She felt like dashing his hand away, but a more dignified way to put an end to his teasing was to say, 'If I have, a night's sleep will cure it. I'm tired now.'

He removed the book she was holding and put it on the lower bunk.

'Lie down and I'll tuck you in.'

'I don't want to be tucked in, thank you. I like the
bedclothes loose . . . and I want to finish the chapter
before I put the light out. May I have my book back,
please?'

'Okay, but don't read too late.' He returned it to her.
And then, to her total confusion, he leaned over and
kissed her lightly on the cheek. 'Goodnight.' He
turned away and left the room.

She didn't read any more. Nor did she sleep. It
wasn't the pain in her foot which kept her awake, but
the feel of his lips on her cheek. Strangely, the gentle
kiss—such as he might have given Emily—had almost
as disturbing an effect as his kiss on Friday evening.

If anyone other than James had kissed her like
that—Raoul, for instance—she would have accepted
the gesture as an affectionate impulse. But although
he seemed fond of his niece, she doubted that James
felt affection for anyone else, and certainly not towards herself.

He was in the mood to take a wife. Because she
happened to be at hand, as it were, he had taken it into
his head that marrying her would be easier than
finding and courting some other young woman. It
might even be that he thought her quite bed-worthy
now. The way he had looked at her shoulders and the
outlines of her breasts had suggested that he did.

She remembered that he had once told her that all
men assessed the women they met as possible bed-
partners. Presumably, after she had slimmed down,
he had looked at her in that light and revised his
original opinion of her.

Certainly she had often thought of him in that way.
The nights when she went to sleep wondering what it
would be like to be his bed-partner, hoping to dream
of him, outnumbered the nights when she didn't
engage in such fantasies. But one thing about him
troubled her.

Women—perhaps not all of them, but certainly her
kind of woman—needed to be loved as well as de-
sired. And James didn't seem to be capable of loving

the women in his life. He had admitted that his relationship with Loretta Fox had been a physical one, and no doubt that applied to his two previous liaisons.

There had also been that other woman—the painter of portrait miniatures—but even with her it might have been the urgent demand of his biological urges rather than calf-love, in the emotional sense, which had been the motivating force on his side.

Perhaps something in his early relationship with his mother had made him fundamentally antipathetic towards all women. Yet if he had had a bad relationship with his father, one would have expected him to turn to his other parent for affection and approval. Perhaps she hadn't given it to him. It could be that her loyalty to her husband and her love for her first-born had made her reject her younger son.

Lady Cranmere had died in her forties, after a long painful illness, and about five years after James's departure for America. Surely, if he had known she was dying he would have returned to see her? But perhaps they hadn't known where he was and had made no effort to trace him.

If he had loved her, it must be a terrible grief to him that she had been ill for months and he hadn't known it. But if he had loved her, he would have written to her; and it was only in Victorian times that husbands intercepted letters to their wives and destroyed them unread.

If he had written to her, surely no woman, least of all someone suffering from a terminal illness, would not want to be reunited with her son, no matter what his past misdemeanours. The implication was that he hadn't written to her, hadn't loved her. And there, perhaps, lay the key to the enigma; the explanation of his lack of heart.

From this train of thought, Summer's mind turned to how she should cope with the situation if, determined to get his own way, he deliberately set out to charm her.

She had an uneasy suspicion that James, if he

chose to exert himself, might be hard to resist, especially as her position in his household made it hard for her to avoid him.

She wished now that, when he had asked her if she were pining for Raoul, she had pretended she was. If she had led him to believe she was losing her heart to Raoul, James wouldn't have suggested she should marry him.

At the beginning of the week of Raoul's party, James left word with Hetty O'Brien that Summer and Emily were to fly to New York in time to have dinner with Cordelia Rathbone on Thursday night.

By the time they returned to the apartment Summer was no longer limping, but hadn't yet resumed her workouts which involved jumping jacks and jogging in place.

From José, they learnt that Mrs Rathbone was staying at the Pierre Hotel. James, who was out when they arrived, would be back in good time to escort them there.

Emily was looking forward to meeting her grandfather's first wife. It didn't seem to strike her as strange that Mrs Rathbone had never shown interest in her until now.

Discussing what to wear, they decided on a Paisley-print dress for Emily and a silver-grey silk shirt and black skirt for Summer. The shirt was the colour of her eyes. With it she wore a string of amethyst beads with silver spacers which had belonged to her mother, and she made up her eyes with a new violet shadow-stick.

They were ready to go when James arrived.

'You both look very nice,' he said approvingly. 'How's the foot, Summer?'

'It's fine again, thank you.'

'I'll be ten minutes shaving and changing.'

An early riser, he had the kind of dark beard which by mid-evening shadowed his lean, hard jaw unless he had a second shave.

They arrived at the Pierre at five minutes to seven.

As the elevator took them up to Mrs Rathbone's suite, he said to her, 'You've changed your scent.'

How unnervingly observant he was.

He said, 'I don't know what it was you used before, but this is Chanel No 5, isn't it?'

'Yes.' Had it been Loretta's favourite scent?

'Cordelia uses it. She knew Coco Chanel.'

The door of their hostess's suite was opened by a neat little woman, dressed to go out, whom James introduced as Paulette. He had already told them that Cordelia had her French maid with her.

'*Madame* is taking a call in her bedroom. She'll be with you in a moment,' said Paulette, showing them into a luxurious sitting room. 'She asks that you help yourselves to champagne. There is lemonade for *mademoiselle*.'

Summer had expected the much-married Mrs Rathbone to be like the rich women she had seen shopping at Altman's and Bergdorf Goodman and Henri Bendel who, in their terror of looking old, had had repeated face-lifts; who had their hair styled several times a week; who thought of little but their appearance and seemed to have no idea that their painted faces had become macabre masks.

However, as soon as their hostess joined them she saw that Cordelia Rathbone was nothing like this preconception of her. In both looks and manner she bore a certain resemblance to Congresswoman Millicent Fenwick whom Summer had seen on television and thought a striking exemplar of how to age gracefully.

Mrs Rathbone came into the room with the light, brisk step of a woman who keeps in shape by her own exertions rather than those of her masseuse and beautician. Her warm smile emphasised the lines that time and perhaps too much sunbathing had engraved on a fine, dry complexion. Her once-dark hair was now brindled to iron grey. She was wearing a dark red shirt-dress with a wide suede belt of the same colour, a single strand of large matched pearls and pearl ear-studs.

'Miss Roberts . . . how do you do? I'm so sorry I was detained.' She took Summer's hand and held it while she gave her a friendly but searching look.

'And Emily.' She turned to her first husband's grandchild. 'How do you do? James tells me you share his passion for computers. I'm determined to live at least to ninety because I want so much to see how the electronics revolution affects our lives in the next twenty years. Thank you, James'—this as he brought a glass of champagne to her.

They had all risen as she entered. Now Mrs Rathbone seated herself on the sofa beside Emily, and went on, 'I feel I was lucky, in some ways, to be born when I was. When I was your age'—with a gesture towards Summer—'travelling was much slower but more interesting. Each country was quite different from its neighbours. I saw Dresden before it was bombed in the Second World War, and Jerusalem before it was ruined by terrible apartments, and the Costa Brava in Spain when it was still a wild coast without hundreds of holiday villas and camping grounds spoiling its beauty. But everything has its price, and the price of being privileged to see those places at their best was a very restricted set of options if you were a girl. Unless you were extremely clever and extremely strong-minded, which I wasn't, you had almost no choice but marriage. Whereas you'—patting Emily's knee—'can be anything you want.'

'And what's the price of that privilege, Cordelia?' James asked her.

'The price is that, if she chooses a career which demands a great deal of time and energy, she'll either have to forget marriage and motherhood or accept the strain of leading two lives,' Mrs Rathbone replied. 'Up to now men with exacting occupations have had wives to look after them and let them concentrate their energy. Some husbands are beginning to accept a share of the domestic responsibilities. But there's a long way to go before those burdens fall equally on a husband

and wife. I don't know that they ever will.'

'What would you have liked to be if you had been born when I was, Mrs Rathbone?' Emily asked her.

'Strangely enough, after my marriage to your grandfather, which wasn't a success, I was content to be a wife. I always enjoyed doing up the many houses I've lived in, and I liked entertaining and bringing together people whom I felt would enrich each other's lives. You mustn't suppose that all my generation were frustrated career-women. That isn't so. To make a house comfortable and beautiful is an art, and a very satisfying one.'

She turned to Summer. 'James tells me that those delightful *trompe-l'oeil* paintings in the Octagon Room as *Baile de Sol* were your father's work. You may be interested to know that I have friends in Virginia who commissioned him to create the illusion that their dining room is a pavilion on an island in the centre of a lake. I'm sure if you'd like to see it they'd be delighted to have you stay with them.'

'I'd love to see it. I once had the idea of trying to trace all his murals and writing a monograph on them,' Summer replied.

To her surprise, James said, 'That's an interesting idea. If you expanded it to embrace other painters of murals, you might have enough material to make a book. I know a publisher who specialises in books on art. If you like, I'll ask him if modern murals are a genre which hasn't been documented, and if he'd be interested in publishing a work on the subject.'

She guessed the publisher was someone he had met through Loretta Fox.

'It's good of you to suggest it, but I have no qualifications for doing a book of that kind, nor have I the time to research it,' she answered. 'It would involve a lot of travelling.'

'In the later stages—yes. Not initially. Anyway, I'll call my publishing contact and ask what he thinks of the project.'

'I could help you, Summer. With me as your secretary, you could write the book on Oz,' said Emily.

They had dinner in the hotel's Café Pierre restaurant. Summer had eaten sparingly the day before
and had had only fruit and yogurt for her lunch in
order to eat freely tonight.

Her precautions proved to have been well-advised
because Cordelia had decided in advance what they
would eat and her choice of menu was definitely not
what Weight Watchers called legal. The first course on
its own—chicken liver *timbales* served with a red wine
sauce—was as much as Summer would normally eat
in the evening.

After the *timbales* came a very special kind of seafood
chowder called *marmite dieppoise* which Cordelia said
she had first eaten at Prunier's, the famous fish restaurant in Paris. As well as prawns and mussels, it
contained fillet of sole and sea bass baked with leeks
and cream and black truffle.

Finally they had a wonderfully light coffee soufflé
flavoured with rum.

While all these delicious things were being consumed, accompanied by a fine French white burgundy
for the adults and Perrier for Emily, Cordelia displayed a talented hostess's flair for drawing out her
guests. From time to time she contributed an amusing
anecdote from a life which had clearly been full of
interesting experiences and personalities.

She had beautiful hands adorned with several unusual rings which Summer longed to look at more
closely. Cordelia must have noticed her interest in
them, because when they returned to the suite, she
slipped one ring off and handed it to her, saying, 'As
you're designing jewels, this may interest you. I found
it in an old-fashioned jeweller's shop in a small town in
England. At that time the stones were in a brooch, not
a very pretty one.'

Summer studied the ring which consisted of a
cloudy bluish stone polished to the dome shape called
cabochon and surrounded by a nimbus of diamonds.

Cordelia said, 'There are some matches on the table,

James. Would you light one and hold it directly above the stone for Summer, please.'

He did as she asked and, as the tip of the match flamed, something came to life in the depths of the cabochon.

'Oh, it's a star sapphire,' Summer exclaimed. 'I've read about them but never seen one before. Did the jeweller know what it was?'

'Yes, but he told me there's less interest in them in England than here.' She slid off another of her rings. 'This, which is one of my favourites, was originally a ruby button from the *achkan* of an Indian prince.'

'What's an *achkan*?' asked Emily.

'That slim-fitting, high-buttoned coat which Indian men wear,' said Cordelia. 'You'll have some beautiful things to wear when you're older, Emily. There are several exquisite pieces among the Lancaster jewels. I remember a magnificent emerald necklace which I never wore myself but which will be perfect with your colouring. But I must say that, although I've had the chance to wear some wonderful jewels in my life, I've never liked *grande toilette* jewels as much as unusual stones like these rings . . . and your intaglio ring, Summer. May I see it?'

When she had examined the rose quarz in Raoul's setting, she said, 'Next time you go to Switzerland, James, you should take these two with you and let Summer visit Marina B's atelier in Geneva. Marina B's full name is Marina Bulgari Spaccarelli. The Bulgaris are jewellers in Rome with branches in Monte Carlo, Paris and Geneva. The New York branch is in this hotel. I've always admired their designs and some time ago James gave me a beautiful old silver coin in a Bulgari setting. I don't have it with me or I'd show it to you.'

So Cordelia, not one of his mistresses, had been the recipient of that lavish gift, thought Summer, remembering how she had read about it during their first winter in Florida.

'As a matter of fact I'm thinking of sending them

to Switzerland for the summer,' said James. 'I've
been offered a chalet at Wengen for them for the hot
weather. They could fly to Geneva and go the rest of
the way by car.'

That night, before she went to bed, Summer wrote a
note to thank Mrs Rathbone for including her in the
dinner party. Next morning, knowing that James
would be seeing her again that evening when he and
Emily went to the theatre with her, she asked him to
deliver it.

'Certainly. What did you think of her?' he asked.

'I don't think she's the tremendous snob you described her as being. Or the bigoted person I imagined. I think she's a delightful person. I hope she
will sponsor Emily—if her health allows it. Although
she doesn't look ill and she has a good appetite,' said
Summer.

'Her generation were brought up to hide their afflic-
tions,' he answered. 'When I called her a snob I didn't
mean she would ever be anything but courteous to
people she considers her inferiors. But don't let her
considerable charm blind you to the fact that, as did
my mother, she married a man she didn't love, or even
like, for the dubious éclat of being a marchioness and
mistress of Cranmere.'

'Perhaps they were pushed into it by their parents.
Mrs Rathbone admitted last night that she wasn't
strong-minded as a girl.'

'I doubt that either her parents or my maternal
grandparents would have forced their daughters into
the marriages if they'd shown any serious resistance. I
like Cordelia. She's an interesting, amusing woman.
But although she was fond of her second and third
husbands, there was never any question of the world
well lost for love,' he said sardonically. 'She would
think that a ridiculous concept. It's my sex who tend to
lose their heads over a pretty face. Not many women
lose sight of the practicalities of life.'

'I don't think that's true. I'm sure most women
marry for love and don't give a thought to the man's

position or his income.'

He didn't argue but the cynical lift of his eyebrow expressed his opinion.

'Think of all the girls who have supported their husbands or boy-friends while they trained to be doctors or lawyers,' she persisted.

'A tiny minority outnumbered by the thousands who, having divorced a man, have lived comfortably on his alimony,' was his caustic reply.

'If you feel like that about women, I think you'd do better to forget marriage and stay a bachelor,' she said shortly. 'Is it worth having heirs if it means spending the rest of your life with a member of the sex whom, in general, you despise?'

She made this retort without pausing to consider the unwisdom of touching on the subject of marriage. The moment the hasty words were out she regretted them.

Fortunately, at this point they were joined by Emily, which put an end to a conversation which might have got out of hand.

It was mid-afternoon when Raoul arrived in a taxi to take her to Grand Central Station to catch a train to Old Saybrook, on the opposite bank of the Connecticut River from Old Lyme.

In the taxi, he took her hand in his and kissed her knuckles, smiling at her.

She smiled back at him, relieved to have escaped for a few days.

Escaped from what?

From the cat-and-mouse feeling she had when James was around. She thought of the shell in its box in her dressing-table drawer. *Lyropecten nodosus*. The lion's paw. That was how it was under his aegis; like being a gazelle aware of a lion near at hand.

As they drove downtown on Lexington, she pushed James to the back of her mind and began to tell Raoul about Cordelia Rathbone's rings.

'What causes the star in a star sapphire?' she asked him.

'Microscopic tubes as fine as hairs. Most stars have four or six points, but occasionally one sees a twelve-point star. A cat's eye is a similar effect, but with one ray of light crossing the stone. A yellowish green chrysoberyl with a good cat's eye effect is amazingly like a real cat's eye.'

'Although I know it's fashionable, I've never been crazy about tiger's eye. Do you like it?' she asked him.

'Not too much. There's a blue variety called hawk's eye which you might like better. As soon as we get on the train I want to see what you've got there.' He tapped the portfolio she had brought with her.

'I hope you won't be disappointed. I'm not sure the kind of jewels I should like to wear are what other women would like. Also, I don't know nearly enough about the technical side. I've been reading about the "trembling" ornaments which were fashionable in the last century, and I've done two designs which should tremble. But they may not be workable.'

It wasn't long before they were comfortably ensconced in the train and Raoul was studying her careful pen-and-wash drawings. She knew her ideas were completely different from the flower motifs of much conventional jewellery or the abstract shapes of more avant-garde designs.

Much of her inspiration came from shapes she had admired at Cranmere, such as the broken pediment on an eighteenth-century bookcase which she had translated into a necklace and bracelet. Several designs were for pieces which had more than one function; a necklace which unclipped to form two slim bracelets or one thick one; ear-rings which doubled as clips; pearls which could be worn as a triple strand or a single long rope.

She waited in silence while he went slowly through the folder. She wished she knew what he was thinking. Perhaps he was bracing himself for the unpleasant task of telling her the designs were no good.

At last he looked up, a slow smile spreading from his eyes to his mouth.

He said, 'Have you heard of the French sculptor, Auguste Rodin?'

'Of course. He sculpted that lovely statue, The Kiss.'

Raoul nodded. 'Rodin said, *I invent nothing. I rediscover*. This is what you've done. You've taken ideas from the architecture of ancient Greece and applied them in a new way. Also I think your multi-purpose designs are very good for the young career-women who want a few pieces of good jewellery to help project a successful image. Memorable jewels are fine for very rich women; the widows, wives or girl-friends of millionaires. But a career-girl needs jewels which can be worn many times like a classic silk shirt or a wool blazer.'

As he had in the taxi, he reached out and took her hand in his.

'It's a failing of most young designers to create for grand occasions only,' he told her. 'Everyday life doesn't inspire them. You've struck a balance between the exquisite flights of fancy and the more practical pieces. That's good. I'm pleased.'

'I'm so glad.' She squeezed his hand in an unselfconscious expression of relief and elation. 'I was afraid you'd think them hopeless.'

'*Au contraire*, they're better than I expected—and my expectations were high. It'll take a little time to set up a promotion, but by next fall we should be ready to launch you. Do you want to use your real name or a *nom de guerre*?'

'I don't know. I haven't given it any thought.'

'Why not use your first name on its own? It's sufficiently unusual to stick in people's minds. That way you won't have to change your name when you get married, or continue to use your maiden name. That can be a problem in Europe although here women often add their husband's name to their own . . . Summer Roberts Rockefeller, or whatever it might be.'

Their hands were still linked but just then the guard came by to check their tickets and Raoul, who had insisted on buying her ticket for her, had to take out his billfold.

After the interruption, he said, 'I think *Summer for Santerre* would look good in our advertisements. How does it strike you?'

'Like a pipe-dream which, by some miracle, seems to be coming true,' she answered, smiling. 'If, three years ago, a fortune-teller had predicted that today I'd be living in America and going away for the weekend with a top New York jeweller who was going to use my designs, I'd have dismissed it as nonsense.'

A man walking past overheard this and turned to look at them in a way which made her realise the ambiguity of her remark.

'You realise he is putting the worst possible construction on that,' said Raoul, with a teasing glance. His expression changed. 'For my part, I'd be very happy if we were going to be *à deux* this weekend. But I think if I'd suggested that, you wouldn't have accepted the invitation.'

She turned to glance out of the window for a few moments. Then she looked at him again, and said, 'No, you're right . . . I shouldn't. For several reasons. For one thing it would have involved either having to tell Emily lies, or not setting the kind of example I want to set her. You can't advise your pupil against something and then go ahead and do it yourself. It's like telling your children not to smoke with a cigarette in your mouth.'

'And the other reasons?' he enquired.

'I don't think people who have any kind of working relationship can be . . . more than friends. Do you?'

'It can complicate life,' he agreed. 'You said "several" reasons. Is there another?'

She nodded, a little reluctant to admit to this one, yet confident that Raoul would never take pleasure in deriding her as James did.

'I know it must seem strange, at my age, but there are reasons why . . . why I've never had a lover,' she told him. 'I guess the longer you postpone it, the more momentous it becomes. Now I'd just as soon wait for my husband. I know it's incredibly old-fashioned.'

He said quietly, 'I don't think so. The permissive society is played out. It's had a long run and now the pendulum's swinging in the other direction, as it always has throughout history. Can I ask you why you've never had a lover? Any girl with your looks must have had to resist one hell of a lot of persuasion.'

She debated telling him the truth, but instinct told her that no one ever liked to be disillusioned.

She said. 'Not really. I'd no sooner started college than I had to go home and nurse my aunt. After she died I was cut off from the world by my job as Emily's tutor. It's not hard to resist temptation when it doesn't come your way.'

He looked at her thoughtfully for a moment. 'You haven't mentioned the basic reason for saying no if I'd asked you to spend the weekend alone with me.'

'The basic reason?'

'That you didn't like me well enough.'

'I like you very much, Raoul; and one of the reasons I like you is that you don't . . . rush your fences.'

They smiled at each other. Then he turned back to the first drawing in the portfolio and began to discuss each design with her.

His house on the outskirts of Old Lyme was an early eighteenth-century clapboard saltbox, simply, even sparsely furnished and in total contrast to the designer-decorated perfection of his apartment in the city.

'The Sinclairs won't be here till later. Andrew flies everywhere in his own plane. They'll be landing at Groton-New London airport and picking up a rental car,' he explained.

'What part of Canada are they coming from?'

'Toronto. He's a vice-president of an international automobile corporation which might make him sound dull. He's not. Nancy used to be a model. Now she has a boutique in Yorkville which is Toronto's most sophisticated shopping area. When she hears about the belt and wrist-band you made for my sister, she'll want you

to design for her. She specialises in unusual clothes
and accessories, a lot of them imported from Europe.'

It was around six o'clock when the Sinclairs arrived
in a Hertz car. Within an hour Summer felt as if she
had known them for years.

Nancy, six feet tall, with the long bones and languid
movements of a giraffe, made Summer feel almost
petite by comparison. She had a cloud of dark hair
with a white streak growing from her forehead.
Whether this *mèche blanche* was natural or put in for
dramatic effect, it was difficult to judge. She was
probably in her late thirties and her husband was some
years older, possibly forty-five. They were already
casually dressed for a country weekend when they
arrived, and Andrew looked more like a farmer or
rancher than a top-level corporation man.

Raoul had arranged for them to dine at one of the
best restaurants in New England, the Copper Beech
Inn at Ivoryton.

'The name of the town comes from the industry
which a family called Comstock set up. A lot of the
ivory keys for pianos and organs were made there,' he
explained, as they drove across the Baldwin Bridge to
the west bank of the river. 'The Copper Beech was
originally the Comstocks' mansion. I'm told that before it was turned into an inn, it was in such a terrible
state that the fire department were going to burn it
down for practice. Now the food they serve is so
good you have to reserve a table a long time ahead, especially at weekends.'

'Didn't Katharine Hepburn start her career at the
Ivoryton Playhouse?' said Nancy.

'I believe so. Her family had a summer place at
Fenwick which is on this side of the river, down by
Long Island Sound.'

'She was always one of my idols,' said Nancy. 'That
incredible voice and those cheekbones. You have
them, too,' she told Summer. 'I wish I did. In my
modelling days I could make up to look like I had them
for the camera, but it took a lot of what my husband

calls "plaster" to achieve that effect.'

Remembering the time when her cheekbones and most of her other bones had been invisible, Summer hoped that tonight she would be able to choose what to eat. Last night's dinner at the Pierre followed by three more nights of gourmet eating could do a lot of damage to her figure. If she wanted to stay a size eight, next week she would have to counterbalance this weekend with a few days on programme.

As they drove through Essex with its handsome houses and tall trees she could understand Raoul's liking for all these unspoilt river towns. Like Nantucket and Cranmere, they had the serenity of places which had a long history and where many people who lived there had known each other all their lives, and their parents and grandparents before them.

'Do you live in Toronto or outside it?' she asked Nancy.

'A few minutes' walk from Bloor Street which is the equivalent of midtown Fifth Avenue or Regent Street in London,' Nancy told her. 'But even though Toronto is a big city, somehow it has a nice friendly feeling about it. I wouldn't ever travel by subway in New York. It's dirty and I don't feel safe down there. In Toronto visitors are always amazed at how clean our subway is . . . the whole city, for that matter. We love living there but I think it may not be long before Andrew has to move to Detroit. Before that happens, Raoul must bring you to stay with us.'

This last remark made Summer wonder if Nancy was under the impression that she was his girl-friend.

She said, 'That's very nice of you. I'd love to see Toronto, but unfortunately I'm not a free agent. I think my pupil's uncle is planning to send us to Switzerland before long.'

'Oh, yes, you work for the man behind Oz, don't you? What's he like?'

'Very nice,' said Summer, making a private joke.

In the sense in which nice was usually used—which was how Nancy would take it—there could scarcely be a less appropriate term to describe the man who employed her. But the true definition of nice was exacting and discriminating, and those were attributes which did apply to him, but Summer didn't feel inclined to give Nancy a more detailed assessment of his character. Apart from the loyalty she owed him as his employee, the ninth Marquess of Cranmere, as James had been for a brief time, was not an easy person to describe.

Charming, when he chose to be. Crushingly sarcastic when he didn't. Sometimes friendly, sometimes withdrawn, the man was a mass of contradictions; an enigma she had yet to solve and perhaps never would.

They dined in the Inn's dark-panelled Comstock Room, making their choices from a menu of interesting dishes which proved to be as good although considerably less expensive than those the best restaurants of New York and Toronto had to offer. The two men decided to begin with baby trout in a mustard sauce followed by Beef Wellington. Summer settled for watercress soup and turbot with shrimps, a choice which made Nancy say, 'I'll go along with that.'

While the men were discussing the wine list, she added, 'Andrew is a gourmet but I'm not crazy about rich food, and especially not anything sweet. I could live for a week on grapefruit and cottage cheese. All my customers are on reducing diets and I have trouble keeping my weight up. Do you have the same problem?'

Summer said, 'Not really. My weight stays pretty constant. But, like you, I haven't a sweet tooth.' Not any more, she added mentally.

She hadn't been slender for long enough not to get a boost from being taken for a naturally slim person.

During dinner the conversation was general, but when they returned to the house the two men fell to talking about America's foreign policy and after a while Nancy turned to Summer and said, 'I have to confess that politics bore me. Could I look at the jewellery designs you've done for Raoul'—he had mentioned them during dinner—'or are they strictly under wraps?'

Evidently he had not been completely engrossed in talking to Andrew because, as Nancy was looking at the last of the drawings in the portfolio, he said, 'You must have modelled several million dollars'-worth of rocks in your time, Nancy. What do you think of Summer's ideas?'

'Original. Stylish. I love them.' She showed one of the designs to her husband. 'If you're worrying about a present for our next anniversary, this little bauble would be fine. Listen, Summer, how about designing some clothes for my boutique? There are lots of very elegant women—with very rich husbands!—in Toronto. It could be a good testing ground for your ideas about clothes. I'm sure you have plenty, and I could have them made up for you.'

It was an exciting offer, but Summer wasn't sure how Raoul would react to it. Perhaps he wouldn't like her diversifying; and there was the book about her father and other muralists which James was going to discuss with his publishing contact. Would she have time for all these projects as well as preparing Emily for Smith or Vassar?

Before she could answer, Raoul said, 'Let her sleep on it, Nancy. I think we should all go to bed. You people have had a long day. My plan for tomorrow morning is to take Summer up the river and, I hope, let her see some bald eagles. I also want to show her the Florence Griswold House. You two have already seen it so you may prefer to do you own thing until lunch.'

Early the next morning, Summer sat on a log by the river bank, drinking coffee from a vacuum flask and eating an apple while the sun rose over the river and a salty breeze rustled the reeds surrounding their breakfast place.

Raoul had entered her room at first light and given her a gentle shake—to have set an alarm clock would have disturbed the Sinclairs sleeping next door. Before dressing she had washed her face and brushed her teeth, but she hadn't put on any make-up.

When Raoul snapped a bar of chocolate and offered half of it to her, she said softly, 'No, thanks. May I look through your binoculars?'

He removed the strap from his neck and handed them to her.

'You may have to adjust the focus,' he told her, as she put the strap over her head and propped her elbows on her knees to steady her hold on the glasses.

'No, the focus if fine. We must have the same kind of eyesight.'

She scanned the far bank of the waterway called Connecticut by the Indians, the name meaning long, tidal river. It was certainly long—its source was in Canada. And for some miles upstream from where they were bird-watching, it continued, so he had told her, to be a wide estuary.

'Not only that; we have a great deal in common,' he remarked.

She lowered the glasses. 'Raoul, what do you think about this suggestion of Nancy's that I should try my hand at dress designing?'

'I think you should. I felt you and she would get along. That's one of the reasons I asked them down this weekend.'

As the breeze caught a strand of her hair and blew it across her face, he reached out to brush it aside. Having tucked it behind her ear, he touched her cheek lightly with his forefinger.

'You do have cheekbones like Katharine Hepburn. In fifty years' time you'll still be a beautiful woman.'

She was conscious that this was a moment which would always be imprinted on her memory. No woman ever forgot the first time she was told she was beautiful, or the man who told her.

'Is that ouside the terms of a working relationship— to say that I think you're beautiful?' he asked, with a slight smile.

'If it is, I can't truthfully say I object,' she answered lightly. 'To be complimented at this hour of the morn-

ing, with a bare face, does wonders for anyone's
morale.'

'A lovely girl may enhance her looks with make-up,
but she doesn't need it,' he said. 'In fact I think a lot of
girls spoil themselves by overdoing their make-up.
Those glistening lips and sultry eyes on the covers of
the glossies aren't attractive from a man's point of
view. Who wants to kiss a mouth thick with goo?'

He was looking at her mouth as he said it. She knew
he was planning to kiss her but giving her the chance
to turn away, if she so wished.

She kept her head still and after a moment he leaned
towards her and kissed her, lightly at first and then, in
a continuation of the first kiss, with a little gentle
persuasion to open her lips.

Perhaps, if a heron hadn't chosen that moment to
take off with languid wing-beats from a nearby reed-
bed, he might have gathered her close. But the wading
bird's sonorous croak before it took to the air made
them draw apart and look up to watch its slow flight.
As, its head drawn back in an S-shape, it headed
north, it drew Raoul's eyes to another bird flying over
the marshes. With an exclamation of excitement he
pointed it out to her; the eagle which was her country's
emblem and which, carved and gilded, with an olive
branch and arrows in its talons, was to be seen above
the lintels of many of the houses in the area.

It was their only sighting, and a distant one, of the
birds he had wanted her to see. Presently they drove
back to Old Lyme to visit the house which, at the
beginning of the century, had been a summer colony
for American artists such as Childe Hassam and Julian
Alden Weir.

By the time they returned to the house, his sister
and her husband had arrived from Boston. The former
Giselle Santerre, now Mrs Scott Adams, was two years
younger than her brother and very much like him in
looks.

Raoul had already told Summer that Giselle had
been engaged to the son of a French industrialist when

she had come to America for a holiday and fallen in love with Scott, a junior partner in a Boston law firm.

It had taken considerable courage for her to upset her fiancé and her family by breaking the engagement a few weeks before her wedding, particularly as at that time Scott hadn't declared himself. But from the moment of meeting him, she had known that she couldn't go through with a marriage based on liking rather than love. As soon as she had returned to America, this time without an engagement ring, Scott had asked her to marry him.

Giselle had brought with her a typically French picnic lunch of pâté, which she had made, crusty bread, good butter, fruit, cheese and—because it was her brother's birthday—champagne.

The six of them sat in the sun in the garden at the back of the house; four people who had found their life partners and two who might be poised on the brink between friendship and love. And yet, enjoyable as it was to be with people who had never known the other Summer Roberts, and with whom she had much in common, she found herself wondering how James and Emily were spending the day and whether they missed her or hardly noticed her absence.

After lunch they drove to the beach and filled their lungs with sea air, the three men walking together with the women following some yards behind. In the course of a conversation ranging over many subjects, Giselle contrived to elicit most of Summer's life history.

It wasn't until she was dressing for dinner that she had a chance to think about Raoul's kiss and what it might or might not presage.

Yesterday, in the train, she had told him she was a virgin and was inclined to remain one till she married. Did he think he could change her mind? Or were his intentions more serious? Judging by his arrangements for the weekend, and that one gentle kiss on the marshes, he was serious.

She closed her eyes, trying to recapture her feelings

while he was kissing her. To her dismay she found herself remembering James's kisses, especially the one following his proposal at Nantucket. Merely to remember that kiss stirred her senses, but when Raoul had kissed her it hadn't made her heart stop beating or produced any way-out sensations. It had been more affectionate than passionate; a nice, tender, chocolate-flavoured kiss which had momentarily revived her desire for the taste of chocolate but hadn't aroused any deeper desires.

Perhaps true love, the 'durable fire', didn't burst into flame at the outset but began as a gentle glow. She felt sure that, if he wanted to, Raoul could ignite stronger feelings in her. There might be no rational basis for the idea that as lovers Frenchmen were superior to other men; but somehow she felt sure that he—if and when they went to bed together—would take her with tenderness and skill.

Meanwhile all she had to do was to let him set the pace of their relationship. She had once read an interesting essay by the English writer Margaret Lane—in private life the Countess of Huntingdon—in which she had analysed the nature of *amitié amoureuse*, the special friendship between a man and a woman who found each other physically attractive but who, for a variety of reasons, preferred to be no more than friends in the old-fashioned sense.

It might be that she and Raoul would never progress beyond an *amitié amoureuse*, although already, by kissing, they had gone beyond the strictest bounds of friendship. Or it might be that he was the one in whose arms at long last she would experience fulfilment.

At this moment she only knew that she felt more for him than for any man she had met—other than James, she thought wryly. He was kind and considerate, and also very attractive, and she always felt comfortable with him. What more could one ask?

Scott and Giselle were staying at the Old Lyme Inn which was where that night's dinner party was held. It was an elegant establishment with a reputation for haute cuisine and a strict dress code.

However, as among the families who had summer
places or winterised houses in the area, those with old
money still predominated, dressing up was low-key.
Overdressing signalled the presence of tourists.

On Sunday they went to the Hunt Breakfast at the
Griswold Inn in Essex. The breakfast was actually a
superb buffet lunch.

'These breakfasts are supposed to have been started
by the British when they captured The Gris in the war
of 1812,' Raoul told her, as they helped themselves
from an appetising display which included bacon and
eggs, sausages, kidneys, kippers, chipped beef in
creole sauce, lobster kedgeree and turkey hash.

The waistband of her butterscotch cotton pants was
feeling too snug for Summer's liking. She seemed to
have been feasting for days and wished there was
some way to avoid doing justice to the lavish spread.
But with Raoul at her elbow there wasn't. She could
only eat very slowly, and plan to revert to programme
the moment she got back to New York.

Unable to stay a second night, at mid-afternoon his
sister and brother-in-law began their journey home.

'I've told Raoul he must bring you to stay with us in
Boston, so I'll only say *au revoir*, Summer,' said Giselle,
before they drove away.

To Summer's relief, instead of going out to dinner
that night, they stayed in and had omelettes and a
green salad.

It was not till Monday, on the train, that she was
alone with Raoul again.

'Next time you come down we'll take a ride on the
Valley Railroad's old stream train. It's touristy, but
fun,' he told her. 'And we'll try to get a closer look at
the eagles.'

As he said this, she could tell by something in his
eyes that he was remembering their kiss.

He didn't kiss her again till the day before she and
Emily flew to Geneva.

As he had an important business engagement that evening, Raoul asked her to lunch with him, and suggested she come to his apartment.

It was a few days before her birthday. After lunch, when they had left the table and were having coffee on the sofa, he produced a small gift-wrapped package.

It contained a cornelian box, carved in the form of a pumpkin with a removable segment rimmed with tiny rose diamonds. She knew instantly that it must be a piece of Fabergé.

'It's beautiful, Raoul—but I can't possibly accept it. Not only because of its value, but because of its associations. It should be kept in your family.'

He said, 'This is a piece which I found on a visit to England. It was in a little back-street junk shop, and the dealer didn't know what it was. She thought it was plastic and marcasite, and I bought it for a song. If it had any workmaster's initials, they've been worn away.'

'You're not making that up to overcome my scruples, are you?' she said doubtfully. How could anyone mistake this exquisite object for a cheap trinket?

'I would never lie to you, Summer.'

He removed the little box from her hand, put it on the coffee table and then took her gently in his arms.

Today he didn't kiss her on the mouth but put his lips lightly against her forehead and began to brush many soft kisses all over her face. Her eyes closed, she felt him kissing her temples and cheeks while the fingertips of his right hand stroked her neck and explored the delicate skin behind her ears and under her chin.

At last his lips came to hers and found them already parted and eagerly responsive to his long, tender kiss.

'I wish you weren't going away,' he murmured presently. 'It will seem a long two months without you . . . more than two months if you're not coming back till September.'

She rested her cheek on his shoulder, one arm round his waist and her other hand playing with a button on his shirt.

'Don't you go to France every summer? While you're there, why not come and see us? The chalet we're going to stay in is quite large. I think it has six or seven bedrooms.'

He stroked her hair and her back. 'Perhaps I will.'

She was suddenly filled with a longing for more than these gentle caresses. Lifting her head from his shoulder, she slid both arms round his neck and pressed herself against him, offering her mouth for another kiss.

This time he embraced her less gently. But just when she was beginning to feel all kinds of pleasurable sensations spreading through her entire body, he suddenly broke off the kiss and put her away from him.

Springing up from the sofa, he said thickly, 'You don't know what you do to me, *chérie*.' He walked away to the window and stood with his back to her.

Watching him, she wondered why he had cut short something they were both enjoying. Was it because of her inexperience? Or because he still wasn't sure of his feelings for her?

Either way, she couldn't see that it would have done any harm to let things go a bit further. However, as he had just said, she couldn't judge his reactions. She only knew how she felt—as if something lovely had been snatched away before she had had time to enjoy it to the full.

Still with his back to her, Raoul said, 'I will come to Switzerland. No one stays in Paris in August. My family have a house near Annecy in the Haute-Savoie. It's not far from Geneva.' He turned. 'You must give me your address and telephone number.'

'I don't know them yet. As usual all the arrangements have been made for us. I'll write to you as soon as we arrive.' She stood up. 'I'd better get back and finish our packing. Thank you for lunch, Raoul—and for this lovely birthday present.'

He accompanied her down to the lobby, but when

he would have asked the doorman to get a cab for her,
she said, 'No, I'd rather walk. Goodbye, Raoul.'

'Perhaps it's a good thing we shall be separated for a
while.' He took her hand in both of his. 'Till August.
Take care of yourself.' He lifted her hand to his lips
and pressed a kiss into the palm.

As she walked home, Summer found her thoughts
and emotions in considerable confusion. Even if it
meant not seeing him till September, she couldn't
pretend to be sorry to be going to Switzerland tomorrow. Travelling to new places was always exciting and
New York, when the temperature soared as it did in
July and August, was not a comfortable place to be for
anyone who disliked humidity out of doors and the
unnatural coolness of air-conditioning indoors.

On the other hand she was conscious of disappointment that he hadn't seized his opportunity and swept
her into bed. Would she have resisted him if he had
tried to make love to her? It was impossible to tell.

Probably she ought to be grateful that he had behaved with such rare old-world chivalry. It was yet
another proof of what an exceptionally nice man he
was. She had told him she wanted her husband to be
her first lover and he, not being ready to ask her to
marry him, had remembered and respected her wish.

If he had proposed, what would she have said? Not
yes . . . not yet. She needed more time. They both did.
Marriage was such an awesome commitment. The rest
of one's life in day and night partnership with another
human being. She felt reasonably certain that she was
never going to meet anyone with whom she had more
in common than with Raoul, but they had known each
other only a few months.

Thinking about marriage to him reminded her of the
proposal she had received—if such a cold-blooded
offer could be called a proposal.

We'll leave the subject in abeyance for a month or two,
James had said.

She wondered if he would visit them while they
were in Switzerland.

PART FOUR

MANHATTAN
LONDON
MUSTIQUE

IN winter a smart ski resort, the village of Wengen, was ringed by high peaks which were white with snow at all seasons. From their chalet, its balconies bright with crimson and pink pelargoniums, Summer and Emily could see across the Lauterbrunnen valley to another mountainside village, Mürren. Just below Mürren the lush, wooded pastures were cut by a tremendous cliff down which plunged the Staubbach waterfall, dissolving in spray before it reached the floor of the valley a thousand feet below.

In spite of the very hot weather throughout their stay, they explored both sides of the valley, toiling up steep, narrow paths to rest in high alpine glades with dazzling views of the Jungfrau, the Eiger, the Mönch and other famous mountains.

One baking August afternoon Summer was alone at the chalet while Emily played tennis with some other young people whose parents had taken a house at the far end of the village.

After a strenuous morning Summer was relaxing on the main balcony. Because it was completely private she had dispensed with her bikini and was lying face down on a sun-bed, browning her already brown back and her paler golden behind.

The local people had been hay-making in a nearby meadow, and the scent of mown grass—the quintessence of summer—wafted on the warm breeze which from time to time caressed her bare skin.

For a while she tried to concentrate on *Pensées*, a book of philosophical reflections by Pascal, a seventeenth-century French writer, which someone had left at the chalet. Then, surrendering to languor, she put the book aside and lay down, her head cushioned on her forearms and the line, *The heart has its reasons, which are quite unknown to the head* floating in her mind like a mantra.

Lost in a drowsy day-dream, at first she thought that the delicate ripple of sensation from her nape to the base of her spine was the breeze. Then it happened again, going the other way and feeling almost like a finger.

By the time she realised it *was* a finger, it had been joined by three other fingers, and a thumb and a palm. A whole hand was passing lightly over her sun-warmed left buttock and down the back of her thigh. A hand which, for all its gentleness, was unmistakably male.

'Raoul?' she queried, without moving.

He was expected to arrive the following afternoon. Naturally her first thought was that he had come a day early. When he didn't answer and the hand returned to her bottom, she pushed herself up on her elbows and twisted to look over her shoulder.

'You!' she exclaimed, aghast.

For it wasn't Raoul who was squatting beside the sun-bed, casually fondling her backside as if he were stroking a cat. It was James.

He gave her smooth rounded cheek a final pat and stood up. His smile mocking her startled confusion.

'Disappointed?' he asked.

'W-what are you doing here?'

'Passing through. I thought you would probably be out and I shouldn't see you till later. It's an unexpected pleasure to find you at home to welcome me.'

As his amused gaze swept from her head to her heels, she wondered if her body was blushing to match her face.

'Maybe I should get into the sun cream market and use you to advertise my product,' he murmured musingly.

Peering up at him, over her shoulder, was beginning to add physical discomfort to her mental discomfiture.

She said, 'If you'll turn your back I'll put something on and . . . and make you some coffee.'

James's reaction to this was not to do as she requested but to seat himself in a cane chair facing the sun-bed.

'I'm not embarrassed by nudity,' he announced smoothly. 'The beaches round the Mediterranean are littered with near-naked bodies. Even in Spain, once so prudish, bare breasts are a common-place sight. Don't cover up on my account.'

As she gritted her teeth, he added, 'And I have seen you undressed before, if you remember.'

There was—and she felt sure he knew it—a big difference between lying on a Riviera beach among hundreds of women in monokinis and being totally naked and alone with a fully dressed man. Particularly this man.

The only wrap she had with her was a large scarf of printed cotton which she had left draped over the back of another chair. To reach it she would have to stand up and turn in his direction, giving him a clear view of her front.

Well . . . so what? her common-sense asked. He's not going to rape you, you idiot. Why are you in such a stew?

Why indeed? The answer to that was too complex for her to analyse it right now. But it wasn't because she was still ashamed of her body. Considering the size she had once been, she was in good shape. A gradual weight loss combined with an exercise programme had succeeded in slimming her down without loss of firmness.

Nerving herself for his scrutiny, she rolled into a sitting position and forced herself to move without haste as she retrieved her scarf and wrapped it round her like a sarong.

'Why did you think it was Santerre who was

touching you a moment ago?' James enquired, watching her tuck in the corner of the scarf.

'He's staying with his family near Annecy. We're expecting him to visit us tomorrow.'

'And I take it his hand on your bottom is more acceptable than mine?' His lion's eyes were no longer smiling and his tone held an edge of sarcasm.

What perverse impulse made her say 'Yes' when it was so far from the truth?

'But Raoul would never touch someone unless he were sure it was welcome,' she added. 'He . . . he would have coughed or something.'

'Damned gentlemanly of him.' It was more than faint sarcasm now. 'He sounds in the same league as Bayard—*sans peur et sans reproche*.'

'Yes, I think he is,' she retorted. 'And I don't know why you should sneer. He's been a very good friend both to me and to Emily. I thought you liked him yourself.'

He shrugged, and his voice was indifferent as he said, 'I have no objection to his coming here if you feel the need to see each other while you're in Europe. I'm only staying here for one night. I shan't interfere with your plans. Excuse me, I'm going to unpack.'

The chalet had four bedrooms. She opened her mouth to offer to show him the two unused rooms, but he was already walking away and she realised that he didn't need her to conduct him upstairs. He had only to open doors to discover which rooms she and Emily were occupying.

Listening to the sound of his footsteps crossing the wax-polished wooden floor of the living room, she wondered for a moment if his snappy remarks about Raoul could have been prompted by jealousy. No, jealousy was too strong a word. But he might feel some resentment that she seemed to prefer the Frenchman's approach to his own.

If only he knew her real reaction to his touch. What her inner self had wanted to do when she looked round and saw whose hand was stroking her behind

had been to turn on her back and give him her most
glowing smile.

What would he have done if she had, she
wondered.

It was something she would never know; a chance
she had failed to take and which would never come
again. Had she been bolder, more daring, she might
now be locked in his arms instead of being left on her
own, regretting her mishandling of the encounter.

Soon afterwards Emily came back. For the rest of
James's stay she was always present and Summer
was never alone with him. He had gone before
Raoul arrived to spend three pleasant days in their
company.

After that, every time Summer sunbathed she remembered James's hand on her flesh. She tried to
close her mind to the memory and to think instead of
Raoul's kiss as they soared high above the fragrant
meadows on the Grindelwald chair-lift. But somehow,
in spite of the heavenly setting, the kiss itself had not
thrilled her.

In mid-September the two girls left Wengen with
unforgettable memories of their Swiss summer. But
although on the long flight west across the Atlantic she
tried not to let herself dwell on that afternoon on the
balcony, it was undeniably the most vivid and disturbing of Summer's memories.

She spent much of the flight attempting to convince
herself that it was Raoul whom she most wanted to see
again. Her mind accepted him as the better man for
her, but her heart denied it. It had its own reasons for
loving James.

Not long after their return to New York, Raoul told her
that Santerre et Cie were giving a party at an hotel to
present the new seasons's designs to selected clients.
He suggested she should buy a new dress.

'Something simple which will set off the jewels I
should like you to wear.'

'What are the jewels like?'

'You'll find out on the night of the party,' he said, with a mysterious smile, and she guessed he had had one of her own designs made up for the occasion.

Emily was going to be out of town that week; staying with Cordelia Rathbone in Bermuda. In any case the party was not an occasion for teenagers. As a matter of courtesy, Raoul had sent an invitation to James which he had accepted with the proviso that, having meetings in Chicago that day and returning on the evening shuttle, he might be a late arrival.

While Summer was dressing for the party, she wondered which of her designs Raoul had made up for her to wear. She hoped it was the one she thought of as the mermaid's necklace.

More than any other precious stone, she loved the clear, shining, sea-water blue-green of a fine large aquamarine. The mermaid's necklace had five in a simple but bold gold setting with ear-rings to match. But whichever design he had chosen, her classic black chiffon dress with its narrow straps, low *décolletage*, close-fitting waist and floating skirt was the perfect foil for fine jewels.

For a change she had had her hair put up at the salon where she had it cut when she was in New York. The upswept style made her look more sophisticated, and she took great pains with her make-up, giving her eyes a more dramatic emphasis than usual.

Raoul was punctual in arriving to fetch her. It was the first time she had seen him dressed for a black tie occasion. She wasn't sure that she liked his claret-coloured tie and cummerbund, or the jewelled studs in his dress shirt. Like his cuff-links they were probably Fabergé, but she felt she preferred the low key black onyx studs and black silk tie which James wore with his dinner jacket.

'You look lovely, Summer,' he told her. 'I like the new hairdo.'

'Thank you. Will you have a drink?'

José and Victoria were off duty, and she had let him in herself.

'Not at the moment, thank you. I want to show you my surprise.'

He was carrying a large manila envelope from which he extracted a flat leather case. Having placed this on top of a table, he put his thumb on the catch and then paused for effect, smiling at her. 'I hope you're going to like it.'

'I'm sure I shall. Do let me see.'

He pressed the catch, lifted the lid and revealed the shimmer of diamonds, the ice-gleam of platinum. It wasn't any of her designs. It was the dew-beaded web she had seen on his drawing-board the first time she had been to his apartment.

She had told him then it was beautiful, and it was. But it was a beauty which went with white mink and Cattleya orchids. She admired the craftsmanship of it, but it wasn't for her. It was too fragile, too cold. A necklace fit for a Snow Queen.

'Let me put it on for you.' He lifted it from its black velvet bed.

The lid of the case was lined with black satin stamped in silver *Santerre et Cie*.

He lifted it carefully over her head and moved behind her to secure the clasp. 'For your ears I have a pair of diamond studs. They're in my pocket.' He handed her a small box.

She went to a mirror to see how the necklace looked on. Seeing the delicate meshes spread on her golden skin, the diamonds winking and flashing, didn't change her opinion.

'It must be worth a fortune, Raoul.'

'It isn't the sort of thing you'd leave in a dressing-table drawer. It would have to be kept in a bank vault. Don't worry: you're in no danger because you're wearing it. I've made special security arrangements.'

She fastened the studs in her lobes. As she turned her head from side to side, he put his hands lightly on her smooth upper arms and let them slide down to her wrists in a gentle caress. Then he bent his head and pressed his lips to her shoulder.

'You don't know what pleasure it gives me to see my
creation on someone worthy of it. I wish you could
always wear it. To me it's a sacrilege when a necklace
like this is worn by an old, ugly woman.'

She turned to face him, smiling, wanting to be
kissed. Raoul started to bend his head but then
straightened again.

'No . . . better not smudge your lipstick,' he said,
stepping back. 'We must go. As one of the hosts I have
to be there before our guests arrive.'

She knew that he was now the only Santerre on the
board of directors, although two other directors were
of French origin, although not, like himself, of French
birth.

Not surprisingly all the board members' wives,
when she met them a short time later, were magnificently jewelled. She saw them appraising her necklace but no one made any reference to it. It seemed to
her that although Raoul's colleagues were favourably
disposed towards his protégée, their wives' amiability
masked varying degrees of hostility.

In the case of one of them, this might be because she
had a daughter a year or two younger than Summer
for whom, perhaps, she cherished matrimonial ambitions which included the company's debonair president. The undercurrent of coolness emanating from
the other two wives could be the antagonism which
some women who undervalued their role as home-
makers felt towards women with careers. Or it might
be that they saw her as a glamorous blonde whose
slenderness underlined their own figure problems,
little guessing the relentless self-discipline which lay
behind her new image.

The Presidential Suite in which the party was being
held gave her a curious sense of *déjà vu* although she
couldn't recall seeing it illustrated in a magazine.

The room was on two levels, the upper level—
where Raoul was going to receive his guests—being
separated from the lower by a wide flight of two or
three steps flanked by flower-banked balustrades. As

well as the waiters who would circulate with the champagne, a butler and two maids had been hired to take charge of the men's coats and show the women to a luxurious bedroom where they could leave their furs.

When everyone had arrived four top models were going to display some of the new season's jewels, after which a buffet supper would be served from the suite's dining room. Extra furniture had been introduced in the very large sitting room so that, at that stage of the party, everyone would be able to sit down.

Sipping her first glass of champagne, she wondered what time James would arrive. Thinking of him made her realise why the Presidential Suite seemed vaguely familiar. Long ago, when he was still her *bête noire*, she had imagined herself, in a setting very like this, giving him the cold shoulder.

As things had turned out she no longer felt bitterly angry with him and indeed, while Raoul was obliged to leave her for his duties as host, would have welcomed the support of James's presence in an assembly of people most of whom knew each other but were strangers to her. Clearly the wives of the other directors did not intend to exert themselves to introduce her, and Giselle and Scott Adams had been prevented from coming by the sudden serious illness of Scott's father.

However, it wasn't long before she was approached by a heavily-built man in his fifties who said pleasantly, 'Raoul has suggested I introduce myself to you, Miss Roberts. My name is Heinrich Brandt. I come from Idar-Oberstein in West Germany which, as you may know, is the centre of the European jewellery trade.'

'How do you do, Herr Brandt. Yes, Raoul has mentioned Idar-Oberstein. Do you come to New York regularly?'

Grateful for Raoul's thoughtfulness in sending him over to her, she spent the next half an hour encouraging the German to talk about himself and his business.

He was an interesting man who had travelled all over Africa and South America in search of fine gems. She could have talked to him all evening, but presently their conversation was interrupted by the ringing of a hand-bell which caused a lull in the buzz of conversation.

As a hush fell over the room, Raoul moved to the top of the steps, repeated his welcome to everyone and introduced the first model whose famous smile, as she stepped into the pool of radiance beneath a downlighter, caused a ripple of applause.

As she walked briskly round the room, she was followed by a second model. By the time the first had disappeared, the third was in view. The whole show took a very short time, giving the people present no more than a tantalising glimpse of the beautiful baubles the models were displaying.

When the last model had disappeared, followed by a stronger and more sustained burst of applause, Raoul held up his hand to indicate he had something more to say.

'Ladies and gentlemen, you've just seen a few of the new designs from our workrooms. As many of you know, my grandfather was a designer for the goldsmith to the Imperial Court of Russia, Peter Carl Fabergé. He achieved his reputation by a combination of inspired design and consummate craftsmanship and we are constantly striving to maintain that tradition. Later this year we shall be launching the first collection by a young designer who I believe has a great future. She's the daughter of a distinguished American artist, the late Thomas Roberts who specialised in *trompe-l'oeil* murals. Some of the most admired houses in the United States are embellished by the delightful fantasies he devised for his patrons. His daughter has inherited his gift for creating beauty . . . and is herself a very beautiful young woman, as you will see in a moment. Will you join me, please, Summer.' He looked towards where she was standing and held out his hand.

She had had no idea he intended to present her to his guests and was both surprised and dismayed at having no choice but to leave her place beside Herr Brandt and make her way to Raoul's side. Another burst of polite applause accompanied her reluctant advance from the edge of the room to the centre of attention. Instinctively she shrank from being in the limelight and felt angry with Raoul for forcing it on her without warning, the more so when, as she took his still outstretched hand, someone nearby took a flash photograph.

Raoul squeezed her fingers, smiling at her.

'The necklace which Summer is wearing is one I designed,' he announced. 'Next time you meet her she'll be wearing the *pièce de résistance* from her own collection; and I think when you see it you'll agree that we have discovered a remarkable talent.'

He bowed to her, kissing her hand with the easy gallantry of his French background. There was more applause, and more flashes. She smiled at Raoul and then at the blur of faces. There were a hundred people present, most of them standing in groups in the lower section of the room, all of them staring at her.

It was an experience which convinced her that being in the public eye was not a sensation she enjoyed. It might be meat and drink to some people, but not to her. She was thankful when Raoul told his guests that refreshments were being served in the adjoining room, and conversation broke out again.

'I wish you had warned me,' she said to him, in a low tone.

'I purposely didn't. I thought it might make you nervous,' he answered.

This was neither the time nor the place to tell him that, had he appraised her of his intention, she would have declined to participate in the ordeal which had just concluded.

'I hope Brandt hasn't been boring you. About eight months ago he lost his wife to whom he was very devoted. It's his first visit here without her. I asked

him to look after you in the hope it would take his
mind off her absence,' he explained.

'I like him—he's extremely interesting. I'll go back to
him now, as you have to concentrate on being host.
I—'

She was interrupted by a woman in scarlet taffeta
who surged up to them, saying gushingly, 'I just adore
this gorgeous necklace Miss Roberts is wearing, Mr
Santerre. Did you design it for her, or is it for sale?'

For a fraction of a second he hesitated. He didn't
glance at her neck which, Summer saw, was encircled
by rubies and diamonds; but probably he knew without looking that she had a dewlap between her chin
and her necklace, and her chest had dull, mottled skin
which a wiser woman of her years would have veiled
with the flattery of chiffon.

'I'm glad you like it, but I'm afraid it isn't for sale,' he
told her.

'You mean it's exclusive to Miss Roberts?'

Again there was an infinitesimal pause before he
replied, 'Yes, it is.'

'I see. Lucky Miss Roberts.'

The woman in red gave her an appraising glance in
which Summer read a supposition she didn't like.

However, at that point they were joined by some
other people and it was some time before she had an
opportunity to say quietly to him, 'Raoul, what possessed you to tell her this necklace was for me?'

'We can't talk about it now. Tomorrow—' He broke
off as once again they were interrupted.

With so many people wanting to speak to him, or be
introduced to her, it was impossible to have any
private conversation. Nor could she resume her *tête-à-
tête* with Heinrich Brandt because on her way back to
him she was intercepted by a couple who wanted to
tell her they had recently stayed in a house where her
father had painted some murals.

Her interest in this information helped to calm her
vexation over Raoul's misleading statement to the
woman in red. She could understand his reluctance to

have his cherished design snapped up by someone
with so little taste that she couldn't see the necklace
was as unsuitable for her as her girlish hairdo and
revealing red dress. But surely he could have found
some other excuse not to sell it to her? It was plain
what inference she had drawn from his reply. And if
she were a gossip, as women of that sort usually were,
she would share her conclusion with others.

Summer began her supper in conversation with
Mr and Mrs Mettinger who told her that since Mr
Mettinger's retirement they had moved to Bermuda,
but frequently flew to New York to attend the theatre
and opera.

Although elderly, they were a pleasant couple with
wide-ranging interests and she would have been happy to continue talking to them. But when, having
eaten the poached salmon which they had chosen
from the cold table, they returned to the buffet for the
second course, she was drawn into conversation with
another, younger couple, the Grigsons.

After they had been talking to her for a while, some
other people joined in. Having started the evening
feeling an outsider whom the wives of the other
directors weren't eager to befriend, she found herself
being almost lionised. It was pleasant to have so many
people wanting to meet her and, if they hadn't heard
of him, to ask her about her father. She found it easier
to talk about him than about herself because, having
had no formal training, there was not very much she
could tell them.

She was being questioned by a woman who seemed
to be at the party on her own when suddenly James
appeared beside them.

By this time Summer had stopped keeping an eye
open for his arrival. She had virtually forgotten he was
coming. As her companion was speaking at that moment, she had to wait for her to finish what she was
saying before she could greet him. And before the
pause came he had bent on her a steely glance which
silenced the words she had intended to utter.

'Good evening, Mr Gardiner.' It was the other woman who spoke to him first. 'I didn't know your interest in art embraced modern jewellery.' She turned to Summer. 'Mr Gardiner is one of the leaders of the computer revolution.'

Before Summer could explain that she knew him, James said, 'I'm also the owner of some murals by Miss Roberts' father.'

'Oh, really? I have another party to attend, so I'll leave you to discuss them. Goodnight, Miss Roberts. I'll look forward to talking to you again at the launch party for your designs.'

When she had left them, James said, 'Do you know who she is?'

'No: should I? Is she famous?'

'She's a columnist. Whatever you told her will be dished up in tomorrow's column for the delectation of her readers.'

'I didn't tell her anything very much. James . . . is there something the matter?'

'Yes,' he said curtly. 'There is.'

Her blood froze for a moment. 'Not Emily . . . ?'

'It has nothing to do with Emily. Where's your wrap? Go and get it.'

She did as he told her. The maid on duty in the bedroom had no difficulty in finding her black cloak—Summer was the only woman at the party who did not have a fur.

When, carrying it over her arm, she rejoined James in the suite's spacious lobby, she said, 'I can't go without speaking to Raoul.'

'I've already had a word with him.' Grasping her firmly by the elbow, he hustled her out of the suite and into the elevator.

'What did you tell him?' she asked, as he took her cloak from her and placed it round her shoulders.

'That you had a migraine.'

'But I never have migraines. Why are you looking like thunder? What's happened? Where are we going?'

'Back to the apartment. We'll talk there,' he told her repressively.

A few moments later the elevator reached the lobby and as soon as the doors slid apart he renewed his grip on her arm and hurried her across the foyer.

Usually, being tall, she wore low-ish heels in which, at least for a short distance, she could keep up with his long stride. Tonight, in black glacé kid evening shoes with closed toes but only the finest of straps attaching the high heels to her feet, she had difficulty in keeping pace with him.

'Would you slow down, please,' she protested.

He cast a swift, glowering glance at her steeply arched insteps and slender strap-encircled ankles, and reluctantly he shortened his stride.

It was the kind of hotel where, except during the hour before curtains rose in Broadway theatres, there was always a cab-driver waiting for the doorman's signal.

Feeling that she had been bundled rather than helped into the back of the cab, Summer wished they were in a London taxi where the passengers were separated from the driver by a glass partition. In Manhattan taxis there was not much leg-room and no privacy, so she was obliged to sit in silence, her feelings a mixture of anger and apprehension, all the way back to the apartment.

By the time they had taken the elevator up to their floor and James had unlocked the outer door, she was keyed up to a pitch at which her fingers shook slightly as, entering the living room ahead of him, she fumbled to undo her cloak clasp.

'Would you mind telling me what this is all about?' she demanded. 'If there's nothing the matter with Emily, and the apartment hasn't been ransacked, why did I have to be rushed back here?'

'Because, whatever you're planning to do with your future, right now you're still on my payroll and I expect you to act with appropriate discretion,' was his harsh reply. 'I hadn't been at the party ten minutes

before I heard two women discussing you in terms
which you wouldn't have liked. Or am I wrong in
assuming you don't wish to be regarded as Santerre's
new mistress?'

Without giving her a chance to answer, he went on,
'A not unreasonable conclusion on their part considering that you're wearing at least a hundred thousand
dollars'-worth of diamonds, which they seemed to
have grounds for thinking he has given you as a
present.'

'They have no grounds at all for thinking that. It's
malicious tittle-tattle. I'm surprised you didn't say so,'
she retorted.

He said angrily, 'I have no authority to repudiate
their conjectures. If Santerre has undermined your
common-sense to the extent of persuading you to
wear that necklace, how should I know what else he's
persuaded you into?'

'He hasn't persuaded me into anything. He's not
that kind of a man. If you'd arrived earlier, you'd have
heard him introduce me as a new designer for *Santerre
et Cie*. Why shouldn't I model a necklace for them?'

'Because you are neither a model nor a member of
Santerre's family. Had you been engaged to him, it
would have been a different matter. But I don't see any
diamonds on your finger. Only in your ears and round
your neck. Take them off and I'll put them in my safe!'

The curt command and the contemptuous look
which accompanied it brought a rush of hot blood to
her cheeks. He succeeded in making her feel as if the
diamonds really had been given to her for the reason
surmised by the woman in red. Her fingers made
clumsy by vexation, she began to remove the stones
from her ears.

'Apart from other considerations, I should have
thought your own taste would have dissuaded you
from wearing that thing,' he said coldly. 'It doesn't
suit you. If he had you in mind when he designed it,
he doesn't know you very well.'

'What makes you think you do?' she flashed back,

her head bent and her arms raised as she struggled to undo the necklace's intricate fastening.

'Perhaps I don't. I gave you credit for more nous than you've shown this evening.'

She continued her futile efforts to release the catch until, finally, she was forced to say, 'I can't get it off. Would you help me, please?'

As he moved towards her, she turned her back. But now she was facing a mirror which reflected them both; a tall, scowling, tight-lipped man, his swarthy colouring accentuated by the snowy whiteness of his dress shirt, and a flushed and mutinous girl in a low-cut dress which revealed her indignant rapid breathing.

It seemed to take him forever to get the damned thing undone, and she was acutely conscious of the brush of his knuckles against her back while his fingers dealt with the difficult clasp.

He said, 'There's certainly no danger of it coming undone accidentally.'

And then, having succeeded in undoing it, he let one end go and the combined weight of the diamonds pulled it forward across her shoulder. It slid, glittering, over her collarbone and the soft swell of her breast to disappear in the valley partly revealed by her *décolletage*.

'Thank you,' she said, in a clipped tone, putting up her hand to catch it before he let go the other end.

He didn't do that, however, because with a suddenness which made her catch her breath, he turned her to face him and jerked the end of the necklace out of her cleavage, tossing it on to an armchair with a casual indifference to its delicacy or its value.

'Perhaps it's time to discover who does know you best. Judging by that thing, Santerre sees you as an ice-maiden. I think he's wrong. Let's find out.'

He jerked her into his arms and swooped on her protesting lips like a hawk on its prey.

It was as traumatic a kiss as his first, in the swimming pool in Florida. Although neither of them was

naked, and she was almost three years older and had
been embraced by other men as well as by him, she felt
the same shock and alarm as she had long ago in the
pool at *Baile del Sol*. Because this time he wasn't being
either gentle or persuasive. This time he was angry,
and the kiss was prolonged and punitive.

Even though she knew from experience that it
wouldn't make him let her go, as she had in the pool,
she resisted. With her arms clamped between them,
she couldn't use her hands as weapons so she drew
back her right foot and kicked him, hard, on the ankle.

He gave a muffled grunt of pain. An instant later,
still with his mouth covering hers, she was swung off
her feet and carried to one of the sofas.

In the twisting and squirming which followed, all
she succeeded in doing was snapping one of her
shoulder straps. And throughout her futile struggles
he kept possession of her mouth, kissing her with a
kind of relentless sensuality which was frighteningly
effective. With every movement of his lips she could
feel her own senses responding and conspiring to
betray her will.

At last, with a moan of despair at her body's
treachery, she gave in and lay still in his arms, no
longer fighting against him but against her own rising
desire to go beyond passive submission and return his
kisses.

As soon as he felt her surrender his hold on her
eased, his hands ceasing to restrain and beginning to
caress. His fingertips smoothed her throat, searching
for and finding the pulse which betrayed the excited
beating of her heart.

'I don't like your hair this way either,' he murmured, his lips to her cheek.

She felt him pull out the pins and release the soft
swathes of her hair while his warm lips roved over her
eyelids before returning to her mouth.

His kisses were like a drug which destroyed or
distorted every normal control. All she knew was that
she was a woman in the arms of a man whose touch

was a magic she had no power to resist.

Soon she was caressing him; feeling the thick springy hair under her wandering hands, the long strong neck leading down to the powerful shoulders.

Without taking his mouth from hers, he got rid of his dinner jacket. Then there was only the fine white lawn of his dress shirt between her hands and the warmth of his muscular body. Without knowing what she was doing until she had done it, she found she had pulled his tie undone and opened the top two buttons, making room for her hand to slip inside and feel the heat of his skin and the heavy thudding of his heart.

At the same time he had discovered the zipper at the back of her dress. Moments later she was naked to the waist and his hands were gently exploring her satiny breasts, making her shiver with pleasure.

When his fingertips touched their soft peaks, piercing shafts of ecstatic sensation shot through her body from her breasts to between her legs and down the insides of her thighs. He seemed to know all the ways to induce deeper shudders of bliss; by nibbling the lobes of her ears and playfully biting her neck, his mouth working lower and lower so that she knew, very soon, his warm lips would replace his fingers, and then—oh, God! Could she stand it?

The feel of his cheeks and chin, not bristly but unmistakably male, as he moulded her breasts with his palms and nuzzled the valley between them, made her wrap her arms round his head, wanting to hold him there forever.

Then his thumbs circled in a caress which made her breath catch in her throat as new pangs of delight zigzagged through her. Seconds later, without knowing how it happened, her hands were clasping her own head and she was arching her spine, not knowing which was more exquisite, the sensuous touch of his fingers on one breast or the hot, hungry pressure of his mouth on the other.

When his hands wandered down her body, tracing the lines of her ribs and exploring the softness of her belly, she was beyond caution. Nothing mattered but these rapturous feelings and the need to experience, at long last, the ultimate ecstasy of all.

As she lay there, throbbing, in his arms, his hand reached the thicket of curls at the top of her pulsating thighs.

'No . . .' she murmured. 'No . . . please . . .'

It was only a token protest and he knew it. The strong, sure fingers continued their gentle, determined exploration while she held her breath and waited, helpless with longing . . .

At first, when the telephone rang, she didn't recognise the sound. It was merely an intrusive noise like a strident alarm clock breaking into a dream. And, as if in a beautiful dream, she resisted waking up.

But the jarring sound went on and on until finally, with a smothered curse of exasperation, James stopped making love to her and heaved himself up from the sofa. He staggered across the room as if he were drunk, or abruptly roused from a deep sleep so that he scarcely knew where he was or what he was doing.

That was how she felt herself. Intoxicated . . . dazed . . . disoriented. She had had no idea that a man's hands and lips on her body could kindle such wild, wanton feelings.

He picked up the receiver. Instead of the usual incisive 'Gardiner speaking', he said, hoarsely and angrily, 'Who is it?'

If the caller didn't get the message that they had chosen a bad time to call, they had to be extraordinarily dense.

'Oh . . . Santerre. What do you want?'

That it was Raoul on the other end of the line was like a douche of cold water on Summer's flushed face and warm, swollen, tender-tipped breasts. In a flash she recovered her wits and realised how nearly her senses, and James's expert knowledge of how to arouse them, had made her make a fool of herself.

Her sprawled posture, her dishevelled clothing, all

the tell-tale signs of her almost total abandonment suddenly filled her with revulsion.

As James said, 'You needn't have called. She's not ill—it's only a headache. By tomorrow morning she'll be fine,' she sprang from the sofa and ran, as if from a rapist.

Although he had had his back to her, she expected him to swing round, drop the receiver and come after her. If he had, she would never have made it to the safety of her bedroom.

But as she tore across the living room, she heard him say something else, replace the receiver and then discover her flight. It gave her just enough time to reach her own room and turn the key in the lock before he crashed against the outer side of the door.

Had it been like most modern doors it would have burst open. But all the doors in the apartment were made of strong solid wood with high quality hinges and fittings. It resisted the impact of his shoulder better than she had resisted his gentler onslaught on her body, and evidently he was not so far gone in lust as to vent his frustration in ways which might bring José and Victoria to see what was going on.

'Open this door!' she heard him demand, in a low, furious voice.

'No . . . please go away.'

For a long time, clutching her dress, trembling with self-disgust, she waited to be sure he had gone. At last, far down the hall, she heard another door close. Only then did she collapse on her bed and burst into tears.

She was roused by an insistent noise which, after a moment or two, she recognised as Victoria's way of tapping on a door.

Realising that she must have overslept, she glanced at the clock on her night table and saw that it had gone eleven. She was late for breakfast by three hours!

Hurriedly scrambling out of bed, she called, 'I'm coming,' and hastened to unlock the door.

When she opened it, she found the stout Spanish woman waiting outside with a breakfast tray.

'Meester Gardiner tell me not to disturb you before eleven,' said Victoria, entering the bedroom. 'You had late night at party—yes? You had a good time?'

'Er . . . yes . . . very, thank you.' She climbed back into bed and tried to look pleased at being presented with a three-course breakfast atttractively arranged on a wicker tray with short legs at either end.

Green and white porcelain . . . a green linen tray-cloth and napkin . . . a white rosebud in a crystal specimen vase . . . butter in dewy curls . . . the fragrance of hot bread rolls emanating from a covered basket—Victoria had been at pains to make Summer's breakfast in bed an enjoyable indulgence.

'Be careful—this plate is very hot,' the maid warned, indicating a plate with a silver lid concealing whatever was on it.

'Has Mr Gardiner had breakfast?'

'Si, si—at his usual time. All the years José and I have worked for him, he has never stayed in bed later than seven.'

Summer picked up the fruit spoon and dipped it into a mixture of fresh grapefruit and pineapple. It was the only thing she felt like eating.

'Is he still in the apartment?'

'No, he went out about ten and he won't be back until this evening. What time you expect Mees Emily?'

'She should be here by two.'

It was a relief to know she had several hours' grace before she had to face James.

Victoria picked up the black dress flung carelessly over a chair, and she clicked her tongue in disapproval.

'You spoil your nice dress if you don't hang it up,' she remonstrated. 'And you not take your make-up off, I notice. You have black marks all round your eyes. That is bad for your skin—and also bad for the pillowcases. Mascara is hard to wash out.'

'I know. I'm sorry,' Summer said meekly.

She liked the outspoken little woman, but right now she wished Victoria would go away and leave her alone with her headache.

But in shaking out the crumpled dress, Victoria had discovered the broken shoulder-strap.

'Tsk, tsk—how this happen?'

'I . . . it came apart while I was dancing,' Summer said, feeling her face burn and hoping the maid wouldn't notice and suspect the truth.

Not that it would occur to her that the man who had made a pass at Summer had been their employer. Victoria was a practising Catholic who had been strictly brought up and didn't approve of the licence which girls had now. She would have been deeply shocked to discover what had happened in the living room last night.

'I'll mend it for you,' she said.

She enjoyed looking after clothes. For her own satisfaction she would take off machine-sewn buttons and replace them by hand. A silk shirt washed and pressed by her would look better than if it had been dry-cleaned.

'Thank you.' Summer watched her leave the room.

As soon as the door closed she stopped eating the fruit and sank back on her pillows to think about how, since this time yesterday, her world had been changed and disrupted and could never be the same again.

She had spent half the night thinking about it, which was why she had a headache and felt more like going back to sleep than getting up and making decisions.

One decision was already made. She had to leave. She couldn't possibly continue to live under James's roof and be paid by him. How could she go on working for a man who had tried and almost succeeded in seducing her? Last night had made her position impossible. She could never look at him without remembering her abandoned behaviour in his arms; the soft gasps and murmurs of pleasure which now made her cringe with shame.

Above all, he had given her a glimpse of the heaven they could have shared if he had been capable of loving her. To stay on, knowing what it might have been like, would be an unendurable purgatory she knew she had to escape.

When, some time later, she took the tray to the kitchen, the dish under the cover and the bread basket were empty. To avoid making Victoria feel she had wasted her time, she had flushed the breakfast down the lavatory.

The Spanish woman said, 'I forgot to tell you: Mr Santerre, he called you this morning. He asked that you call him back when you wake up.'

'Did he say where he would be?'

Victoria produced a slip of paper. The number she had written down was Raoul's Fifth Avenue number. Summer went back to her room and telephoned him. After giving her name to the girl on the switchboard, she was put through to him immediately instead of having to speak to his secretary first.

'Are you feeling better?' he asked, in a tone of concern.

'I'm fine, Raoul, thank you. I hope you haven't been worried about the necklace. I should have taken it off before leaving last night.'

And perhaps avoided what happened after James took it off for me, she thought.

'It's in a safe,' she went on. 'I don't know the combination so I can't get it out until this evening when James comes in. He's not here at present.'

Thinking about the moment when she would have to look at him and speak to him made her inside churn with nerves.

'I have it on my desk,' Raoul answered. 'James delivered it in person soon after we opened. I didn't see him myself—he handed it over to the manager downstairs.'

'I see.' She wondered why he had put himself to that trouble instead of leaving it to Raoul to recover his property.

'Are you really better?' he asked. 'Well enough to have lunch with me? I must talk to you, Summer.'

'Yes, I want to talk to you, but I can't meet for lunch. I have to be here when Emily gets back about two.'

'Then have tea with me. I can't wait till this evening to see you. Let's meet at the Plaza at four-thirty. In the Palm Court.'

Assuming his impatience to see her was because he wanted to discuss the party, she agreed to this arrangement.

By two o'clock she had packed an overnight case, booked a room at the Barbizon on Lexington Avenue, and written a brief note to James.

In the circumstances, I prefer to leave immediately. I shall tell Emily we have had a serious disagreement.

'A disagreement? What about?' asked Emily, an hour later, after Summer had helped her to unpack and heard all about the trip to Bermuda.

'Specifically about my wearing a very valuable diamond necklace at the party last night. But that was really just the tip of the iceberg. We've both made an effort not to show it because of our affection for you, but the fact is that James and I have never really seen eye to eye. Last night our mutual antipathy came to the surface and . . . and we lost our tempers and said things which make it impossible for me to go on working for him.'

Emily looked baffled. 'I knew you didn't like each other at first, but I thought that was over ages ago. I—I thought you got on very well now. I was even beginning to think that one day you might get married and we'd be together forever,' she said, in a low voice.

Summer felt a lump in her throat. Striving to keep her tone level, she said gently, 'We can't be together forever because one day *you* will get married and who knows where that may take you? Back to England perhaps, or to the ends of the earth. But wherever we are we'll never lose touch with each other. We'll write and telephone and visit. I'm only moving out of this apartment—I'm not going far. Maybe to the other side of the Park, or down to SoHo . . . wherever I can find a place I like at a rent I can afford. We'll still see a lot of each other. You can help me to furnish my place.'

'But I'm not in New York all the time. What about Florida? What about Nantucket? You won't be there.'

'Well . . . no. But neither will you if you go to college. We were going to be separated then in any case. It's just happening sooner, that's all.'

Although she tried to speak cheerfully, the look on the younger girl's face made Summer feel sick at heart. This was all James's fault—damn him! If *he* hadn't lost *his* temper and behaved unpardonably, this sudden and premature severance need never have happened. Emily herself would have been the one to make the break.

'It must have been a terrible row if you can't say you're sorry and make it up. What did he say to you? What did you say to him?' the younger girl asked bewilderedly.

Summer flushed and avoided her gaze.

'I—I'd rather not discuss it. Anyway, as I've already said, the row was the culmination of frictions which, as you realise, have existed from the beginning. For a time we managed to keep them submerged, but no one can do that indefinitely. There was bound to be a clash sooner or later.'

'I can't understand it . . . why you don't like him, I mean. He's so nice, Summer . . . so are you. If I love you both, and you both love me, how can you not like each other?'

Summer sighed. 'It's one of those inexplicable things. Think of all the married couples who adore their children but find they can't live with each other and have to split up. James and I are just incompatible.'

'But he isn't with us very often,' Emily persisted. 'You're with me more than with him. Can't you put up with him for the short time he does spend with us? I don't want to be on my own till I go to college.'

'Probably, if I'm not around, James will try to spend more time at home; and I'm sure Mrs Rathbone will want to see more of you, too.'

'She's nice but she's old. I can't talk to her the way I can to you.'

'What you need is more friends of your own age.'

'No, I don't. I need you,' said Emily. 'Please, Summer—don't go away. James will cool down. So will you. If you only had this row last night, you're both still up in arms with each other. It's silly to act in haste or in a temper. You've often said so.'

The trouble was there was no way of making Emily understand the situation without telling her the truth—which was impossible.

She was too young and idealistic to understand the combination of factors which had triggered last night's débâcle. Summer herself had not understood it at first. Only after lying awake for several hours, her body tormented by unsatisfied desire and her mind in a ferment of angry confusion, had she begun to understand—although not with the forgiveness which understanding was supposed to induce.

It was her reluctant recognition of how much he had made her want him which had been the clue to comprehension. He had needed a woman—any woman. It might be that he hadn't had sex since ending the affair with Loretta. A long time for a man of such powerful animal vitality to live like a monk. Probably his sexual appetite had been gnawing away at him for days; a slow-burning fuse which he would have kept under control if it hadn't been for his outburst of anger and the contact with feminine flesh when he had had to unfasten the necklace for her. What had driven him to make love to her, she had realised, had been straightforward primeval lust; the fierce driving force which kept the human race going.

There was something immeasurably degrading in being made love to by a man who didn't want you, yourself, but only your female body. But it wasn't that she could never forgive. It was that he had made her a party to blind desire. She had wanted what had almost happened. If it hadn't been for Raoul's call, she would have permitted and welcomed James's possession of her. That was what she couldn't forgive. And, having done it once, he could do it again. He must know that. He might never act on the knowledge, but it would always be there in his eyes when he looked at her.

Once he had despised her for being a compulsive eater. Now he would despise her for being a push-over.

'I'm not acting in haste,' she said, in answer to Emily's last remark. 'Striking out on my own has been on the cards for a long time. Now it's been precipitated, that's all. It's come as a shock to you, I know. But try to take it in your stride. You must know how fond of you I am. I wouldn't hurt you for the world. But I have to leave . . . I just have to.'

Holding her hand at a secluded table in the Palm Court of the hotel which had been a Manhattan landmark for almost fifty years, Raoul said quietly, 'I want you to marry me, Summer. I've been thinking about it for some time. Suddenly, last night at the party, I was sure we were right for each other. Tell me you feel the same way. You do, don't you? Please say you do.'

His tone, his touch, his whole tenderly chivalrous manner were balm to her raw self-esteem. Her impulse was to say *Yes*. Yet somehow her lips wouldn't form the words he wanted to hear. Some deep, inexplicable instinct made her hesitate to commit herself.

'I—I don't know, Raoul,' she answered with a troubled sigh. 'I am very fond of you . . . I know that. But marriage is such a big step.' Suddenly, to her own surprise, she found herself adding, 'Perhaps . . . perhaps we should try living together for a while.'

He looked at her long and intently. It was difficult to gauge his reaction.

At length, he said, 'I thought you wanted your first lover to be your husband?'

'I know I said that at one time. But . . . circum-

stances alter cases. My ideas have changed. I think
now—'

But her thoughts were in too much confusion for her
to explain them to him. She only knew that she had to
find some escape from the memory of last night's
embraces.

The gravity of his expression made her say, 'Have I
shocked you? Are you disappointed in me?'

He smiled then. 'I could never be disappointed in
you. Will *you* be shocked if I suggest that we leave
this'—with a gesture at the tea he had ordered—'and
go to my place?'

Suddenly there was an ardour in his eyes which she
had never seen in them before.

'No. I—I should like it,' she answered.

He squeezed her fingers, then lifted her hand to
press a kiss on her knuckles. After leaving some bills
on the table, he rose and recaptured her hand and led
her away. A few moments later they were in the back
of a cab, travelling the short distance across town to his
apartment.

Raoul fondled her hand, stroking her palm with his
thumb and playing with the soft webs of skin between
her fingers. It was impossible not to notice the bulge
alongside his zipper—after being restrained for so
long, he couldn't wait to get her into bed. She wished
she felt the same way. But in spite of the erotic things
he was doing to her hand, she felt no response.
Perhaps it would be better when they were alone and
he kissed her.

But it wasn't. The moment the door of the elevator
had closed, he took her in his arms and pressed a long,
passionate kiss on her mouth. She put her arms round
him and opened her lips, but she felt no thrill of
excitement.

When the elevator stopped at his floor, reluctantly
he raised his head. His face was flushed, his blue
eyes were slightly bloodshot, and when he unlocked
the door of his apartment, his fingers shook with
impatience.

Standing beside him, Summer found herself feeling nervous that, for all his restraint in the past, he might now be too wildly aroused to wait for her passion to match his before he took her. At the moment she felt no reaction at all. The burning desire which James had kindled last night hadn't even begun to reanimate.

To her relief, when they entered the apartment he didn't make straight for the bedroom. By the sofa where once before he had held her and kissed her, he drew her against him. With their arms round each other, kissing, they subsided on to the cushions.

In the moments which followed, Summer strove hard to recapture the feelings he had roused in her last time. But even when he began to undress her, her heart didn't beat any faster.

Although he had fumbled with his latch-key, he was deft and swift in removing her shirt and bra. Soon she was naked to the waist and his hands were exploring her breasts while he told her, in French, how lovely they were, and how often he had wanted to caress them.

She lay in his arms, willing herself to respond. But all the time he was stroking her, and pressing his lips to her neck, and murmuring husky love-words in her ear, she experienced no stirring of pleasure. All she felt was miserably guilty; as if she were doing something wrong . . . giving her body to a man who had no right to it because . . . because in her heart she belonged to someone else.

'No . . . no . . . I can't,' she exclaimed suddenly, pushing him away.

He misunderstood her outburst. 'Don't be nervous, chérie. I won't hurt you.'

'It isn't that. Please . . . let me go.'

Not unnaturally Raoul was determined to overcome her resistance. The tussle which followed was in many ways very similar to her struggle with James the night before. Raoul wasn't as powerful as James, but he was a man and, as such, much stronger than she. The difference was that with every moment in James's

arms her power to resist him had weakened and her
longing to surrender increased. In Raoul's hold she
felt no such weakening but rather an increasing des-
peration to escape. Suddenly, to have his mouth glued
to hers and his hot, eager hands on her body was
as revolting as if he were a stranger. As she understood the difference between last night's kisses and
these, she gave a convulsive shudder and began to
weep.

At this, Raoul gave a muffled groan and broke off
the kiss to sit up. As soon as he let her go, she crossed
her arms over her breasts, instinctively covering herself.

With tears on her cheeks, her lips trembling, she
stammered, 'I—I didn't mean this to happen. Forgive
me, Raoul . . . please forgive me.'

At first he ignored her apologies. She could see it
was difficult for him, perhaps even physically painful,
to control the surging desire which her sudden tears
had frustrated. As difficult as it was for her to suppress
the uncharacteristic need to weep.

She lay still, watching his profile as he sat, shoulders
hunched, glowering at the carpet while his breathing
quietened and the fever in his blood died down.

When eventually he turned his head to look at her,
his eyes were puzzled rather than angry.

'What happened? What made you change your
mind?'

It was impossible to tell him the truth; to confess that
in his arms she had found out there was only one man
to whom she could ever give herself. To say that
would upset him even more. Yet what other explanation was there?

To her astonishment, he said, 'You're in love with
James Gardiner, aren't you?'

She gaped at him. What had made him say such a
thing when, ever since they had known each other,
she had been desperately striving to overcome her
feelings for James?

When she didn't answer, he said, 'I've suspected it

for a long time, but I didn't want to believe it. The first time I saw you—at the Bernier lecture—I saw how you looked at him. But after a while I thought you might have got over it . . . as I've tried to convince myself that I'm over Louise.'

He sank his head on his hands in a posture of weary despair.

'You mean you're *not* over Louise?' she ventured uncertainly.

At first he didn't reply. Then he sat up and shrugged. 'I guess not. To be truthful . . . when we were kissing . . . I found myself thinking of her. I didn't want to, but it happened. I shouldn't have brought you back here where she and I—'

He broke off, left the sentence unfinished and then, on a note of anger, said, 'What a mix-up life is! You and I are so right for each other. We have almost everything in common. We could build a good life together. Except that neither of us feels whatever it is that makes the difference between affection and love.'

Summer had never expected to find herself staying at the Barbizon Hotel for Women a few blocks from Bloomingdales.

It was one of a number of all-women hotels in the city, and although most of its rooms were occupied by permanent residents, some were available for transients. She had checked in and left her luggage there before meeting Raoul at the Plaza, secure in the knowledge that there was no possibility of James invading her room and insisting she return to the apartment.

The Barbizon was very security conscious and claimed to be the safest hotel in New York. The elevators were attended and male visitors were not permitted in any part of the building other than the lobby and the public lounges.

Her room had a private bath and was attractively furnished, but it seemed very small compared with the spacious rooms to which she was used. Not that her surroundings mattered to her as she lay on the bed,

staring at the ceiling and trying to come to terms with
the total disruption of her life which had taken place in
less than twenty-four hours. This time yesterday she
had been preparing for the party with no sense of
impending chaos.

The telephone rang. Summer sat up, but she didn't
immediately reach for the receiver. She had told Emily
where she was planning to spend the night and it
might be Emily who was calling. Or it might be James.
She had a strong intuition that it was James.

She wanted to hear his voice and yet she was afraid
of speaking to him. What would he say? What was
there to say?

It was curiosity to know how he would handle the
situation which made her answer the call instead of
ignoring it.

'Hello?'

Without any preliminaries the familiar, deep,
slightly clipped voice said, 'Is Emily with you?'

'No . . . no, she isn't.'

'She left the apartment soon after you did, telling
Victoria she'd be back before dinner. She's still out.
Have you any idea where she might be?'

He didn't sound unduly anxious, but the instant he
had said, 'She's still out' Summer felt a stab of alarm.
Emily had never been known to miss a meal before, or
even to be late for one.

'No, I haven't . . . no idea at all,' she answered
worriedly.

There was a short pause before he said, 'She may
have been involved in an accident. If so, she's going to
need you. I think you'd better come over right away.'

'Yes—yes, I will. I'll grab a cab and be there in five or
ten minutes.'

She replaced the telephone receiver, grabbed her
room key from the night table, thrust her feet into her
shoes and moments later was dashing along the hall to
the elevators. On the way down to the lobby she
shrugged into her raincoat and looked in her purse for
dollar bills to pay the fare.

Fortunately, she had no trouble getting a cab and the traffic in the streets was light. Even so it seemed to take forever to drive the short distance to the apartment. All the way there, and while she was going up in the elevator, she had nightmare visions of Emily being injured in an accident and rushed to hospital with no identification on her so that no one would know who she was or how to contact her family.

Is this my fault, Summer wondered, with a pang of anguish. Was she not looking where she was walking because she was worried about my leaving? The thought that she might be indirectly responsible for Emily being badly, even fatally hurt was agony to her.

José opened the door looking worried and, she thought, accusatory. But perhaps it was only her own sense of being to blame which made her see reproach in his expression. He took her raincoat and told her she would find his employer in the study.

James was on the telephone when she entered his sanctum. His desk chair was on a swivel base. When she opened the door he was facing the window with its view of the East River. As she crossed the threshold he swung round and indicated with a gesture that she should take the chair in front of the desk. As their eyes met she gave no thought to what had passed between them the night before. Concern for Emily had driven everything else from her mind.

'Yes, that's a good idea, Morton. If you can get hold of him, bring him with you. We may be over-reacting, but the way things are—'

He left the sentence in the air and concluded the call with a brisk goodbye.

As he replaced the receiver, he said, 'That was my lawyer, Morton Eliott. He's going to organise a check on hospital admissions. Then he'll try to contact a friend of his, a very experienced senior police officer who's recently retired and who can advise us what to do if we draw a blank at the hospitals.'

He paused, his expression grim. 'I'm afraid we can't

dismiss the possibility that Emily may have been kidnapped.'

This was something which hadn't occurred to Summer, and which was even more horrifying than the thought of Emily lying unconscious in an emergency department. Suddenly the room began to sway. Although it had never happened to her before, she knew she was about to black out.

Something must have shown in her face. As she tried not to let the great wave of dark fog engulf her, she saw James spring up from his chair and come round the desk.

The next thing she knew was that she was sitting bent double, looking at the toes of her shoes and the legs of the chair and the twisted wool pile of the carpet, with something heavy on her back holding her down.

As her head cleared she realised that it was his hand. Seeing her about to keel over, he had pushed her into this position and was keeping her there till she showed signs of recovery.

'I'm all right now,' she murmured.

The weight was removed from her back, and James took hold of her shoulders and helped her to sit up.

'Sorry about that . . . the last thing you need . . .' she apologised muzzily.

'When did you last eat?'

She tried to recall, but what came back into her mind was the psychological shock which had caused her to faint.

We can't dismiss the possibility that Emily may have been kidnapped.

Without waiting for her reply, James leaned across his desk and touched a key. When José's voice said, 'Yes, sir?' he gave instructions for a glass of milk and some sandwiches to be brought to the study.

Then he sat on the front of the desk, his arms folded, looking down at her.

'Tell me what happened here today? What explanation did you give Emily for moving out?'

Miserably Summer repeated the gist of her conversation with Emily. But it was remorse for inflicting
such a painful shock, not embarrassment, which made
her hang her head. Her anxiety for the girl who was as
close as a sister to her still outweighed every other
feeling.

'Did she seem greatly upset?' he asked.

She nodded.

'Did she cry?'

'Not then. Perhaps she did later . . . after I'd gone.'
She looked up at him, pale and distraught. 'I shouldn't
have left her alone. If I'd stayed, she wouldn't have
gone out . . . this wouldn't have happened.'

'Maybe nothing has happened. Five minutes from
now she may walk in here, right as rain.'

'But where could she have been all this time?'

'Walking around, thinking things out. Sitting in a
coffee bar, maybe.'

She shook her head. 'Not all this time.'

'People can lose track of time when catastrophe hits
them. You and I are Emily's family. A split between us
is bound to have a traumatic effect on her.'

José brought the food he had asked for. Seeing the
sandwiches made her realise that apart from fruit at
breakfast, she had eaten nothing all day.

James said, 'I'm expecting Mr Eliott, José. When he
arrives, we'll have a large pot of coffee.'

'How long do you think it will take to check the
hospitals?' she asked, when they were alone again.

'Not too long. A teenage girl with red hair is more
easily identifiable than someone with common-place
colouring.'

She forced herself to eat a sandwich. She still wasn't
hungry, but she knew that it was partly lack of
nourishment which had made her pass out momentarily. That and a sleepless night and almost twenty-
four hours of emotional stress, starting with James's
arrival at the party last night.

Now it was essential she should pull herself
together and be ready to give sensible answers to any

questions which might be put to her by the lawyer and the former police officer.

Barely twenty minutes after her own arrival at the apartment, James's lawyer was introducing the man he had brought with him, John Hurst.

Both men had the brisk but calm manner of people accustomed to handling crises. The lawyer, one of the city's leading attorneys, had a telephone in his car on which he had made several calls while being driven across town to collect the other man.

As they seated themselves in the chairs which James had drawn up for them, he said, 'It appears unlikely that your niece has been involved in a street accident, James. No one answering to her description has been admitted to any of the midtown hospitals. So let's check through some other possibilities.' He addressed himself to Summer. 'Has she ever been late home before, Miss Roberts?'

'No, never. She hasn't many girl-friends. When she does go out without me, she's always back by the time arranged. Emily isn't a rebel. She's mature for her age, and considerate. She would realise how anxious we'd be if she didn't come home at the right time.'

John Hurst leaned forward. A big, burly man with grey hair and bushy eyebrows, he said, 'How about boy-friends, Miss Roberts?'

'She sometimes spends time with boys who share her passion for computers. But she doesn't have dates in the usual sense.'

'She's almost seventeen and she doesn't date?' Clearly he found this surprising. 'Is she pretty?' he asked.

'More than pretty. She's on the brink of being beautiful.' She hesitated, reluctant to betray Emily's confidence but realising that, if she kept silent, they might follow a lead which led nowhere. 'The reason she isn't interested in boys is because she's in love with an older man. Not much older—he's twenty-four. Probably she will grow out of it, but meanwhile he far outshines any of the boys who might like to date her.'

She saw John Hurst's next question coming and forestalled it by adding, 'But he can have nothing to do with her disappearance. He lives and works in Florida. I know Emily very well, Mr Hurst. She isn't secretive. For a long time we've been more like sisters than tutor and pupil.'

He gave her a searching look before switching his keen gaze to James.

'You won't like this suggestion, Mr Gardiner, but please think about it carefully before you dismiss it. Is it possible your niece could be on drugs?'

It was Summer who reacted indignantly. 'Absolutely not!' she said sharply.

Mr Hurst turned to her and said mildly, 'Miss Roberts, if you went to any one of the drug rehabilitation centres in this city, you'd find the patients include many young men and women from wealthy, socially prominent families. Often the habit starts in school and continues for years before it's discovered by the parents. It's been estimated that twenty million Americans have tried snorting coke. What makes you so sure that Mr Gardiner's niece isn't one of them?'

'I'm equally sure of it, Hurst,' James intervened. 'Emily is a girl with a lot of character. Even if she'd been to school, which she hasn't, it's unlikely she'd have been persuaded to try pot or pills or whatever. She hasn't even tried cigarettes. Both she and Miss Roberts are on the exercise kick. They work out every day. People who do that aren't usually inclined to abuse their bodies in other ways.'

'No, I guess not,' the older man agreed. 'How come she hasn't been to school?'

Briefly, James explained the origins of Emily's private education. 'But the last time she had an attack was two years ago in a garden full of exotic plants in Florida. I doubt that her asthma has anything to do with her failure to come home tonight.'

It seemed to Summer that they were wasting time, ignoring the worst possibility. She said, 'James . . . Mr Gardiner thinks she may have been kidnapped.'

'I doubt it,' said John Hurst. 'If that had happened, I'm sure you'd know about it by now. Kidnappers usually make their demands not too long after the snatch and before the victim's relations are seriously alarmed. Also, although Mr Gardiner's a public figure, the fact that he has a niece living with him hasn't been publicised. I'm not saying we can rule out kidnapping, but at this stage I think we should consider other reasons for her absence. I'd like to go through the details. Who was the last person to see her?'

James told him and Hurst asked to speak to Victoria. At that moment José came in with the coffee and James requested him to bring his wife to the study.

As soon as she entered it was clear that the little Spanish woman had been weeping and was distressed and nervous. James made her sit down and spoke to her quietly in her own language which seemed to help her to compose herself. In answer to Hurst's questions, she said that Emily had left the apartment about an hour after Summer had gone out.

'How was she dressed, Mrs Perez?'

'The same as when she arrived . . . in her raincoat.'

'Arrived? She had been away?'

Victoria nodded, and James said, 'My niece had been visiting Bermuda. She got back this afternoon. I wasn't here but Miss Roberts was.'

Hurst said, 'Mrs Perez, how did Emily look before she went out? Did she seem her usual self?'

The cook-housekeeper nodded. 'Yes. I ask about her trip. She say she had very nice holiday with Mrs Rathbone. I ask her why she going out. She say to buy tape of some music she hear on her trip and like very much. I tell her tonight for dessert I make pineapple mousse especially for her. She say, "Oh, you very kind, Victoria". Then she go out.' Tears filled her dark brown eyes and she fumbled for a handkerchief.

'Thank you, Mrs Perez. That's all for the moment.'

Hurst indicated to José that he should take his wife away.

When they had gone he turned to Summer. 'Tell me what happened between Emily's return to the apartment and the time you went out, Miss Roberts? Did you go to the airport to meet her?'

'Yes, I did. It was the first time she'd been away on her own. Coming back from the airport she told me what she'd been doing and the people she'd met. Then when we got back to the apartment I helped her unpack. She was wearing a blue Madras shirt with Ralph Lauren's logo, a polo player, machine-embroidered on the cuff, and a navy skirt and navy leather loafers. I haven't been to her bedroom to look, but probably she's still wearing those clothes. Would you like me to check?'

'If you would, please.'

When she returned to the study a few minutes later she said, 'As far as I can see there's nothing missing except the clothes she was wearing when I left her. Oh, and her shoulder-bag.'

Hurst asked her to describe the bag and Emily's raincoat, making notes as she did so.

'You left the apartment before she did. Where were you going, Miss Roberts?'

'I had a date to have tea at the Plaza.'

'Did Emily mention that she planned to go shopping later on?'

'No, she didn't.'

'Did she tell you about this music which she mentioned later to Mrs Perez?'

She shook her head. 'Before I went out I had to tell her something which came as rather a shock to her. But whether it has any bearing on her disappearance, I don't know.'

'What did you tell her.'

'That I was leaving.' She flashed a troubled glance at James, wondering how he would react when Hurst started probing for the reason for her quitting her post with such suddenness.

'Emily's known for some time,' she went on, 'that when she didn't need me any more I was going to give up teaching and concentrate on designing. While she was away I decided to change careers sooner . . . in fact right away.'

It was Morton Eliott who said, 'You announced this change of plan and then left her alone to digest it? If, as you tell us, you and Emily have grown very close, wouldn't it have been wiser and kinder to break the news later in the day . . . after dinner maybe?'

His tone and the way he looked at her gave Summer an insight into how it must feel to be on the witness stand facing cross-examination. She didn't try to refute the censure implicit in his question.

'Yes . . . it would,' she admitted. 'But I wasn't coming back for dinner. I—I wasn't coming back at all. Mr Gardiner and I had had a major disagreement and I had resigned my job here.'

The lawyer gave an exclamation. 'This explains the girl's disappearance,' he said, as if resting his case.

'Does it? I wouldn't be too sure of that, Morton,' was James's curt comment.

'It would seem a highly probable explanation, Mr Gardiner,' said John Hurst. 'A serious dispute in the home is often the reason for teenagers running away. If you and Miss Roberts have been Emily's surrogate parents, the news that Miss Roberts was leaving must have been a great shock to your niece.'

'Naturally. I accept that,' James agreed, with a snap in his voice. 'But I know my niece better than you do. She's not a hysterical type. She's unusually intelligent and rational, and she would realise that running away wouldn't solve anything. Would you agree with that, Summer?'

She nodded. 'It was because I believed in her level-headedness that I felt it was all right to leave her on her own until her uncle came home,' she told the two other men. 'But since he called me to say she was missing, I've been wondering if I was wrong to rely on her acting sensibly. Yet I'm sure if she had run away, she would have contacted us by now. However hurt and upset she was, she would never put us through this agony of uncertainty . . .' Her voice cracked. She felt her lips tremble and put her hand up to hide them.

For some moments nobody spoke. Then Morton Eliott said thoughtfully, 'Unless it occurred to Emily that worrying about her might bring about a reconciliation between the two of you.'

Above the hand masking her mouth, Summer's anxious eyes widened. Could Emily have conceived such a plan?

She said, 'But where would she go? Where would she spend the night? Nobody who knows her uncle would agree to put her up without informing him. No responsible person would be party to letting her hide with them.'

'There are plenty of hotels where she could stay,' the lawyer replied.

'A young girl of her age . . . with no luggage?' she said doubtfully.

'If she paid for the room in advance, there are places where they wouldn't ask questions.'

'I don't think she'd know how to find that kind of hotel. I shouldn't myself,' she pointed out. She turned to James. 'Do *you* think what Mr Eliott suggests is a possibility?'

His long fingers were drumming a devil's tattoo on the dark red leather of the desk top. It was unlike him to fidget.

'Anything is possible, but—'

He was interrupted by the telephone. For an instant all four of them froze.

As she watched him lift the receiver Summer sent up a prayer that he wouldn't hear a voice saying *We have your niece, Mr Gardiner* or, worse, Emily pleading for help.

'Gardiner speaking.' His face was grim but his voice was normal.

'For you, Hurst.' He handed over the receiver.

Almost sick with relief, she relaxed, but only for a

moment. Who knew what bad news was being imparted to John Hurst?

All the horrific details she had ever read about crime in this city came flooding from the recesses of her memory. Up to now she had felt that the media exaggerated the dangers. With its broad avenues, towering buildings and acres of Central Park greenery, Manhattan had always seemed a friendly, exciting place to live. But then neither she nor Emily had ever had to use the squalid subway or pass through the seedier neighbourhoods. Supposing Emily had asked a cab driver to take her to a cheap hotel and—

Hurst stopped listening and said, 'Thanks, George. Yes, do that, would you? G'bye.' He replaced the receiver. 'That was the result of a more exhaustive check on admissions. Negative. Wherever Emily is, she's not in hospital. The question now is whether to put out a general alert for your niece. But if we do that, some reporter is sure to get hold of it and, if Morton's theory is correct, you're going to incur a lot of unwanted publicity.'

James looked at his attorney. 'What's your advice?'

The lawyer rubbed the bridge of his nose and pondered his reply for some moments. Then he said firmly, 'In your place I would sit this out overnight. My hunch is that Emily will reappear early tomorrow. This is not a young child who's missing, or even an early teenager. From what you say about her, your niece is a young adult. We've eliminated the most obvious cause for alarm—a street accident. Had she disappeared on her way to or from a class, or any other activity which she attended regularly, then I'd be more concerned that she might be being held under duress. A kidnapping is a premeditated crime. When Emily left this afternoon she wasn't following a pattern which someone could have watched and noted. She hadn't planned to go out. It was a sudden decision.'

James turned to Summer. 'What do you think?'

'I think Mr Eliott may be right. I hope so . . . oh, God, I hope so!' she added fervently.

He ceased the restless tattoo and swung his chair to
face the window, his profile a study in concentration.

She watched him making up his mind and she felt
deeply stirred by her love for him.

James swung back to face them. 'I agree with your
reasoning, Morton. We'll give it twelve hours. If she
hasn't shown up by then we'll call in the police.'

In the early hours of the morning, Summer roused
from a restless doze to find that James had covered her
with a blanket.

She was lying on one of the sofas in the living room,
having refused to go to bed. He had wanted her to take
a sleeping pill, but she had been determined to share
his vigil.

Now, as she opened her eyes, she saw that he was
no longer attempting to concentrate on the papers
which he had been studying when drowsiness over-
came her. He was stretched on the opposite sofa, his
shoes off, his tie discarded, his folded arms rising and
falling in rhythm with his deep, even breathing.

She had never seen him asleep before. Stealthily,
afraid of waking him, she put off the blanket and sat
up.

He was lying with his face turned towards her, its
stern lines relaxed. But his jaw hadn't slackened, and
his lips remained firmly compressed. He was sleeping
as lightly as she had slept. The least sound or movement might rouse him and cut short her study of him.

She gazed at him for a long time. She wished she
could kneel down beside him and lay her cheek upon
his and feel his strong arms slip round her. It seemed
incredible now that he had once asked her to marry
him and she had refused; that the night before this he
had wanted to make love to her and she had seized the
chance to escape. What a fool and a coward she had
been. Afraid to take any chances. Wanting the moon
on a platter instead of being ready to settle for whatever he could give her, as she would now, if either
opportunity recurred.

But opportunities never came twice.

His eyelids flickered and opened. For three or four seconds their eyes met. Then, as instantly alert as if he had never been asleep, he swung himself into a sitting position.

'What's the matter, Summer?'

'Nothing. I just woke up. I didn't mean to disturb you.'

He looked at his watch. 'Four forty-six. Would you like some more coffee? Tea?'

She shook her head. 'No, but if you would I'll be happy to make some.'

He pulled on his shoes and stood up. 'Maybe I'll have some fruit juice.' He bent to pick up the tray from their last snack which they had had at two that morning.

They had been awake most of the night, sometimes talking, sometimes wearily silent as the slow hours of waiting dragged on.

She followed him to the kitchen. While she added the used cups and saucers to those already in the dish-washer, he opened the refrigerator and surveyed its contents before selecting a can of tomato juice.

'Maybe I'll join you,' she said, opening a cupboard full of glasses.

It wasn't that she fancied a tomato juice. But drinking it was something to do . . . a way to release some of the tension. Some people chain-smoked. Some people chewed their nails. She and James drank coffee . . . and more coffee . . . and now, for a change, tomato juice.

'I wonder if Emily is sleeping?' she said, in a low voice, as he poured out the juice.

'Like a log, I shouldn't be surprised. The young do, no matter what happens.'

'Did you sleep the night you left home?'

'I guess so. I can't remember. It was a long time ago. Where's the Worcester sauce kept?'

Had he really forgotten, she wondered, as she found the sauce for him. She hadn't forgotten the night after her parents' sailing accident.

The long night wore on.

The next time she woke from a doze the sky was beginning to lighten. James was standing by the window, watching the dawn break. At first he was only a dark silhouette. Gradually, as night dissolved into day, his tall frame took shape and form.

Even if he had managed to nap again, he must be exhausted, she thought. The ordeal of waiting must be even worse for him than for her because it had been his decision not to notify the police immediately. The fact that three other people had seconded that decision wouldn't help if it turned out to have been the wrong one. He would feel the misjudgment was his alone, and he wasn't the kind of man who could forgive himself for a mistake . . . certainly not one involving the safety of someone dear to him. Emily was the only family he had . . . the only person he loved.

He turned. Seeing that she was awake, he said, 'I'm going to take a shower and change my clothes. I suggest you do the same. Then we'll have an early breakfast.'

Her bathroom was as she had left it, suggesting that James hadn't informed Victoria that she had gone and wouldn't be back. Yet he must have accepted her decision because he hadn't got in touch with her until Emily's disappearance had forced his hand.

Her toilet bag was at the Barbizon, but the bathroom cupboard contained a spare toothbrush which she hadn't packed and sachets of shampoo and body lotions which she had collected on their travels. Her hair-dryer was at the hotel, but Emily had one she could borrow.

Emily . . . Emily . . . where are you? Summer thought, standing under a hot shower and shivering with fatigue and dread that today might bring back that terrible pain and desolation she had been through before when they told her her parents were dead.

Fortunately, the clothes she had worn the day before had survived the night without looking too scruffy. She could have borrowed one of Emily's shirts, but somehow she shrank from doing so.

When she returned to the living room José was there, laying the table at which she and Emily often ate when there were only the two of them in the apartment. While she was talking to him James reappeared. Now the early sun was gilding the tops of the highest buildings and she could see how haggard he looked, his lean, angular face seeming even more rawboned than usual, with bruise-dark shadows under his eyes.

When José left them, he said, 'I think you should call the Barbizon in case there've been any calls for you.'

'But nobody knows I am staying there except you and Emily.'

'Precisely. Emily might call you. I'll look up the number.'

When the hotel operator answered, Summer said, 'Good morning. This is Miss Roberts. I checked in yesterday but an emergency came up and I left the hotel last evening and haven't been back. If anyone calls me, would you tell them where I can be reached, please? It's very important.'

Before she could give the number of the apartment, the operator said, 'What is your room number here, Miss Roberts?'

'Oh, God . . . I don't remember. Wait a moment. I have the room key. I was in too much of a hurry to leave it at the desk.' As she spoke, Summer signed to James that the key was in her bag.

He was quick to find it and hand it to her. When she had given the number, the operator said, 'There's already been one female caller for you. I remember it because we don't have many incoming calls that early, and also we couldn't reach you.'

'Did the caller leave a name?'

'No, no name and no message.'

'It was definitely a girl? You're sure?'

'Yes, I remember her accent. I think she was British.'

Summer gave a gasp of relief. 'If she calls again, would you tell her I'm at home now . . . permanently.

She'll know the number. Thank you. Goodbye.' She replaced the receiver and turned to him. 'A girl with a British accent called me. It *has* to be Emily. Oh, James—'

She wanted to fling her arms round him and weep on his shoulder. But instead she collapsed in the chair beside the telephone, covering her eyes with her fingers, holding her emotions in check.

There was a pause before he said, 'She must have called you to see if her strategy had worked. If you weren't there, she'd guess it had. I'd better have a word with Morton.'

His cool reaction amazed her. She could have sworn he had spent the night racked with anxiety. Yet now, speaking to his lawyer, he sounded calm and unemotional.

Seconds after he finished the call the door opened and his niece walked in. She must have entered the apartment by using her key rather than ringing for José to admit her.

'*Emily!*' Summer sprang up, intending to rush across the room and embrace her.

But James grabbed her and kept her beside him, his hard fingers painfully tight on her soft upper arm.

'You're just in time for breakfast,' he said mildly. 'But perhaps you've already had it?'

Emily shook her head. She came forward, moving rather gingerly, obviously uncertain of her reception.

'I—I'm sorry if you've been worried.'

'Wasn't that the object of the exercise?'

'I had to do something, James. I couldn't let you and Summer—'

Her explanation was cut off as he let go of Summer and transferred his grip to his niece, seizing her by both shoulders and towering over her, rage erupting from him like lava from a volcano.

'Worried! I'll say we've been worried. We've spent the whole bloody night thinking the next time we saw you would be on a slab in a mortuary. Don't you know what can happen to girls alone in this city? Don't you read the papers? Have you any idea what it's like to spend a night waiting to hear that someone's been mugged, raped or murdered?'

He began to shake her so violently that her neck seemed in danger of snapping and Summer sprang to the rescue.

'James . . . for God's sake . . . stop it! You'll hurt her,' she protested, grabbing his arm.

He ignored her, roaring at Emily like a man demented. The savagery of his anger was terrifying.

And then, quite suddenly, while the girl's head jerked back and forth and Summer clung to his arm, shouting, 'Stop it . . . stop it,' he stopped.

All at once the wild rage evaporated. Ceasing the brutal shaking, he pulled Emily into his arms and held her close. Whereupon she began to cry and Summer let go of his arm and fell back and stood watching them hug each other, her own eyes brimming.

Before noon she recovered her belongings from the Barbizon. After lunch she caught up on some lost sleep. They all did.

Half an hour before dinner James called her into his study. He came to the point with his customary directness.

'I don't want you to come back under pressure of emotional blackmail. Emily won't repeat last night's folly.'

'I acted equally foolishly. I realise that now that I've had time to think things over.'

He said stiffly, 'You have my assurance that the . . . circumstances which upset you won't happen again.'

She said nothing. What could she say?

There was an uneasy silence which he ended by remarking, 'Last night you told Hurst that Emily was in love with an older man. I take it you meant Skip Newman? How long has she had that idea?'

'He's been her hero since our first winter in Florida. Please don't let her know I told you. I wouldn't have mentioned it except that it was the only way to explain her lack of interest in dates.'

'I shan't say anything to her, but I don't approve of a girl of her age building an adolescent crush into something so important it kills her interest in boys of her own age. Maybe she should spend next winter somewhere other than Florida.'

'I think she'll be terribly disappointed if we don't go to *Baile del Sol*. My feeling is that loving a nice person like Skip can't do her any harm, even if it doesn't come to anything. And who's to know that her first love won't be her last love? It happens sometimes.'

'Skip's a nice guy, agreed. But he's not up to Emily's weight. As you said last night, she's on the brink of being a beauty. She also has brains and breeding, not to mention substantial private means. Rushing into an early marriage would be a mistake she would almost certainly regret. I think you should try to discourage her from taking this calf-love too seriously. Skip is already committed to the family business and the same small-town life as his parents. Emily still has a lot of the world to see.'

In the weeks following Emily's drastic method of repairing the rift between her elders, James spent less time away than he had before her disappearance.

He was in New York most of that autumn. When business took him to the West Coast, he took Summer and Emily with him, showing them the birthplace of his empire, the area south of San Francisco, between Palo Alto and San José which because of its soil and climate had once been verdant with orchards of cherries and apricots, and the plums which, dried in the sun, became Californian prunes.

To Summer it seemed rather tragic that so richly fertile a region should be despoiled by a sprawl of factories making silicon semiconductors and other products of the electronics revolution, hence its new name, Silicon Valley.

Although Emily agreed it was a pity the factories couldn't have sprung up in a desert, she was thrilled at being introduced to many of the still-young pioneers of the industry.

The trip intensified the intellectual bond between her and her uncle, and made Summer wonder if he could ever be happy with a woman unable to grasp the complexities of his life's work.

But it wasn't till the day he told them to pack for a trip to Europe, and added that he was coming with them, that she began to question his motive for spending so much time with them. The more she thought about it, the more uneasy she became. For Emily's beauty was blossoming rapidly now. People in the street turned to stare at her—especially men.

Sometimes, when he thought himself unobserved, James watched her; with the hint of a smile playing round his hard, sensual mouth, and a look in his eyes which forced Summer to face the painful fact that he might have fallen in love with the one girl he could never have.

In London they stayed at the flat where they had spent their last night in England after leaving Cranmere. It seemed half a lifetime ago. This time they didn't wander, wide-eyed and wonder-struck, round Harrods but went to Bellville Sassoon, in a quiet street behind the great store, where the Princess of Wales bought clothes, and to Caroline Charles in Beauchamp Place, another of her favourite designers.

And instead of having supper at the Chicago Pizza Pie Factory, they dined at Tante Claire in Chelsea, a mecca for London gourmets where the chef had once been a pupil of the renowned Roux brothers and now was himself a master of superb French cuisine.

'It's much better being seventeen than thirteen,' said Emily, sitting between them in the taxi which took them back to the flat.

'Almost seventeen,' James corrected her.

Watching them smile at each other, Summer wondered if he knew what was happening to him? Surely he must; and yet, if he did, how crazy to stay in their company. He ought to go away and find himself another mistress. To come under the spell of any girl of not quite seventeen was folly for a man of his age. To fall in love with the daughter of his elder brother was madness.

A few days later he took Emily to Cranmere to see how skilfully the house had been converted into sixteen houses and flats. Summer opted out of this expedition—she was reluctant to return to a place where she had experienced much loneliness and unhappiness, and where everyone who remembered her would be sure to express astonishment at her transformation. Emily was disappointed that she didn't want to go with them, but James accepted her decision without argument. She suspected he was glad to be rid of her for a day.

Wondering if she could be mistaken about his feelings for his niece, and worrying about the outcome if she were not mistaken, she spent the morning idly window-shopping.

In Bond Street an arcade devoted to antiques lured her inside to browse at stalls selling jewellery, porcelain, silver and bric-à-brac. A stairway led down to a lower floor with more stalls, among them one devoted to portrait miniatures.

Summer spent some time admiring the many tiny portraits on display before the friendly face of the women behind the counter encouraged her to ask, 'If one wanted to trace a miniature painted about twenty years ago, without knowing the name of the artist, how would one go about it?'

Ten minutes later she left the arcade on her way towards Trafalgar Square. For although, according to her adviser, it would be a laborious business to locate a portrait of a undistinguished sitter, the whereabouts of a painting of the younger son of a marquess might be known at the National Portrait Gallery.

'I'm afraid we haven't a photograph of Lord James Lancaster,' said the girl who dealt with Summer's enquiry. 'But it has been shown in a number of exhi-

bitions and we have a note that it's in the possession of
the artist, Miss Diana Kendall.'

'How would I track down Miss Kendall?'

'The Royal Society of Miniature Painters would put
you in touch with her.'

By mid-afternoon Summer had the artist's telephone number. Rather than ring from a call-box, she
went back to the flat which gave her time to think of a
way to introduce herself to the woman who had
known James before his metamorphosis.

The telephone was answered by a man who, when
Summer asked to speak to Miss Kendall, asked who
was calling.

'My name is Summer Roberts. Miss Kendall doesn't
know me. It's about having a miniature painted.'

'Would you hold on, please. My wife may be painting, in which case I shall have to ask you to ring back.'

A husband who took his wife's work seriously,
thought Summer, as she waited. That he was at home
during the morning suggested that he might also be a
painter, or had retired. Diana Kendall could have been
as much as fifteen years older than James when they
met. In which case she would now be fifty and her
husband might be sixty or more.

After a short interval a woman's voice said, 'I'm
sorry to have kept you waiting, Mrs Roberts. I was in
my studio. You want a miniature painted, I understand. Of one of your children?'

'No, of myself. I'm not married.'

'Ah, I see. The majority of my commissions are for
portraits of children, and my husband said "Mrs
Roberts" so I jumped to the wrong conclusion. I'd be
pleased to paint you, Miss Roberts, but I'm very busy
at present, and indeed for some time ahead. I doubt if I
could manage it before Christmas. Do you live in
London?'

'No, in America.'

'I thought I detected a slight American accent. How
long are you over here for?'

'Only until the end of the month. I realise a well-

known artist is booked up a long time ahead, but I felt
there might be a slight chance that you could have had
a cancellation through illness or something.'

'I'm afraid not. In fact I'm even busier than usual at
the moment. How did you come to hear of me?'

Summer said, 'I'm tutor to Lady Emily Lancaster,
the granddaughter of the last Lord Cranmere. I think
you used to know Lord James Lancaster.'

There was a pause before the artist said, 'Yes . . .
yes, I did. Do *you* know him?'

'We live with him. When Emily's grandfather died,
James took her under his wing.'

There was another pause. Then Miss Kendall said,
'Even if I can't paint you, Miss Roberts, I should very
much like to meet you and hear how James has been
getting on since I last saw him. Are you free this
afternoon? Could you come and have tea with me?'

'I'd like to. Thank you.'

'Come at four. You know the address, do you?
Yes . . . good. Till four o'clock then. Goodbye.'

Shortly before four Summer's taxi arrived in a part of
London rarely discovered by tourists and unknown to
many Londoners.

Lying to the north of Paddington Station, the area
called Little Venice was the neighbourhood surrounding the junction of the Grand Union Canal, once a
busy link between the Rivers Thames and Trent, and
the waterway to the Paddington Basin.

The house where she was to have tea was an early
Victorian building with an elaborate white stucco
façade which had recently been repainted.

Soon after she had rung the bell, the door was
opened by a stout middle-aged woman who said,
'Miss Kendall's up in the studio. This way, please.'

The whole of the staircase wall was covered with
framed architectural drawings, not of the present century, which suggested Miss Kendall's husband might
be an architect who collected the drawings of his
forerunners.

On the landing at the top of the flight there was a large full-length portrait of a girl in the clothes of Queen Elizabeth I's reign. The wall of the second flight of stairs was hung with about twenty samplers.

The top floor of the house, where once there would have been several attics, had been converted into one large, light room. As Summer was shown in, a woman who had been bending over a table at the far end, looked up and transferred her spectacles from the bridge of her nose to her red hair.

Some grey hairs at her forehead and temples had toned down the colour, but when she was younger it must have been as fierily red as Emily's hair. The realisation made Summer's heart sink. It seemed yet another piece of evidence to support her theory that James had fallen in love with his niece.

Diana Kendall rose from the table and came swiftly across the room to greet her.

'Miss Roberts . . . how do you do? Come and sit down over here.'

She indicated a large sofa over which was flung an antique Paisley shawl. In front of it was a large cabin trunk transformed into a colourful table by being painted all over with the pine cone motif which patterned the shawl.

'I'm interested in your reason for wanting to have your portrait painted in miniature,' said Miss Kendall, as they sat down. 'Is it to be a present for someone?'

This was a question for which Summer had no ready answer. After some hesitation, she said, 'Yes . . . in a way. I thought I might give it to Emily when my time with her is over. It would be a nicer memento than a photograph.'

'Much nicer. How long have you been with her?'

'Since she was twelve and she's almost seventeen now.'

'And James must be in his middle-thirties. How life flies. I'm surprised he remembers me. What did he tell you about me?'

'That you met on a ski-lift years ago and you taught

him to recognise fine antique miniatures. When he came to Cranmere after his father's death, he showed me a miniature by George Engleheart of Lady Maria Lancaster, one of Emily's ancestors.'

At this point the woman who had let Summer in reappeared, carrying a tea tray which she put down on top of the trunk.

'Mrs Brown is the mainstay of my life,' said Miss Kendall. 'Without her, all would be chaos. Sometimes it verges on chaos even with her, doesn't it, Mrs Brown?'

This remark was acknowledged with a chuckle as Mrs Brown arranged the tea things which included small brown bread sandwiches and half a home-made cake.

After she had left them, Miss Kendall said, 'I'm so lucky to have Mrs B. Not least because she never utters when a nod or a shake of the head will do. Alex, my husband, is an architectural historian. He's away a good deal, but when he's at home we enjoy entertaining, and I also have four grown-up step-children who often stay with us. In order to paint professionally, I have to delegate almost everything domestic. Now, tell me about James. Is he married?'

Summer answered her questions, discreetly studying her as she poured out the tea. The youthful lines of Diana Kendall's figure were emphasised by narrow black trousers and a short-waisted sweater patterned like tortoiseshell. She wore a necklace of old silver beads interspersed with polished lumps of reddish-brown copal resin, and swinging silver ear-rings. Seen from a distance she would have seemed still in her thirties, but close to her age showed in the lines on her neck and the crow's-feet surrounding her eyes. They were hazel, like Emily's, but her skin was not freckled.

'So he's still a bachelor. What a pity.' She explained this comment by adding, 'Having been twice married—very happily—I think everyone needs a mate. My first husband was killed, and I was a widow when I knew James. I was lonely and he was lonely and, in spite of the difference in our ages, we became friends. Obviously you knew Lord Cranmere. Did you ever meet Lady Cranmere?'

'No, I didn't.' Summer explained a little of her own background.

Having handed her a cup of tea, her hostess offered the sandwiches.

'You have very beautiful eyes, Miss Roberts,' she said. 'I noticed their shape and colour the moment you came in. Unfortunately, there's no possible way I can make time to paint your portrait before the end of the month, but I could paint one of your eyes which used to be done at one time. You may have seen some eye miniatures in the form of brooches or lockets. Would that be an acceptable compromise?'

Any arrangement which would enable Summer to spend more time talking to this intriguing woman was acceptable. She agreed to the suggestion with enthusiasm.

'I believe you did a miniature of Emily's uncle,' she said. 'It would be interesting to see how much he's changed. But perhaps you don't have it any more.'

'Indeed I do. It's one of my best pieces of work.'

Miss Kendall rose and crossed the room to a tall cabinet of shallow drawers.

'I keep most of my collection of early miniatures in here because often the pigments are fugitive. Light, particularly sunlight, fades them. This top drawer contains various relatives and friends whom I've painted for my own pleasure.'

As she returned to the sofa with a miniature and a magnifying glass, she went on, 'Like his niece now, James was almost seventeen when I did this. Most people aren't at their best at that age. But occasionally one sees a girl who has an almost magical freshness about her, or a youth who looks like a young god. He was one. He outshone all the dashing ski *lehrers* who usually bowl the girls over, but he was never one of the *après-ski* crowd. The friend whose family he stayed with was a tremendous flirt, I remember—

but not James. He was rather serious and aloof. He skied brilliantly, and sometimes with terrifying recklessness.'

The small oval portrait she handed to Summer showed a sun-burned, unsmiling young face which was recognisably James Gardiner but without the air of authority and the penetrating gaze he had developed in the meantime. Nor had his mouth and eyes acquired the hardness and the cynicism which characterised his expression in repose, only disappearing when he was amused or listening indulgently to Emily expounding a brainwave.

'If he's changed—if his hair is thinning and his neck thickening—please don't tell me,' said Diana Kendall. 'We all have to age and decay, but I'd rather remember James as the "golden lad" he was then.'

'That's what he said about you,' Summer told her. 'He gave me a beautiful miniature of an "unknown lady" in a blue silk dress for my last birthday. I asked then if he was still in touch with you. He said that, after a long interval, it was a mistake to go back to places or to seek out old friends. I—I think he was in love with you.'

The older woman smiled. 'Perhaps. It's a long time ago. I was not so much older than you are.'

Summer looked again at the portrait. The white open-necked shirt he was wearing emphasised the dark sheen of his hair and the burnished bronze of a naturally dark skin exposed to dazzling alpine sunlight. The portrait radiated health and strength, yet the eyes, when she studied them through the magnifying glass, held a curiously sombre expression as if, in spite of his looks and his privileged birth, he hadn't been a carefree young man.

'Let me look in my diary and see when I can fit you in,' said Miss Kendall. 'It shouldn't take more than two hours. Could you manage next Thursday morning, rather early . . . at a quarter to nine?'

When Summer had agreed and, reluctantly, given back the portrait—which she would have liked to study for much longer—she was shown some of the finest examples in the artist's collection.

James wasn't mentioned again, or only indirectly. But she went away feeling that perhaps, next time, she would learn something more; something which would help her understand the complex personality of the man she loved.

On Thursday Mrs Brown let her go up to the studio unescorted. As she mounted the upper flight she heard the sound of a typewriter and found that the typist was Miss Kendall, using two fingers but tapping away at great speed.

As Summer entered, she stopped. 'Heavens! Is it a quarter to nine already? Let me take your coat. Shall we use each other's first names today?'

Having directed Summer to a chair and hung up her raincoat in a corner concealed by a Chinese screen, she went on, 'I'm an early riser and between eight and nine I try to keep pace with my correspondence. At the moment I'm writing to one of my godchildren who is very unhappy because her parents are divorcing. Were Emily Lancaster's parents happily married?'

'I think they must have been reasonably content with each other. I was told that Lady Edgedale couldn't have any more children. In which case, if they hadn't been happy, I imagine her husband might have changed wives in order to secure the succession. Nobody seems to have expected James to reappear. But the reason why he left Cranmere is a mystery I've never fathomed.'

'You've been with him some time. Couldn't you have asked him?'

Summer shook her head. 'Even Emily, who's very close to him, has never raised that subject. Do you know the reason?'

'Yes, I do—but it was told to me in confidence.' The artist picked up her magnifying glass and came to where Summer was sitting. 'I'm going to study your eye in detail for a few minutes. Don't try not to blink.

Look at the pictures on the wall behind my desk and try to ignore me.'

Knowing that she had been too precipitate in speaking about James's rift with his family, and had been deservedly snubbed for her inquisitiveness, Summer flushed.

'I wasn't sure what to do about eye make-up so I left it off,' she murmured.

'You don't really need it, except perhaps in the evening. You're lucky to have naturally dark eyelashes. I have mine dyed,' said Diana. 'Eye miniatures don't always include the eyebrow but I shall put yours in. They were sometimes framed with a lock of hair at the back. Do you want to have yours made up as a locket or a brooch? Or you could have it mounted to hang as a tiny picture. I'll send you to my favourite framer and let him show you the alternatives.'

While she was making one or two preliminary sketches of Summer's eye from different angles, Mrs Brown brought up two cups of coffee.

Putting aside her pencil to drop two minute white pellets into her cup, Diana said, 'The other day you suggested that I had been James's first love. Am I right in suspecting that you would like to be his last love?'

An even deeper flush suffused Summer's face. 'What makes you think that?'

'Something in your expression when you were looking at the portrait of him—and the fact that, unless he's changed a great deal, it would be difficult not to love him.' She paused. 'I did. It began as a friendship, and ended as a love affair. Ending it, as I realised I must, was as painful, in a different way, as losing Ben, my first husband. I loved James with all my heart, but the age gap between us was too great. He was too young to be bound to anyone.'

She sipped her coffee, her hazel eyes kind and understanding as she looked at her sitter over the rim of her cup.

Summer said in a low voice, 'I don't aspire to be James's last love, but yes—I love him. It isn't just idle curiosity which makes me ask if you knew why he seems to have hated his father.'

'Lord Cranmere wasn't his father. James is the son of an American army officer, a hero of the Second World War who ended his career as a four-star General at the Pentagon and, as far as I know, is still alive.'

There was a long pause before Summer said, in a stunned tone, 'So that's why he looks so unlike the rest of the Lancasters.'

'Yes, and it was because he took after his natural father that his legal father loathed him and made his early life hell for him. Even his mother was never nice to him. He adored her and couldn't understand why she was cold and unloving. In the end he found out—he was a living reminder of her lapse from grace . . . an affair with the commanding officer of a post-war American base not far from Cranmere.'

At last Summer understood why James had always referred to the Marquess as 'Emily's grandfather', never as 'my father'.

'I don't blame her for that,' Diana continued. 'In the different social climate of those times, she'd been pushed into marriage with a middle-aged man who preferred horses to women but needed an heir. She supplied him with one. Probably she would have had other legitimate children, but my guess is that heavy drinking had made Lord Cranmere impotent. Then, at a hunt ball, she met a dashing American who was everything her husband wasn't. Who can blame her for losing her head? Whether he, being unmarried, tried to persuade her to leave her husband, is something which will never be known. Perhaps he didn't. Being involved in the divorce of a member of the House of Lords, with all the attendant publicity, might not have improved his career prospects.'

'But if he had been a war hero, and he loved her, would he have cared about that?' Summer interjected.

Diana smiled. 'Most people aren't all of a piece. A man can be physically brave, but not have moral courage. Possibly the General didn't love her. Perhaps for both of them it was what the French call an *amourette* . . . an affair of the body rather than the heart. Anyway, although there appears to have been a lot of gossip at the time, nobody could have proved anything if James's splendid dark looks hadn't made him an obvious cuckoo in the nest.'

'How did he find out?'

'His brother—who was actually his half-brother—enlightened him. They'd had a quarrel about something and the older boy—was his name Gerald?—called James a rotten little bastard. In a flash, James realised it wasn't just an angry epithet. Somehow Gerald had found out something which explained why Lord Cranmere disliked him and his mother was never affectionate. He went to her and asked if it were true. She admitted that it was, and she made him feel it was his fault rather than hers.'

Summer remembered the night at her cottage in England when James had said: *No man with my income is ever avoided by women. If a man has power and money he can be the biggest bastard ever born; there'll always be plenty of women prepared to overlook his defects.*

Her retort had been: *Are you a bastard, Mr Gardiner?*

No wonder he had glared at her. Unwittingly she had touched him on a raw spot.

She said, 'Like you, I don't blame his mother for her affair with the General, but I find it hard to forgive her treatment of James.'

'She must have been a flawed personality to have made such a marriage in the first place. Her situation, following the birth of her second son, would have tested a strong, sound character,' Diana said thoughtfully. 'I've no doubt her husband gave her hell. He may not have minded her having affairs. He might even have accepted James, if he'd looked like her. But to have his wife's infidelity confirmed and advertised by the boy's resemblance to her lover must have galled him beyond endurance. What an atmosphere to grow up in!'

'Yes . . . terrible,' Summer agreed. 'It explains a great deal about him which I've never understood. May I ask you something very personal? How long did you know him?'

'For nearly three years. For a long time after that skiing holiday I saw him only spasmodically. I was still missing Ben and even though James was so tall I thought of him as a boy. It wasn't until he kissed me that I realised he wasn't; and that, if I didn't do something about it, our friendship would get out of hand. So I went to Greece, to the island of Patmos. Unwisely I wrote to him from there. Three weeks later he turned up.'

She paused to finish her coffee before going on, 'By that time he was almost of age . . . almost eighteen. I was renting a house built by a Patmian sea captain in the days when the island had a merchant fleet. I told James he could stay for two weeks . . . for a holiday. A year later, we'd been to most of the islands together. I didn't care if people thought me a cradle-snatcher. I was very happy. So was he, and for him that kind of happiness was a novel experience. The family who took him skiing had always been kind to him, but no one had loved him before. It was good for him . . . good for both of us.'

They were sitting almost knee to knee and now she rose from her stool to fetch a wheeled table of the type with a single leg so that it could be used in bed and for various other purposes. Reseating herself, Diana pulled it over her lap. On the table was an old-fashioned writing slope to which she had taped some white paper with a small oval piece of ivory gummed to it horizontally.

She said, 'One could live very cheaply in Greece then. James had a little money and sometimes earned a little more. He learned to speak Greek in no time. So he paid his way, or would have done if I hadn't sometimes insisted on paying for better accommodation than he could afford. But I knew that our wanderings couldn't go on indefinitely. As he was half-American I thought he should go to America where perhaps his real father could help him get a start. He refused to go without me and, because I couldn't bear to part from him, I agreed.'

As she talked she was using a fine sable brush dipped in Venetian Red to outline the shape of Summer's left eye and her eyebrow.

'We spent some time in New York and James made enquiries about his father. When he found out how important he was, and that he had a wife and children, he changed his mind about approaching him. He became determined to make good on his own. Somehow I felt sure he would, in spite of the difficulties. He had incredible energy. He could study until three in the morning and wake up at seven, ready to run in the park. After a while I knew he'd be better off without me. In the note I left for him, I said I wasn't coming back to England but I didn't say where I was going. I left him some money—as a loan—and I wrote that I'd be in New York in twelve months' time if he wanted to see me. Then I flew back to Europe and went to stay with some friends with a villa in Tuscany. It was there I met my husband—although at the time I was too unhappy over James to pay much attention to Alex.'

She fell silent, concentrating on her work, her glance flicking from her subject's face to the piece of ivory and back again as, with a larger brush, she washed in the local flesh tints.

'And did you meet him the next year?' Summer prompted.

'Yes, by that statue of the girl outside the Plaza Hotel—New York's equivalent of Eros in Piccadilly Circus. We had lunch together, and that was the last time I saw him. My feelings hadn't changed then, but his had. For him it was over. He was absorbed in his new life. Having repaid the loan, and given me a miniature by Richard Cosway which he'd discovered in Boston, he rushed off to catch the bus back there. I was sad for myself, but glad for him. And after a while

I thought less about James and more about Alex until I was thinking about him most of the time.'

She began to mix another colour. 'Ivory isn't absorbent like paper. One can't take off superfluous colour. One has to work with a much dryer brush than when painting an ordinary water-colour.'

She tested the colour on the paper alongside the ivory before beginning to apply it.

'Don't be jealous of my little share of James's love. It was a long time ago and, for him, less important than for me.'

'I'm not jealous. I'm envious,' said Summer. 'I—I would give my soul for what you had. James hasn't changed physically since you knew him—or only for the better. He's still devastatingly attractive. But I think he must have changed inside. He's had three long-term affairs, all with clever, independent career-women. Some time ago he decided it was time to start his dynasty. Because I was conveniently to hand, as it were, he asked me to marry him.'

Diana looked up. 'And—loving him—you refused?' she exclaimed, with obvious perplexity.

'Wouldn't you have done the same?'

Instead of answering the question, Diana said, 'What reason did you give him?'

Summer told her the gist of their conversation on the subject. It was not one she was likely to forget.

'So you didn't tell him you were in love with him?'

'No! How could I?'

'Why not? Men have been laying their hearts at our feet for centuries, and they haven't always been turned down gently and tactfully. Equal rights involve equal risks. If you laid your heart at his feet, I doubt if he'd kick it or trample on it. He'd be flattered and possibly delighted. For all you know, he may have discovered that he feels more warmly towards you than he did at the time he proposed.'

Summer shook her head. 'I—I think he may be beginning to fall in love with someone else.'

'Will she make him happier than you would?'

'No.'

'Then fight for him, my dear. Who is this other woman you think he may be interested in?'

But this wasn't something which Summer felt able to confide. 'I could be mistaken. Anyway he can never marry her.'

'In that case you've nothing to fear. From my knowledge of his character, James is not the type to allow his life to be blighted by a yen for a woman he can't have. If she's married and won't leave her husband because of children or whatever, I'm sure he will cut his losses. He has a romantic streak but he's primarily a realist— as I am.'

She paused, concentrating on her work for some moments before adding, 'I've loved three men in my life and I know that, if I hadn't met them, I shouldn't have gone through life alone. There are other men in existence whom I could have loved equally deeply had my life taken a different course. I don't expect you to believe that because at the moment, for you, James is the sun and the stars. Perhaps he always will be. There are women who love only once. But one thing I do know for certain is that, when you are my age, it's the chances you *didn't* take, the opportunities you *didn't* seize, which you regret. If I were you, my dear, I shouldn't dither any longer. I'd go back and tell James how I felt.'

When Summer returned to the apartment she found a message waiting for her. The other two, who had gone to Cambridge for the day so that Emily could meet one of her heroes, Sir Clive Sinclair, a pioneer of British electronics, were dining there and wouldn't be back until late.

This threw her into a fever of impatience. Never had time passed so slowly. She attempted to read and, when she found she couldn't concentrate, to watch television. That didn't grip her attention either, so she switched off the set and began to pace restlessly about, rehearsing ways to tell James how much she loved him.

Many times during that interminable evening, her courage faltered. What if he turned her down? How could she bear it if he rejected her: either the immediate mortification or the long-term despair of facing a future without him? For if, however tactfully, he made it clear that he didn't want her, she couldn't possibly stay on as Emily's companion.

It was after ten o'clock when she heard the scrape of a key in the outer door. Sitting down with the discarded book, she took some deep breaths to steady her vibrating nerves. When Emily burst into the room, exclaiming, 'You should have come with us. We've had a fabulous day,' she was able to put the book aside and say calmly, 'Have you? Tell me all about it.'

Emily's description of the delights to be found in the Fitzwilliam Museum, and of their meeting with the admired Sir Clive Sinclair, took a full fifteen minutes. By the time she paused for breath, James had been to the kitchen to make coffee for himself and Summer and to fill a glass of milk for his niece.

'What have you been doing with yourself?' he enquired.

'Exploring London . . . nothing special.'

She thought he looked rather worn; not as if he had been enjoying himself.

He said, 'I think we've spent enough time here. Tomorrow we'll move on.'

'Where to?' asked Emily.

'To Austria. I was planning to spend Christmas there and then return to New York early in January.'

'What fun! I'll go and start packing. Thanks for a super day, James. 'Night.'

Carrying her glass of milk, she dropped a kiss on his head and blew one to Summer before she waltzed out of the room.

As the door closed behind her, James slid down in his chair, stretched his long legs across the rug and leaned his dark head on the backrest.

Watching him lounge with closed eyes, his hands thrust into the pockets of his trousers, Summer wished she knew what he was thinking.

After some moments of silence, she said quietly, 'Are you exhausted?'

At once he opened his eyes and rolled his head to look towards her. 'No, not at all. Just glad to relax in your restful company.' He smiled at her.

It was the encouragement she needed. 'Actually there's something I'd like to discuss with you.'

'Go ahead.'

'A long time ago . . . in Nantucket . . . you said that we . . . you and I . . . had the makings of a "workable marriage". Do you remember?'

She paused, half expecting a frown or a look of discomfiture at the reminder of an offer which he now regretted. But although he looked surprised, James didn't appear to be embarrassed.

'Yes, of course I remember,' he said evenly.

'You said at the time that you hoped to make me change my mind . . . and you'd raise the subject again at a later date. But you never have.'

There was a considerable pause before he answered, 'Are you telling me *you* have changed your mind?'

She swallowed, her mouth dry with nervousness. 'Yes . . . yes, I have.'

James sat up. His expression as he watched her make this difficult admission had never been more poker-faced. She felt herself redden under his thoughtful scrutiny. At last he said one word.

'Why?'

'A lot has happened since then. We're not the same people we were. The objections I raised last time are no longer valid. I—I think now we *could* make a life together . . . if you're still willing to try?'

'Perhaps . . . I'm not sure,' he said guardedly. 'As you say, the situation has altered since you turned me down flat in Nantucket. However, I hadn't realised that your views on marriage had undergone a transformation. At that time, I recall, you were adamant that the only basis for marriage was both parties loving each other to the extent of being unable to live without each other.'

'I still believe that's the ideal. But if the ideal isn't possible then one has to compromise. When we talked about this before I—I didn't think you were capable of taking *any* woman seriously. Your detachment repelled me. It seemed so . . . inhuman. Now I know that you are capable of caring for someone, it makes all the difference. Even if you can never feel that way about *me*, having loved someone and not been able to tell her must make you more understanding of other people's emotions.'

His dark eyebrows drew together in a forbidding frown. 'I don't know what you're talking about.'

She could see he was deeply displeased by even an oblique reference to his hopeless passion for the one girl who could never be his.

'Don't be angry, James,' she appealed. 'Surely you know you can trust me with your secret?'

When he continued to scowl at her, she went on, 'After tonight I shall never speak of it again. I realise how painful it must be. I wouldn't have mentioned it now except that I've come to realise that you are too strong a character to let it affect your whole life. And I don't believe that, after being in love with Emily, you can ever revert to those soulless relationships you used to have with women.'

It was in the open at last. Would he deny it? Would he be bitterly angry with her for divining the cruel come-uppance which life had had in store for a man who had once dismissed love as nonsense?

Being James, whose reactions were never predictable, he didn't deny it, nor did he lose his temper with her. For some seconds, which seemed like minutes, he sat in silence, looking at her, his eyes narrowed almost to slits, the muscles of his jaw bunched under the taut brown skin, showing how tightly his teeth were clamped together.

When at last he spoke, his voice was quiet and controlled.

'You're ready to marry me . . . believing me to be in love with Emily?'

She nodded. 'You see I've changed as well.' Unconciously she lifted her chin and squared her shoulders before she gave away her own secret. 'I've discovered I love you. I've known it for quite some time and . . . and it seems to me that, if you can never have the person you really want, you might as well settle for me, as you once intended to.'

For a few ghastly moments she thought he was searching for the least humiliating way to reject her proposal.

Then, slowly, he rose to his feet and came to stand towering above her.

'It seems to *me* that we don't know each other well enough to marry. I was under the impression that you'd never been at ease in my presence since the night I tried to take you to bed. And if you seriously believe I'm nursing an incestuous passion for my teenage niece, you're way off beam about my feelings. The girl I want isn't Emily?'

'She isn't?'

He reached down and grasped both her hands. 'Of course she isn't . . . you dumb blonde.'

The next instant she was in his arms, held close to his tall strong body with her face pressed against his shoulder.

'Oh, God—it seems like a decade since I held you . . . touched you,' he exclaimed hoarsely. 'How could you possibly believe that I felt this way about Emily? Not only is she my niece, but she's years too young for a man of my age.'

'But she isn't fully your niece . . . and she is such a darling.'

She felt him tense slightly. 'What do you mean? Not fully my niece?'

Summer lifted her face to look up at him. 'I know you and Lord Edgedale were only half-brothers . . .

that you're the son of a high-ranking American army officer.'

His face didn't darken with anger as she feared it might. He seemed no more than surprised. 'Where did you hear that?'

'I went to see Diana Kendall. After I'd admitted that I loved you, she told me. Oh, James, I can't believe you care for me.'

'I thought I was making it plain enough by spending most of my time with you. How was I to know you'd dream up the crazy idea that Emily was the magnet who drew me?'

'I feel I may be dreaming this . . . being in your arms at long last. Kiss me before I wake up.'

He bent his head and pressed a soft, tender kiss on her upturned mouth. Her lips quivered under his. She couldn't believe that it was happening; that one simple act of courage had brought this amazing reward.

The kiss deepened, igniting the passion which had blazed between them those precious times before. This time her response wasn't forced from her. She gave it willingly, eagerly.

'We've wasted so much time already. Need we waste any more?' he asked, in a husky murmur, a little later.

For answer she pressed herself closer, as impatient as he was to give full rein to their desire. 'Not a single minute,' she whispered, against his hard cheek. 'I want to sleep in your bed . . . in your arms. I never want to sleep alone again.'

Holding her by the hand, he switched out the sitting room lights and led her swiftly to his room. There he locked the door and crossed the room to close the curtains, shutting out the faint glow from the street lamps and plunging the room into deeper darkness. But only briefly.

A few seconds later a pool of light from a reading lamp illumined the wide double bed. James took hold of the linen cover and flung it back. With another strong jerk of his wrist the blanket and top sheet were thrown back exposing the smooth white undersheet, clean on that day.

Then he beckoned her to him.

It was neither shyness nor last-minute uncertainty which made her move forward slowly. After waiting so long for this night and never really believing it would ever come about, she wanted to prolong every blissful second of it.

When she reached him, he took her face between his hands and his thumbs gently traced her eyebrows and the slanting line of her cheekbones.

'How lovely you are,' he said quietly. 'The first time we met I was struck by the colour of your eyes—even though they were glaring suspiciously at me.'

'I thought you only noticed how . . . enormous I was.'

'That, too, but it didn't obscure the beauty of your eyes and this exquisite skin'—caressing her cheeks.

She closed her eyes, the better to enjoy his touch. From the lobes of her ears to the centre of her chin, his fingers brushed lightly back and forth. Instinctively she let her head fall back, exposing her throat. His fingertips left her jawline and trailed softly, slowly down to the base of her neck and from there to her nape and back again in a necklace of delicious sensation.

For her solitary evening she had changed into a loose velour robe, buttercup-yellow with a long white zipper down the front. She felt the slight tug as he started to open the fastener, sliding the tag down till it was level with her navel.

Still without haste he pushed the robe off her shoulders. The loose sleeves slid down her arms and the whole garment fell to the floor, leaving her naked except for a lacy white bra and matching briefs.

She heard James give a kind of low groan and opened her eyes to find him looking as if he wanted to tear them off her. But his hands remained gentle as he fondled her waist and hips for a moment or two before pulling her against him and giving her a long, hungry kiss.

Summer twined her arms round his neck and returned the kiss with abandon. She felt him unloose the ribbon which tied back her hair. Then his hand glided over her back to the clip between her shoulder-blades. Next she found herself lifted and placed in the middle of the bed and her loosened bra peeled away.

He took her breasts in his palms as if they were ripe, perfect fruit which would lose their bloom if not handled with the utmost care.

'The last time I did this you seemed to hate it,' he said, as he stroked her.

'Only seemed. I wanted to hate it . . . but I didn't really. I could never hate anything you did to me.'

He smiled and his dark head swooped, but not to kiss her on the lips. She gasped as his warm, sensual mouth brushed lightly over the soft flesh he held plumped into pale golden domes, each one topped by a circle of pink with an unfolding bud at its centre.

When his lips touched her there, she stifled a cry of delight at the lovely sensation which shot from the tip of her breast to the deep inner core of her body.

'Oh, God! That's divine,' she muttered, clutching his head, beginning to shiver with excitement.

Pausing halfway to her other breast, he said, 'We've hardly begun yet,' and she wondered what could be in store if she felt so much pleasure in these first moments of her first night of love.

'I—I can't stop shaking,' she gasped, a little while later, when he paused once again to glance at her flushed, bright-eyed face.

'Don't worry . . . you will,' he assured her, the once unreadable eyes now warm and loving.

His hands glided down past her ribs and her quivering belly to take hold of her flimsy briefs. She lifted her bottom to help him, and he pulled them down over her thighs and then past her knees till he could throw them away.

'Why don't you take off some clothes?' she murmured, watching him look at her now naked body.

His response was to loosen his tie and, when that
had been discarded, to unbutton his shirt and pull
it out of his pants. A moment later she was looking
at the muscular torso so often admired but rarely
touched.

'Oh, James . . .' She sat up and flung her arms
round him, pressing her breasts to his chest. 'I didn't
know what I was missing.'

'You still don't.' He kissed her mouth. 'But we're
going to make up for lost time.'

They kissed for a long time, his hands still exploring
her body and hers roving over his shoulders, feeling
the strength underlying the chamois-soft skin.

Presently, still sitting up, embracing him, she felt
his hand on her legs, first stroking her outer thigh
from hip to knee and back again; and, after some
moments of that, moving to the inner side of her leg,
his fingertips brushing slow circles from her knee to
where her thighs joined.

The last time his hand had been there, she had tried
to resist, and what had followed her surrender had
been a few guilty seconds of ecstasy before they had
been interrupted by Raoul's telephone call.

Now there was no need to resist or to feel any guilt.
Tonight she had no inhibitions, only a longing to yield
herself utterly to him, giving all that he asked, receiving all he could give her.

Although she could feel his heart pounding an
urgent tattoo, he had his own feelings under steely
control as his fingers searched for and found her most
sensitive spot. When he touched it she shuddered
convulsively, her head falling back and her whole
body shaking and twitching.

She was vaguely aware of being propped against his
raised knee while he pulled the pillows together and
lowered her against them. Then, with hands and lips,
he launched a gentle but relentless attack which soon
had her writhing and jerking in uncontrollable abandonment, the back of one hand pressed over her

mouth to muffle the groans of pleasure which rose in her throat.

When it was over, when the final paroxysm of delicious feeling had engulfed her body and left her limp and panting, she opened her eyes and saw by the fierce gleam in his how much he wanted her.

'But you didn't . . . you haven't . . .' she whispered.

'We have all night. I can wait.' He took a tissue from the box on the night table and lightly blotted the moisture which had broken out on her forehead and under her eyes. Her breasts were wet from his tongue. Very tenderly, he dried them.

'I want you to be drunk with love before I hurt you, my darling,' he told her softly.

'I don't mind if it hurts for a moment. I want you to take me . . . now,' she pleaded softly, lifting her arms to pull him down to her.

He shook his head. 'Not yet. Just lie still and rest for a minute.' He moved down the bed and, picking up one of her feet, began to play with her toes. 'You have very pretty feet. I noticed it at the beach at Nantucket.'

'You have nice feet, too . . . nice everything,' she said admiringly.

He gave her a wolfish grin. 'You haven't seen everything yet,' he reminded her.

She looked at him through lowered lashes. 'If it matches what I can see, I should have no cause for complaint. You remind me of that bronze at Cranmere, "The Dying Gaul".'

She remembered once furtively stroking the statue of the magnificently naked wounded man; imagining what it must be like to have such a man as a lover, never dreaming one day she would.

James nibbled her smallest toe between his white teeth and flicked his tongue slowly along the backs of the others. She closed her eyes, filled with lazy, luxurious well-being.

It was when he was kissing her knees that she felt her half-drowsy enjoyment become recharged with excitement. She glanced down and saw the dark head

between her knees and felt his palms under her calves
and the slightly rough feel of his cheeks against the
smooth flesh of her thighs as he inched his way
higher. His lips seemed to burn her skin, or was it her
skin which was burning? She lay still, almost not
breathing, her eyes tightly shut, her clenched hands
gripping the sheet as she waited for him to come closer.
Would he bypass the centre of her body and follow the
line of her hip, or would that hot sensual mouth . . . ?

When she found out, a cry burst from her. Her spine
arched in a spasm of intense, electrifying sensation
which zinged through her whole nervous system,
followed by another and another as he quickened the
delectable friction.

When it suddenly ceased, her eyes blinked open in
dismay.

'Why have you stopped?' she asked faintly, her
body throbbing and aching with the need for him to go
on.

In a rapid continuous movement James removed his
shoes, socks, pants and undershorts. She had a brief
glimpse of his hard aroused maleness but, before she
had time to be nervous, he was making love to her
again, swinging her legs over his shoulders, his hands
snaking upwards to enclose her quivering breasts and
force her to new heights of rapture.

At the peak there was a fleeting instant of such
paradisiacal feeling that, when it was ebbing, she
wanted to burst into tears. But then, while that
wonderful wave of erotic delight was still in her mind
and her bloodstream and every last cell of her being,
another wave came; and this one was James surging
upwards and plunging into her body with one swift
decisive thrust which gave her a second of pain immediately succeeded by the joy of having him as close
as it was possible to be.

What followed was not, for her, as physically blissful as what had gone before, but she knew that was
only because it was the first time. Emotionally, the
experience of holding this long-adored man in her

arms and learning the rhythm of love was something she would never forget.

There was a moment, when they were still and he lay with his face buried against the side of her neck and his weight pressing on her, when she thought she wouldn't mind dying, not now she had known the high point of living.

Then James raised himself on his arms and began to kiss her softly on the eyelids.

'Shall I let you go? Are you hurting?' he whispered tenderly.

'No, no . . . stay with me, please . . . it's lovely like this.' She caressed his broad back and pressed little feathery kisses along his collar-bone. 'How can people who've done this together ever turn against each other?' Then, before he could answer, she added, 'I guess it isn't like this for everyone, and the first time can be a disaster. You made it wonderful. Thank you.'

He was silent for a while before he said, close to her ear, 'It was a first time for me, too. I love you very much, Summer. There's no way to describe the difference. I didn't know what I was missing either.'

Presently they had a shower together and James went to the kitchen for a bottle of wine which they drank sitting up in bed with Summer leaning against his chest while he wound silky strands of her hair round his fingers.

'I think I was in love with you when I asked you to marry me in Nantucket, but I didn't want to admit it to myself,' he told her. 'Love makes people vulnerable and that's a condition I've tried to avoid.'

'Because your mother rejected you when you were a small boy?'

'No, I don't think that was as painful as Diana Kendall walking out on me. I was nineteen and as crazy about her as a kid of that age can be if an attractive older woman exerts herself to be nice to him. It was one hell of a shock to come home one day and find her gone. Of course it was the right decision. I wasn't sufficiently mature to be anyone's permanent partner. But it hurt like hell for a long time, and from then on I tried to avoid giving anyone the power to repeat the process.'

'Sometimes being hurt can be good for people. It was for me. You don't know it, but you hurt me terribly soon after you arrived at Cranmere. I overheard you talking to Dr Dyer about me. But although I hated you for them, the cruel things you said were the spur I needed to change myself. If you hadn't said them, I probably shouldn't be slim, and I certainly shouldn't be here in your bed.'

'I wouldn't say that. It isn't only your body I love. It's the inner you . . . the girl who made Emily happy and whom everyone at Cranmere liked, regardless of the way you looked. You didn't often show that side of yourself to me, but I heard things from Mrs Hardy and many other people which indicated there was a very sweet, warm personality behind the prickly defences you put up when I was around.'

'All the same, love is partly a physical thing and you wouldn't have enjoyed making love to me the way I was.' She had finished her wine and she put the glass on the night table and wriggled herself round to face him, sitting back on her heels. 'How long does it take for men to recover their energy?'

He grinned. 'It depends,' he said, putting his own glass aside. 'For a boy of seventeen maybe not more than ten minutes. For a man of seventy maybe four or five days.'

'And for someone of your age?'

He cupped her left breast in his palm and took one of her hands and placed it upon his own body. Then he put his hand behind her neck and pulled her towards him, at the same time leaning towards her.

Before their mouths met, he said, 'Not long.'

From the nest of dark curls at the base of his flat, hard belly she felt his resurgent power stirring, strong and warm, under her fingers; and, inside her, a melt-

ing readiness to make him as welcome in her body as
he had long been in her heart.

On a morning, two weeks after Christmas, she opened
her eyes and saw on the pillow beside her the sleeping, beard-shadowed face of the man who was now
her husband.

He had been her lover every night since that first
night in London, making slow, ravenous love to her
and teaching her how to please him. When not locked
in each other's arms, they had opened their minds,
finding as much delight in that as in freely exploring
each other's bodies.

From that first night on they had been married in
spirit, but because of their different nationalities there
had been minor complications attached to making the
bond official. For two reasons they had decided to
postpone their legal marriage till after Christmas;
the first being that it was unthinkable not to spend
Christmas with Emily, and the second being to spare
her the uncomfortable feeling of intruding on their
honeymoon. Whether she had guessed they were
sleeping together in Austria, Summer wasn't sure. But
it would have been impossible for them to spend their
nights apart.

Now Emily was in Palm Beach with Cordelia
Rathbone and this was Summer's first awakening in
the place James had chosen for their official honeymoon.

She still didn't know where they were. It had
amused him to make a mystery of their destination.
All she knew was that they were on a small island
somewhere in the Caribbean, having spent the previous night at an hotel in Barbados before flying from
there to St Vincent and transferring to a specially
chartered boat for the final lap of the journey. It had
been dark when they arrived and a taxi had brought
them from the jetty to an isolated house on a headland
which she hadn't yet explored because James had
been impatient to make love to her.

Luxuriously stretching her naked body, Summer decided to leave him sleeping while she slipped out of bed and had a look round their home for the next three weeks.

A few minutes later, wearing the white trousseau nightgown in which she had yet to sleep, she returned to the large, high-ceilinged living room she had seen briefly the night before.

Someone, presumably the maid who had welcomed them to the house, had opened the folding double doors under the wide-ribbed fanlight which reminded her of those she had seen on early New England houses. Now it was clear why the cushioned bamboo sofa and armchairs were placed facing those doors for, through them, was an incredible view of near and far islands lapped by the bluest of seas under a blue morning sky.

Adjoining the living room, beyond some more folding doors, was a pillared dining veranda with another glorious sea-view.

She had explored the garden with its swimming pool and palm-thatched gazebo when James appeared on the sun deck outside the living room and she hurried to join him.

'Darling, what a lovely place! But isn't it time you revealed to me where we are?' she said, after they had kissed good morning.

'These islands are the Grenadines. The one we're on is Mustique and out there is Petit Mustique, Canouan, Union and Carriacou,' he said, keeping one arm round her and pointing them out with the other.

'Mustique . . . isn't this where Princess Margaret has a holiday house?'

'Yes, a place called *Les Jolies Eaux*. Mustique used to belong to an English family who lived in St Vincent, but about twenty-odd years ago it was bought by Colin Tennant who's a friend of Princess Margaret. When she married he gave her some land at the southern end of the island as a wedding present. Some years later she commissioned Oliver Messel, the famous theatrical designer who was also an architect, to design a house for her.'

'Which end of the island is this? Are we anywhere near the Princess's house?'

'Yes, but you won't see anything of her. She won't be here while we are.'

'How do you know?'

He grinned and kissed the tip of her nose. 'Because this is *Les Jolies Eaux*.'

'*This* is Princess Margaret's house?' she exclaimed in amazement. 'Do you know her? Has she lent it to you?'

'No, I've rented it. When the Princess isn't using it herself, she lets other people enjoy her retreat from the world. When I was considering places where we could be alone together this seemed an ideal spot. There's a cook and a gardener, and a car if we want to get about. However, as I'm told we have one of the best and most secluded of the island's beaches on our doorstep, I don't think we'll want to go far. Shall we have a swim before breakfast?'

They spent most of the day on the beach. It was while she was lazily floating in the crystalline sea that Summer suddenly had an idea for a spectacular evening belt incorporating the pearls James had given her and her lion's paw shell. It pleased her that, after eluding her for so long, the perfect design should have been conceived on her honeymoon.

After dinner they danced for a while. But it wasn't long before she had both arms round his neck and his hands were stroking her hips, pressing her closer to him.

'Another early night, d'you think?' he suggested huskily.

'What a good idea.'

In the middle of the night, her body not yet adjusted to the change from European time, she woke up and, knowing she couldn't lie still for the hours until sunrise, went to swim by moonlight in the Princess's pool.

She hadn't been in the water long when James came

to find her. Coming down the steps from the house he looked like a magnificent naked savage.

'The last time we did this you made a tremendous fuss,' he reminded her teasingly, when he joined her in the pool.

'Naturally. What did you expect? You behaved disgracefully, and I was scared out of my wits.'

'You weren't really afraid of me, were you?'

'Considering that I was a virgin who'd never even been kissed before, you were lucky I didn't have hysterics. Who would have thought that the next time I went skinny-dipping I'd be your wife?' she murmured happily, hugging him.

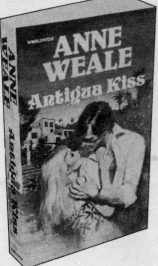